The Rebel Christian Publishing

ISBN: 9781957290348 (eBook)
Print: 9781957290355

This is a work of fiction. Any references to historical events, real people, or real places are used fictitiously. Names, characters, and places are products of the author's imagination. Inclusion of or reference to any Christian elements or themes are used in a fictitious manner and are not meant to be perceived or interpreted as an act of disrespect against such a wonderful and beautiful belief system.

Cover designed by Valicity Elaine
Cover image provided by Envato Elements

The Rebel Christian Publishing LLC
350 Northern Blvd STE 324 - 1390
Albany, NY 12204-1000

Visit us: http://www.therebelchristian.com/
Email us: rebel@therebelchristian.com

D1596975

Contents

Other Books by A. Bean

The End of the World Series (End Times Fiction)
The Woof Pack Trilogy (Romantic Suspense Trilogy)
Too Young (Children's Fantasy)
The Scribe (Fantasy)
The Living Water (Contemporary Romance)

A Note from the Author

The heavenly realm depicted in this story was created by me. It is Biblically inspired, taking elements from Heaven, and using them to create a realm for the characters in this story. While Biblically inspired by the truth of the Word of God, there is NO Biblical evidence of the existence of the fictional realm used in this novel. It is completely made up and is ONLY my own interpretation of what life *might* have been like before we reached Earth.

Please do not take this depiction as literal, but only as an element in the story and a look into my own imagination.

Thank you,

A. Bean

The truth is not controversial, and we should not be silent.

Singlehood

By A. Bean

A Rebel Christian Publishing Book

1

Glimpses

"Alright," Michael said. "Who's next?" He glanced around at the new recruits, each of them stared in disbelief at the grueling fields across the chasm before them. Ropes, water, animals, cones—things they hadn't even known existed waited for them on the course. The course was meant to be challenging, and to teach the recruits endurance and faith before their name was called for the 'Earth' assignment.

"Come on, Benny." A brown-haired child of Jehovah shoved his friend forward.

"Benedict? You volunteer?" Michael called, crossing profoundly muscular arms over his chest.

Benedict whirled around with eyes as large as the moon below and glared at the callous act of his best friend. "Um…" he returned his gaze to Michael. "I guess—"

"Good enough!" Michael yelled before he could finish.

Sighing, Benedict stepped off the platform and made his way through the grass to Michael.

"Now, I'll only explain this once, so listen closely." Michael leaned down to his face, hulking over him at a height that was not given to the children of Jehovah. "You've been learning about time in preparation for Earth, haven't you?"

Benedict nodded, remembering his studies on time and the way it existed on Earth as a tool of measurement.

"Good," Michael nodded, "because once you cross the chasm, time is going to begin, and your body is going to change. You won't be as fast as you are now, and you will feel the full velocity of negative emotions in that place."

"Why?"

"Because you need to learn to control these things before your Earth assignment. The more you train and work on self-control, the better you'll be when your time comes."

"But…" Benedict paused, scratching his youthful face free of stubble, "won't you be there to help me on Earth?"

Michael sighed. "I will only be there if Elohim allows me to be. If He does not approve of your petition, or there is no need for me to be there, I will not have permission to pass into the earthly realm. You probably wouldn't see me anyway, and if you did, you most likely wouldn't even remember me."

Benedict frowned slightly, it was a subtle disapproving look, however, in this place, anything besides a smile was strange. Recruits, however, were allowed to experience negative emotions in preparation for Earth.

"So, I'll be alone on Earth?"

Michael shook his head. "The Great God Jehovah will be there with you. His Spirit will reside in your heart, and the sacrifice of the Lamb will protect you. You remember the Lamb, don't you?"

Benedict smiled widely and nodded. He'd aced a test he'd been giving by a bald man who taught many classes to the recruits. He often told of his experiences from when he was on Earth—endless teachings after an encounter with the Christ that caused him to be knocked off his horse.

"Good." Michael patted Benny's back. "Just be cautious out there. You're going to be tested on everything you've learned. The things you'll feel may be overwhelming at first, but if you believe and call out to the One who helps, He will rescue you. Got it?"

"Yes," Benedict said.

"Alright then…" Michael paused and glanced around. There was a bell ringing out in the distance. "Class dismissed for today," he said abruptly.

"Wait," Benedict called. "I thought I was going to—"

"Another day!" Michael yelled as his wings burst forth around him, and with a mighty push, he flew into the air, disappearing within seconds.

"Whew!" Benny's friend ran over to him, staring at Michael as he flapped his wings in the distance. "You just escaped the training."

"No thanks to you, Joseph." Benny shoved his friend playfully before the two took off in a sprint. They raced at neck-breaking speed, rushing through the fields as the sweet smell of fruit danced on the wind.

"Slow down!" a woman called.

"Sorry, Mother Eve!" Joseph shouted as he raced by.

Benedict zipped by without a word, trying to catch up to his friend before they were caught. The wind galloped beside the two friends, rustling through the fields, whispering cool breezes over their sweating bodies as they raced. The dirt did not sink beneath their feet, and the grass did not wither. Flowers were not disturbed as they raised their heads above the grass to watch the playful interaction.

3

Without notice, Joseph stopped, and Benedict rushed to a halt, almost slamming into his staring friend. He raised his eyes and found what Joseph was looking at. The recruits for the assignment, 'Armageddon,' were gathered around the great King David who was dressed in armor that looked like it weighed more than he did despite being a big, bulky man. Large feet, thick muscles, broad shoulders, King David was every bit the warrior, and he was proud of it. The crown of gold on his head never let anyone forget who he was.

"If my name isn't called, I'm going to join the Armageddon force," Benny said as he stood beside his friend.

Joseph grunted. "You serious? I was considering it."

Benny nodded. "Yeah, I think I'm actually going to do it."

"And Adar? What did she say?"

A rosy hue grazed Benny's cheeks as the mention of his crush tickled his ears.

"I actually haven't talked to her yet."

Joseph gasped. "You can't be serious."

He shrugged. "I don't know how to bring it up."

"Well, you'd better think of a way," Joseph said.

— ☙ —

I sat up out of my bed, holding my head and gasping for air. Those dreams always felt real, like I'd somehow stepped out of my body, watching myself interact with people and things I've never seen before. Somehow, the dreams fade after I wake up, and by the time I realize I'm no longer asleep, I've forgotten what I dreamed.

I've tried to remember many times before, but my mind always drew a blank, like it never happened. All I'd have left from the encounter was an empty feeling within, like someone had called out to me, I just didn't

4

know how to answer.

I sighed as I swung my legs over the edge of the bed. I brushed a hand over my curls, trying to push that empty feeling as far away as I could. Today was my graduation day, and I didn't need or want any distractions. My last piece of the high school puzzle would be put into place in just a few hours; I wanted to enjoy the entire day, not be stuck wondering or spaced out about a dream I couldn't even remember.

Sinking my elbows to my knees, I whispered to myself, "It doesn't matter, it was just a dream."

I crossed the floor to the bathroom and stared at myself in the mirror. Tan skin and big loose curls stared back at me. I was getting my hair cut today for graduation, but mostly because I wanted to ask Lia Sunohara out. This would be my last attempt to ask her since I didn't have her number and probably wouldn't see her again once I left for college.

Lia was the prettiest girl I'd ever seen. I'd been crushing on her since my freshman year. Watching her grow from her slick black hair and geeky glasses to contacts and red highlighted hair. Lia was beautiful. I didn't care about her glasses or anything like that, she was cool, and good at volleyball. I used to watch her practice sessions every day, or rather, I was honestly just watching *her*. The way her spandex shorts—

"X! Are you up? You'll miss your appointment if you don't hurry!" my mom called.

I groaned and pulled open my door. "Yeah, Mom, I'm just going to freshen up and then I'll be down." I closed my door without waiting for an answer. The only good thing about going to college across the country was that my overbearing parents couldn't baby me anymore.

To be fair, I couldn't blame them for the way they treated me, since I was late for school all the time. Especially once I started driving myself. There had also been a few nights with my friends that I knew would make my very Christian mother scream and keel over.

I try to forget those nights.

But I was eighteen now. I really didn't think I needed someone babying me.

After cleaning up in the bathroom, I rushed downstairs into the kitchen where my brother and mother were eating and chatting.

"Morning, X," Jax said as he grabbed his crisp bread from the toaster, he blew on it before taking a crunchy bite.

"Hey, Jax," I replied. I slipped between him and my mother to grab a slice of bread.

"You're going to be late again," Mom pestered.

I rolled my eyes behind her, and she snapped, "Roll your eyes again and you're not going to that graduation party."

"Sorry, Mom."

She turned to smirk over her shoulder, full lips glossed in a shimmering pink color. Her hazel eyes and tan skin matched mine right down to the birthmark we shared on our wrists, a cloud shaped patch of skin a little darker than the rest of my body. I glanced down at it before leaning over to kiss her forehead, then I stuffed my bread into my mouth and grabbed my keys.

"Be back soon!" I called as I pushed open the screen door and headed out.

2

The Wrong Idea

Matt slapped my back and said, "Sunohara, twelve o'clock."

I whirled around so quickly; I almost spilled the punch in my hand. At the sight of Lia, I squeezed my red cup tightly, trying to still my nerves.

"You've got to go talk to her," Matt was saying into my ear. We'd been friends since daycare. Played on the same community soccer team when we were kids, and in the fifth grade, Matt transferred to my middle school. We ended up going to the same high school, but this would be our last summer together since Matt was going to Europe to study abroad and I was going to New York.

"I know," I said through the panicked breaths I was trying hard to control.

"Well, what are you waiting for?" He slurped the spiked punch, and stared ahead at the dancing couples, kissing friends, and suddenly confident nobodies letting the punch boost their secret egos.

"I don't know. What if she rejects me?"

He shrugged. "It's a party. There's special punch," he waggled his eyebrows, "and plenty of other girls looking to have fun."

"Have fun," I deadpanned.

He slapped my shoulder again. I gripped my punch.

"Do you know what the freshmen wave is?"

I did, but I shook my head because I knew he'd tell me anyway.

"Girls who want to get their first time over with before going to college." Matt sucked the punch off his teeth as I glanced over at him, hoping the thumping music was loud enough to confuse what he'd said. I guess I looked stupefied because he leaned closer and repeated himself.

"I said, there are plenty of girls looking to have their first before college."

I shook my head and took a dramatic step to the side to see all six feet and two inches of Matt. I was only two inches shorter, so it didn't take much for me to look him over in one quick glance.

"Excuse me." A girl with cocoa skin and curly brown hair was trying to step by me. I'd stepped back from Matt so suddenly, I'd bumped into her. She was smaller than Lia, but thicker *in all the right places*, as Matt would say with a waggle of his thick eyebrows.

"Sorry." I waved at her, but she threw a hand over her shoulder and walked into the crowd. I didn't get a good look at her, but I did see the silver bracelet she wore as she waved me off. A cloud-shaped charm was attached to it, the sight made me subconsciously press my left thumb into my right wrist, right against my birthmark.

"Come on," I said, returning my attention to Matt. He was eyeing the girl snaking through the crowd.

"She's not as pretty as Lia."

I knew what he really meant, and the thought made me shake my head. "I'm not interested in a freshmen wave; I just want to ask Lia out."

"Are you kidding me?" Matt asked. "You go over there right now, she's going to take you to a bedroom, and you're going to get laid."

"She's not like that." I glanced over at Lia who was dancing with two other girls, swaying her hips left and right.

"Yeah, she is." Matt grabbed my shoulder. "She's exactly what you've been wanting. I don't know why you're so hesitant today. You spent all these years watching her at practice, now's your last chance. Just do it." He shoved me forward before I could protest, and I stumbled into the crowd.

Nodding a few apologies, I glared back at Matt who only raised his cup and his brow. I shook my head, maneuvering through the crowd toward Lia and her friends.

I could feel the seconds ticking by as I stood there like an idiot, staring at her.

"Do you know this guy?" one of her friends asked.

I stuttered, "N-No! I came over to introduce myself."

Lia placed a hand on her thin hip and raised a brow. "You want to introduce yourself to me?"

I nodded nervously.

A wicked smile stretched across her lips and her hooded eyes seemed to suddenly draw me in. "Well, it's a little loud here," she grabbed my hand, "let's go somewhere quieter."

Lia nodded at her friends, and they all smiled and waved at me as she led me through the crowd of people. We made it around the hall where couples lined the walls. Some whispered, some were kissing, a girl was crying as a guy frantically tried to explain why it was best for them to split.

Lia opened a bedroom door and pulled me inside. "Sit," she said as she flopped onto the bed. It belonged to neither of us, in fact, I'd never been to this house before. I think it was Stacy Miller's place, some girl in my class I hadn't even known existed until Matt got us invitations to this party.

"We don't really need to be in a bedroom, do we?" I said, still standing at the door.

"Oh, come on," she purred, "we can't do this out there."

My stomach knotted as she began to unbutton the cropped pink cardigan draped over her shoulders. There were eight little white buttons, and she'd already unbuttoned three.

"Lia, I think you've got the wrong idea." I set down my cup on the desk beside the door.

Lia frowned, the look in her eyes shifting from intrigue to burning desire—like my subtle rejection had excited her instead of disappointing her. She sprang to her feet, crossing the room to me in an instant. Before I could protest, Lia pressed her lips to mine, and thus I had my first kiss.

It was invigorating, and my heart thumped erratically within its chamber. She pressed her hands against my chest, deepening the kiss. I wasn't sure exactly what to do, so I let her guide my hands, slipping them beneath the cut off shorts she was wearing. I could feel Lia's tender skin melting in my hands. I groaned into her mouth as she worked on the button of my jeans.

But … suddenly, nerves reached up my throat, and I pulled away abruptly.

"Lia," I panted, "I think we should slow down a second."

"For what?" She raised a brow. "I thought you wanted this."

My chest rose and fell dramatically. I wanted to run away. This wasn't *exactly* what I wanted, and it felt wrong. It *was* wrong. I knew it was wrong. Just being at this party was wrong.

I'd lied to my mother about the graduation party and had her drop me off at Katelynn Beck's house, the valedictorian of my class. I'd told her that Katelynn was having a little get together, but my mother didn't know Katelynn like most guys in our school did.

Katelynn's spot was the cover up place everyone told their parents they were going. One by one, we arrived there and, one by one, we left to go to Stacy's house where the real party was at.

Matt had picked me up—somehow half-drunk and talking stupid

before we'd even gotten to Stacy Miller's place. I don't think I have to tell you my sanctified mother wasn't fond of Matt, but his parents were cool (and rich), so my mother never suspected that Matt was the one who brought the booze and had even convinced me to start drinking it with him.

I knew it was wrong. I knew Believers didn't do that, but Matt was my best friend, and I couldn't let him down.

This was no different. I didn't want to let Matt down since I knew he was expecting me to *get laid*, but inside, I screamed for help. The pleasure was indescribable. The way Lia, the one girl I'd been crushing on forever, was kissing me. She apparently knew what she doing because even though I wanted to stop her, I couldn't.

Please God, I cried in my heart, *help me out of this and I swear I will never do this again! I promise! I promise I'll wait until marriage!*

Just then, Lia pulled loose from me and tugged my jeans open.

"Lia!" I said quickly, but she didn't pay me any attention. Lia unzipped my pants, her eyes widening.

"Are you just being nice?" Her thin lips curled into a cunning smile. "I love shy boys, they're always secretly wild once the shyness wears off." She reached for the band of my underwear, but I shoved her away before she could touch me.

"What are you doing?" Lia snapped, stumbling backwards.

This was an awful idea. This was a nightmare.

Only some lonely sack would shove away a girl like Lia. A *willing* girl like Lia. But I just couldn't do this.

She glared at me with a clenched jaw. "What's your problem?"

"I—" shouting cut me off.

"Police! The police are here!" someone yelled outside the door.

Lia swore loudly, but instead of storming off, she took my hand. "Come on! Or else the police will catch us!"

We'd only been having a party, like most kids after graduation, but there was tons of booze here and a crowd of kids handing out edibles, plus someone from the track team bought a hookah to share. The party was legal, but everything else was not.

I could not get arrested for underage drinking, not when I was just a few weeks out from going off to college. So I gripped Lia's hand and rushed into the hallway with her. Everyone was scattering. Running in every direction.

"X! X!" I heard Matt calling for me, but Lia pulled on my hand and said, "This way! Let's go around back!" I nodded and we ran down the hall. Down two flights of steps we found the back door and sprinted out. We raced across the lawn, and I saw Matt running to his car in the distance.

"Matt!" I screamed. "Matt!"

"Matthew!" Lia shouted. He looked around for a second, scanning the area, then he spotted us running towards his car. There were cars all over the lawn, thankfully, Matt had parked on the outside of the vehicles, near the sidewalk.

"Come on! Get in!" he shouted as we ripped open his doors and piled into the back. He swerved the Jeep around on the grass and zipped off away from the party.

I exhaled heavily, sitting back against the seats as the sirens began to fade into the background.

"That was incredible!" Matt hooted, slapping the steering wheel in excitement. Lia leaned forward to slap his shoulders.

"What a way to end high school, right?" She laughed.

I couldn't respond. My stomach was in my throat, and my mind was spinning. I sat with my head back, thinking of everything that'd almost gone wrong.

"Come on, X." Matt glanced up at the rearview mirror. "You can't tell me that wasn't fun!"

"No," I sat up, "it wasn't."

"You didn't even have fun with me?" I glanced over to find Lia pouting, not at all fazed by the fact that we'd just sprinted away from the police like criminals. To make things worse, she smirked at me when I didn't answer her question and reached up to unbutton the rest of her cardigan.

"Oh God." I sighed and pinched the bridge of my nose. Not this again.

Lia yanked open her cardigan, shocking me as I realized she had nothing on underneath. Matt whistled as he glanced over his shoulder, swerving the car a little.

"Matt!" I snapped, making him focus on the road again.

Lia scooted closer to me.

"Don't—" I began, but she pressed a finger to my lips.

"We got interrupted," she whispered.

"Man," Matt cooed, "if he's too scared, I'm not."

Lia eyed the rearview mirror, then she glanced back at me. "*He* wants to."

I looked away.

"Don't you?" Lia asked, cupping my chin and turning my head so I'd look at her again.

My mouth went dry as I stared at her breasts. I couldn't look away, despite every effort I tried to make. I glanced at the mirror for help, but I knew I wouldn't get any when I realized Matt was already looking. His mouth was hanging open.

I didn't know if I should be angry that Matt was staring at the girl I liked, instead of trying to help me calm her down. But Matt always had an aggressive appetite, one I could never keep up with, though Lia wasn't the type of girl he preferred. But preferences didn't matter right now because I couldn't feel anything but relief.

I didn't want to have sex with Lia, I just wanted to ask her on a date. While I also didn't want to give her up to Matt, at this point there wasn't

13

much that could be done. Whatever Matt wanted, he always got it, no matter what. Even if he wanted a woman. A woman I liked. A woman who didn't like him. It didn't matter—he was that kind of guy.

"Forget him, Lia," Matt rasped. "Get up here with me."

Lia pulled her cardigan off completely and leaned forward. Matt craned his neck, flicking his eyes between the road and Lia. A heartbeat of silence passed between them before his eyes dropped to her bare breasts. Before I could blink, Lia leaned forward.

My heart hammered in my chest as I watched my best friend kiss my crush. I dragged my eyes to my window, feeling defeated yet relieved, but all that was washed away when a blaring horn bellowed out on the dark street. Bright white lights flashed at us, and I felt the car swerve violently.

Matt gasped but didn't pull away from the kiss. Lia giggled like it was funny to have our lives at risk.

"Matt! Look at the road!" I shouted.

He glanced forward for half a second, the smirk on his face vanishing as he realized it was too late.

3

Just Be Honest

"Adar!" A thin woman stood in a field of flowers, leaning over to greet each rose, daisy, and lily. They danced in the wind for her, waving back at her greetings. "Adar!" Benny called again. The woman stood, brushing a loose curl behind her ear, she smiled as she watched Benny make his way through the flower field.

"Benny, are you done with training?"

"Yeah," he palmed the back of his neck, "Michael was called off. The bell rang and he took off immediately."

She nodded, dipping her head slightly. "I see."

"I was wondering if you were free right now?" Benny asked. He shuffled back and forth in what earthlings called a 'nervous tick.' Nervousness was connected to fear, a negative emotion, therefore, only new recruits were able to feel it as part of their Earth training.

"I am." She blushed. "What is it, Benedict?"

"Well... I wanted to talk to you about something. It's important." Benny and Adar had only recently begun speaking to each other. They'd grown up only streets apart in the 'New Recruit' sector. In that district, the children were raised by prophets of old, and teachers from the Word. Each child was placed in the care of a man or woman of Jehovah based on their Earth assignment.

"Alright then," Adar said as she sat down in the flowers. "I can't train until Michael returns." She patted the grass softly, and Benny sat beside her.

— 🌱 —

I grunted as my eyes fluttered open. Swallowing thickly and blinking back the piercing white lights, the dizziness I'd felt was beginning to fade.

"Where—" I tried to speak, but there was a breathing mask on my face. I raised my arm to pull it off when I noticed it was bandaged. I tried to move around, but my entire body ached. A beeping noise ticked behind me, and when I glanced around, I realized I was in a hospital.

"X? You're awake!" Jax yelled. "Mom! Dad! He's awake!"

I could hear my parents rushing in; Mom immediately shuffled to my side.

"Mom?" I asked, still feeling dazed.

Tears rolled down her cheeks, she looked frightened. Dad looked tired, but not an ounce of worry was tethered to his features. Which didn't provide any help for what state I was in. Mom was overdramatic, and Dad was usually indifferent. I don't even think getting my head blown off would make my father react the way any other human would. Work had hardened him, and he'd become distant over the years.

"Xavier Miles! What were you doing in that car?" Mom snapped, like, *literally* snapped, bursting into tears and sinking at my bedside as she wept.

"You could've died!" she sobbed.

"Mom," I pulled down the oxygen mask, "I'm sorry." My voice was raspy, and it hurt to speak.

"Get some rest for now," Dad said. "We'll—"

"*No.*" Mom snapped her head up. "We are talking *right now.* I've waited all night and morning for you to wake up." She lifted a trembling hand to her mouth, trying to control herself. "You don't even know what's going on or what condition your friends are in. You walked away with some burns, some scratches." She shook her head. "What if you hadn't walked away at all?"

"Mom, I'm sorry," I said again.

"What were you doing!?" she shrieked.

My entire body jolted away from her. I'd never seen my mother so … broken. Dad tried to wrap an arm around her shoulders, but she shoved him away and rushed out of the room.

Dad sat a moment, sighing heavily. "Just be honest," he said quietly, then he stood and left the room.

I lay there, wondering how much trouble I was actually in once things calmed down. Maybe Mom and Dad wouldn't go so hard on me since this was my first offense on this scale and I *could've* died. But then again, maybe they'd go hard on me *because* I almost died the first time I snuck out. Well, the first time they knew of.

I groaned as I tried to sit up. Jax moved over to me and gripped my hand, helping me sit up slowly. My entire body ached, like I'd been forced to lift weights heavier than myself.

"How bad was it?" I asked Jax. He sat down, brown eyes glancing away for a moment, and I knew something wasn't right.

"Jax," I called. "Say something."

His eyes met mine. "You have to speak with the police."

I blinked. "The police?"

"Things are worse than you think, X."

I gulped hard, gripping the blankets. Everything still felt like a dream, I could barely remember what'd happened. I knew I was in an accident, and before the accident I was at a party with Matt. I twisted the blankets in my hands, trying to force myself to remember when Mom stormed into the room.

"Honey, a nurse is here to see you. She's going to check you, and then someone else is going to come talk to you."

"Who?" I asked, even though I already knew. The words just came out as an effort to fill the throbbing silence.

"Some detectives."

"Mom, what's going on?"

She gripped her purse, a sympathetic look on her face. "Something very bad has happened, I just want you to tell the detectives what you know, okay?"

"Mom, why won't you just tell me——"

"Just do as I say for once!"

My hands flinched, and I dropped my eyes to my blankets, nodding. A moment later, a nurse came inside. Her blue scrubs swished with every movement, and she tried to look optimistic as she stepped over to my bedside.

"Xavier, how are you?"

I licked my chapped lips quickly, trying not to let the sudden rush of anxiety overtake me. "I'm alright."

"Just alright?"

I nodded. I could feel her eyes watching me, and then she said through her mask, "Well, you managed to sit up, so it seems to me like things are going to be okay. If they're not," she stressed, "I can't discharge you and you'll have to stay an extra day to make sure you're completely ready to go home."

My mother chimed in, "You hear that, X, you'll stay a while longer if you're not better. It's okay if you're not better."

Everyone was acting strange without reason. I tried to shift, to shake

18

off the uncomfortable feeling tensing my muscles, but I was so sore, I settled for an awkward adjustment in the bed instead.

"Alright," the nurse nodded, "I'll let the detectives know you're ready."

Mom rushed to my side, her black purse falling from her shoulder to her forearm, but she paid it no attention. "Listen, Xavier, the longer you stay in the hospital, the longer we have to keep the detectives from a full interview."

"Mom, what's going on?"

"It's bad, X. I can't tell you anything, but just be honest, alright?"

Mom was gripping my hands in the bed, and my stomach did flips like never before. I chewed my lip as she pulled away, trying to think of everything that could've happened to bring in detectives. But the bigger question was why my mom couldn't talk to me. Dad had told me to be honest, and I thought he meant with Mom, but now I know he meant with the detectives.

Two women in suits stepped inside my room, lifting their badges before standing before my bed. The woman in front held a manilla folder, the one behind her clasped small hands together as she waited. Brown skin and tight coils that were pulled back into a ponytail, a blue suit jacket, and a white button down, the woman with the folder looked like your typical television detective. It was so absurd I almost thought it was a joke, until she came around the bed, and I caught a glimpse of the gun on her hip.

"Oh," she pulled her jacket closed when she noticed me eyeing her weapon, "don't worry about that, it's just for safety reasons." She sat in a chair by my bedside and retrieved a document from her manilla folder. "I'm Detective Vean, this is Special Agent De Luca." She motioned to the other woman who stood glaring at me from the end of my bed. "Your name is Xavier Miles, correct?"

"Y-Yes."

"And how are you feeling, Xavier?"

"I'm alright."

"Just alright?"

I nodded. She lifted a sheet of paper and read something quickly before placing the paper back onto the folder. "Do you know why I'm here?"

"Not really." I glanced at my mother, but Special Agent De Luca stepped in front of her. Sweeping my gaze back to Detective Vean, I said, "Everyone just keeps telling me to be honest."

"When you say everyone, you mean your parents?"

I nodded.

Detective Vean smiled. "You've got good parents, kid."

"Better than mine," De Luca added. The two women chuckled before Detective Vean continued. "How much do you remember about what happened yesterday?"

"Um," I tried to stall, but their intense stares made me so uncomfortable, I just wanted to get this over with. "I can't remember much … Just a party."

She nodded, and then leaned forward to read something in her folder. "Do you know who the house of the party belonged to?"

"I…" I paused, shaking my head, "I don't remember."

Silence rang out. I was beginning to suffocate from their tortuous glares.

The detective offered me a gentle smile and waved her hand. "That's enough for now, Xavier. You may have bumped your head harder than we thought. We're going to need you to come down to the station once you're discharged. Give us a statement of what you know."

"What?" I asked slowly. "Why?"

"There have been a few tragedies since your accident, and we just need someone to point us in the right direction. Do you think you can do that?"

"Tragedies?"

"That's enough," my mother said loudly. "Your five minutes are up, detective." She pushed past De Luca. "You both need to leave now."

The detective stood. "We'll be seeing you, Xavier."

Stiffly, I inclined my head. My mother eyed them both as they left the room, but De Luca stopped right in front of her. In a low voice, she said, "We had a deal," and left the room. My mother's fierce frown melted into a defeated look. She stood against the wall an extra second, trying to regain her composure.

"Mom," I called.

Mom closed her eyes at the sound of my voice. "Not another word from you."

I ended up staying in the hospital an extra night for a total of three days. During that time, Jax was the only one who spoke to me besides the nurses. Mom was absentminded the entire time, watching over her shoulder at every cop and detective that passed our room. Dad wasn't there at all; I don't know if he was working or just decided to stay home.

Jax talked to me like nothing had happened, although his eyes drifted from mine to his phone a lot. But I knew better than to ask any more questions until we got home. Mom was on edge, Dad was gone, and Jax was trying to be normal.

Something was up, and it had to do with the detectives.

On the ride home from the hospital, I thought over Special Agent De Luca's last words to Mom, *we had a deal.* I didn't know what she meant by that, and I was afraid to ask. I figured that was why everyone was acting so secretive, but it was eating away at me. Detectives came to my room to question me, and they mentioned tragedies. I didn't know what that meant, and I wasn't sure I wanted to know. I wondered if Matt had to be interviewed too—or if he was even alright.

I'd spent the day of my discharge trying to piece my memories together. I began to remember more, like how Lia was my first kiss and almost my first *time* all in one night. I remembered Lia getting undressed in the car and then kissing Matt. Everything after that was a blur. I didn't know if they were alright, or if they were being interviewed, or if they knew anything about these tragedies or deals. But it didn't matter, because the next day after my discharge, I was taken to the station to find out exactly what was going on.

"Xavier Miles?" the prissy voice of a bony-looking woman chirped through the room, jarring me from my thoughts.

"Yes." I raised my hand.

She waved me over, and my parents followed me to the counter. "They're ready for you in room two, down the hall."

"Thanks," I said. I took a deep breath and glanced at my parents. We hadn't spoken much lately. When I tried to ask about Matt, Mom scolded me for lying to her about him, but that was it. No one answered any of the questions I had. I was left in the dark, but I wasn't sure if that had something to do with the deal the agent mentioned or some form of punishment from my parents.

4

Interrogation

"Good morning, Xavier," Detective Vean said as she watched my parents and me file in.

"Morning," I said. The room was all black. The only thing in it was five chairs, a wooden table, and a recording device with a folder on the table. I glanced around, dark mirrors reflected my tired and emotional face.

"Yes," the detective said, catching my eye, "there are others listening and watching, so please speak up."

I clenched my fists tightly and moved to a seat across from the seated detective and the standing agent.

"You elected to no attorney, is that correct?"

I nodded.

"I need a verbal answer," Detective Vean said.

I gulped. "Yes."

"Good. And they read you your rights before you came in?"

"Yes."

"Perfect, then we can get started." Detective Vean scribbled a few things down as Agent De Luca moved from behind her chair to sit on the edge of the table.

"How are you feeling, Xavier?" Her voice was tough to read, like her questions were always loaded, or trying to trip you up.

I looked at the bright skinned woman. Freckles traced the bridge of her nose and her cheeks while dark loose curls hung down to her shoulders.

"I feel fine," I answered.

"Have you talked to Matt by any chance?"

His name made my brow raise, and I clasped my hands together beneath the table, trying not to let myself get too anxious. "I haven't." I shook my head. "I texted him, but he hasn't responded. Is he alright?"

"That's what we're here to talk about." She stood and grabbed the folder Detective Vean had been fingering through. "Tell me why you think we asked you here."

"You told me you needed me to give a statement."

"You don't know why you're giving a statement?"

I shook my head. The detective flicked her eyes to my mother quickly before looking back at me. "Good. We wanted you to hear this information from us, and not give us a skewed story."

"Story?"

"I want you to walk me through exactly what happened at that party."

"Why?" I asked. "What happened?"

"Like I said before," she opened her hands, and a serious look rolled onto her face, "there have been tragedies. We need to piece this all together."

"Piece what? No one's told me anything since I woke up."

"You want to know what happened?" De Luca snapped.

I wanted to shrink away, but I gritted my teeth and forced a 'yes' between them.

"*This* happened."

The folder made a loud cracking noise as it hit the table. I jumped at the noise, and my eyes fell to the photos.

"Do you recognize this person?" De Luca pointed to what looked like a severely beaten person.

I leaned forward, trying to make out the figure lying in the grass.

"You don't, do you?"

"No," I whispered as I began to realize just how much trouble I could actually be in.

"That's partially because you probably didn't know the guy. He's in critical condition as we speak."

"What happened to him?"

"He was hit by a car." She shook her head and began listing his injuries. "A crushed ribcage, collapsed lung, and a punctured lung, to name a few things."

I looked around the room. My mother's mouth was sagging into a frown as she tried not to burst into tears, and my father wouldn't look at me. If this situation was different, then maybe I'd be grateful that my dad was showing some kind of emotion, even though I wasn't sure which one this was.

My eyes returned to De Luca. "Did we…" I cleared my throat. "Did we hit him?"

"Who is *we?*" De Luca pressed.

"Matt and I."

"No one else?"

I paused, wondering if I needed to bring Lia into this. I didn't have to if I didn't need to.

"You're going to a fancy private college in New York City, aren't you?"

"What?" I blinked from my thoughts to focus on Detective Vean's soft voice. "A private college in New York City, that's where you're going?"

"Oh, yes. But what about the man—"

"You're going on a full ride scholarship. Even got a book stipend, and housing. You're a smart kid, Xavier."

"That's right," Agent De Luca added, "smart kids make dumb mistakes sometimes though, don't they?"

"What do you want with me?"

"We want the truth. That's all," the detective said. "As long as we get the truth from you, you get to keep your scholarship, and this whole thing gets swept under the rug like it never happened."

"What are you talking about?" Anxiety shot through me.

"You're going to need to calm down, Xavier," De Luca said. But I couldn't. No one was making sense or telling me anything.

"Am I a killer!?" I yelled. My chest felt like it would collapse with pressure and all the air in my body felt like it had been pumped out as I gasped.

"Xavier!" My mother's voice snapped my head straight, and suddenly, I took a deep breath. De Luca and Vean began to blur as tears filled my eyes.

"What do you want?" I whispered as I dropped my head.

"Just the whole truth. If you can tell us the whole truth, then this will be painless, and quick. You walk away from here with a clean record. Does that sound good?"

I studied the floor, trying to hold back the tears that were burning my eyes. Although my vision was blurred from the tears, everything else had begun to make sense. If I told the truth, I could walk away with a normal life, as if none of this had ever happened.

What other choice did I have?

Shakily, I raised my head to answer, "It sounds fine." I glanced over at my mother, and she nodded at me. Her wide-open eyes pierced me, and I wondered how much she'd really known.

26

"Good, now name the three people in the car," De Luca said sternly.

"Naming each person, that's turning them in, isn't it?"

"If you want to see it so negatively, then yes." De Luca leaned over the table. "You can see it as a way of saving yourself."

"What if I ... What if I don't want to save myself?"

"*Xavier!*"

I snapped my vision to my mom; she was clenching the black strap on her purse. It was the one I'd bought her. Cheap and pleather, but it was all I could afford with my part-time job at the time. Her knuckles were fleshy white, but her hands trembled around the strap. "Xavier, they made their choice, now you have to make yours," she said.

"But, Mom, that's not right. I can't do that to Matt."

"Xavier Miles, you have no idea what you're talking about," she said hotly.

"X," my father said, "listen to your mother for once."

My eyes darted between my parents but the clicking of the tape recorder caught my attention. I looked over to find Detective Vean had moved from the table to flick a switch on the wall. "Listen, Xavier," she said, folding her arms over her chest as she crossed the room to me. "I know we haven't said much yet, because we don't want to scare you, but what's happened here is much bigger than you think. There's no need to be a hero when your life is on the line." She paused. "I know it seems wrong to turn your friends in. This is a big thing we're asking for. But trust me when I tell you, this case involves more than just your friends. So I need you to cooperate with us. Because, honestly, we really don't have anything to charge you with."

"*Detective,*" Special Agent De Luca snapped. Her face was blood-red now, and she was fuming, but Vean only waved a hand at her.

"So why are you making me do this? Why can't you get someone else to help you?" I asked.

"Just because we don't have anything to charge you with, doesn't mean we can't find a charge to tack on." She came around the table to sit again. "If you don't tell us what we need to know, you could be an accomplice, an associate, we can grab any charge along those lines and tack that onto you. With the loss of life involved in this case, those charges can start at four years behind bars. Do you really want that?"

"Wait a second, loss of life? I thought the guy we hit had injuries."

"Injuries that killed him."

Vean glanced over at De Luca, and the agent moved to flick the switch on the wall. Detective Vean pressed the button on the tape recorder and lifted her eyes to mine. "Can you give us your word that you'll cooperate?"

I glanced at my parents and in perfect unity, they nodded at me. I didn't know what I was getting into, but I didn't see a way out. I didn't know what else to do.

God, please help me.

I sighed and nodded. "I will cooperate."

Detective Vean nodded and opened a second folder. "So how about this, we'll tell you something, and you tell us something. This way, everyone knows what the other person knows. Sound good?"

"Yeah." I sniffled.

Detective Vean began to flip through some pages. "Can you answer Agent De Luca's question? We need the names of everyone in the car. And we need the placements, like where everyone was seated."

I took a breath and tried to tell myself I wasn't betraying Matt or Lia. "Matthew Leslie, he was sitting in the driver's seat."

"Matt was the driver?" Vean confirmed as she wrote on a yellow pad.

"Yes."

"Who else was in the," she paused, lifting her legal pad, "2021 Jeep Wrangler?"

"I was. I was sitting in the back."

"Which side?"

"Back right."

She mumbled my answer to herself and nodded. "Anyone else?"

I swallowed hard. "Lia Sunohara. She was sitting back left."

Her pen stopped, and Detective Vean looked up at me and then at the special agent. De Luca raised a brow and took a deep breath. Their awkward gestures made the nerves that were already stirring in my belly begin to boil.

"What's wrong?" I urged.

"There was no one in the front seat? The passenger front seat?"

I shook my head.

"We need a verbal answer," De Luca said sternly.

"No." I still shook my head. "Matt was driving, and Lia and I were in the back."

"Is Lia your girlfriend, Xavier?" De Luca asked as she placed her hands on the table.

"No." I glanced over at my parents. "I don't have a girlfriend." When I looked back at De Luca, she eyed me a moment and then looked over at my parents.

"Are they going to be a distraction? Keep you from being honest?"

"No," I said slowly.

"Because if they are, then they'll need to leave."

"*No*," I said firmly, "I-I-I won't do this without them."

"Fair enough," the detective said. "We just need you to state for the record that your parents, by name, are not a distraction, and you will remain honest and cooperative with us."

"My parents, Tanya Miles, and Dylan Miles, won't distract me, and I will remain honest and cooperative."

"Excellent. So tell us the truth now." De Luca hunched forward. "Was Lia your girlfriend?"

"No," I said loudly, "she wasn't."

"She was found shirtless."

"*Found?* What are you saying? Is she dead?" Before panic could set in, the detective cut in and said, "No threads, or evidence of clothes were found on her torso, which means they had to have been removed before the accident."

I shook my head, trying not to get overwhelmed.

Is Lia dead?

"Xavier, we need you to stay focused," the detective said.

I chewed my lip and nodded. My voice was quiet as I said, "Lia took her shirt off because she had the wrong idea about what I wanted that night."

"What do you mean?" the detective asked.

"She thought I wanted to hook up with her." I glanced up at my parents. My father was cradling my teary-eyed mother, and my heart almost broke. I'd done all that sneaking around, and all it amounted to was devastation. "But I didn't want to have sex," I said, looking back at the detective. "I went to the stupid party just to ask her out since we'd all graduated, and I didn't know when I'd see her again. She was going to a college here in Fresno, but I was going to New York, so I wanted to take a shot at her."

"So, Lia wasn't your girlfriend," the agent said. "She was your crush."

"Yes."

"Whose house was the party at?"

"I think her name was Stacy Miller."

"You remember now?" The detective smiled as she wrote.

"Yes. Can you tell me what happened to Lia or Matt?"

De Luca sighed and nodded at the detective who set her pen down and steepled her fingers on the table.

"Lia Sunohara didn't make it, Xavier. Her body was thrown from the car, through the windshield, and found some distance away."

30

I covered my mouth, swaying in my chair, wondering if I'd heard them right.

"But Matt Leslie did make it. He's at the hospital being treated right now for two broken legs."

I couldn't even feel relieved. I couldn't feel anything right now. Lia was dead, Matt had broken both his legs, and there was a man I didn't even know who'd lost his life.

Nervously, I asked, "Is that all?"

"Why do you ask that?" Vean sat back in her chair, looking me over closely.

"You said there were multiple tragedies. What else happened that night besides the car accident?"

De Luca eyed me for a moment. "Who called the police at the party, Xavier?"

"I don't know. Lia and I were in a room, and we heard someone screaming that the police were there. When we came out, the entire house was in an uproar, so we left out the back door."

"That's where Matt picked you up?"

"Yes. But I don't understand." Tears spilled from my eyes. "What's going on?"

"The reason the police showed up was because a girl made a call claiming her friend had been assaulted at the party."

Assaulted… Just a fancy word for rape. That realization made bile claw its way up my throat, and I clamped a hand over my mouth to keep it down.

"When the police arrived," De Luca continued, "the name of the girl given to them was not the name of the victim they found. The girl who called the police had been knocked unconscious."

I gripped the armrests of the chair just to keep myself from tipping over. "What does this have to do with me?"

"We need to identify the rapist. We also need to identify the true

31

assault victim. And," the detective paused.

"And what!?" I snapped.

"And we needed to know what the driver of the Jeep was doing."

I went numb. This was so much bigger than I thought. Whoever had been driving was responsible for killing Lia and that man we'd hit.

"They're dead because of us, aren't they?"

"We need to know what was going on in that Jeep, Xavier. Why was Matt distracted?"

"She kissed him," I answered absently as the memories of Lia kissing my best friend erupted in my mind. "I wouldn't kiss her, but Matt said he would. They were both drunk."

"And you weren't?"

I shook my head. "I never finished my cup of punch."

"You only had one?" The detective's voice was gentle now.

"Yes. But I didn't finish it."

"How many drinks did Matt have?" De Luca chimed in.

"I don't know. He had already been drinking when he picked me up for the party."

"How many drinks did Lia have?"

"I don't know."

"Do you know what the punch was spiked with?"

"I don't know!" I snapped.

"I think that's enough for today," the detective said before De Luca could ask me anything else. "We'll be in touch sometime later. For now, just keep us posted on whatever new information you remember, Xavier, alright?"

Barely able to speak, I murmured, "Alright."

5

Silent Progression

I lay in bed, but I couldn't rest. I couldn't stop my mind from wandering all over. Lia was dead, possibly two women had been raped, and Matt was going to be charged for killing two people—one of them was my own crush.

I didn't know how to feel. I didn't know what to make of everything.

"That was my last chance to tell her how I felt," I choked on my words, slapping a hand over my mouth as tears spilled from the corners of my eyes. I hadn't cried since the interrogation four days ago, but I'd been stuck in this state of numbness. Nothing going on. No thoughts, no appetite, just fear and questions I couldn't answer. Special Agent De Luca barred me from visiting Matt or his family. They didn't want me discussing the case with anyone related to him; they said talking about it could put myself in jeopardy.

I sniffled, wiping my nose on the back of my hand as my mom came into my room. "Xavier? How are you today?"

"I'm fine, Mom," I said.

She sat on the edge of my bed and stared at my dresser across from us. No one in the family had asked me about the case. They'd left me to myself mostly. Mom and Jax came to visit me, Dad didn't, but I hadn't expected him to.

"Lia's funeral is tomorrow," Mom said softly. "Do you want to go?"

I shook my head. "I don't really think it's a good idea."

"Do you think you'll regret it?"

"Like I regret everything else?"

Mom shot me a look of sympathy. "Don't blame yourself for what happened—"

"Who am I to blame? I got Lia killed because I did something I shouldn't have done. Aren't you mad I lied? Aren't you mad I caused all this?"

She sighed. "Would punishment make all the guilt go away? You can't figure out who to blame, so you blame yourself and deem yourself the sole reason why this catastrophe has happened." She stood and walked across the room, looking at a picture of Jax and me from when we played baseball together. We were three years apart, but one year, we got to play varsity together in elementary school. He was really good, and wanted to go pro, but I'd only played because Matt had played. Just like I'd only been at that party because Matt had gotten us invitations. Just like I'd done a lot of things and had kept a lot of secrets because of Matt.

"When the police arrived at my house and told me there'd been an accident, I thought my heart would stop." Mom stared at the photo, her short hair swinging into her face. Slowly, she touched her thumb to the inside of her right wrist, rubbing the cloud-shaped birthmark. I wasn't even sure if she was aware she was doing it as she said, "They told me, 'Your son has been involved in a terrible accident, and he's at the hospital.' I nearly left in the middle of the conversation to find you. Your father ... he was dazed after the police left, just standing in the doorway. But I rushed around the house, making certain I never let a single bad

34

thought into my head." She teared up, swiping at her eyes. "I couldn't lose you. I wouldn't. What would Jax do without his older brother?" Mom turned to face me. "When we got to the hospital, the doctors told us they had no idea how the accident had happened, but you were the only one they were certain was going to wake up soon.

"When I finally saw you, I collapsed at your bedside, holding your hand, and weeping praises to God." She took a deep breath. "And in that moment, I realized I was like Mary, Jesus' mother. You remember when Jesus was at the temple, and Mary and Joseph thought He was lost? They had to go looking for Him?"

"Mom, I'm not Jesus. He was out doing good. I was out doing wrong."

She nodded. "I know, but you needed to be found and brought back. Taught that you can't do things like this anymore. You learned about consequences in ways that were harsher than any parent would like."

"Isn't that more like the prodigal son?"

She chewed her lip, her tan nose turning pink. "You'll be the prodigal son when you come back to me on your own, Xavier. When you can realize where this was all wrong for more than just a court case. You think I care about that? You think Mary cared that Jesus was teaching? She was just relieved that He was alright. I am no different." Mom crossed the room and grabbed my hands. "X, all I want is for you to come back to me. You've lost your way, but I don't think there's any discipline in the world that is needed right now to guide you. There are no words to scold you or antagonize you. I just want you back… I want *my* son back."

She pulled me into her embrace, and I knew things had to change.

Mom didn't yell at me, she didn't take a belt to my bottom, she didn't do anything you'd think of as discipline. But her wretched plea for the old Xavier, the one who believed in Christ and followed Him wholeheartedly, to return to her was more than enough discipline for me.

Mom was right, so far, I'd only thought what I'd done was wrong because of the circumstances. But what if things had gone right, and the cops weren't called, and the accident never happened, and I got Lia to understand that I just wanted to date her? Would I feel bad that I'd lied to my parents? I probably wouldn't have thought much about it since I'd have Lia, and no one would've known. But that wasn't who I was supposed to be. I'd somehow lost myself along the way, and now, I had to rediscover myself through Christ.

Months passed and summer ended without another interrogation which surprised me. I thought I'd be testifying in court within days but this was real life, not some true crime television show. Criminal cases took a lot longer to sort out, months—sometimes even years.

Nevertheless, things began to settle down, and I started going back to church. It was the only place for a long time where my mind didn't wander. I was always focused during service, listening to every word from the preacher, clinging to it for dear life. I'd felt like I was suddenly thrown into a sea of chaos but, somehow, Jesus had met me right in the center of it and was leading me out of it.

"Alright, X, don't forget you're to see the counsellor, and make sure you join that Christian group on campus like you promised."

I nodded as I stood at the car with my family. Mom's smile was weak, somewhere between worried, reluctant, and happy. But I'd already promised myself I'd never screw up like that again. I needed to avoid problems and run-ins with the police at all costs.

"Mom, you don't have to worry," I said, throwing an arm around her. "I'll be fine."

She squeezed me tight. "Just be careful, Xavier Miles."

I leaned down and kissed her head. "It won't happen again, Mom, I promise." The hissing of the locusts in the trees filled the awkward silence before Dad called, "Come on, Tanya, or he'll never make friends."

Dad nodded at me, it was firm and emotionless, but it was a passage of trust. My parents were only letting me go to college in New York because they wanted me as far away from Fresno as possible. They wanted me to try to start over without the case looming over my head.

I gave my father a nod back as I held the door open for Mom to climb in.

Jax rolled down his window and pulled one of his Air Pods out. "I'm going to wear your clothes, just so you know."

I rolled my eyes and slapped his head which was shaved into a mohawk now. "Fine, just put them back." He cracked a smile before rolling the window up.

"Alright," Mom said from the front seat, "we're off. I'll shoot you a text as soon as we're off the plane."

"Sounds good, Mom."

"I love you," she called.

I chuckled and leaned into the window to give her one more kiss on the forehead. "I love you too, Mom. See you for Christmas." The car pulled off, Mom waved out the window at me, tears on cheeks and pursed lips trying not sob.

"So, your family's keeping a secret—obviously."

I whirled around to find a dark-skinned guy with close shaven hair and a wicked smile on his face standing behind me.

"Secrets? What do you mean?"

"You've got to go see the counsellor. Means there's something wrong with you, doesn't it?"

"No." I turned to leave but he followed behind me, his floppy shoes slapping loudly against the parking lot blacktop.

"I've got to see the counsellor too," the annoying guy said. "I've got a phobia of bugs." I stopped walking and turned to face him.

"Like spiders?"

He shook his head and began to itch. "*All* bugs, man. They all freak me out. But what girl is going to want a guy who's scared of bugs?"

I raised a brow, and he shrugged. "Yes, I've got bigger problems, but girls are my real problem. If they were just nicer to me, then I'd probably be less afraid of bugs."

I paused and squinted at him. "I don't think I see the correlation."

"Who cares?" He shrugged, slapping a hand to my back. "What's your name?" He shoved me along, and we began walking to the main building. The campus was huge and stunning. Smooth concrete buildings with glass tunnels and sleek windows. The campus looked like a modern-day castle, not an educational institution.

"My name's Xavier."

"Alright, I'm gonna call you 'Secret X.'"

"Why?" I asked as we stepped over a speed bump.

"Because your family clearly has a secret, and until you tell me why you're going to counselling, you'll be Secret X." He paused, grinning slyly. "*Sex* for short."

I stopped abruptly and shoved his arm away. "You can't call me Sex!" A woman and her daughter stopped their teary goodbye and blinked at us as we stood in the middle of the parking lot.

"He means he can't wait for sex! He's so hormonal!" the guy shouted goofily.

I snatched him by the shirt and dragged him to the grassy fields away from the staring eyes of the lot. "Would you stop that??" I snapped.

He flashed me his pearly whites and began to laugh loudly. "Come on, lighten up. I'll call you X, alright?"

I rolled my eyes. "Fine."

He nodded. "I'm Junior Calliway, but just call me JC."

"Junior?"

He ticked a brow before swiping a hand over his face. "Alright, first embarrassing story of brotherhood happening right now." JC grabbed my shoulder and pulled me closer to him. "My mother doesn't know who my dad is, so she named me Junior, like the actual word, 'junior.' She said she wanted to name me after my father, but since any one of the men she'd been with could be him, she opted for Junior."

"You're kidding me, right?"

He shook his head. "Afraid not. But you'd better not tell anyone."

I snorted. "I wouldn't even *want* to tell that to anyone."

JC patted my back. "We're going to be good friends, aren't we?"

"I hope." I smiled.

"Come on, I'll show you to the counsellor office."

"I'm guessing you're not a freshman," I said as we crossed the field.

"I am, actually. My sister went here two years ago, so I got to know the campus a little from her events and random visits."

"I see."

"You're not from here," he said, "you say everything funny."

"You mean I don't have a New York accent."

"Are you insinuating that *I* have an accent?" JC teased.

"I'm from Fresno," I said as we finally made it to the big glass doors of the main building of the campus.

"Fresno. That's Cali, right?"

"Yeah." I nodded.

"There's a lot of hot girls in Cali, right?"

I stopped, as thoughts of Lia sprang into my head.

"Hey, man, you alright?" Junior asked when he noticed I'd stopped walking.

I sank my hands into my pockets and nodded, staring at the tile floor. "I'm alright."

Mercifully, JC changed the subject. "There are two counsellors here every day. It's more than likely that you'll meet with one of them instead of the other three counsellors who're only here three days a week, and some weekends."

"Who are they?" I asked as I pulled out a folded piece of paper. Weaving through the crowd of mousing students, I read my counsellors name, only stopping to pay attention when I walked right into a girl, and she dropped her backpack.

"Sorry," she murmured, leaning down to grab her bag. "I was looking all over." She chuckled, waving her hand—and I caught a glimpse of the silver bracelet on her wrist. From it dangled a cloud-shaped charm.

I blinked, trying to remember where I'd seen that charm before, but she was speaking again, snatching my attention away from her bracelet. "This place is so big, I wasn't sure where I was going."

She looked familiar. Sweeping red hair fell over her shoulders, obviously a wig, but undeniably still beautiful. I couldn't even find any words as she reached for the papers that'd fallen from her bag.

I swooped to the floor and grabbed them for her.

"Thanks—" her mouth hung open as she suddenly frowned at me, staring. She had cocoa brown skin, a small bulb nose, and almond eyes that blinked rapidly at me.

"Do I know you?" I asked, leaning forward, but she snatched the paper from me and stood, scurrying off without giving me an answer.

"What was that about?" JC asked.

I shrugged, standing slowly as I watched her snake through the crowd. "I think I've seen her before."

6

Introductions

"Hello, Xavier, I've been expecting you," the counsellor said. He was shamelessly tall. And he wore square black framed glasses and a sweater over his button-down in the middle of the hot summer. His office was cooler than the rest of the building, however, I felt like he dressed that way because it was more of his style than because of the coolness of his room.

"Please," he gestured to the center of his wide office. "Have a seat."

I nodded and sat in a chair. His office was set up like a psychologist's office. A big comfortable chair for the patient across from a more studious looking chair for the doctor. There was a desk off to the side, brown and black, with a mini fridge. I've never been in a counsellor's office before, but I don't think they usually have mini fridges.

"You want something to drink?" he offered.

"No thanks," I said.

He sat across from me.

"Where's your clipboard or notepad? Don't you need to write some things down about me so you can laugh at how crazy I am?" I have to admit, that was a shallow statement, but I didn't want to go to counselling in the first place. My parents were worried I'd spiral out of control in college, so they'd signed me up for counselling without telling me until the day of our flight.

"Well," he said, setting an ankle on his knee, "I'm just here to introduce myself and talk to you. And I don't write things down because I think you or any of my students are crazy."

"I don't think I'll ever feel comfortable talking to you." I shrugged. "I don't even know you." Hopefully, I could be annoying enough for him to pass me off, but he smiled at me, and I knew I was in for the long haul.

"That's alright, Xavier. Part of these sessions is for you to get to know me. I believe that it's great for my students to come to understand that I was a young person once too."

"You still look young to me."

He nodded, and his dusty blonde bangs sagged in his face before he shoved them back. "I appreciate that." He blushed. "I'm thirty-four this month, so I'm glad all my youthfulness hasn't disappeared yet." He chuckled lightly, but it was so awkward and not funny, I forced myself to give him a stiff smile.

"But, anyways," he said, still smiling, as if he didn't just embarrass himself, "let me introduce myself. My name is Elijah Ross, you can call me Ross, or Eli if you'd like."

I sighed and adjusted in my seat. I couldn't care less if his name was Jon with an 'h' or without one, I just wanted this session to be over.

"You know, Xavier, these sessions will go by faster if you talk a little."

"I don't feel like talking right now."

"I see." He shrugged. "Nothing can be done then. Our sessions are one hour every Tuesday at one. Starting next week. So, I'll see you at the next session."

I raised a brow. "Wait, you're letting me go?"

"Yes." He chuckled. "I won't always do this, but sometimes it's better to step away than to try and force someone to talk. Generally, I figure my students will tell me what they need to when they feel like it. That way the conversation is more open, less forced."

I thought it over for a moment and then shrugged. "I guess so."

He stood and motioned toward the door. "Like I said, I won't always do this, but I see a bright future for us, Xavier, one where our conversations won't be forced."

"Right." I made my way to the door.

"I'll see you next week." Elijah held the door open for me as I nodded and walked out.

"Whoa, that was fast," Junior said as he stood and walked beside me.

"Yeah, he told me that he doesn't normally let his students out early."

"So why'd he let you out?"

"Something about not forcing the conversation." I made dramatic air quotes that won me a snort from JC.

"He's so cringe," he said as we made it to the main stairs. The long winding staircase was glass and spilled into a lobby with couches, student boards, folding tables with all-too-friendly students, and a long hall that connected you to another building if you took a left, and on the right were administrator offices.

"Want to get some food?" JC asked as we raced down the steps.

"Sure, but I haven't even found out who my roommate is. He wasn't there when I moved in this morning."

"Alright, then we'll go to the dorms and see if he's there."

I followed JC around the campus to the dorms. All the way there, he told me about himself; how his phobia of bugs began with ants, and

43

grew to spiders, then worms, then dragon flies to actual flies, and he's been downhill ever since. I don't know how he's survived this long, especially since his sister moved to the south last year and he goes to visit her. He says the heat brings out all kinds of bugs, but he just stays indoors.

"Let's cut through the girls' dormitory, it's shorter than walking all the way around."

I didn't get the chance to protest. JC moved like a dart, zipping into the building, and hiking up the stairs.

"Why are we going upstairs?" I asked, jogging up behind him.

"Because my high school crush is staying in these dorms."

We stood against a wall and peeked around the corner.

"Right there. Jocelyn Keifer, or Jay. She's a stone-cold fox."

"How old is that slang?" I teased.

JC threw a hand and pointed as Jay stepped out of her dorm to retrieve a box on a bellhop. Long, sugar brown legs were exposed beneath her short jean shorts, and she wore a navy-blue lace bralette. Loose curls were tied into a messy bun, and her pouty pink lips lifted into a smile as she glanced over her smooth shoulder, laughing with whoever her roommate was.

"Wow," I whispered.

"Hey, she's off limits." JC swatted my stomach, and I belted out a cough, drawing Jay's attention to us. We tried to scramble around the corner, but she called out, "Junior? Is that you?" His eyes darted to mine, and he whispered, "She's *my* crush, so don't get any ideas."

"Right." I nodded. I'd keep my word too. I knew how it felt to have your crush swept into the arms of the only friend you trusted. I pushed away the thoughts of Lia and Matt as we walked around the corner.

"Hey, Jay," Junior said.

"What are you doing here?" Her voice sprang out with joy, and her eyes shifted to mine.

"I'm showing my new friend Xavier around." JC suddenly sounded nervous.

I glanced over at him and back at Jocelyn who hadn't pulled her eyes away from me. "Hi," I said shyly.

She adjusted the box in her hands to set it on her hip. "Hi."

JC looked between us.

I shook my head.

"I'm here with Junior, just trying to get to my dorm."

"Yeah, this hall is like a shortcut to the boys' dorm." Jay smiled. "At first, I thought it sucked because there'd be a lot of traffic, but," she paused and chewed her lip, her eyes flickering over me, "maybe it's not so bad." Before either of us could say more, Jay turned and went into her dorm room, and JC shoved an elbow into my side.

"Ouch!" I cradled it.

"What was that between you two?"

I shrugged. "I don't know."

"Come on." He pulled my arm, and I stood upright to follow him into Jay's room. "So, who'd you get saddled with?" JC said sarcastically as he stepped into Jocelyn's room.

She set her box on her bed and opened a palm to her roommate. "This is Madeline Jones. And I didn't get *saddled* with her, she's actually pretty cool."

"Madeline Jones? You're the girl Xavier bumped into downstairs."

Madeline glanced over at me before turning away to dig through a box on her bed.

"You two know each other?" Jay asked.

"Not very well," I said. "We stumbled into each other in the main lobby."

"Before she ran off like a total psycho," JC teased.

Madeline didn't say anything. She continued to unpack, pulling notebooks and paper out of the box while her cloud charm dangled on

45

her bracelet. I rubbed my birthmark as I stared at it, still trying with all my might to remember where I'd seen it from. The little shape reminded me of so much. My home … my connection to my sweet mother—everything I'd left behind.

Madeline pulled out a composition notebook. It was blue with a white sticker on it that read, *Face it, Tiger, you just hit the jackpot.* I'd seen that notebook before, read that sticker a million times, but since the accident, a lot of my memories had been foggy, and I couldn't remember where that notebook was from, just like I couldn't remember where I'd met Madeline from. However, I was able to remember that quote.

"That line," I said, stepping forward.

Madeline looked over her shoulder at me as I came to stand beside her at the bed. "Those are Mary Jane's first words to Peter Parker."

Her eyes widened and there was a sense of confusion before a small smile traced her lips, "Yeah, how'd you know?"

I smiled too. "I'm a big Spiderman fan. Or at least I think so."

"What do you mean?" she asked.

I touched the sticker on her notebook. "I got in a car accident not long ago, memory's been fried ever since."

The room shifted, and I could feel everyone's eyes on me.

"I'm alright," I said, turning to face JC and Jay.

Jay looked concerned, but JC blurted out, "That's your secret. That's why your family was all moody in the lot. They're scared you're going to forget who you are."

I sighed. "It's not like that."

He burst into laughter and came over to look at the sticker. "Huh, I never would've known where that was from."

"Well…" Jay slipped her hands in her back pockets. "You guys busy? I could really use a hand getting the rest of my boxes inside."

"No," JC said quickly, "we are absolutely not busy." He turned on his heels, nearly slipping to the floor to retrieve boxes for Jay. I walked

46

out to the bellhop and grabbed one to bring it inside. I was carrying it to Jay when Madeline said, "That one's actually mine."

"Oh, sorry." I carried it to her bed and set it down for her.

"There's a party tonight," Jay said, eyeing me again. "Everyone's going to be there."

"Everyone?" I asked.

"Yeah. It'd be cool if you came by." She pressed her glossy lips together before releasing them into a pout.

"Well…" I swallowed thickly. "I don't know. It's my first day here and I'm—"

"Perfect," she interjected. "First day here, you need to make some friends. Come on out, it'll be loads of fun. And bring a friend if it'll make you feel more comfortable."

I took a deep breath and nodded. "Alright, I'll be there."

Jay smiled. "Good, I'll see you tonight at eight. By the docks—it's a boat party."

I nodded, passing a glance to Madeline. She swiped her fire engine red hair from her face, there was a gentle smile pursing her lips.

"Well," I said, looking back at Jay, "we'd better get going."

"I'll walk you out." She turned, and my eyes dragged down her slender frame. Her hips swayed, and her bottom peeked out from beneath her super short shorts. I closed my eyes, suppressing every urge to do something I'd regret as I followed her to the door.

"Hey, Xavier," Madeline called. Her voice snapped me from my thoughts of Jay, and I whirled around to face her. "You dropped this." She extended my counselling papers to me. It was what I'd been digging for when I'd stumbled into her back in the lobby.

"Thanks," I took it and headed out of the dorm.

7

Will History Repeat?

"I think that Madeline girl likes you," JC said as we stood in his dorm. He wanted to stop by his room before going to find out who my roommate was.

"Why do you say that?"

"Did you see the way she looked at you when you knew where that quote was from?" He jogged into his bathroom and left the door open as he used it.

"She was shocked," I said, sitting on the bed. "She didn't expect anyone to recognize it."

"She was happy!" he said loudly. "And she likes you." He flushed the toilet and washed his hands before stepping out. "I think you should go out with her."

"What?"

"Yeah. You could be her Spiderman, while she's MJ. Come on," he teased, "she's got the red hair and everything."

"That doesn't mean anything."

"Are you defending her?"

"No," I said, standing. "I'm just saying, her red hair could be what she likes."

JC sighed. "Yeah, thirty-six inches of the fakest, reddest hair in the world is definitely an interest and *not* someone pretending to be someone else."

"The real MJ didn't even have long hair like that."

"It doesn't matter." JC waved a hand and crossed the small room to his dresser. "You two need to hookup."

"No," I said firmly. "And you're only saying that because you think I'm interested in Jay."

He stopped digging through his drawer and sighed. "You didn't see the way she looked at you."

"You can't keep her from every guy, Junior. And I don't even like her." I shrugged. "She's a nice girl, but I'm not interested in her. Which is why I'm not going tonight."

"What?" he gasped. "Yes, you are going because I'm your plus-one!"

"Or you can go in my place," I said.

"I wasn't invited." He frowned and began digging through his drawer again.

"You're taking this way too seriously."

"You're not taking it seriously *enough*. Everyone will be there! It's an important party and I wasn't even invited."

I sighed. I didn't want to go, but I knew JC would never let me live it down if I didn't go. "Fine, but I'm only staying for an hour." I looked away from him. "I had a bad experience at the last party I went to. I don't want to go out ever again."

"Good—great!" JC slammed his drawer closed and held up a pair of white socks. I'm not even sure he heard a word I just said. "I'll put these on and then we can head to your dorm."

We took the elevator to the fifth floor and walked toward my room. The men's dorm was much different from the women's. It didn't *look* different, they were built the exact same way, it was just the atmosphere. The women's dorm was mostly quiet, a few giggles and chatter, but it was charming. The men's dorm... it was loud, and messy already. Luggage, bedding, garbage, and clothes were sprawled throughout the blue carpeted halls. Someone's dorm was open, and they were playing music loudly inside. There was a guy riding his hoover board right towards JC and me, squirting everyone with a water gun. We jumped out of his way, but he still managed to shower us in something I realized wasn't water.

JC smelled himself and frowned. "Who puts lemon juice in a water gun!??"

I laughed at his misery.

"This hall has a mix of freshmen and seniors, but I bet you'd never believe it," JC said as we finally made it to my dorm. "Everyone is so immature. You can't tell what year anyone is in."

I unlocked the door and walked in. Moon shaped eyes looked up from a suitcase in the middle of the floor. "You must be Xavier," he said.

"Yeah," I came inside, and JC followed, "I am."

"What's your name?" Junior asked.

I rolled my eyes. "This is Junior, just call him JC."

He nodded. "You two come from the same school?"

"No, JC and I just met earlier today."

He adjusted his glasses and glanced between us. "You guys look close already."

"Which means there's no room for you," JC interjected.

"Stop." I shoved him and crossed the floor to my new roommate. "What's your name?"

"Glenn Michaels." He extended a hand.

"Nice to meet you, Glenn." I took his hand. "I'm Xavier, but you can just call me X."

"Sounds good."

I sat on my bed as JC stood in the middle in the room watching Glenn unpack.

"So, Glenn," I said, "you like partying?"

He shrugged. "Never been partying."

"Wow, you're a loser." JC frowned down at him, but Glenn didn't pay his remark any attention.

"No, you're not, Glenn," I told him. "I think avoiding parties is a good thing."

"I don't avoid them," he stopped packing, "I've just never been invited."

"Oh, well, good news. There's a party tonight and I'm supposed to bring someone."

"You're taking me!" JC whined.

"It's a college party, no one's actually going to care if I bring two people." I rolled my eyes. "You should come, Glenn." I wanted to start off on the right foot with my roommate, but I also needed someone to bring Junior home in case I left early.

"Seriously?" Glenn moved from the floor to his bed and tossed the pile of clothes in his arms on it.

"Yeah, it starts at eight. On the docks."

"Sounds fancy," he snorted.

"Yeah," JC said flatly.

We arrived at the docks at ten, walking by three people who were passed out cold before we even got to the yacht that was blasting with music and cheers. JC and Glenn rushed in ahead of me, but I couldn't get my feet to move. The last party I'd gone to, things had gotten out of control, and I almost lost my own life.

"I shouldn't be here," I whispered to myself. "I can't do this."

As I turned to leave, I heard a familiar voice call out to me. "Xavier! What are you doing out there?" It was Jay, walking over in a sheer top, and a mini skirt. Her slender hips swayed like the boat behind her as she reached me. The repulsive smell of alcohol filled my lungs as I breathed in her scent when she got close.

"Hey, Jay, I was just getting some air," I said nervously.

"Air." She folded her arms, tapping her bare foot on the wooden dock. "You just got here, and you need air already?"

I sighed, I didn't want to bring my Fresno problems to New York, so I swallowed the vivid party memories and flashed her a smile.

"Let's go inside." She pulled on my arm. "I want to dance."

There was no breathing air inside the yacht. Everyone was high or drunk. And if you weren't, you were getting secondhand intoxication. The haze in the room made the strobe lights and flailing limbs look like a club, and less like a college party. Jay dragged me out to the middle of the floor, pushing through people and knocking some out the way. She hooked her arms around my neck and began to dance. She swayed on her feet, while she hung her head back.

When the next song began, she leaned forward, a dizzy look in her eyes. I thought she might kiss me, but she quickly let go of my neck and twirled around to press her bottom into me. I caught her by the hips, letting her dance against me. I wanted it to stop, but just like with Lia Sunohara, I also wanted her to keep going.

JC popped into my head, and I reflexively let go of Jay. But that didn't stop her. She stood up straight, sweeping her sweaty curls to one side, and stepped back to let me watch her dance. She groped herself, twisting her body in every direction. I tried to look away, but I didn't want to. She was sexy, and she liked me. It was hard to be loyal to JC right now. Considering I barely knew him, I wanted to think it was okay to do this. But something stronger than JC, *Someone* stronger than JC, was tugging at my eyes, at my heart. I could hear the words so clearly in my head, like there was no music playing anymore.

For I do not understand my own actions. For I do not do what I want, but I do the very thing I hate…

I closed my eyes, trying not to hear the Voice in my heart calling out to me. Trying not to identify with the words pounding in my head. I wanted to stay, but I knew I should go. *But I'm already here… No! Leave X!*

I opened my eyes, feeling dizzy and sweating. I looked around, trying to find an exit when I spotted Jay. She had left me already, moved through the crowd to cuddle up with Madeline in their own corner of the dancefloor. I shook my head, stumbling through the crowd and tried to find the exit.

I moved around dancing couples, singles, and potheads too high to move. I didn't care, I just wanted to get out of there. It felt like my heart would thump out of my chest, like I would faint any moment if I didn't move fast enough.

My movements became irrational as the verse from earlier kept repeating in my head. I tripped and shoved a man to the floor to keep from falling. I didn't even care if he stood up and retaliated. Maybe he would knock me out and stop the calling in my head.

Finally, I made it to the exit, and crashed through the drunks at the door as I tripped up the stairs. When I finally made it out, I fell down on the dock, panting for air. The hollow sound of footsteps came closer and when I looked up, I was shocked to see black flamed glasses reflecting the light of the moon. I blinked as he stepped closer, a tall gentleman leaned over me.

"Eli?" I muttered. *My counsellor?*

He smiled pleasantly. "You won't believe this, but I got a tip there was a party going on out here." He shrugged. "Nothing wrong with college kids throwing a party, but I doubt everyone in there is old enough to consume alcohol."

"Right…" I said, still confused.

"I came to break up the party. The cops are on their way over here right now, but I don't want my students to end up behind bars before the semester starts. So, if you don't want to get caught, Xavier, I suggest you leave now."

"But … Eli, I swear it's not what it looks like," I said, trying to stand up. I was weak for some reason, like it took everything in me just to get up. I didn't look like a kid fleeing from sin, I looked like another drunken student wobbling his way out of a crazy party.

Eli looked down at me, but there was no judgment on his face. I think that made me feel worse.

"Just get out of here," he said, extending a hand to me.

I took it, and he pulled me up. "Thanks," I mumbled.

He nodded and headed for the yacht.

8

Sherbet Pink

"I know we were interrupted last time," Michael said, "but today, Benedict will begin his earthen experience."

"Hey," Joseph whispered to Benny. He was standing in line behind him, watching as Michael went over information at the podium. "How'd it go with Adar?"

Benny twitched at her name, gripping his pants.

"I guess not so good?" Joseph prodded.

"I don't want to talk about it."

"But I guess she said no."

Benedict shrugged, not wanting to remember the conversation where Adar snapped at him. It was out of concern, but Benny had never seen Adar so upset before, he'd never seen *anyone* upset before. The more human the ones above became, the closer it was to their assignment. Feelings of negative emotions were always the telltale signs of a child of Jehovah's earthen assignment upon them.

"I'm trying to listen," Benny whispered back.

"Now," Michael said, catching their attention, "this whole exercise is designed by God as a fulfillment of the written Word that on the hearts of those on Earth, Elohim has put His law so that you will always know righteousness from unrighteousness."

"I don't think I understand," Benny said.

Michael folded his thick arms and nodded. "Then I will explain further. What you are about to experience is the way the Earth works. The way darkness works. God is fair and just, therefore, He is giving each of you a chance to experience Earth before you officially go, because He would never send you without preparing you."

"So how is this then written on our hearts?" Joseph asked behind Benny.

"You will experience and learn what righteousness and unrighteousness looks like on Earth in every possible situation your dust form will be able to handle. With this knowledge, it will never leave you. You will always have guidance in your heart, stemming from this training."

"What if we don't remember our training once we arrive?" A small girl in the back raised her hand.

"You will not need to remember this exercise," Michael explained. "You will know without a doubt, what is wrong and what is right. Whether or not you choose to do what's right will solely be up to you."

The small class grew quiet, each student beginning to understand just how serious going to Earth was.

"Benedict," Michael called, "you're up."

I sat up, rubbing my eyes, I'd had another one of those dreams again. The ones where I couldn't remember anything. But I wanted to remember.

I sighed, swinging my legs over the edge of the bed. I spent my first night in my dorm mostly alone since I came back from the party early. I rubbed a hand over my face, thinking of how much of a fight it'd been to get myself to leave that party. With Eli showing up and letting me go, I was grateful that I didn't stay. Last night could've been a repeat from the graduation party.

When I glanced at my phone on the bedside table, I groaned in annoyance. I had thirty-six unread messages. Thirty of them were from JC, three from Glenn, one from Mom, and two from scammers. I opened the message from Mom, she told me their plane had landed and the house felt empty without me.

I stood and I tipped to the bathroom. I don't remember Glenn coming in last night, and I'm sure he doesn't either, but I tried to be quiet as he snored loudly. I closed the bathroom door and sat on the toilet to call my mother. The phone rang twice before she answered.

"Hello? Mom?"

"Xavier? What's wrong?" I heard her shifting around in bed, panic setting into her voice.

"Nothing, Mom, I'm just calling to say hi. I … I missed you guys."

"At four in the morning?"

I turned my wrist over and read my watch. It was seven in the morning, Mom's usually up by now.

"Did you forget we were three hours behind?" she asked into the silence.

I exhaled dramatically. "Sorry, Mom, I totally forgot."

Her chuckle came with a sigh of relief, and I heard my father waking up on the other end.

"What is it? Is something wrong with X?" His voice was panicky like Mom's had been, and I realized just how much I'd put my family through since the accident. Everyone was afraid they'd be getting bad news from me, and it was the worst feeling in the world. It made me feel even stupider for going to that party last night.

I swapped ears with my phone, as I listened to Mom have a short conversation with Dad.

"No, he's alright," she was saying. "He forgot about the time difference."

"Oh! Alright," my dad said drowsily, "tell him I said hey."

"I will," Mom told him. I could hear her moving around, probably leaving the room so she wouldn't keep Dad up. "Sorry about that, X," she said softly. "How was your first night?"

I shrugged, trying to decide how to tell her I went to another party that almost ended the same way the last one did. "It was alright," I muttered. "I did a little unpacking, met some friends, and turned in."

"You made friends? That's wonderful!" The excitement in my mother's voice made me smile as I thumbed the pattern on my shorts.

"Thanks, Mom, they're good people."

"I'm sure they are, you have good judgement. I trust you."

Trust... I didn't like that word. It was loaded with all kinds of expectations I didn't know whether I could uphold.

"X? You there still?"

"Yeah," I said abruptly, "I'm here, Mom."

"Did you meet the counsellor yet?"

I had only thought about Eli in passing this morning, but thinking about his appearance at the party, and letting me go, I figured I should thank him.

"Yeah," I said after a moment of silence, "he's alright, I guess."

"Good. You think you'll be able to talk to him?"

"About the case? No."

"Xavier, you said you'd give it chance." All traces of happiness vanished from Mom's voice, replaced by annoyance.

"I know, Mom," I said. "And I am."

"No, you're not. You're purposely keeping your guard up when you

58

said you wouldn't."

"I told you I'd give it a *try*. I tried it, and I don't like it."

"Xavier Miles, you better learn to *love* it," she snapped.

I sucked my teeth. "Fine, Mom. I've gotta go. I'll call you later."

"Don't you dare hang up this phone," her words were sharp, and her accent reappeared. It always came out when she was angry at me or my brother. My mother doesn't speak Spanish to us, she only speaks it *about* us to her mother sometimes.

"Mom, I'm serious," I said, standing up at the sink, "my roommate might be up soon, and I've been in here for a while. He'll need the bathroom."

"Fine, but you better call me later."

I nodded, as if she could see me. "I promise. I love you, Mom."

"I love you too. Bye now."

"Bye."

I hung up the phone, stretched my hands across the counter. I needed to find Eli, and ask him why he let me go, or thank him. I wasn't sure which one I wanted to do more, but I was afraid to thank him because it might come off as too desperate, and then he would know something's up. I grabbed my toothbrush and decided on just asking him why he was there, and why he didn't make me answer to the police.

After cleaning up, and doing a little more unpacking, Glenn still wasn't up, and I hadn't heard from JC. I decided to head to the Sullivan Center, the campus' dining hall, for breakfast. I wanted to go with JC, but it didn't matter. All he'd want to do is tell me about last night, and I wasn't sure I wanted to hear any more about that party.

Shoving my wallet into my sweatpants, I left the dorm and headed for the dining hall. I opted for the long way to the dining hall to avoid Jay or Madeline, who I caught *together* last night. I thought Jay liked me, but I guess she doesn't, or maybe she still does? It didn't matter, I didn't like her, and JC liked her, so she was forever off limits from now on.

As I crossed the campus into the dining hall, I noticed a table where three girls were set up right at the entrance. It was a long white folding table with blue and white balloons (our school's colors), and pamphlets, and papers and even candy on the table.

"Isn't it a little early for candy?" I said as I approached the table.

A girl with natural red hair, big blue eyes, light freckles, and long lashes blinked up at me. I thought my heart stopped, or my mind froze. Her lips curled into a smile, and I swear she hypnotized me.

"But it got your attention, didn't it?"

I grunted, lost for words at her perky voice and bright white teeth. "Well," I cleared my throat. "I guess so. What is all this for?"

"It's our club, the Crusaders."

I arched a brow. "Like, the medieval crusaders or the religious ones?"

"The religious ones." She crossed her arms. "We're a Christian group looking to recruit some freshmen."

I slipped my hands into my pockets and looked around at the table. Bibles, and information were available for anyone to take, and there was a signup sheet taped to the table.

"You look shocked," the blonde on her right said.

"Oh, I just didn't know this college had a club like this." That was a lie. I knew they did and had promised my mother I would join.

"A Christian club?" the blonde asked.

I nodded as I flipped through a pamphlet.

"You know, this college was founded by a Christian couple long ago. It's a private Christian college."

I looked up from the pamphlet. "I didn't know that."

The red-headed girl stood. "My name's Carly, and I think you should join our group."

I snorted. "Alright, Carly, why do you think I should join your group?"

"Because only a Christian, or someone interested in Christianity, would stay at this table for this long."

The blonde-haired girl glanced over at the quiet brunette. "Or you're still here for a different reason." Her eyes shot to Carly, and then she looked at me with a teasing grin.

"I'm a Christian," I said slowly, as I looked back at Carly. "But I don't really know if this is the right thing for me to do."

"Why not?" Carly asked with a grin. "Because you're afraid you'll get made fun of?"

"I'm afraid I'd join for the wrong reasons." I looked Carly over once more and winked at her before tossing the pamphlet onto the table. "Thanks anyway." I turned to leave with a flurry of giggles erupting behind me.

"Wait!" Carly called.

I turned to see her walking around the table, she had on a sherbet pink dress that flared at the knees. "Who said your reasoning was wrong?"

The two girls sitting at the table fell quiet and watched the exchange between Carly and me. I chuckled, taking a bold step toward her. "Fine, my name is Xavier Miles, you can put me on your list."

She smiled slyly. "Then I expect to see you here on Monday at six in the evening."

I smiled too, and she began to blush. "I'll be here."

9

Say Something About Yourself

Eli was out the rest of the weekend and wouldn't be in until tomorrow. Since I was scheduled to see him Tuesday, I didn't make a fuss about getting in early before my appointment. I spent the rest of the weekend avoiding the ladies' dorm and unpacking with Glenn and JC. Glenn and I didn't have much to unpack, so we ended up spending time in Junior's dorm helping him out. His roommate had a girlfriend on campus, so he didn't spend much time in the dorm, it was mostly just his place to crash when he and his girlfriend argued. JC didn't care at all, he wanted the place to himself anyway.

I'd been avoiding the girls' dorm since the party, it just felt awkward to see Jay, even though I'm sure she didn't remember anything that'd happened. But it didn't matter because when I showed up to my last class early, in the hopes of finding a seat in the back corner of the room, Jay and Madeline were sitting together in the exact spot I'd been hoping to get to.

I stopped in the doorway when I saw them. I almost let out an exaggerated sigh when Jay raised her hand and waved at me. Her genuine excitement to see me almost made me wonder if that party was a figment of my imagination but I adjusted my pack on my shoulder and headed to their table. I sat beside Madeline, and Jay reached over her and hit my arm.

"Hey, you, haven't seen you since the party."

"Yeah," I scratched the back of my head. "I got out of there, started not to feel well." I'd been refusing to let myself remember why I had actually left the party. The intense sweat I broke into, the dizziness I felt, it was like I was on the verge of passing out, but never actually making it past that verge. It was hard to describe, and awkward, so I decided not to tell anyone. I decided not to even think about it.

"I see." Jay pressed her blue pen to her lips. "You missed out. Madeline and I wanted you to join us. But you were gone."

I gulped as nerves tickled up my spine.

"Yeah, I didn't know you two were like *that*." I couldn't stop the images of Jay and Madeline from popping into my head. They had been dancing together the same way Jay had danced with *me*. Like they were more than just innocent friends.

Jay grunted, and I looked over at Madeline who hadn't said a thing since I came over.

Jay smiled. "Well, we *are* like that. We weren't at first. But that doesn't mean we're not interested in you too. Right, Maddy?" She leaned toward the shy girl. Maddy smiled nervously at Jay, and then at me.

"Well," I cleared my throat, "I'm not really into that kind of thing."

"Come on," Jay winked, "isn't it hot with two girls?" She pressed her red painted lips to Maddy's cheek. Maddy seemed shy, but Jay was her friend, so she tried to smile a little brighter when she left the lipstick outline of her kiss on her cheek.

"Can you guys stop?" I huffed, glancing away. I couldn't even describe how uncomfortable I felt about this. I wasn't the type of guy who thought this sort of interaction was *hot*. But I knew if I said that,

Jay would get offended. So I had to sit there and endure her flirtation.

Jay laughed at me, sensing my discomfort. "Calm down, we're just messing around."

Maddy still didn't speak, she pulled out two notebooks and set them on the table.

"You're weird," Jay said, getting her own things from her bag. "Most guys love when girls are together like this."

"I'm not like most guys then," I said without looking at either of them.

"Well, why—"

"Secret X!" I looked up to find JC walking in wearing baggy shorts, a t-shirt, and socks with slides.

"Hey, Junior," I said, relieved. "You've got this class too?"

He set his books down and took the last seat beside me at the table of four. "Yessir." He leaned forward and grinned at Jay and Madeline. "Hey, ladies."

"Hi, JC," Jay said flatly. She brushed a dark curl behind her ear, and I watched Junior's eyes light up. He was obsessed with Jay, and I wouldn't be the one to tell him she swung whichever way the wind blew her. I doubt he would believe me anyway. I hardly believed it myself.

"Madeline's here too," I said, catching his attention. He almost frowned, but she looked up, red hair shaking from her face to reveal plump dimpled cheeks.

"Oh no," she waved, "it's alright."

"Maddy is so shy, it's adorable." Jay kissed her cheek again. I held in a sigh.

More students began to file in, a few I'd seen all morning, while others I hadn't seen at all. A short man entered with them, bald, white skin, and green eyes. He carried a briefcase, and wore his shirt tucked in as he rushed in and sat at the table at the front of the class. More students came in as the clock ticked down to start the class, and our professor set out papers on the front table. When he finished, he looked at his watch and clapped.

"Alright class. Welcome to Gen 210, The History of the United States. I'm your professor, Michael Daniels, but please just call me Mr. Daniels. This is a level 200 class, and I know most of you are freshmen, but don't worry, it's not anything you haven't seen before, it's just more in-depth."

"Why do they put freshmen in level two hundred classes?" a girl in the back of the class asked.

"What's your name?" Mr. Daniels asked.

"Dianna," she responded.

"Alright, Dianna, to tell you the truth, I have no idea. But, in this class, we do have order, and my number one rule is to raise your hand to speak. This class is open, and it's meant to be a conversation, however, we can't converse if we all talk at once or shout at me. Understood?"

The class collectively nodded, and Mr. Daniels smiled, the crow's feet digging deeply into his face. "Good. So, we'll go around the room, everyone say your name and one thing about yourself, and today I'll let you go early. But don't get used to it." He chuckled. "This is the only day I'll be letting you all go early, and that's because I have somewhere I need to be in an hour. Pick up a syllabus on your way out, and we'll go over it briefly on Wednesday." He glanced around and nodded. "Alright, we'll start here, and make our way back and around to the front."

The guy in the front began, and it took a while to get to our table. Some people took the exercise seriously and tried to show off. A woman in front, whose name was Cheryl, decided to tell us that she was a child actor until she was twelve. But she named films no one had ever heard of, and she was almost fifty now so no one really cared.

Another guy named Samuel was born in Costa Rica, but moved to the United States eight years ago, to Colorado. Someone else had won a snowboarding contest, and another was on some television show about losing weight.

I nearly nodded off listening to everyone when Junior was called on. He stood up, his chair scraping against the floor snapped me wide awake.

"My name's Junior Calliway, and I have a dog."

The class chuckled as he went to sit, but Professor Daniels stopped him and asked, "Junior what's your first name?"

JC cleared his throat, darting his eyes to me. I shrugged slightly, not sure what to tell him.

Junior stood and offered the class a tight-lipped smile. "My first name?"

Daniels nodded.

"Well, that's a good question." He nodded too. "Uh, it's Gunner."

"Gunner? What a fascinating name."

"Yeah, well I like to go by Junior because it gives me a little individuality."

Mr. Daniels nodded quickly, seemingly enjoying what JC was lying about.

"I believe that is wonderful, Junior. Thank you for sharing."

"Of course," Junior said sarcastically as he flopped back down in his seat.

I heard the professor call for me to speak as I held in a snicker with Junior. I nodded and stood. "My name is Xavier Miles. My mom is Spanish and Black and my dad's white." I shrugged, hoping that was good enough.

Mr. Daniels raised his brows with a smile, and I offered one back as I sat. Madeline stood next, her hands trembling at her side. "My name's Madeline Jones, and I like experimenting with hair color."

Mr. Daniels added, "I love that red. It's very cool."

Madeline nodded and sat.

66

Jay shot to her feet, and I knew she was going to have something annoying to say. But I couldn't take my eyes off her. She was wearing an incredibly short top, that left everything except her breasts out, and pants so tight, if she made one wrong move, I was sure they'd rip.

I closed my eyes, forcing myself to look away and hoped that JC hadn't seen me checking her out... he hadn't. Because when I opened my eyes, he was almost drooling on the desk.

"My name's Jocelyn Keifer, and I like girls."

The class gasped. Some laughed. Some cheered. I rolled my eyes and hoped no one saw.

Jay added, "I'm kind of into boys too. Just depends on the day."

"Thank you, Ms. Keifer, you may sit." Mr. Daniels shook his head as the next student stood. When the class finally finished, we headed out, grabbing the syllabus as we left.

"So, what's this I heard about you joining the Christian club?" JC said as we walked together.

"I only joined because there's this cute girl there." That was, technically speaking, ninety-eight percent true. Carly was incredible to look at. Her warm ivory skin, freckles, and curly red hair were captivating.

"Bro, you're going to be labeled if you stay in that group."

"Labeled as what?" We moved through the crowd of people, heading to the dorms since we were done for the day.

"At best? They'll call you a weirdo. At worst?" He shook his head. "You know what they say about religious people these days."

I did know, except they didn't say it about *religious* people. They only said things about Christians.

Closed-minded. Old fashioned. Nutjobs. Brainwashed. Far-right bigots. The list could go on and on.

I grunted as JC said, "No one's going to want to hang around you if you join that group."

I frowned at him. "I thought this was a private Christian college. Shouldn't there be tons of Christian students here anyway?"

JC laughed like I'd just said the stupidest thing in the world. "You do realize this is the 21st century, right?"

"I don't get it."

He bunched his shoulders like his next words were hard to say. "I don't think you're going to find any serious Christians at this school, even if it *is* a private Christian college." He laughed. "I don't think you'll find any serious Christians in *church* these days. They don't take their own faith seriously. So I don't get why you would by joining their stupid group."

"It's not stupid," I said defensively, even though he was right. I called myself a Christian and look at everything I'd done so far. The saddest part was that my story wasn't unique.

There are millions of Christians in this country alone living lives identical to mine, giving people like JC more reasons to laugh and criticize us.

He's right. We've made our faith look like a joke.

Still…

"I want to join the Crusaders," I said quietly.

JC groaned. "No one's going to want to hang around you if you join," he repeated. "Which means no one will want to hang around *me*."

"You don't really have any friends besides me, so who cares?"

He huffed. "Just drop the group and try talking to that cute girl another way."

"I'll think about it. This may be fun. You should join too."

"Please," JC waved his hand, "I grew up in a Christian household, and it is *not* for me. I mean, my grandmother was Christian, but I just can't do it."

I chuckled as we made our way out the doors. "I have a meeting with the club tonight, I'll make my decision then. But don't count on me changing my mind." I shrugged. "They might not be a bunch of fakes. And it might actually be fun."

JC sighed as he grabbed my shoulders. "You're so weird."

I opened the door to the dining hall and found the Crusaders sitting around in a large circle in the middle of the room. The dining hall was closed every few hours before the next meal rush. Dinner started at seven here, and from six to seven in the evening, there were no students allowed inside. I guess the Crusaders took advantage of this and booked the dining hall for their club room.

Carly was standing in the middle of the group when she noticed me walking in. Waving me over, she called, "I'm surprised you came."

I grabbed a seat in the circle. "I said I'd be here." I shrugged. "So, I'm here."

She placed a hand on her hip. "You're late, you missed prayer."

"Sorry," I apologized.

She tried to hold in a smile as she blinked away to the rest of the group. "Well, we're just starting now. Everyone's going to introduce themselves with their name, their year and major, and their favorite scripture."

I nodded.

"I'll start," she said. "My name is Carly, I'm a sophomore majoring in criminal justice with a minor in behavioral science." She tapped her chin for a moment, polished pink nails looked freshly manicured as she thought. "I can't pick a favorite scripture, but I really like second Thessalonians three and three, where we're reminded that God is faithful and will protect us from the enemy." She tucked her peach skirt beneath her legs and sat.

I watched her as a boy named Joe stood and talked. Carly glanced over at me, her eyes suddenly met mine, and I forced a nervous smile. Hers was genuine though. Perfect pink lips pulled into a pretty grin. Then she nodded and looked back at Joe, who'd apparently made some joke that everyone else had caught besides us two.

I turned my attention back to the group to see the blonde girl from the other day standing for her turn now. The quiet brunette who'd been with them was sitting beside her, waiting to go next.

"My name is Julia," the blonde said. "I'm a junior majoring in psychology. I don't know if I have a scripture. Probably John three-sixteen." She shrugged a shoulder and sat down as the brunette stood.

"I'm Gertrude, a sophomore studying criminal justice. My favorite scripture is about wisdom, how she'll protect you. It's from Proverbs chapter four, verse six." She sat, and the next girl, Tabitha, stood.

I listened intently, trying to think of any scripture I could remember on the spot. The guy beside me stood, and the nerves twisting in my gut almost made me dizzy. I didn't want to be the only one who didn't have a favorite scripture. But I hadn't thought about that ever. *Every* scripture was important, right?

I couldn't say that though.

"My name's Phoenix, I'm a senior, and I'm studying international affairs. Favorite scripture," he gripped his pants, "I'm really not sure. But I can tell you my favorite book is probably the Book of Daniel."

"Good enough, I guess." Carly laughed.

He sat down, and I took a deep breath before I stood. My eyes immediately fell to Carly's which made me even more nervous, but I couldn't run away now.

"I'm Xavier, you can call me X." I paused and looked around at everyone. There were only three people left after me, and I didn't want to be the only one without a scripture or copy Phoenix and just say my favorite book. "Uh, I'm majoring in aviation management, and—"

"Aviation? You mean, like, flying planes?" Joe asked.

I shrugged one shoulder. "Yeah. I want to own an airport, but I figured I'd probably manage one before I did that."

"You don't want to just be a pilot?" Julia asked. She popped her red gum, and I gave her my full attention.

"Well, I want to get my piloting license, but the overall goal is to own my own airport." I palmed the back of my neck. "It's just, I've always loved airports. Probably because I've only flown on a plane like five times, including my flight here."

The group chuckled as Carly said, "That's quite a dream."

I tried not to smile too hard at the fact that I'd impressed her.

"Well, Mr. Aviation Manager," Carly went on, "tell us your favorite scripture."

I nodded. I'd almost forgotten about that. "Right. I don't know if I have a favorite scripture, but there is one that's stuck with me all my life. Romans seven, verse nineteen, it says—"

"For I do not do the good I want, but the evil I do not want is what I keep on doing," Carly finished.

"Yeah…" I eyed her.

She gave me a delicate smile. "It's a powerful scripture, and says a lot about your struggle, who you are, and who you want to be."

I swallowed and glanced around at everyone before sitting. As the last three people went on to speak, I kept catching Carly's eye. I wasn't sure why, but she'd been looking at me ever since I'd given my scripture.

When the last person had finished, Carly stood and clasped her small hands together. "Alright everyone, thank you for sharing. All of us, except for Xavier, are returning members, so we know the ins and outs. I do want to say that this year we are looking to do a Christmas event for the school and for *ourselves* before the break starts. So get your ideas in soon. Friday, we meet here again; we'll start discussing our plans and events for the semester. Sound good?"

We all agreed, and Carly dismissed us. She got caught at the end, talking to everyone she hadn't seen since last year, passing out hugs and whatnot. I wanted to stick around and ask her why she was so moved by the scripture I'd given, but I took my leave instead and headed back to my dorm.

10

Penance

"I love flowers and trees," Adar said as she walked beside Benny into a field of red poppies. "The way they can be so colorful, the way trees can change the color of their leaves. It's like the world is painted with their beauty."

Benny was silent as he walked with Adar. He'd gone through his training, seen things he never knew were possible, experienced feelings and emotions he still couldn't quite grasp. The Earth was different from the realm around it. It took Benny thirty-three earthen years to finish part of his training before he was killed by accident. He wasn't sure he'd ever be ready to experience death again.

Benny looked at the field of flowers, wondering why the Earth couldn't be the same. Why did things die there? Why did people die? He knew why, of course, because of the fall of man, but he didn't want to accept it. He didn't like it. And he didn't want Adar to ever experience the earthen training. He wanted her to stay here. He would go to Earth for both of them and return back to her. But he knew that wasn't possible.

Only those who have been requested by Jehovah, or was an acceptable recruit, could return to the Realm. Everyone else must go to Heaven. The swirling thoughts brought Benedict to a stop in the field. When Adar noticed his stillness, she turned to him, placing a hand on his shoulder.

"What's wrong, Benny? You've been different since your training."

He reached up and took her hand from his shoulder, holding it in his own. "Adar, things die on Earth."

She nodded. She'd received the same teachings as Benny and knew that death was part of the fall of mankind.

"The trees, the flowers, the people," he whispered. "They all die. I don't want you to experience that."

Adar placed a hand on his cheek. "Benedict, if I don't train, you'll go without me."

"I don't want you to go." He dropped to his knees and for the first time, a tear slipped from his eye. It was so sudden, his feelings of brokenness stopped, and shock overtook him as he wiped at his eyes. "I've never shed one before."

Adar stepped away from him, staring at the salty wetness on his fingertip. "You are so very close," she said quietly. "You'll be called soon."

"Maybe they'll never call you."

"I want to be called. If I'm not called, who will you be with?"

Adar and Benedict had promised to be with each other here in the Realm, and on Earth. They began to feel things in their hearts for each other, and they never wanted that to fade. They promised that in their Earth suits, they would find each other, and they would complete their earthly mission together.

But Benedict had learned that there were distractions on Earth, and the scariest thing about Earth was that Benny couldn't remember a single thing about the Realm.

—— ✤ ——

"Xavier? Xavier?"

I blinked, snapping into consciousness. Madeline was shaking my shoulder. I was dazed as I glanced around, the world finally clearing up from the blurry awakening.

"Madeline? What is going on? Where's Adar?"

"Who?"

My eyes shot open, and I looked around. "What did I just say?"

Madeline's brows came together as she looked worriedly at me. "You just asked where Adar was."

"Adar? What is that? Who is that?"

"I don't know. You must've been dreaming about whoever or whatever that is."

I flipped my bag around and dug for paper, repeating 'Adar' over and over in my head.

"Are you alright?" Madeline asked.

I nodded as I chomped on a pencil and ripped a piece of paper from my notebook. Scribbling on it quickly, I wrote down the day, the time, the location, and the name 'Adar.' I didn't know why I was so sure it was a name. I didn't care either, it was the first thing I'd ever remembered from one of those dreams. It left me little information as to what I was actually dreaming about, but apparently it involved someone named Adar.

"I woke you up because you were crying in your sleep."

I looked up from the slip of torn paper to find Madeline wearing a flat smile. I reached up and patted my cheeks, there were tears running down them. For a second, a memory came into my head—a field of red poppies.

75

I thought I could see myself crying at the feet of someone, but when I jerked back out of the memory, I couldn't even remember why I was looking at my fingers.

"X?"

I glanced over. Madeline was offering me a tissue.

"You should wipe those before Eli sees them. He'll think you're super screwed in the head, and you'll be hiked up to three sessions a week."

"Right," I said, taking a breath. I took the tissues and dabbed my eyes. It was no use trying to remember now, but I wish I could. I wanted to remember and wanted to know why I was having these dreams. Maybe I could ask Eli, but he'd probably think I was crazy, and like Madeline said, increase my sessions.

"It's alright," Madeline said, adjusting in her seat, "crying is good sometimes."

"I guess so."

"So, you gonna tell me why you're here?"

I looked over at her, but she continued to fidget with the Spiderman keychain hanging from her backpack. We were sitting in the waiting area outside of Eli's office. I guess I dozed off while waiting for my appointment.

"Are *you* going to tell me why you're here?" I asked Maddy.

She shrugged. "Maybe someday I will when I'm better. But I'm not better now, not at all."

I sighed. "I'm better, but not completely. I still need to talk about some things. I just don't know who to trust."

She smiled a little as she tucked her red hair behind her ear. The entire cuff was pierced. Black and silver rings and a pole were pierced through the cartilage. Madeline wasn't slender like Jocelyn. She had big round hips, bigger breasts than Jay's, and she wasn't petite like Carly. She was cute though; I'd even say pretty. The way her nose looked like

76

a button, and her dimpled cheeks made her face look more youthful. Her incredibly smooth brown skin didn't look bad with her vibrant hair.

For some reason, I couldn't help but think I've seen her before. I knew her. I could almost believe I knew her really well while still feeling like I didn't know her at all. Just in passing.

She looked up at me, catching me off guard.

I looked away.

"What?"

"I just," I paused, "I didn't know you had all those piercings in your ear."

"Yeah, I got them done over the summer." She turned so I could see her other ear. It had matching piercings.

"Did they hurt?"

"Not initially, but healing? That's a totally different story." She giggled. It was the most girly thing I'd ever heard. I don't even think Carly, who was super girly to me, could produce a giggle so sweet and charming the way Madeline's sounded. I wanted to hear it again, wanted to see her smile the way she just had.

For a second, it felt like Madeline and I were connected, or at least connect*ing*. But the door to the office opened, and a guy walked out, followed by Eli. He looked between the two of us and smiled happily.

"Madeline, I wasn't expecting you today."

She stood, tossing her pack onto her shoulder. "I was just waiting with Xavier. I saw him as I was passing by." She looked back at me. "I just wanted to chat until you were ready for him."

"Well, that was really kind of you," Eli said.

Madeline looked over at me once more, and I nodded in gratitude that she didn't tell Eli about the real reason she was here, although, I didn't know she'd only stopped for me.

She turned and left, and Eli said from his doorway, "Come on in, Xavier. I'm excited for our first real session."

I grabbed my bag and shoved my tissues from Madeline into my pocket. "Yeah, me too. I guess." I followed him into his office but stopped as the door closed behind me. "Eli," I said. I hadn't forgotten the question that'd been burning me.

He turned around, brows raised above the dark frames of his glasses. "Why did you let me go?"

"Was joining the Crusaders some kind of penance?"

I frowned. "How do you know about that? And no."

He sat and gestured to the seat across from him for me to sit in. "I'll tell you, if you tell me why you joined the Crusaders."

"Fine." I sat. "But you first."

"Fair enough. I let you go because you looked ill, and you were leaving anyway. I wasn't the one bringing the cops, someone else called them. I was just there to break up the party. Unfortunately, I got wind of it a little late, and couldn't get enough people out before the cops came."

"Oh," I said, looking off.

"Now it's your turn." He rested his ankle on his knee.

"I joined the Crusaders because..." I bit my lip, trying to think of a way to say this. "Everything is confidential in here, right?"

He nodded.

I blew air between my lips. "I like the leader of the Crusaders. Carly is her name. I kind of want to get to know her."

He chuckled. "That's a big commitment just to talk to a girl. You're a handsome guy, you don't need to go through such great lengths, do you?"

"Well, that's the thing," I said. "She called me out. She said I was only at the table because I was a Christian or looking to convert."

"Which was it?"

"I am a Christian. At least I think I am. I just ... I haven't been a very good one."

"Why do you say that?"

"Come on, Eli," I said, finally looking him in the eye, "you saw me coming from that party. Does that seem like a place a Christian should be?"

He gave me a slow nod, like he understood what I meant. "It isn't an appropriate place for a Christian. So, why were you there if you think you are one?"

I shrugged. "I don't know. I just didn't want to let my friends down. I really didn't want to go, like at all." I shook my head, trying to shake away the thoughts of Lia Sunohara.

"Did something happen that makes you not want to go to parties?"

My eyes shot back to his. "N-No, not at all. Why?"

"The way you said 'at all' seemed like you were truly repulsed by the idea. Yet, you went anyway. I'm just curious if something is keeping you from partying."

"I had a bad experience at a party."

"Recently?"

"I don't know." I shrugged, trying to avoid the topic.

"Does this bad experience come up when you arrive at the party or before you go?"

"What does it matter? I said I don't like going."

"You did." He adjusted his glasses. "But you also said you had a bad experience, and when I was on my way down to the docks, I saw you. You came bursting out of the yacht and collapsed on the dock."

"You saw that?" I said nervously.

He nodded. "Yes. So, you want to tell me what was going on?"

I rubbed a hand over my face because I'd been trying to forget this, but now Eli was talking about it, and I couldn't stop the memories from vividly replaying in my head.

"I don't know how to explain it," I said, sinking my head into my hands. "I just suddenly felt dizzy, and I broke out into a sweat."

"Had you been drinking?"

"No, I'd just gotten there. I danced a little, but something felt off. It felt wrong."

"Why did the party feel wrong, Xavier?" His voice was the only thing I could hear above the booming music in my head as memories of the party replayed. I had completely fallen back into the party scene. I could see Jay dancing, the strobe lights, the people packed like sardines, and the music throbbing in my chest. I could feel myself sweating again. I felt like I was swaying suddenly as I recalled that night.

"For I do not do the good I want, but the evil I do not want is what I keep on doing," I whispered. My breaths became short, and I thought I would faint when I felt Eli's hands on my shoulders.

"Xavier!" he said firmly.

I lifted my head and glanced around. I was sitting in his office, sweat dripping down my face, panting for air.

"You were reliving that moment, quite physically. You murmured something." Eli slid back into his own chair.

"It's a scripture from the Bible, for I do not do the good I want, but the evil I do not want is what I keep on doing." I tried to calm myself as I spoke through shaky breaths. "It's what I heard that night. Like a Voice calling out to me, trying to steer me away from indulging any further in that party."

"What you experienced was civil war. Internally."

"What?"

"Inside of us is our soul and spirit, and between the two is the Holy Spirit, or guidance, telling us to do what's righteous. You were fighting within yourself, your spirit versus your soul, to do the righteous thing which was to leave. Because even though you wanted to do evil, it's in you to do righteous."

"I don't understand." I swallowed. "I didn't really want to leave."

"But at the same time, you did, didn't you?"

Slowly, I agreed.

"Exactly. It's just like when an addict is trying to get off whatever he or she is addicted to. They call them withdrawals, and while the physical body may be experiencing a 'withdrawal' or lack of the particular drug, the spirit is warring within. What the body actually feels is the war raging within."

"There was a war raging inside of me?" I asked as I placed a hand on my stomach.

"Very much so," Eli said softly. "Your spirit was fighting with your soul, your flesh, to do the righteous thing the Holy Spirit was telling it to do. Thus, you broke into a sweat because it was such a tough decision."

My breathing had finally slowed now. Eli's light brows were lowered as he peered at me through his glasses. "We wrestle not with flesh and blood, but with powers and principalities. That doesn't just mean with someone else, it can also mean within ourselves."

"But," I swallowed, "I thought I wasn't feeling well."

He laughed. "You weren't, as a result of the war."

"So then, did I win that war?"

"Looks like God won it for you."

"How do you know all this?"

He smiled. "Well, when I'm not here, I'm serving as a young adult pastor to my church."

I blinked. "You're a youth pastor?"

"I am, and I'm the Crusaders club adviser, actually. I've been the adviser for eight years now."

I sat back in my chair, staring at Eli, or rather, *Pastor* Eli.

"This is going to be a crazy semester for me, isn't it?" I asked.

"You have no idea," he assured me with a smile.

11

Pick A Side

"Have you found a church yet?" Mom said over the phone.

"Not yet, but a friend of mine from the Crusaders has invited me to her church twice. I'm considering going next week."

"You should, you've been there a full month and you haven't been to church. And don't mention your club, those meetings don't count as church."

"I know, Mom," I said as I sat on the dryer, highlighting notes in a textbook.

"Detective Vean came by yesterday."

I froze mid-highlight and waited for my mother to say more. When she didn't, I asked, "What did she want?"

"She was looking for you, something about new information on the case."

"Have you heard anything around town?"

"Only that the Leslies have an attorney."

"So ... that means—"

"Yes, they're really going after Matt."

I closed my book and sat there. I didn't know what to say or what to even feel. Being here in New York, I'm away from the suffocation of that case. But it felt wrong that I was here, living and moving on, while Matt was stuck there in Fresno.

He's going to lose everything; his scholarship, his family, his future. But it was an accident, and it just didn't seem fair that he would be charged. But, if there was one thing I knew, the price for a life was another life. It'd been that way for all eternity. I just wondered if eternity knew the strings the Leslies would pull to keep their name clean. Or the strings they'd cut...

Matt was between a rock and a hard place with this case. If his parents didn't believe in his innocence, he'd have no help. His life would be over.

Life must be given in order to gain it. To gain eternal life, we have to die to our old selves. To live the life of a celebrity, you have to give up a life of privacy. Life hung on a pendulum, swaying back and forth throughout our years on this Earth, gaining and losing momentum from the force of each side, giving, and taking.

Those are the only two options you have, give up something to receive another, or take something to make things fair in your own sight. Every time we give, we push the pendulum far enough away that it won't swing back and hit us. But every time we take something, that pendulum rushed towards us again in a never-ending cycle. I don't think life was meant to be like this, however, we're too afraid to explore any other way.

"Xavier, it'll be alright," my mother's voice called me back from the darkness that was consuming me.

"Right. When do I need to be home?" The door to the laundry room opened, and MJ walked in. She waved as she walked to the washing machine, and I watched her silently. There was something about her that was so distracting and inviting simultaneously. I didn't know what it was about her that made me want to be around Madeline, because she wasn't special. She hardly talked, and she wasn't cute and girly like Carly, or hot and wild like Jocelyn. She had her own look, pretty, with assets I couldn't ignore, but nothing more than that. But I think that if I wasn't swooned by Carly, and intrigued by Jay, I might actually—

"No, I told them you're at school and you don't need to be bothered with this. When you come home for Christmas, that's when they're expecting you."

"Oh," I nodded. I'd drifted off into my thoughts, my mother's voice had startled me. "Well, I've got to go now, so I'll give you a call sometime later. Night, Mom."

"What's the rush all of a sudden?"

I glanced up at MJ who was putting laundry into the washing machine. "I don't want to disturb the other people who're here now."

"Oh, I see. Well, give me a call later. I think your brother wanted to talk to you."

"I'll call him." I hung up the phone and waved a hand at MJ. "Sorry."

She looked up from her basket. "You weren't bothering me."

"Oh, well, then—"

"I don't care that you used me as an excuse to get off the phone. Parents can be trash sometimes."

"I guess you don't like your parents?"

She shrugged again. "Don't know. Never met them."

"Oh."

She sighed. "They died. I lived with my grandmother, but she didn't like me. Said I was shameful and brought the family down. I'm over it though."

"That's hard to believe, considering you're here at a private college. There's gotta be something good about you."

She was looking at me, a rush of red as vibrant as her hair took over her cheeks and she dropped her gaze back to her basket.

I hopped off the dryer in the silence and began packing up.

"Thanks," she muttered as I reached the door.

"For what?"

"Nothing. Just small talk. It keeps my mind busy."

I nodded. "I know what you mean. Well, night, MJ."

"Night."

I waved over my shoulder as I left the laundry and headed to my dorm.

— 🌿 —

The next evening, I was late for the Crusaders club again. Carly was going to chew me out until Julia caught her off guard with a question, "Are we doing something for Hallows Eve this year?"

Carly lowered her balled fists from her hips as she turned to answer Julia. "Actually, I kind of wanted to do a little midnight bowling this year."

"Midnight bowling? On Halloween? Won't that look bad?" Phoenix asked.

"Why would it look bad?" Carly replied.

"Because it's still Halloween, and we don't celebrate Halloween," he said.

"I do." Joe leaned back in his seat.

Phoenix narrowed brown eyes at him like he was ready to pounce, but Carly interjected, "Some Christians do, and some don't. We didn't last year, and we're not again this year."

"Hold on," Julia said, "we should celebrate it this year since we didn't last year."

"What do you mean some Christians celebrate Halloween?" Phoenix asked.

I sighed and hung my head, but that only caused more of a problem.

"Well, sorry this obviously doesn't interest you, Xavier," Phoenix hissed, "you never have any input anyway."

"Hey," Carly snapped, "don't be upset with him."

"Whatever." Phoenix stood from the circle. "I'll come back *after* Halloween, when everyone remembers their faith again."

"It's not even in the Bible," Julia yelled over her shoulder as Phoenix waved a hand.

"But… does it have to be?" Gertrude's voice was timid and shy. She brushed a brown lock of wavy hair from her face and peered around the group. "We know that Halloween is the celebration of darkness and evil, why would we participate in that?"

"It's an innocent day for candy." Joe shrugged. "I don't see what's the big deal. It's a *costume*."

"So, you'd rather dress up for candy than just buy your own?" Gertrude's face was pinched now as Joe sat forward.

"It's not just about the candy."

"Then what is it about?" With her timidness gone, Gertrude was sitting on the edge of her seat, looking past Julia at Joe.

"It's about the fun and the memories."

"Memories can be made at any given moment," Gertrude said. "I was always taught to lead by example. You can't lead people from the darkness if you put a lampshade over your light for a day and call it a costume because it's Halloween."

I quirked a brow. I'd never heard it explained like that before. I was always taught that the root of Halloween was a perversion of Hallows Eve which was the celebration before All Saints Day. All Saints Day was a memorial of all the people who'd passed on from the faith.

Catholics celebrated the day as a way to remember all the people they canonized. Christians celebrated the great generals in the Body of Christ who passed away but left legacies behind. However, that was all I knew. I'd never heard anyone say that we were basically hiding our identity as Christians for a day to look like the world.

I glanced back and forth between Gertrude and Joe, JC's words ringing in my ears.

I don't think you can find any serious Christians in church *these days. They don't even take their own faith seriously. Why should you?*

"Do you know why we're called Light?" Gertrude started again. "Because natural light never stops shining. The Earth may turn its back on the sun, but the sun always shines."

"Well," Joe said after a moment of silence, "I still don't think it's a big deal. I mean, they know I'm a Christian and I'm just having fun."

"And what do you do the other three hundred and sixty-four days of the year?" Gertrude asked.

"I crack my Bible open and try to find a scripture that says don't celebrate Halloween."

Gertrude stood abruptly with a look of complete shock. Her face was so astonished, like she couldn't believe someone would say that. I watched her carefully, wondering if she really had a scripture to combat Halloween. I'd never heard a single one my entire life.

"Ephesians verse five and eleven tells us to take no parts in unfruitful works of darkness, but instead expose them. First Corinthians ten and twenty-one," she slapped her hands to her hips, "You can't drink the cup of the Lord *and* the cup of demons. You can't partake of the table of the Lord *and* the table of demons."

"Well, they're just saying—"

"Just saying what? To celebrate Halloween because the Bible didn't use the *specific* word 'Halloween'? Well, when God made a distinction with the Israelites when the plagues hit Egypt, the death angel knew which doors to steer clear of. How could that angel steer clear of you if you look just like the world—just like the pagan-worshipping Egyptians? Dressed up like them. *Identical* to them, not to Christ." She shook her head. "There is no distinction. No leader. No follower."

The room fell silent.

"Jesus never stopped looking like the Son of the Living God," Gertrude told us sternly. "We should never stop looking like His followers. Not even for an innocent night of candy and fun."

Joe rolled his eyes, his voice came out almost a snarl. "You just keep hurling scriptures at me but not even understanding where I'm coming from. This is why I don't talk about it. I do what I'm going to do and hang out with the people who understand me. It's crazy because *they're* not judgmental. I'm more accepted by unsaved people than by Believers."

Gertrude laughed. "They accept you because you're just like them."

"Okay guys." Carly finally stepped into the center of the circle.

"Hold on," Gertrude said, still looking at Joe. "You think I'm judgmental because I'm *correcting* you?"

"Oh, I forgot to add to the list that Christians always think they have the moral high ground." He crossed his arms.

"We do," Gertrude said flatly.

He chuckled, shaking his head in amusement, but I was amazed at Gertrude's fearlessness, her accuracy. "Do you know why we have the moral high ground? Because morality was created by God for us. He is the originator of morality because He *is* purity. When your morals come from Him, there are none higher."

"That's enough," Carly said, stepping into Gertrude's face.

Gertrude wasn't fazed or intimidated. "Those who were ready went in with Him to the marriage feast, and the door was shut." She slung her bag over her shoulder. "Don't be caught without oil in your lamp." She walked off in silence, the clicking of her heels was the only noise in the dining hall.

We all sat there, blinking around, avoiding eye contact as we took in Gertrude's words. I never knew all that, never looked at Halloween that way. I knew it was wrong, and that was enough for me, but hearing the scriptures, hearing Gertrude stand up so fiercely, it was amazing.

At first, I almost sided with Joe just to smooth things over because I didn't know how to explain that Halloween shouldn't be celebrated. Yet, Gertrude did it so effortlessly, leaving me in awe.

"I think that's enough for today."

Joe shot to his feet with his bag in hand and didn't wait for a dismissal. He left grumpily without another word.

I turned back to a defeated Carly. Her shoulders sagged as she stood there staring at the floor. Quietly, everyone began to pack up and leave. I stayed though, until it was only Carly and me left.

"I bet you think I'm an idiot."

"For not jumping in? No way. Who could've stood between them?"

She lifted a corner of her mouth before shoving strawberry colored hair behind her ear. "I wish I could've done something."

"What would you have done differently?" I asked as I came over to her.

She shrugged. "Honestly? I didn't step in because I didn't have an answer. I didn't know what side to pick." She shook her head. "I'm the leader of this group and I can't even efficiently explain why Christians shouldn't celebrate Halloween. There are kids in *children's* church who know the answer. But I didn't."

I couldn't tell her that I was on Gertrude's side because I didn't know which side she was truly on and I didn't want to ruin my chance at spending some extra time with her.

I thought for a moment, trying to decide what to say when I blurted, "Well, the bowling is scheduled already, isn't it?"

She nodded.

"Then we'll go. You'll see, everyone will show, and if they don't, who cares? More food for us."

She laughed, looking up from the floor for the first time. Her icy blue eyes chilled the sweat she could make me break into. "I guess you're right." She chewed her lip. "I'd better go, but will I see you this Sunday for a change?"

I slipped my hands into my pockets as I watched her pack up her pink backpack. "If it means you'll go on a date with me."

"A date?" She leaned down and grabbed her books, red hair spilling over her shoulder, exposing porcelain skin peppered with freckles. "This is your salvation; you know that, right?"

"Yeah, I know. That's why I want to share it with you, someone who believes like me."

She immediately looked up from the book she was cradling in her arm. She blinked away the bewilderment and let a glowing smile stretch across her face. "Alright, Xavier Miles, if you come on Sunday, *on time*," she stressed and we both laughed, "then I'll go on a date with you."

"Seriously?"

She nodded.

"I'll camp out there."

She leaned back and laughed, covering her mouth with a dainty hand. Her nails were painted powdered blue. "Don't forget the salvation part."

"Right," I nodded, "how could I?"

She eyed me a moment. "I'll see you Sunday then."

"Yeah, you will."

12

Try Again

I buttoned my green shirt before tucking it into my khakis. I was nervous about going to church today, and it wasn't just because of Carly. I was also nervous because I hadn't been to church since I got here. I'd been avoiding it because I'd been spending my Sundays with JC doing whatever he wanted. But, if not for Carly, I don't know when I would've started going.

My reasoning for going to church again might be a little skewed, but I'm kind of grateful she kept pestering me the way she had. *Maybe...* I thought for a second, *maybe I need a girl like that. Someone to help me walk the right path, someone who connects me with my faith. Maybe I found her, maybe Carly's the—*

No.

I jerked my gaze up from my buttons and stared at my reflection. *Did... Did God just speak to me?*

"You alright, man?" Glenn was sitting on the bed flipping through a book as I caught his eye in the reflection of his full body mirror.

"Yeah." I shook my head. "I thought I heard something."

"It's probably someone next door." Glenn returned to his book, but then our door opened, pushing away the thought of the Voice in my head.

"Morning, losers, I'm here to take you two..." JC trailed off as he stared at me in the mirror. "Why are you dressed like that?"

"He's going to church," Glenn said.

"*Glenn!*" I whirled around.

He shrugged, turning a page in his book. I'd told him to let me tell JC if he arrived before I left.

"Going to church? For what?" His shoulders dropped. "Don't tell me it's the crazy Crusaders again."

"No, it's me. And they're not crazy." I pushed past him to grab my tie. Throwing it around my neck, I began tying the silky piece of cloth as Junior turned with his hands on his hips.

"This is why I told you to drop the group. Now you're acting like one of them."

"What if I *am* one of them?"

"You're not!" he snapped as he trotted across the room to me. Grabbing my face, he squeezed it and said, "You are *not* one of them. We're best friends, remember? Not Crusaders."

"Why can't I be both?" I strained to speak as he continued to squeeze my face.

"Because you can't, alright? It'll bring me down when Jay is *finally* coming around."

I started to tell him that she wasn't interested in him at all, but I let it go as Glenn chimed in. "I don't see what's wrong with it."

"Of course, you don't," JC said, finally letting go of my cheeks.

"I'm serious." Glenn sat up. "I'm a Buddhist, and I'd never let someone take that from me. If there was a group for Buddhists here, I'd join it no matter what anyone thought." He looked over at me. "I don't think you're doing anything wrong. It's your faith. Screw what JC

92

thinks."

I chuckled but JC shouted over my light laughter, "No! Man, don't listen to him. Just go to church today, but don't come back all preachy or whatever. And promise me you won't skip out on me next Sunday."

"I don't know." I tucked my wallet into my pocket. "I'll be dating Carly by then so I might start leaving you stiff more often."

"Wait a second!" he called as I walked to the door.

"Thanks, Glenn," I said before dipping out and avoiding JC.

I barely made it to Greater Is He Church on time. It was just after ten when I walked inside. The comfy space wasn't too big, but it wasn't small either. Rows of wide teal chairs holding diverse people sat on a green carpet. The wall was lined with pleated white curtains, and there was a wooden Cross above the elevated pulpit. I walked along the back wall, trying not to be seen when I was met by an usher.

A bald brown man with thick glasses and a black suit extended a gloved hand to me. "Right this way."

I nodded and followed behind him as he took me past smiling faces, and people clapping along to the music. The entire time we walked, I scanned the faces for Carly. It would be nearly impossible to spot her now.

The usher found me an aisle seat in the third row from the front. I wanted to protest, tell him that was too close for a visitor, but he dashed off before I could say a word. When I glanced over my shoulder, somehow, in three seconds flat, he'd made it back to the entrance and picked up a family to lead them towards me.

I took my seat and continued looking around. I didn't want to be too obvious, so every few minutes, I glanced around. There was a woman sitting with her baby beside me. The baby was on her lap blowing spit bubbles as her son sat on her other side.

"Sorry," she whispered as she wiped the baby's mouth.

I gave her a tightlipped smile as I glanced off to the front. Disappointment was beginning to settle over me as I started to think Carly had set me up just to come to church. It was a weird way to get someone to the House of God, but I guess it was worth it since I did promise my mom I'd start going again.

I needed this for myself anyway, I needed to get my feet back on the path of righteousness. So, for today, I shoved away the thoughts of Carly and lifted my hands and clapped along.

As worship service ended, announcements began, and the pastor was welcomed onto the stage. A heavyset woman with tight coils came out on stage along with an entourage of people. My heart nearly stopped when I spotted Carly. She walked out a few people after the pastor in a long pink dress. Her hair was twisted into a neat ponytail, and her small hands were clasped together as she took her seat at the front of the church. Another figure I recognized came and sat beside her, Eli Ross, my counselor. I knew he was a young adult pastor, but I didn't know it was here, at this very same church.

I think my frozen stare at Carly forced her to find me in the crowd. She was looking pretty glum up there, sitting with her head lowered and her face sagging. But on the chance when she glanced up and found me in the crowd, she smiled. I smiled back. We were smiling at each other, and it was like our love story had just begun. But the thought was cancelled when I remembered the Voice in my head today telling me that Carly wasn't the one for me.

That wasn't you, God, was it?

No answer.

I exhaled as my row was called and I led them to the offering baskets. Carly gave me a small wave as she stood on the stage, and I nodded at her. I was glad I got to see her and that she hadn't set me up. Which meant Carly and I would be going on a date sometime this week, and the thought nearly made me jump for joy.

"We're talking about the ten virgins today, the five wise and the five foolish." Pastor Tosh was up at the podium speaking into the microphone.

I let go of my date ideas at the sound of her voice. I remember Gertrude mentioning not being caught without oil in our lamp. At first, I thought she meant don't turn out your light, but now I remembered the oil lamps in this story.

I tried not to make it so obvious that I was interested, until I remembered I was in church, and this was the best place to be interested in a sermon. It'd been hard keeping my faith with Glenn and JC. Glenn wasn't really a problem, but JC was so adamant about staying away from anything Christian, it was hard to be me... the real me, the Christian I knew I was.

"We all know the story," the pastor continued, "so today's sermon will be short, because all you're doing is applying today. Somebody say, 'applying today.'"

"Applying today," everyone said around me.

I nodded and whispered it in my heart.

"You already know the story, and if you didn't know the story before you came in here, it's alright, I'm going to retell it. There were ten virgins in all with oil lamps. Five of the ten were wise and brought spare oil, the others didn't bring any spare oil. They're the foolish virgins."

Heads bobbed as the pastor continued. She read the short story aloud to us as we followed along in our Bibles. I was a little embarrassed because I was so focused on looking nice today to impress Carly, I hadn't brought a Bible with me. I hadn't even had one downloaded on my phone. Thankfully, the Wi-Fi in the church was good enough for me to download a Bible app and read over the short passage.

"Now," Pastor began, "let me retell this story so that y'all can look deeper than the surface of being prepared. Ten people get saved and start coming to church. New babes in Christ, they sometimes drift away, and like the ten virgins, they fall asleep in their spirit." Pastor Tosh paused and grabbed some water, giving me a chance to take a glance at Carly. She was writing notes with a pink pen in a violet notebook.

"But, all of a sudden, everyone starts realizing the signs of the time. Now, I just want to add this in and tell y'all that this world is ending, and it's timeout for the foolishness. The King is returning to rapture His Bride, and we gotta be ready."

People began to clap but the pastor made everyone stop by raising her hand in the air.

"No, everyone just wants to clap along and shake their heads, but there's no application of what you're learning. You're not even understanding. Many of you just sit in church being preached at but not taking any of it in, you're falling asleep in your faith, just like the virgins. And you know what? When you hear that the end is near, you want to shake yourself from your slumber and try to get a little of the Word in, but it doesn't work like that."

She took another big gulp of water, and the church was hushed as she set her glass on the stool beside her. "See, the five wise virgins brought extra oil, which means they're sitting in church and even though they may fall asleep spiritually, when they awaken to themselves, they've got some roots in Christ that'll prepare them and keep them ready for when the King arrives. But woe to those of you who are the five foolish virgins!" She shook her head, coils moving with the motion. "All of you who wake up and hear that the King is coming and don't have any roots, y'all aren't going to make it. And you sit in church Sunday after Sunday. You pray with false tongues; you have a form of godliness, but you deny the real power. You raise your hands and cry every Sunday because you're so moved but Jesus is going to turn to you and say, 'Go! I never knew you!'"

Her cry rippled in my chest, and I took a deep breath to steady myself. It was like something had suddenly awakened inside of me.

"If you are not walking in purity, that means denying sin, making sacrifices daily for God, then you are not going to make it. You don't have any extra oil, you don't have any roots in Christ to tug you awake."

Tears rolled down my cheeks as I realized I was a foolish virgin. I was walking in a false sense of the Spirit; I wasn't actually in the Body of Christ. I had no purity. I had no focus on God. I was just alive, doing a little to say that I was a Christian, but there was no distinction in my lifestyle than from JC's or Glenn's.

I thought of what Junior had said again. *They don't take their own faith seriously.*

Pastor spoke again. "I want you all to understand that you can recommit yourself today to Christ and trim your lamp with your spare oil. A lot of people are walking around with a lamp, some of the flames been burned out, and we know there are others who are burning brightly. But some of you have a lamp with a flickering flame. And you don't want that light to burn out. If that's you, and you want to recommit yourself to Christ today, I want you to stand to your feet."

I looked around the room as people stood. Some were crying, some were holding back the tears. I didn't know if I should stand or not, but I wanted to. I wanted to stand like everyone else, but I didn't want anyone to know what I was going through. I didn't want Carly, who was nearly perfect, to know I wasn't committed. That I wasn't perfect like her.

I want my son back.

My mom's words twisted in my gut, and I knew this was my chance. I knew if I stood right now, everything would change, even the pastor was saying so. I absently pressed my thumb into the cloud-shaped birthmark on my wrist, thinking of how broken she was when she'd said that to me.

"You'll have a transformation in the Spirit," Pastor Tosh said.

"Everything will change. You'll lose friends. You'll be separated and alone for God to work on you. But in that time, the spare oil will be trimming your lamp, prepping you for the return of the Groom. You'll be trained in your calling." She was shaking her head and walking around the pulpit now.

She said into the microphone, "I feel this in my spirit. The spirit of obedience wants to be in your life, the spirit of commitment wants to live in you, but you have to want them. You have to want *God*, and He will send His Spirit, who is able to keep you committed and help you be obedient. Do it today. Don't wait."

I chewed my lip as the music began to play louder. I squeezed my eyes shut, begging God internally to help me. I didn't want to stand; I didn't want to be like everyone else. I didn't want everyone to know.

Humility brings submission. Submission brings obedience. Obedience brings commitment.

What?

Come back to Me, Xavier.

Shakily, I gripped the chair in front of me, and pulled myself to my feet.

Ok, God, I said in my heart, *I want to return to You. I want to recommitment to You, come back to You. Help me to be obedient. Help me to walk in humility and meekness. Help me submit to You, God. I don't know what I'm doing, but I'm going to trust You. I know You wanted me here for this. So please, don't leave me out here. Help me, God, in Jesus' Name, amen.*

When I opened my eyes, my hands were lifted, and tears were streaming down my face. I didn't care who saw me. I didn't care what changes needed to be made. I hadn't felt this good in so long, I was wondering if I was dreaming. But before the doubt could wedge its way into my mind, I heard God in my spirit.

Welcome back, My son.

13

Get to the Root

After service I didn't get to speak with Carly. I didn't feel upset, but I did feel let down since I'd been looking forward to talking to her. That feeling only intensified when I returned to my dorm and realized Glenn and JC were gone—plus, neither of them answered my texts.

I wondered if it was beginning already, the loneliness Pastor Tosh spoke about when you recommit yourself to Christ. She said it was a purification process, weeding out all the bad in your life to make room for the righteousness that's coming. I was afraid, honestly. I didn't want to be alone, I hated being alone. Being lonely was the entire reason I stuck by Matt's side, even when I knew I shouldn't. Even when he did things I knew were wrong.

I hated going out with Matt most nights, and I especially hated the things he did. But I hated being an outcast even more. That's crazy because now I had no choice but to be an outcast. JC was right, no one would want to hang around me once they realized I was serious about my faith.

I sighed and shook all those deep thoughts away. I didn't have

Carly's number, so I'd have to wait until the next Crusaders meeting to see her and ask her out. I kept up my end of the deal, I was hoping she would keep up hers. The thought of seeing her made me ooze with joy for the rest of the day. I was smiling as I entered Eli's office for our session on Tuesday morning.

"It was nice to see you at church," Eli said before sipping coffee from his favorite plain black mug. "What brought you to service?"

"What brought me?" I gulped, clenching my hands together.

"Well, your inability to come up with something doesn't speak for your grades. You're doing very well in your classes so far."

"Really?"

He nodded and grabbed a folder from his desk. "I was given your grades from your first big tests of the year, and you scored high across the board. That's very good."

"Why'd you get my grades before me?"

He chuckled, closing the folder. "I have to know these things in order to help you."

"I see."

"Just like I wanted to know why you came to church on Sunday. So I can help you."

"Help me with what?"

"With your reasoning. I know you came because you made a deal with my sister. She was so adamant about being on time on Sunday, I knew something was up. And when I saw you—"

"Who's your sister?" I was sitting on the edge of my seat now, nervously bouncing my leg. Eli sipped more coffee, letting the agony rush over me a little longer.

"Xavier, I want you to tell me one thing first; why did you stand on Sunday?"

The question threw me off. My leg stopped bouncing, and I forgot all about the secret identity of Eli's sister. "I stood because I … I wanted to recommit myself."

"To what or who?"

I paused. It was still hard to verbalize, and with Eli's frozen blue eyes, the pressure to say the right thing seemed to intensify. I'd planned to keep my recommitment a secret for as long as I could. I didn't want JC to know, or he would fly off the rails, which was why I'd been avoiding him since Sunday. I knew Glenn wouldn't care, but I didn't want him to mention it to JC, so when he returned Sunday evening, we chatted like nothing had happened.

"To ... Christ," I said softly.

"Why?"

"You said one question."

"I know, but, in this case, I needed to ask a second question."

"Why?"

"Because your relationship with God needs to be for you, not anyone else."

"It's *not*," I said defensively. "It's not..."

"Something happened?"

"There was a Voice." I reached up and covered my ears. "It was so clear."

Eli nodded. "Not everyone hears the Voice of God."

"How are you so certain it was Him?"

"Isn't that a question you should be asking yourself?"

I sighed and covered my face. I knew that Voice was God, it was undeniably clear. I just didn't want it to be, because then He was real. He was real and I'd have to walk the straight and narrow, I'd have to hold myself accountable from that point forward. But I already knew God was real, I just thought if I ignored Him long enough, He'd go away.

I came to learn that God never goes away, we just try to get away from Him. We do what we can to drown out the Voice, the Thumping in our chest to do the right thing. Sometimes, we even try to appease Him by reading a scripture in the morning just to say we're still part of the faith or liking something spiritual on social media. But after Sunday, I learned that wasn't good enough. What I'd been doing was only a *form* of godliness, but there was no purification or sanctification. The path I was on wasn't going to get Jesus to know me when He returned.

Frustrated, I folded my arms over my chest and pouted like a child. I still wasn't willing to come to terms with this transformation, as Pastor Tosh called it, in front of Eli.

"Isn't it against some law for you to be asking about my religion?"

"Not when I double as your counsellor and as Carly's guardian. I can ask whatever I want."

"Carly's what?" I sat up as Eli raised his mug and gave me a smug nod before sipping the black sludge.

"Carly is my little sister. But our parents died four years ago, so I took Carly in and became her legal guardian."

"Oh my goodness, could things get any worse!" I yelled as I erupted to my feet. Pacing the room with my face covered, I could hear Eli chuckling. "This is not funny! I'm stuck with you as a counsellor and as Carly's guardian!"

"That's right. But you know, Xavier, I am concerned for your wellbeing."

"Of course you are," I snapped as I continued to pace.

"When I asked about your faith, I was just interested in it. I wanted to know where you were coming from. It really didn't have anything to do with Carly. This room isn't about you and her, it's about you, and what you want to talk about with me."

"I don't want to talk about anything." I stopped and faced him. "I don't like this. I come in here every week, and just talk nonsense! It's annoying. I hate this!"

"You're frustrated, and you've *been* frustrated. You think you can't trust me."

"I don't like you psychoanalyzing me!"

"That's my job."

"No!" I shouted, "your job is to help me! I just…" all the frustration about Matt's case, about JC, about being rededicated to Christ, it peaked for whatever reason, and tears were pricking my eyes as I hung my head. "I just want help. I want all the thoughts to stop. I'm tired of pretending to be okay when I'm not."

"It's okay to not be okay, Xavier. There's no written rule anywhere that says you need to have it all figured out, and you never need anyone or anything to help you. Because if that was the case, then why do you serve God?"

"But why do I have to talk to you? Isn't that wrong?" I shrugged. "I've always been taught that Christians couldn't go to counseling. That GOD was our ultimate counselor."

Eli smiled. "God *is* our ultimate counselor. But sometimes telling someone else what you're feeling helps you open up to God. It helps you put your thoughts and feelings into words so you can really explain what's going on."

"But He's all knowing, He should understand me."

"And He does. But do you always understand Him?"

I wiped at my eyes. "No."

"Exactly. So not only am I here to help you talk through what you want to talk with God about, but I'm also here to help you understand when He speaks to you, and sometimes, when He doesn't."

Eli was sitting with his mug in his lap. He wasn't frustrated or angry with me. He seemed happy, smiling over at me as I tried to regain my composure in the corner of the room. Maybe it was okay to talk to Eli. I always thought it was wrong to tell people about your feelings because you were cheating God. But maybe Eli was here because I haven't been talking to God, and until I'm able to stand on my own two feet and have a conversation with God one on one, Eli can help me.

"What we talk about is confidential, right?"

He nodded.

I came back to my seat. "And you won't tell Carly?"

"No, I won't tell her a thing."

I nodded. "Something happened back home, and when I go back over the Christmas break, I'll have to deal with it."

"Can you say what it is?"

"I don't … I don't want to."

"That's alright. Can you at least tell me how it makes you feel?"

"I feel so bad, like it's all my fault. I don't deserve to be here, to be free, while everyone else suffers. Especially my best friend." I squeezed my eyes shut, wondering if I'd said too much.

"Aren't you suffering too? This internal struggle, it's eating away at you, isn't it? That doesn't count as suffering?"

"Well…" I tried to find words, but Eli was right. I was suffering just as much as anyone else; I just hadn't recognized it.

"And you know, you don't have to suffer. Christ suffered for us, so you can take your problems, your guilt, and place it on the cross. That's why we look to it, it's our emblem of hope, and our reminder that that's where all our problems were finished."

I sat against the chair, playing with the fraying on my jeans as I thought over what Eli said. I didn't have to suffer, but I felt like I should. I really wanted to know how to convince myself to stop feeling like I should suffer, but we only had a few minutes left in our session, so I decided to pack up instead.

"I'll let you go early today. You did really well, X."

"Thanks."

"I'll see you next week," he said as I headed for the door.

I waved but didn't say anything else as I left.

Right outside the door, JC was asleep on the sofa in the waiting area

105

with his backpack under his head. I was going to sneak by when he snorted into consciousness, blinking at me through blurred vision.

"X, where've you been, man?" Junior said as he grabbed his bag and began down the hall with me.

"I've just been sorting things out," I said.

"Something happen?"

I looked up at him, and he was full of concern. Junior was my friend, my closest friend on campus. It couldn't be wrong to hang out with him. God's not like that. He wants me to stop suffering, so I'm not going to anymore. I'm going to fully embrace Junior as my new best friend, and deal with Matt whenever I need to. The thought made me smile at Junior, and he winced away.

"What's that look for? It's creepy." He jabbed me with his elbow, and I laughed.

"I'm just happy that I now have my best friend with me, and I basically have a girlfriend."

"I bet you're getting ahead of yourself."

"Maybe a little." I shrugged. "But she definitely likes me."

He frowned. "I'm not surprised. You're like six feet tall—maybe an extra inch. You've got good skin, good hair, and you're not bone thin like me."

"We could always hit the gym together. I've been wanting to go anyway."

"You're absolutely missing the point."

"Oh."

"Never mind!" He flung his hands in the air and walked ahead of me.

"C'mon, JC!" I called as I jogged up to him. "You're handsome too. You've got a nice brown color, and you're the only guy I know who can still rock a box cut."

He rolled his eyes, refusing to smile. "I'm the only guy you know *with* a box cut."

I leaned back and laughed loudly as we waited by the elevators. When they opened, my laughter stopped, and I sucked in a breath. Carly stepped off, hand in hand with Madeline.

"Hey, Carly," I muttered, totally shocked.

She brightened and waved. "Hey, X."

I glanced at her hand interlocked with MJ's, and when my eyes traced back to hers, she blushed and began explaining, "This is Madeline, my lab partner for our general science class. She's crazy smart, and really cool. We even have matching red hair."

"Yeah," I said flatly.

MJ's brown cheeks were a shade of red now as she let go of Carly's hand. She and I both knew Carly didn't have a clue what holding her hand really meant to her.

"I'm going to head to Ross's," MJ said.

"Oh, no rush. My brother can be a time stickler but if you're with me, he'll be cool about it."

"It's fine," MJ started but JC interjected, "You're Carly!? Man, Xavier won't shut up about you! He's always talking about how cute you are and how—"

I shoved him, and he tripped, laughing as he fell into a nearby locker. Carly's cheeks were as red as her hair, and I gripped my bag nervously as we stood in a painful silence.

"I'll see you at the club," Carly said. "C'mon, Madeline." She grabbed MJ's hand and trotted off before I could say anything else.

"Bro, what was she doing with MJ?" JC said as we stepped onto the elevator.

"I don't know. But MJ had a weird look, didn't she? Like she knew she was wrong or something."

"She definitely looked nervous," JC said. "But I don't think it's anything to worry about. If Carly doesn't swing that way, then MJ's

107

probably just her lab partner like she said. You don't need to worry."

I grunted as the doors opened. I couldn't shake the feeling that I *should* be worried, but I forced myself to let it go anyway as we made our way off the elevator for a late lunch.

14

Bible Study

Since I became a member at Greater Is He Church and joined the recommitment program after Sunday's service as a way to help me stay focused, I started attending the freshmen Bible Study group twice a week. It all seemed like a good idea until I remembered that JC would throw a fit if he found out.

"Please, Glenn," I begged as I sat on my bed. I'd been asking him to cover for me when JC comes looking for me while I'm out.

"Why don't you just tell him yourself? You'll have to at some point."

"I know, but I can't right now. It's all too fresh for him. He won't understand."

"And he never will until you stand up for yourself."

I gripped the blankets on the bed as I stared off at the floor. Glenn was right. He could only cover for so long before JC got suspicious. But how would he react over this? Over me trying to take my faith seriously? Will I lose my best friend because of this? Is my faith worth it? Or rather, when did my faith become so important?

"Fine," Glenn said in an exasperated tone. "But only if you promise to tell him before the semester ends. I can't keep this up forever, you know. What happens if I can't make it to a temple and decide to just go to church with you one day? Then what?"

I felt a little relieved. "I guess you're right. I just don't know how to tell him. He's so against it."

Glenn sat up and tossed his book on the bed. "Who cares? You believe in your God, right?"

I nodded.

"Then that's all that matters."

"But I'll lose JC, and I…"

He stood from the bed and a lanky arm reached across and patted my shoulder. "Is JC worth more than a relationship with a supreme being, especially a being like your God? I mean, He claims to be the Creator of everything, and you're worried about a friendship with a being He created?" He chuckled and patted my shoulder again. "I wouldn't worry so much. Besides, He'll just give you a new friend, right?" With that, Glenn walked off to the bathroom and closed the door.

I was left alone to feel like an idiot.

Someone of a completely different faith just taught me about my own. I looked over at Glenn's empty bed. He was a quiet guy. He'd go out if invited, and when he wasn't invited out, he was here, reading. Or doing homework. I never actually saw him reading anything that looked remotely religious, yet he claimed to be a practicing Buddhist and knows an awful lot about Christianity.

Whatever the case, I was grateful that Glenn was here to be a friend, and to cover for me. I wondered if I'd ever be strong enough to stand up to Junior the way Glenn was strong about his faith. I shrugged, grabbing my things and left the dorm.

When I arrived at the freshmen Bible Study, I knew Carly wouldn't be there. It was a little disappointing since all of this started because I

110

wanted to ask her out on a date, but that still hasn't happened. She cancelled the Crusaders meeting on Monday via school email, and since I don't have her number, I have no way to contact her. I wondered briefly if she was avoiding me, but that made my stomach feel bad, and I didn't want to believe that. Because the only explanation could be that she was interested in another guy or MJ, and both of those options were terrible.

So, I partially came to Bible Study today because I knew they'd be expecting me, and I didn't know if word would reach Eli since he's a pastor here. Then I'd have to hear it from him. But I also came because I didn't want Carly stuck in my head all day and when I call Mom tomorrow evening, I know she'll be so proud of me. It'll make her smile, knowing that I'm back in church. I wondered briefly as I stepped into the sanctuary how much smiling Mom had been doing since the case.

My thoughts stopped as I glanced around and found a man sitting on a stool scrolling through his phone. Blonde hair whisking over his dark glasses, and his gentle demeanor filled the room.

"Eli?" I said aloud. The question turned a few heads from the small crowd of people who looked as young as I was. Some I recognized from campus, others I didn't. I knew this was the freshmen class, but I didn't know they actually meant freshmen in college, I just thought they meant beginners in the faith.

"Xavier." Eli was smiling as he stood and slipped his phone into his back pocket. "I didn't know you were coming."

"I didn't know you'd be teaching."

He chuckled and gestured toward the sanctuary. "Let's get started."

I forced a smile. Now I'd have to see Elijah four times a week; at Sunday service, at Bible Study twice a week, *and* at my counselling sessions. I fought the urge to drop my head and feel annoyed. Instead, I took a breath and found a seat.

"Alright everyone, welcome to our Bible Study," Eli said as he raised his hands at the front of the room. We gave him our attention as he went on to give an introduction. "All of you are new here from many of the neighboring campuses, which is good. Some of you are just in this group because you are in the age range."

A girl with sandy blonde hair and blue eyes raised her hand from the front row. Eli nodded at her.

"I'm not a college student," she said. "So what is the age range?"

"The way our classes work here is based on where you are in life. Right now, we have adult studies for everyone twenty-six and up. There's also a quarterly singles Bible Study and marriage Bible Study. Those classes are led by Pastor Tosh. We also have a children's study, and that's from high school and below, seventeen to about five. They're broken into different age groups amongst themselves."

"Everyone else is lumped together, then?" the girl asked.

"Not exactly. I teach you guys, the freshmen class, but there's a sophomore class, junior class, senior class, and one more class for everyone twenty-three to twenty-five."

"Why are they called freshmen if not everyone's in college?" a guy in the back asked. His voice was full of baritone, making me believe he was in the wrong group.

"We just mean newcomers." Eli shrugged. "But this group did start as a college only session. But I felt like what I was teaching should be taught to young adults in this age category regardless of whether they're in college or not."

"What are you going to teach us?" another girl asked.

Eli looked so calm and bright at the front, like he was truly in his element. He was always nice in our counseling sessions, but the way he smiled every time a question was thrown at him made me feel like this was his favorite job between the two. I shouldn't have been surprised, in our counseling sessions, he's technically not supposed to talk about God. Here, he can speak freely about the Lord and encourage us to do the same.

I felt that freedom too. In here, I didn't have to hide or wonder how others would react to me being a Christian. I could be myself. I could shamelessly work toward becoming the person God created me to be. For the first time, I understood the scripture, forsake not the gathering of the saints. Going to church wasn't a burdensome commandment at all, it was a benefit—in more ways than one.

Eli seemed to glow as he explained the lessons he had planned for us. "For the next four years, you guys are going to learn how to enjoy being single, which is secretly preparation for marriage and your life in general."

It was uncomfortably quiet, but Eli's unbroken smile made it even more uncomfortable.

"I know," he lifted his hands in defense, "everyone either has someone they're interested in, or is already dating someone. Or you guys were hoping to change your status on social media, right?"

The class chuckled, and Eli nodded in laughter with us. "I'm not going to tell you to pull your phones out and dump whoever you're with. That's a decision for you to make once we get into the material and the scriptures."

"Well, what if I don't want to be single? I want to get married," a girl said.

"Let's start with that," Eli grabbed the stool and took a seat as he pulled a red ball from his bag and played with it. "Alright, I'm going to toss the ball around the room. Say your name, if you're a student or not, and whether you want to get married. If that's too personal, then you can just share what you think of marriage." He raised the ball and tossed it to a girl in the back.

We all shifted to see her, there weren't many of us, so this would go relatively fast, which meant I needed to be thinking of my own answer.

I hadn't really thought of marriage, mostly just dating. And if I don't soak my mind in thoughts of dating Carly, I think of Lia, and I get emotional. However, Carly's been the only girl I've ever considered being the one for me. But I can't forget how the same Voice that welcomed me back into His arms, is the same Voice that told me Carly wasn't the one. I've been avoiding that topic for a while. It could've just been the nerves talking and not the Voice of God.

I've been nervous about Carly because of things going haywire with Lia, and so my apprehension plays all kinds of tricks on my mind. Like thinking Carly actually likes MJ when she's the leader of the Christian group *I'm* part of. I see her at the meetings, she's a real Christian. There's no way she isn't. There's no way she's involved with MJ. That would go against everything we believe in.

"My name's Marlo Joanna but call me Marlo Jo. I'm a fitness instructor at Rogue Gym, and I think marriage is good. We're supposed to get married as Christians to enlarge the Kingdom. At least that's what I always thought."

"Thanks, Marlo Jo." Eli nodded at the strong looking woman. Thick muscles and long dreads that were freshly twisted were as brown as she was. She had a pretty face to match her strong lean figure.

Marlo tossed the ball back to Eli, and he tossed it away.

A short lanky guy stood. Rushing a hair through his dark hair that seemed black against his pale skin, he said, "My name's Julius. I'm a freshman majoring in Chemical engineering, and I believe in marriage."

"Thanks, Julius, go ahead and toss the ball to whoever."

The lanky boy locked eyes with me, and I felt my stomach turn because I still didn't have an answer. But the ball flew right past me into the hands of a girl sitting in the row ahead of me.

She stood, wearing a pink chiffon skirt and white top. There was a pink band tied around her very short hair. It was a pixie cut. She was amazing to look at, rivaling Lia and Carly for her girliness and Jay for her figure.

114

"My name's Daisy," she said in a girly voice. But it was surprising because I've never heard a Spanish accent sound girly. It's usually seductive or sultry to me. "I want to be a student, but I just can't afford it right now. I work at a diner, the old-fashioned one up the street from here."

"Retro Three Thousand? I've always wanted to go because I thought it was futuristic," a girl with similar tan skin giggled beside her.

"I know," Daisy fanned at her, "it's very misleading. But that's the one."

"And what are your thoughts on marriage?" Eli asked.

"I don't know, honestly. I've never thought about it, but I'm so focused on bettering myself, I don't know if I have time for someone else."

"So, you don't want to get married?" Marlo Jo asked from the back. Daisy shook her head. "No, I don't. I'm not really interested in it."

"Fair enough," Eli said.

Daisy gave him a smile and passed the ball to the girl beside her.

"My name's Daytona," she said. "I'm a student studying biology, I want to become a surgeon. I'm really kind of open to anything." She tossed her thick curls over her shoulder, and I could see her full lips and round nose. She seemed friendly as she spoke. Eli nodded when she finished, and she tossed the ball to the girl with the blonde hair.

Emily was her name, and she was looking for work. Right now, she was just a babysitter, but she was hopping between part time jobs. She wanted to get married but was afraid she'd never be able to because of her poor finances—she said she didn't want to burden anyone.

Without hesitation, she tossed the ball to me. I caught it and stared at it for a moment. I could feel my shirt sticking to my back with sweat and every muscle tensing in my body. I hated icebreakers, and I wanted to escape. But I took a breath to calm myself and stood up.

"My name's Xavier, I'm an aviation student, and I'm—"

"Aviation? Like airplanes?" Daisy asked. She blinked big, beautiful eyes at me, and I almost caved for her.

I cleared my throat. "Yeah, like the airplanes."

"That's amazing," she beamed.

I gave her a smile and returned my gaze to Eli. "I think marriage is cool, I guess."

"Cool?" Eli laughed. "Fair enough. Go ahead and pass the ball."

Nervously, I glanced around the room. There were only three people left, so I passed it to the guy sitting in the back a few seats down from Marlo. As he stood, I couldn't stop staring at him. He was tall and strong and handsome. But his eyes... they were two different colors.

"I'm Sky," he was the owner of the baritone, "and I'm in welding school. I want to get married, but it's not a big deal to me."

"Welding school, that's only a few months, right?" Eli asked.

He nodded. "Yeah. I'm in a nine-month program. But if you're wondering if I'll go through this Bible Study for the next four years," he shrugged, "I've got nothing better to do."

We all laughed, and Marlo lifted her hand.

"Yes?" Eli inclined his head to her.

"I wanted to ask about Sky's eyes," she said timidly.

Sky shrugged one broad shoulder. "It's melanoma. My right eye is green, which is my natural eye color, but my other eye is brown. My mom brought me to Pastor Tosh when I was a kid, I was losing my eyesight in my left eye. She laid hands on me, and the power of God cleared my vision and healed my eyes."

"Why didn't He change your eye color back, then?" Daytona asked.

"I don't know, but I'm kind of glad He didn't. It's a reminder every day that I have something to be thankful for, even on my hardest days."

We all blinked at him, and he nodded stiffly before sitting.

"Ladies," Eli called, "a real gentleman and a man of God, right there."

We laughed together and Sky passed the ball to the girl sitting further down the bench from me who introduced herself as Tracy. She was a student going for her associates in accounting. She and the last guy, Kevin, didn't want to get married. Tracy believed that marriage was for most but not for her, she said she didn't want to be a slave.

Eli made no remark, only smiled and nodded at her, while Kevin sneered back at her and said he wanted to be a dominant force in the marriage and if he couldn't have that, he didn't want to get married.

"Well, we are going to cover everything we talked about today," Eli concluded. "And in our study on singleness, we're going to discuss how to enjoy this period. Marriage will come for most, bust for some it won't. How do we accept that? And how do we accept when God says no to someone we want to say yes to? We're going to cover all of that as we progress from singleness to friendship, to courting, engagement, and then marriage." He glanced at us and asked, "Does anyone have any questions?"

Julius raised his hand. "What do we do during the summer? I'm not from here, so I don't know if I can attend during the summer."

"Good question," Eli said. "During the summer, everyone attends the general Bible Study, and when you all come back, we start again in September as sophomores. I always wait to start with my freshmen because they have adjusting to do, and finding a church is not always at the top of the list. So usually around October is when the freshmen sessions start, but you guys will be sophomores next year, so we'll be starting in September."

Julius and the rest of us nodded in agreement.

"And this only goes by age, right? Because what if I drop out of college but still want to attend the Bible Study?" Tracy joked.

There was a low chuckle that came from the small group collectively before Eli answered, "Yes, this is based on age. So from eighteen to nineteen you'll be freshmen. And then nineteen to twenty are the sophomores, and you guys get it." He waved his hand and we nodded. "Good questions. No one has any questions about the material?"

"I have a question," Kevin, the one who wants an inhouse slave, spoke up. "What makes you qualified to teach us? I don't want to learn about being single or married from someone who hasn't done any of this."

"Well, then you definitely want to back out now," Eli said gently. His charm seemed to hush Kevin who was just a loudmouth. Eli stood from the stool and paced the room. "I am single," he said, and I almost gasped. Even though I figured he was. I never saw a ring on his finger in our sessions, but it was just so weird for him to say it so openly and unashamedly. "I've been single for a while now. Ever since I became a youth pastor."

"Why?" Emily boldly asked.

"Truly, I am not interested in marriage. I've found that my life is fulfilled doing what I do right now. However, I am still open to marriage, and I believe that if you find someone special, you should hold on to them for this life."

"How'd you decide to stay single? I mean, you never get lonely?" Julius asked.

Eli smiled like Julius had just issued him a challenge. "Not at all. That's why I'm the best person to teach you about being single, and about preparing for marriage." He turned to Kevin. "I've never been married, so I don't teach on *how* to be married, mostly, I teach what a Biblical marriage consists of. But I have had girlfriends, and I've been on dates. I have experiences that have rooted me in Christ, and others that tried to uproot me, but what you'll learn here in this Bible Study is what the single life is all about from a Godly perspective. And you'll find that preparation for marriage is intertwined with singlehood."

118

15

Smile, Because Something's Up

"Alright, what are we doing tonight besides shooting coins into bottles?" JC said as he tossed another coin. It missed and plopped onto the carpet beside the bottle.

"Well, I've got a—"

"Don't even say it." JC held up a bony hand.

"Club meeting," Glenn said from the bed.

JC groaned loudly, and I sighed, never even glancing back to see Glenn.

"I have to go tonight. I've got to ask Carly for her number." I tried to make it more acceptable, but JC didn't care today.

"She's probably just avoiding you, dude, lay off the Carly thing. Skip the stupid meeting and just hang out for once. You're busy all the time now, leaving me with Glenn."

Glenn didn't say anything and neither did I. He'd been covering for me, telling JC that I was doing club work or schoolwork with a tutor.

I sucked in a breath and tossed the rest of my coins down. "I'll see you tomorrow, Junior."

He shook his head, and I could see the anger in his eyes as he said, "Don't even bother. I've got my own things to do tomorrow."

I glanced at Glenn. He shrugged and looked back at his book.

"Sorry, JC," I said as I grabbed my wallet and headed out the door.

I was running late so I took the shortcut through the girl's dorm. Jay was leaning against the wall, a short skirt on, letting her slender brown legs crawl out from beneath it. She wore a white spaghetti top that showed off her arms. Jay had always been slender, but today she looked even thinner for some reason. Unnaturally thin.

"Hey, you." She stepped in front of me.

"Hey, Jay, I'm running a little late."

"Oh." She relaxed and stepped back. "Alright then."

I squinted. "What's going on?"

"Nothing."

"Is MJ alright?"

She rolled her eyes and stepped so close there was definitely no room for the Holy Ghost between us. I could smell her flowery perfume, but I could also see the thinness in her face. The way her cheekbones protruded, like she had suddenly lost 50 pounds right in front of us this semester. She didn't look healthy. She didn't look okay. She looked like she was struggling with something, but whatever the issue was, my sympathy vanished when she opened her mouth and said, "They're hotboxing in the bathroom. I didn't want you going inside and letting the smell get out or the smoke. It'll set off all the alarms."

"Hotboxing?" I frowned. I'd heard of it in high school, Matt was a fan. Of course. Admittedly, he'd gotten me to try a few times, so I was immediately angry at Jay because I knew what hotboxing was. I knew what MJ was doing in there. And now I knew why Jay looked so thin and unhealthy.

Hotboxing was a way of getting high. Like, *really* high. Locking yourself in a room while you smoked weed with the windows and doorways covered so no air could get in or out. The fumes would be concentrated, making the experience that much more intense.

I've done it. I'm not proud of it. But I'm also not that person anymore and I thought MJ and Jay weren't those sorts of people either. Judging from Jay's hollow cheeks, they'd been those sorts of girls. I just hadn't noticed before.

I shook my head. "Why is MJ hotboxing?"

"Why does anyone hotbox?" Now she was squinting, but I was still squinting too because *I* don't even know why I asked that question. I knew why people did it. It felt good, even I can admit that. But feeling good doesn't make it right.

"Well," I said disappointedly, "I really can't be any later than what I already—"

The door opened, bumping Jay. She stumbled into me, but the giggling that came from the room sounded familiar.

"Sorry, Jay!" Carly's voice rang out behind the door before she popped her head out. When her eyes met mine, they widened ten times their normal size. That's when I gasped.

Jay had said *they're* hotboxing, but it hadn't dawned on me until that moment. Someone else was in there smoking with MJ. *Carly* was in there smoking with MJ. Doing drugs. Getting high before our meeting.

I took a step back—the reaction was shared—Carly stepped back too, almost bumping into the closed door behind her. "Xavier? What are you doing here?" She swallowed loudly, clutching her Bible in her hand along with a notepad.

"I was taking a shortcut," I said plainly.

Carly's eyes were filled to the brim with emotion as she looked me over, but she lifted her head and flashed me her winning smile, and there wasn't even a hint of guilt or remorse left in her eyes.

"I just came to share some notes with MJ and lost track of time. You ready to go?"

"That's not what Jay said," I answered flatly. "Carly, what's going on?"

"Jay probably told you there's people in here hotboxing. That's our coverup. I'm doing a mini Bible Study and I don't want my brother to know." She shrugged. "He thinks I'm not ready. But I'm going to show him that I can change people too."

I glanced over at Jay and she laughed. "Sorry, X, I couldn't let anyone know. MJ said she's seen you around his office. So we're keeping things lowkey."

"R-Really?" I felt relieved as I looked over at a smiling Carly.

Carly laughed and linked her arm with mine. "Did you really think I was hotboxing? Did you really think I'd show up to the meeting with red eyes and smelling like that?"

"Oh, right. That was probably dumb. Sorry."

"Relax, as long as you don't go telling everyone, then it'll be fine."

I nodded, feeling giddy about having a secret with Carly as we walked off to the meeting. I'd been right before. Carly was a good Christian; she was meeting with these girls in secret to share the Gospel. How could I ever think otherwise?

"Can I start coming to your group sessions?" I asked, glancing back at Jay and her thin face and her hollow cheeks. Carly wasn't involved with drugs, but something was obviously up with Jay. I wanted to help her too, if I could.

"Well, uh…" Carly paused as we reached the outside. "Maybe next time. Today was unplanned—like a spur of the moment thing. We usually meet during your Bible Study time at the church. I'm a sophomore, so I come on a different day."

"Oh yeah," I sighed, "I forgot."

"But don't worry," she said, squeezing my arm a little tighter, "we can hang out whenever."

"You still owe me a date," I reminded her as we made it to the doors of the cafeteria.

Carly laughed lightly as she unhooked from my arm and stood right in front of me. "I do owe you a date, don't I?"

"CARLAY!" Three guys came jogging over. They each stopped and stared at her like she was the last rib at the lunch buffet.

"Hey guys," she smiled widely, "what's up?"

"We were wondering if you're tutoring again this year. We know you did it last year, so we wanted to get in on it early."

Her smile was genuine, but there was something cunning in her eyes as she sized each guy up. They were juniors, if not seniors, but that didn't seem to bother Carly. *How could a sophomore tutor juniors and seniors? Maybe general education classes?*

"I've got a meeting right now, but I'll stop by the library before I go home. Make sure your names are on the list there."

"Oh, most definitely," the hungriest of them said.

"Good looks, Carly, we're gonna head there now," another told her.

She waved bye as the three of them took off, slapping each other up and hissing with laughter. Suddenly my efforts to ask Carly out seemed fruitless, like maybe she wasn't interested in a guy like me. Everything seemed wrong. Carly wasn't being herself. But I couldn't put it in words what or who she was acting like.

"Earth to Xavier?"

"What? Sorry." I shook my head. "Who were those guys?"

"Students."

"Aren't they a little old to need tutoring from a sophomore?"

She folded her arms and there was a scowl crossing her face as she said, "Are you suggesting something, Xavier?"

"No—I'm saying, don't you think they're up to something?" I tried to change it quickly before she realized I was accusing her.

She softened a little and asked, "Up to something?"

"Yeah, like, they don't really need tutoring, they're just asking for, like, schoolwork. There's a class I'm taking where I've got to have someone from the tutoring center sign off on my work—so maybe…" My voice trailed off. I hoped I was making sense.

Carly nodded slowly, and I added just to make it better, "Sometimes people grab a tutor who's younger and may not know what exactly the work is just to say someone looked it over."

"Oh." She dropped her arms, and I released a breath. "You're right. I didn't even think about that. I just try to help people so much." She shrugged. "I never thought someone would just take advantage of my kindness."

I nodded. "Aren't you glad you've got me around now?" It was supposed to just be a joke to get me out of the neck-high water I was in with her. But she smiled at me, and my heart fluttered.

"I'm glad you're here, X." She touched my arm, her small hand traced down my wrist and grazed over my hand. Her finger prodded mine, and then they were intertwining with mine.

"Come on," she smiled, interlocking her fingers with mine. We were holding hands. I could hardly stop myself from smiling. "Let's go inside before they get too upset."

"Yeah," I said, trying to hold back the excitement coursing through me. I was holding hands with Carly. She liked me… She and I were becoming something right in front of everyone and I couldn't stop my heart from dancing with happiness. But deep down, I knew when the excitement wore off, that uneasy feeling I swallowed earlier to make room for the happiness, might claw its way back up my throat.

16

A Truthful Glimpse

Things began to heat up between Carly and me. She started coming by my dorm, and we actually went on a date, like, a *real* date. We talked about God, and we talked about how well her Bible Study classes were going. She told me she's thinking about bringing some of the people who attend the study to church sometime soon. She's eager to prove her brother wrong and show everyone at church that she's not in his shadow. Carly just wants to be her own person, and I can respect that.

"I've got classes and then tutoring later," Carly said as she squeezed my hand while she walked me to Eli's office.

"Tutoring?"

She looked up at me, a surprised look on her face until realization settled in, then a smirk appeared. "You think I'm tutoring those guys, don't you?" I could see her smirk fading into a goofy grin. "Is Xavier Miles jealous?"

I harrumphed. "Not at all." I tried to keep a straight face until I glanced down at her and we both laughed. "Alright, maybe a little. I'm *sorry*," I said as we stopped at Eli's door. "I can't help it." I leaned down and kissed her right on the lips in front of everyone. She smiled against my lips and wrapped an arm around my neck to deepen the kiss. It felt like nothing in the world really mattered whenever Carly kissed me. Carly Ross was kissing me… it didn't get better than that.

The door behind us opened, and before I could pull away, Carly held me tighter a second longer. I could feel Eli's eyes on us, but I kept my eyes closed until Carly pulled away.

"Good afternoon, Carly and Xavier," Eli said in his normal kind voice. There wasn't even a twinge of anger in his tone or on his face when I finally raised my eyes to meet his.

"Hi," I said weakly.

MJ stepped out, and when our eyes met, my heart almost stopped. A field of red poppies bloomed in my head, but before I could remember anything, the memory fizzled out and Madeline was the only person I was looking at. Cute dimples and glowing brown skin covered by the long tresses of the red ocean of hair she had flowing from her head. Dark cat eyes roved over me as she stood in the doorway. And even though my girlfriend had just kissed the slob out of my mouth, I almost couldn't stop drooling.

Why can't I look away from her? … I don't want to look away… She's so—

"X, you alright?" Carly grabbed my hand, jerking me from the swelling thoughts. I looked at her for a sense of stability, a sense of reality and peace, but when my eyes landed on Carly it was like looking at a storm calling you out to sea. The waves crashed and the winds hollered, but the sound of it all was alluring. The depth of the ocean was worth exploring, but there was an uneasy feeling when I looked at her, the same one I've been smothering just to be with her.

"Yeah," I sighed, "I just…" I glanced over at MJ and felt dizzy. "It was like I almost remembered something for a second, but it disappeared." I tried to play it off, and Carly bought it, but Elijah didn't. His smile was gone, and he was looking at me dead-on. His cool blue

126

eyes sent shockwaves of fear all over me as I passed my focus back to Carly.

"Well, if you remember, text it to me. I'll be a little busy tonight."

"Ok," I said as she pulled me down to kiss my cheek.

"MJ," she extended a hand to her, "let's go to class together."

Madeline only nodded and took Carly's hand. I watched the two of them walk away without Madeline ever speaking to me, or anyone else.

"Xavier, come in." Eli was smiling again but I knew this session would be a long one. "You've been coming to church, coming to Bible Study, going to the Crusaders meetings, and apparently dating Carly. Seems like everything's going perfect," he said as we took our seats across from each other.

I set my bag beside my comfy chair and shrugged. "It's hard to believe it, but everything seems perfect. Except JC, of course, he's still giving me a headache but—"

"A headache? About what?"

"Well, everything, really. He's upset about me being part of the Crusaders, and I haven't told him that I've actually joined the church. It's hard to talk to him about everything."

"Doesn't seem like a very good relationship to be in." Eli sat back in his chair and looked me over. "Why are you so desperate to hold on to JC?"

"What?" I frowned. "I'm not desperate for anything."

"Why are you clinging to him?"

"I'm not," I said forcefully.

"Let's say that you are, what reason would you have to cling to him?"

I sighed and slumped in my chair. "I ... I don't know."

In the silence, I tried to come up with something to say, but I didn't think I was trying to cling to JC. He was my best friend. I didn't want to dismiss him just because we had different beliefs. I know we're unequally yoked, but he hasn't come between me and God. So it's not a problem.

At least, I don't feel like it is.

"I don't want to turn on Junior like I turned on…" I looked up at Eli and then back down at my hands. I'd mentioned very little about the case back home, but now it felt like it would spill out any minute.

"Have you called home lately?"

"No," I said.

"Why not?"

"Because I don't want all the good stuff happening to me to be clouded by all the problems at home. I just want to be away from all of that."

"And what is all the good stuff happening?"

"Well, I'm dating Carly now." I smiled to myself.

"I see. That makes you very happy."

"I don't want to make things awkward between us." I glanced up.

He raised a shoulder and said, "I only know you in a professional setting, Xavier. In this room, and at church, I am a professional."

"So, you're saying it doesn't bother you that Carly and I are dating?"

He shook his head. "Not at all. My only concerns are your concerns."

"You're not worried because Carly's perfect." I sat back and stared up at the wall, thinking about my strawberry-haired girlfriend, until an image of a woman standing in a field of poppies appeared in my head and I lurched forward.

"Adar," I whispered.

"Are you alright, Xavier?' Eli asked.

I blinked at him and then at the wall. I couldn't remember anything.

I sat back in my chair and said, "I have these dreams that I can't remember. But there are bits and pieces that show up every now and then, and I can't tell what's reality and what's a dream."

"Maybe they're both reality," Eli suggested.

"They can't be. I'm living in reality right now."

"Do you believe in the spiritual world?"

"Well, yeah, God's a spirit."

"He is," he nodded, "and things happen in the spiritual world that coincide with the earthly realm. So maybe you're seeing the future, or something else."

"Like a prophecy?"

"Could be." He shrugged.

"Why can't I remember it? I've tried, but nothing comes back."

"Sometimes it's better not to try, and just wait for God to reveal it to you."

"This is so complicated." I dropped my face into my hands and Eli chuckled, leaning forward to rub my back.

"It'll be alright, Xavier, I promise."

Halloween rolled around, and the Crusaders took a school van to the bowling alley. Everyone except for Gertrude and Phoenix showed up, but we weren't surprised by that at all. The only surprise was Joe showing up in a costume. No one said anything, but we all knew he did it just to spite Gertrude, but her absence burned him enough which somewhat made up for his insolence.

When we arrived, there was another school van waiting in the parking lot. Out stepped Jay and MJ, hand in hand, and others just like them.

"Okay, guys," Carly said as she put the van in park. "I invited another group to go with us to keep the price down. So, try to be nice, alright?"

I turned in my seat to look at everyone else.

"We seriously couldn't afford bowling?" Julia said as she stared out the window. I was staring too, but not because I thought we didn't have the budget.

"Well—"

"Of all the clubs to invite," Tabitha interrupted, "you chose the LGBT Club?"

Joe laughed. "You forgot a letter. It's LGBT*Q*—and they call themselves Love Unlimited."

Julia just rolled her eyes, focused wholly on Carly who tried to explain, "Jesus ate with sinners, why can't we? Jesus wouldn't turn them away."

"No one said to turn them away," Tabitha said, her breath fogging up the window as she stared at the LGBTQ Club emerging from their van. "But Jesus never invited sinners out to eat. He attended a banquet thrown for Him by a man *He* saved. That's much different from what we're doing right now. And when Jesus was with sinners, He was feeding them the Word—not hanging out for fun."

"You don't have to quote the story, Tabitha, I know it," Carly snapped.

"It seems like you don't. Jesus only went out because He was invited. If it was alright to just hang out with unsaved people, why didn't God want the Israelites marrying the Egyptians? Why does Paul tell us to get away from the sexually immoral?"

"Why are you trying to preach right now?" Sam asked. "We get it, but is it that big of a deal?"

"That's the problem," Allen said from the back. "It's literally *bowling*, we could've done this another day or time. With people from any other group except this one. If we wanted to *hang out* with them, we could have invited them to a Bible Study session and hung out at church. Not this." He was usually quiet, but there he was, letting it rip for the first time.

"Alright," I said as I eased my hand over Carly's. She was gripping the steering wheel in frustration. "We're already here. Might as well

130

enjoy, right?"

"Yes, thank you!" Joe said loudly.

I didn't agree with holding the event with Love Unlimited either, not just because I thought Carly only invited them to hang out with Jay and Madeline, but also because we didn't *need* to be out on Halloween, and we didn't *need* to be associated with this club. But I was a sucker for Carly, and the Crusaders thought we'd be safe if we went bowling at midnight and no one ever saw us out on Halloween. But we were wrong. Now we're grouped in with Love Unlimited; there is no distinction between them and us.

We looked like supporters of their cause, not a group of leaders standing firm in their faith. Everyone always shouts *hate the sin, not the sinner*, but how do we show them that we hate the *sin* if we're always approving it? Never taking a stand.

I couldn't say it aloud, but Allen was right. If Carly truly wanted to *eat with sinners*, the place to do it was in church—where we could feed on the Word and possibly save the sinners we claimed to want to reach. Just as Jesus did.

I took a breath and gave Carly my best smile, and she seemed to accept it. She gave me one back and interlaced her fingers with mine.

"Come on!" Jay was yelling from outside the window. "It's freezing out here!" She was wearing a skimpy bunny outfit, while MJ wore regular clothes. Some of the others from Love Unlimited stepped out in costumes. Some were dressed sexily; others were dressed in silly costumes.

As our group exited the van, I tried to think of a way to bring this up to Carly tomorrow. The Bible always made it clear that we weren't to associate with sinners. We don't have to treat them poorly, but we're supposed to be separated from them to lead them to the Light. The kindness of God leads us to repentance, that's what pastor Tosh taught this past Sunday.

She said that being kind to unsaved people doesn't mean associating with them. Being kind means showing brotherly love when they come to church. It means being compassionate as they come to learn about God and being compassionate when they make mistakes.

It means being the Light in the darkness so that they'll know which direction to run to and reach God. But every time you make an excuse for sin, or you don't stand flat footed against sin, your light dampens.

None of these people from Love Unlimited can follow us to the Light because they don't see us as being *in* the Light. We're 'cool' with them, we're their friends who have accepted them and their sin tonight. Being 'cool' with them means you're just like them or close enough to them that there's no problem.

But Jesus came to divide. He came to separate the saved from the sinner. He came to give us a light, and as we're the Light dwellers on this Earth, we can't afford to be cool. We have to be hot or else God will spew us out. Or else being too cool might make our fire go out instead of heating up the room and bringing Light into the dark places. It just means we have to stand out even when it feels uncomfortable, and tonight, the Crusaders didn't do that at all... *I* didn't do that at all. So now there's no way to reach the people of Love Unlimited. Bringing up the Word of God now would only offend them and push them away. All because Carly thought it was a good idea to be friends with everyone.

"Hey, Xavier!" Jay let go of MJ and latched on to me as Carly exchanged me for MJ. The two girls were holding hands, snickering quietly as they walked ahead. "They're cute, aren't they?"

"No," I said flatly as I watched the widening eyes of Tabitha following our leader who was walking hand in hand with a member of Love Unlimited. I was getting a little worried she would explode from surprise when Jay said, "Come on, everyone knows you two are a thing, and MJ and I are a thing. They're just friends, which is good for MJ, she needs more of those."

"They just seem close," I said.

Jay straightened as we entered the bowling alley. "I know you don't want to be seen with me, so I'm going to take my leave now. But I hope you watch me bowl when Carly's not around." Her voice was laced with all kinds of seduction as she crossed in front of me, forcing me to stop abruptly and stare at her. My eyes trailed from her white stilettos, up her long legs wrapped in fishnet stockings. Her bunny outfit was revealing, and if it wasn't so shameful, I might've given in to Jay's antics this night since we'd already screwed up.

I didn't know how I'd keep myself together all night, looking at her alluring eyes, but somehow, I'd have to manage.

17

Who's Strong and Who's Weak

"Being single doesn't mean that you're alone."

"Um," Kevin raised his hand, "I'm literally alone."

The group chuckled, except for me. I wasn't in the mood. The Crusaders Halloween night was a failure. Jay snuck in alcohol and got drunk at the bowling alley. She sat on my lap twice, and Carly was alright with it, more alright than she should've been. But that's because Carly was preoccupied. She sat snuggled up, and I mean *snuggled up*, like sharing a jacket with MJ all night.

Carly clapped for Jay when she sat on my lap. She cheered her on and told her she was a stick of dynamite. But that was just the first time. The second time she sat on my lap, Carly chanted for us to kiss. We didn't, but when Carly went up to bowl, I let my hands wander all over Jay's frame. She was curvy and she smelled good, and I liked the way it felt having Jay in my lap. I didn't even think about JC because I spent the rest of the night letting Jay toy with me. I spent the rest of the night touching Jay in places I shouldn't, keeping her close to make Carly jealous but also to keep the ecstasy I was feeling from leaving me.

I was sick with embarrassment the next morning, and I wasn't surprised when I woke up to an email from Carly saying the next Crusaders meeting was cancelled. The only thing that brought me comfort was that we did have fun… too much fun, which also made my stomach churn in agony.

Our night out did not look like a gay club and a Christian club, it looked like a hormonal teenager club, unsupervised edition. Kissing, making out—I heard three different couples had sex in the bathrooms, and there were other favors and theatrics going on. But it wasn't just the sex that bothered me. There was also drinking and smoking in the girls' bathroom. We didn't get home until seven in the morning because when the alley closed, we found an open restaurant to burn off the high and sober up.

"Xavier? You've been spaced out all evening."

I found Pastor Ross's eyes were full of concern. I missed classes today without reason, and he probably found out from my professors. I had no privacy.

"Yeah, just tired." I wanted to tell Eli what'd happened. I wanted to cry and beg God for forgiveness, but everything I did last night was intentional. I wanted to keep Jay in my lap longer every time she sat there. Then I wanted to get her undressed and lose my virginity right there with Carly's blessing. And it scared me. I didn't have a sip of alcohol, not a puff of smoke, yet I was intoxicated with the night. I didn't know what to do, or how to feel except for pitiful and guilty.

We were all hypocrites. We all criticized Carly, whether internally or externally, yet not a single one of us Crusaders tried to go home. No one tried to leave early or wanted to be dropped off when we rode to the restaurant. In fact, we all didn't even ride together. Some of the Crusaders rode in Love Unlimited's van while Jay, MJ, a guy named Ricky, and a few Crusaders rode with Carly and me.

It *was* fun, but was it worth it? Would my behavior last night ever be

135

forgotten by those who aren't part of the Body of Christ? How will I look anyone in the face, and tell them Jesus loves them even though—

"You've messed up," Eli was saying. His words caught my attention, and I kept my head down, but I listened intently. "You feel like you'll always be alone, and because of your past, you'll never be able to love someone, or someone will love you. All the shame and guilt are heavy."

"We know Jesus took it all away though," Daisy's voice chimed in. "What does that have to do with being single?"

"Because one of the biggest elements is not just knowing Jesus took all your mistakes and sins away, it's about not making those mistakes again. You see, singleness is all about transformation. It's about transforming and never going back to who you used to be, but rather picking up your cross and starting your new journey."

"Ok, but what if I'm already doing that?" Sky asked.

"There's a possibility that you've picked it up and begun carrying it, but there's also a possibility that you've picked it up and set it down a few times too."

I heard Sky and the others chuckling and Eli went on. "The sin nature must be broken. You must *want* to be transformed; you must *want* to submit to God. And when you're single, you're less distracted. You have more time to focus on Christ and figure out how to stop doing the things you don't want to do. There's a scripture that I often quote to this class—"

"For I do not do the good I want, but the evil I do not want is what I keep on doing," I said as I erupted to my feet. "I'm sorry," I whispered, and I could feel the tears of embarrassment burning my eyes. "I'm sorry, but I feel like it's wrong to be sorry after what I've done. After I had a chance to stop myself, but I didn't. Why can't I stop doing the evil, and start doing the good?" I looked up at him, and a tear rolled down my cheek. "Please help me."

"Me too!" The screeching cry belonged to Tracy. She was weeping

136

into her hands about doing things she shouldn't but never stopping. Julius was nodding along but didn't say anything, and as I looked around, I found that nearly all of us felt the same. When my gaze returned to Eli, he was smiling at me.

"Resist him, standing firm in the faith, because you know that the family of Believers throughout the world is undergoing the same kind of sufferings." He paused and glanced around as we all began to wipe our tears and try to refocus. "That scripture is an encouraging one. We're reminded that we can resist the temptation, not only because of Jesus, but also because you are not alone. There are other Believers counting on you to win the battle so they can learn from your journey."

Eli pointed his finger around the room at each of us. "The people in this room, and everyone around the globe who is part of the Body of Christ is tested the same way. We are all tempted and, knowing this, we are able to pray for one another. But also, in learning this, we reach the first step at the bottom of the ladder."

"What's the first step?" Marlo Jo asked as I sat down.

"The first step to growing in your singleness is understanding that you are not alone. When you're married, you know you've got your spouse, but when you're single, who do you have? Some have parents, some have friends or siblings, but no one can replicate the love that you get from a spouse. So who can fill that void?"

"God?" Daytona asked.

"God," Eli confirmed. "Technically, He doesn't replicate a spouse's love," he laughed, "your spouse replicates *God's* love the best way they can, but it doesn't compare to the wholeness of Christ. The fulfillment of the love of Christ is powerful, and you need to experience that on an individual basis first. Experiencing the love of God will make you feel like your whole world is complete, and so that prepares you for what you'll be receiving in marriage."

"How can we be loved like that by humans? Isn't it impossible?"

137

Daytona asked again.

"Yes, God's love is stronger than any earthly love," Eli agreed. "But your spouse will give you the next best thing. Specifically, husbands to wives."

"A man will love a woman more than a woman loves a man? There's no way," Tracy said as she wiped her tears.

"Actually, that's how it's supposed to be." Eli shrugged. "Men were given a commandment to love their wives as Christ loves the church."

"But we only have to love a *submissive* wife," Kevin corrected. "We don't have to love a woman who won't submit to us."

"How do you figure that?" Eli raised a brow.

"Because…" Kevin struggled, "the Bible literally tells wives to submit and *obey* us. It's right there." He pointed, as if there were an open Bible in the air for all of us to see.

"Well, if husbands love their wives as Christ loves the church, and more often than not, the church is unruly and not submissive, but God still loves us, right?" Eli said. "He still protects us and gives to us. So, what's the difference between a husband who continues to love his wife even when she's unruly? Doesn't that demonstrate righteousness? Doesn't that demonstrate the way the love of God draws us to repentance?"

Kevin gave a huge sigh, but it wasn't a defeated one, just an agitated one. "But that's only for a *submissive, obedient* wife. A person is literally submissive if they're a Christian. So making a mistake here and there is overlooked. If a wife is submissive, a mistake once or twice can be ignored." He shrugged. "Honestly, I'll overlook anything as long as she's obeying me like the *Bible* says she's supposed to."

Elijah loved a challenge, and I could tell that Kevin's ferocity was only adding coal to Elijah's fire. "Do you know why women are told to submit to their husbands?"

"Because they're weak. They need someone to protect them," Kevin mocked.

Marlo Jo gave him a nasty look, but said nothing, and the whole room felt tense. I don't know when I stopped thinking about the night before, but right now, all I could focus on was what Eli was explaining.

"That's very true," Eli agreed, and I heard the gasps around the room and watched Emily visibly stiffen. "Women are the weaker vessel between the man and woman. Eve was the one tempted, not Adam, even the scripture says that."

"I've never read that," Daytona said.

"Check first Timothy chapter two, verse fourteen. Adam was not deceived, Eve was. And if you look at first Peter, chapter three, verse seven. It's there. Women are the weaker vessel, but what else does that verse say?"

We opened our Bibles, and the rustling of pages filled the sanctuary as we searched for the scripture.

"It says that husbands are to love with their wives in an understanding way," Eli said as he set his Bible on his stool. "Because they are weaker than you. Let's pause right there. Women are weaker than you, in a marriage, but that's it. Because if you finish out the verse, it says that women are heirs *with* their husband in grace. That means women are *equal* to men under grace."

"It just said that women are weaker than men." Kevin looked angry. "We all get grace, but they're *still* weak. And they *still* have to obey men. Period."

I sighed. At this point, I would have cheered if Marlo Jo socked Kevin right in the mouth. The saddest part was that his way of thinking and interpreting the Bible was not uncommon. The church was filled with men who believed women were supposed to bow and obey their husbands without thought or question. And if they didn't bow and agree to be their husband's personal slave, then they were labeled as a Jezebel woman on a one-way trip to hell.

This was the state of the church.

It was no wonder there were so many single Christian women out there. I'd stay single too if Kevin was the only sort of man available to marry.

Eli's voice caught my attention. "Do you have any idea why Peter made it clear that women are equal to men in grace? The first is to make a distinction between women under grace and women under the law. Secondly, it was a deterrent to keep men from putting a value on the word, *weaker*." Eli's eyes bore into Kevin who'd begun to fidget. "Being weaker doesn't diminish the place of a woman beside her husband—nor does it place her *behind* or *underneath* her husband. She is the more *delicate* vessel. She is a vessel that needs to be protected."

"But I don't need anyone's protection," Marlo said. "I can protect myself."

"I understand where you're coming from, Marlo Jo, but let me show you this same information another way." Eli flipped through his Bible in silence. I watched in awe as he calmly searched the Word of God. He wasn't nervous or shaken at all. His demeanor made me feel like I could trust whatever he was about to explain.

I thought Kevin would explode and Tracy might cry, and Marlo might leave while everyone else hid what they really felt. The tension was high in the room because all that'd seemingly been said was that women were weak, and men were strong.

"Genesis two and fifteen." Eli paused and looked up at me.

I fumbled, flipping through my Bible to read the verse. "That's God placing Adam in the Garden to work in it."

"And what else?"

I glanced back down. "To keep it?"

"That's right." He nodded at me and looked out at the students. "Adam was given work before he was married. Which means, as single people, before you can even consider marriage, you need to know what your calling from God is, and you need to be walking in that calling. That means God will prosper you to work in the place He wants you to work in. And I know everyone thinks prosperity is *money*," he held up his wallet, "but prosperity is the divine capability to fulfill your assignment."

"What does that mean?" Julius asked.

"This was next week's lesson, so I'll only give you a little before returning to our topic," Eli said. "God has given each one of us a purpose. Your purpose is your assignment. Our assignments must be fulfilled so that the plans of God for the entire Body of Christ can move forward. So, what that really means is that we have to be intentional about our calling, and we have to be successful. But the only way to fulfill a heavenly assignment, or be successful in our heavenly orders is what?"

"To have heavenly help," Sky answered.

Eli nodded with a grin. "Heavenly help is divine skills, it is prosperity. So, before you get married, you should be prospering in your calling. That doesn't mean you have to be wealthy, but it means you have to be successful in what God's called you to do, and He will make provision for your success."

"And that's because of Adam?" Marlo asked.

"Yes, because Adam's story sets the tone for a lot of things in our life. Adam is given work before marriage, which means we are given our divine assignment before marriage. His assignment was to keep and tend to the Garden. Keep can also be swapped with the word, *protect*."

"Oh! So that's why men protect women?" Daisy said aloud as she jotted something down in her notebook. "Because they're supposed to keep them—take care of them and maintain their needs."

"Correct," Eli agreed. "But women were given that same charge."

"When?" Daytona asked.

"Right there in Genesis chapter two, verse fifteen."

"How?" Kevin shrugged. "It's just Adam."

"Yes, but Adam means *man*, and man is used for *both* male and female, hence the fall of man referring to *all* humans. And while Adam was the only *physical* being there, women were there too. Which is why Eve knew God's commandment was not to eat of the tree of knowledge. Because she was there too when it was given."

"Where?" I asked. My voice sounded dumb when I spoke, but Eli turned to address me with no malice or anger.

"A marriage is the joining of two flesh becoming one. When two flesh are as one, the man becomes the head of the marriage. He becomes the protector, but so does the woman because she is his rib. And what do ribs do?"

It was silent for a moment.

"They protect," Eli said. "They are the protectors of vital organs. So, the commands issued to Adam fell onto Eve as well because she was and is a part of him. And when a man is called to be a protector, a wife, who is part of him, is also called to be a protector."

"I'm not understanding any of this," Tracy whined. "I thought women were weak, but now they're part of men and they're not weak anymore?"

"They're still weak," Eli laughed, "because ribs can be weak. They're bendy little things that can snap pretty easily, depending on the rib. However, their job is to protect the heart, the lungs—all the vital organs. Although a wife may be weaker, she still has a job to protect her husband because it was commanded of her back in the Garden."

"Because Eve was part of Adam, she received the commandment to protect, and not to eat off that tree?" Tracy looked confused still but when Eli nodded, she brightened.

"So that still makes no sense," Kevin said, stretching in his seat. "If she knew better, then why did she eat the fruit?"

"As a rib, as a protector of vital organs, she failed on her part as the

142

helper to Adam. The role of the helper, the protector in a woman as a wife, means she's praying for her husband. That's why she's a rib because she's dealing with the things you can't see. While the husband deals with everything you *can* see. So why did Eve's curse fall onto relationships and why did Adam's curse fall onto the ground?"

"Because those were their assignments," Marlo said quietly. "She was a helper, tending to Adam's needs because he was alone in the Garden. But Adam's assignment was to tend to the Garden itself."

"Very good, Marlo Jo." Eli was proud now as he smiled around the room at us. "Eve was the helper, and since Adam listened to the helper, instead of God, he was cursed in his work because he did not fulfill his assignment to tend to the Garden, to *protect* the Garden."

"This makes sense!" Emily chirped. "Because cherubim were placed at the Garden to protect it, right? Because Adam failed to."

"Absolutely." Elijah nodded happily. "And, if we look at Eve, we see that not only were women cursed in childbirth, but women were cursed in one more way." He held up two fingers so we could all see. "They were cursed with the desire to lead over her husband since she gave him the fruit and led him to eat it. But, in response to that desire, her husband would rule over her as a curse."

"So ..." Julius tapped his chin with his pen. "A submissive wife is a *cursed* wife?"

Eli shook his head. "No, a submissive wife is a *blessed* wife. Helpers serve and respect authority. It's when they *won't* serve or respect the authority of their husband as the protector and provider, that's when they're operating under the curse, which can lead to other things, but I won't get into that today."

"Thank God because you almost lost me," Daytona said.

I chuckled quietly as I nodded in agreement while the rest of the group laughed... except for Kevin.

"So, you're telling me," he said forcefully, "that a wife is equal to a husband, but she's still gotta submit to him? Well then, we're back to square one."

"No, you missed everything in between," Eli said as he confidently stepped around the stool. "Because of grace, women and men are equal no matter what. Wives are to submit to their husbands as the weaker vessel for protection, as husbands are to submit to their wives as the stronger vessel for *spiritual* protection."

"We don't submit," Kevin said flatly.

"According to Ephesians five and twenty-five we do." Eli turned and flipped there. "It says right there that husbands are to love their wives as Christ loves the church. Christ *died* for the church; you know that right? He *served* the church, washed the feet of His disciples who eventually established the first church. He catered to the needy and the sick—the *weaker vessels* of society—because He is strong enough to do it."

"And He's still doing it," Daisy said weakly. "He's our mediator, so technically, isn't He still serving us?"

"He is." Eli nodded at her. "Christ is still serving us, which is symbolic of marriage. The never-ending cycle of a husband serving his wife, and a wife submitting and serving her husband as the church does for Jesus here on earth." He took a breath. "Husbands and wives are to submit to *each other* the same way we submit to God. That means giving up ourselves for the other's sake."

"Not doing whatever we want," I said weakly as the thoughts from last night came bombarding back into my head.

"Exactly," Eli said. "But it's heavier on the man because he's the head of the marriage."

"But women still have to submit," Kevin said, sounding satisfied.

"As do men," Eli told him. "It's actually a curse to rule over a woman in a marriage. Just as it's a curse for a woman to rule over a man. No one rules over anyone. We make sacrifices every day for each other, but the man has to sacrifice more. To much is given, much is required."

"The church sacrifices herself through baptism though, right? We die to our old selves," Tracy said.

"We do, and that's a representation for women in a marriage to give up that desire to live the way you used to before marriage. Now, you're not an independent woman, you are dependent upon God and your husband."

"This makes it seem one-sided then." Kevin shrugged. "She's my equal *and* I've got to die for her?"

"Women are the prize for our toil," Eli said as he grabbed his Bible. "The church is God's prize. Bringing us home to Him when our time is over here brings Him great joy. We have to look at Christ's relationship with the church to understand the way marriage is supposed to be."

My hand was tired of writing, my mind was getting foggy with guilt again, but Eli wasn't finished. He looked up from his Bible with a smile and said, "Ecclesiastes chapter nine, verse nine, this is the English Standard Version: *enjoy your life with the wife whom you love, all the days of your vain life that He has given you under the sun, because that is your portion in life and in your toil at which you toil under the sun.*" He set his Bible down and lifted his phone, scrolling for a minute. "In the New Living Translation, it says: *live happily with the woman you love through all the meaningless days of your life that God has given you under the sun. The wife God gives you is your* reward *for all your earthly toil.*" He closed his phone and blinked around at us. "In order to thrive in your singleness, you must first understand your purpose in this life, and you must understand the future roles in a marriage in order to prepare for it. Now, that's time for today. Next week, we'll get back into that prosperity I was telling you about."

"Thank God! Today was so hard," Daisy complained to Daytona as we packed up.

Kevin stormed out, and I heard Sky telling Marlo and Julius bye as he left. I stuffed my things into my bag when I felt a warmth on my shoulder.

"Xavier," Elijah was standing beside me, smiling down at me. "Can I talk to you?"

"Sure," I said as I pulled my bag on. We left the sanctuary, and he took me around the corner to his office. It was literally the same layout and furniture from his office at school.

Eli noticed me staring before I realized it, and he said, "I like consistency."

"Right." I took a seat in the comfy chair across from his.

"You had an outburst today, what was that about?"

I sighed. "Eli, I messed up last night. The Crusaders went bowling and we stayed out all night and I did things I shouldn't have."

When I looked over at him, his brow was quirked, and the shame of it all was about to break me when he said, "The Crusaders went bowling last night?"

"Yeah." I shrugged. "Didn't you sign off on it? Carly turned in all the paperwork so we could have a van. We couldn't get a van without an adviser's signature."

"Right, of course."

It was the first time I ever saw Elijah look human. There was a sense of confusion that washed over him briefly as he thought over what I'd said.

"So, what happened that makes you feel like you can't stop doing evil?"

"It's Jay," I said, shaking my head, not even caring that I was being open with him tonight. *Really* open. I felt like I was cold and would never get warm if I didn't get right with God right that instant.

"Jay?"

"Jocelyn, she's a girl that my best friend likes, and she's the same girl I danced with on the boat at the beginning of the year. I don't like her, but other parts of me do, and I can't stop thinking about last night. And

146

even though we went with the LGBTQ Club, we had fun, which I know is wrong."

"Was Carly there?"

"Yeah," I waved a hand, "she invited Love Unlimited. We all gave her flack about it until we got inside and became the world's biggest hypocrites. But I don't even think Carly cared." I shrugged. "She was all cuddled up with MJ. Which is another thing that's bothering me because MJ isn't straight, but she's always cuddling with her and swears they're best friends."

"MJ as in Madeline Jones?"

"Yeah, red hair? Comes to your sessions?"

He nodded.

"How do I make things right with God? I thought being on this recommitment journey was enough to keep me from wanting…"

"Sex?"

I nodded sheepishly. "It's like I can't make it stop now. I want to go see Jay, but everything in me is telling me no. And I'm scared to go back to campus because I know I'll go see her."

"Wanting to recommit and actually recommitting to Christ are totally different things, Xavier. What you're doing right now, the fighting, you're warring again. You're actively participating in spiritual warfare, despite what happened last night."

"But I'm only doing it because I'm guilty! I want to fight because I love God!"

"Because you love God you are filled with regret and guilt. No one is blameless, and that's why Jesus had to die. A sacrifice that can purify every single sin, even the ones we do on purpose. Only the Blood of Jesus can purge and purify us completely."

I ran my hand over my head and took a deep breath. "So, what do I do?"

"You pray. Ask God for forgiveness with a sincere heart, and ask

God for obedience, the desire to do His will. He'll give it to you, and you'll experience a transformation within."

"Like what Pastor Tosh talked about?"

"Yes." Eli was smiling again, but something seemed off about Pastor Ross now. I was in no position to try to figure it out, so I grabbed my bag to give him some space.

"Well, I guess I'll do that then."

"When you return to the dorms," he said as I headed for the door, "call home and keep your mind busy so you can avoid that girl. And as soon as your dorm gets quiet, pray."

18

Falling Apart

"Hello?" I answered drowsily as I sat up out of bed.

"Xavier? Sorry I missed your texts. I've just been busy."

"Carly?" I pulled my phone away from my ear and stared at the ungodly bright light. It was almost three in the morning. When I walked home from Bible Study, I didn't feel like calling my mother, so I called Carly instead. She didn't answer the first or second time. But I left her a voicemail, just asking her to return my call when she got the chance... I guess now's the only chance she's got ... Two weeks later.

She cancelled the Crusaders meeting again and didn't return any of my texts either. I thought we were breaking up and had even accepted it because of what'd happened with Jay at the bowling alley and the restaurant. But now, Carly was calling at nearly three in the morning and I had no idea what to even expect.

"Yeah." She laughed gently. I'd forgotten how soothing her voice was. "Who'd you expect?"

"No one," I said quickly as I tossed the covers back. I didn't want her to think I was still thinking about Jocelyn because I wasn't. I was over that night, those mistakes. I'd taken the last two weeks to work hard at my recommitment to Christ, and by my own standards, I'd been faring well.

"I just wasn't expecting you to call at this hour."

"I know. I've been such a terrible girlfriend, I wanted to make it up to you."

"Oh." I looked over at Glenn. He was snoring loudly with a pillow over his head. He always burrowed beneath it and emerged like some kind of slug every morning.

"What's wrong?"

If I told her I thought we'd broken up and had spent the last two weeks getting over her and trying to get closer to God, I thought she'd be mad. So, instead, I said, "Well, I'm just surprised, that's all."

"I know we haven't talked lately, but I've just been busy. So, I wanted to invite you to Thanksgiving dinner with me and Eli."

"Thanksgiving? Wouldn't I be imposing on you guys?"

"Not at all," she said cheerfully. "You are definitely welcomed here, and you're my boyfriend, X, how could you ever impose?"

My heart fluttered when she called me her boyfriend. The words sent a shudder of warmth through me, and I could feel myself smiling in the dark.

"Well, I was staying here anyway, so if you guys don't mind, I guess I'll come over."

"Great," she said happily. "I'll make arrangements. And don't think you're leaving after dinner either. We're going early Black Friday shopping."

"Oh," I laughed, "okay, then."

"Perfect. I'm sorry about calling through the night, I just missed you and felt guilty."

"No." I was smiling ear to ear now. "I'm glad you did. I've missed you a lot, Carly."

In the silence, I grinned like a dork. I was patching things up with my girlfriend and making Thanksgiving plans with her. We were a real couple, two people who'd fallen in love, and I was finally part of something. I was finally part of what I'd missed out on in high school. I was finally one of those happy people who had everything—a girlfriend, best friends, their faith, and good times.

What more could I ask for? I had a lot to be thankful for this Thanksgiving, and I intended to show my complete thankfulness.

"Well," Carly said, "I'm going back to bed, but I'll see you tomorrow at the Crusaders meeting."

"Yeah, I'll see you tomorrow."

"Goodnight, X."

"Goodnight, Carly."

When she hung up, I flopped back into my bed and clutched the phone to my chest. I was happy. I was *so* happy. Carly and I had our first fallout, but we made it through. We could make it through anything if we came back from that. We can forgive each other in the future, and still stay together. Maybe Carly really *was* the one, and that's why I was so happy.

Carly is not who I have picked for you.

I sat up fast and glanced around the room. Glenn was still snoring, and the room was still. No moonlight reached in through the windows, only darkness of the night sky, and the stiffness of the room.

God? Is that you?

My sheep know My voice.

I gasped. *No, it's not.* I covered my ears, but His voice resounded in my heart.

I will tell you things before they happen, I am the Lord Your God.

"What are You telling me?" I whispered with my hands still over my ears and my eyes closed tightly.

Carly is using you.

"What? No, she's not!"

"Xavier?"

I lifted my head from my hands quickly to see Glenn sitting up now.

"Did I wake you?"

"Yeah." He leaned over and turned on his lamp. A low glow chased the darkness away as Glenn grabbed his glasses from the nightstand. "You were yelling just now."

"I didn't mean to. Sorry." I shrank away, staring at the blankets.

"Who were you talking to?"

"I … I was just—"

"Was it God? Did He speak to you?"

I slowly blinked at him, he'd turned over and was staring up at the ceiling, waiting for my answer.

"Yeah, God was talking to me."

"What'd He say?"

"Something about," I paused, wondering if I should tell Glenn, "I don't know. He talks in riddles and stuff sometimes."

"It must be nice, having your supreme being speak to you."

"Yours doesn't?"

He shrugged. "I hear voices quite often. Whispers. The chatter of children."

I flinched. "That … That sounds kind of scary."

"What does God's Voice sound like?"

"Well, I don't know. It's hard to describe."

He nodded and took a breath. "Is He at least nice?"

I wanted to say *no* because there was no way Carly was using me. We'd made up from our behavior at the bowling alley, so how could she be using me? *I won't believe it,* I told myself, *not until I see her in person. If she's questionable, then maybe I'll believe it.*

"I guess so," I shrugged. "Why are you so interested in Him?"

152

"Just a comparison in my head." Glenn rolled over and clicked out the light. I got back beneath the covers as he added, "The semester is almost over and I'm running out of excuses."

He was talking about JC … And his unreasonable dislike of religion. Particularly Christianity. Glenn was still covering for me, keeping the secret that could end up being the death of our friendship. It was a burden I'd been avoiding well so far. Somehow, I felt my time with this secret was running out. There would come a time where I would have to choose between God and JC. And Glenn would witness it all.

"You need to tell him something," my roommate said.

"I know." I stared at the blank wall. "I know."

I could barely sleep last night trying to get Glenn's conversation out of my head … and trying to forget what God said too. I didn't want to believe it, not about Carly. She'd never do anything like that. Carly was nice and helpful, she was a good Christian woman, how could she use me? How could she not be the one?

"Xavier," Professor Daniels called. I pulled my eyes to meet his and he waved. "You're spacing, kid, stay focused."

"Sorry, professor."

He nodded and went on to explain something. I still wasn't listening, but that was partially because JC was elbowing me, asking if I was alright, and for the first time in this class period, I noticed it was just me, JC, and MJ.

Jay wasn't there.

Not that I was looking for her, but she never missed class. Not a single one so far this semester. She'd come in late before, but she'd never skipped out entirely. I tried not to feel worried, but I couldn't help it.

Mostly because I wanted to make things clear to her about Carly and me. What happened on Halloween won't and can't happen again. But also because I couldn't get the image of Jay's thin frame from my mind.

Carly hadn't been smoking drugs and hotboxing that day I caught her in MJ's room. But something was wrong with Jay. Something that made the back of my neck bubble with sweat.

I leaned over and whispered to JC, "Have you seen Jay?"

"No." He squinted. "Why do you care?"

"Because she's out today and she's never out." And she's also deathly thin and probably hiding a drug problem that no one seems to notice because Jay was so unpredictable and rambunctious. She was proudly bisexual and got around quite a bit. She didn't miss parties any more than she missed class. And JC honestly wasn't the type of guy to pay close enough attention to notice the little changes I'd seen in Jay. He just wanted to sleep with her. Why would he notice anything else about her?

"Everyone misses a class or two, X," he said, giving me the side eye.

"Not Jay," I said before leaning over to tap MJ, but the professor called me out again.

"While I'm glad you're awake now, Xavier, I'll need you to keep quiet."

"Right, sorry."

He sighed and turned back to the board, explaining a historical flow chart to us.

"Where's Jay?" I asked MJ.

She raised a brow, and I noticed the fresh piercing in it. I blinked at it, before my eyes traced down to her eyes.

"She's out sick."

"Is she alright?" I whispered.

MJ shrugged, tucking loose red hair behind her ear. "She'll be fine."

I nodded and sat back in my seat, tapping my pencil to the table. I could feel JC's eyes on me. He was wondering why I was interested in Jocelyn, but I was just concerned. He didn't know that she was smoking a lot and had gotten drunk at the bowling alley. And he didn't know she'd almost taken my virginity two weeks ago, and I was hoping to keep it that way, so I turned and flashed him a smile. I tried to make it genuine and normal, but the forced smile he returned told me he was questioning me.

When class was over, JC left without a word. He didn't ask any questions, didn't try to figure out why I was concerned. I was a little surprised that he wasn't more worried about her. Maybe I was overreacting, but a regular student not attending class out of the blue seemed weird to me.

"X," MJ called in the hall.

I whirled around as she marched up to me, throwing her flowery smelling red hair over her shoulder. Her hair, the redness was familiar, but not because I'd seen it on her all semester long, but because I'd also seen it somewhere else.

"Jay's fine," she said, catching my attention.

"Oh, good. I was a little worried since she's always in class, but she wasn't today."

"You must really like her," she joked.

"No." I scratched my head. "I just noticed she was missing. I've got a lot on my mind and the worrying from that was just feeding the worrying over Jocelyn."

"I see." MJ nodded. "Well, I'll see you around."

"Madeline," I stopped her. "Is there anything going on between you and my girlfriend?" I was looking for the smallest wince, or flinch, or flicker of surprise, but nothing came.

MJ said, "We're friends. She's my lab partner. The most I can say is that she treats me like an actual human being, so we're close. She pities me more than anything."

"Right," I said. "I'm sorry, Madeline."

She looked back at me, and the entire building changed to a field of red poppies. In the distance, there was a woman standing there, like she was waiting for me. I gasped and was sucked back to reality.

"It's no big deal," MJ was saying, waving a hand. Her cloud-shaped pendant winked in the sunlight as it dangled from her bracelet.

"Wait!" I called. "What was that name …" I trailed off as I stared at her. She was prettier today. Glowing. But I think I always said that about Madeline. I don't know what it is about her, but when I'm too close to her, I feel winded, and my words die on my lips.

What was it about her that was so… familiar? She was inviting, like I knew her well, like I wanted to know her even better. There was a strange feeling I got from her. The only way I could describe it was feeling like I'd found something, but I had no idea what I was looking for, though I knew it was important.

"What?" she said with a frown. "I'll be late if you don't hurry up." MJ had gotten bolder over the semester. She used to be shy and very quiet. But now she was showing more emotions, feeling more things, and experiencing things. It was like we'd done this before somehow.

"Sorry," I muttered, stepping back to break her dizzying gaze. "What was that name I said that time outside of Eli's office? Do you remember?"

"Adar? I didn't know it was a name."

"Adar…" the name sent a wave of nostalgia over me, and I suddenly felt like I wanted to weep. "I've gotta go," I said, backing away. "Thanks, MJ."

I turned and raced through the hall before she could say anything else. Down the stairs, I rushed for the exit and burst through the doors for fresh air. I hunched over, trying to breathe and make the feeling of crying go away.

"Xavier?" I looked up, and Carly was standing there holding her

156

books.

"Carly, hi." I erected immediately and felt the tightness in my chest suddenly soothing at her presence. She smiled, and it felt like I could breathe again.

"What are you doing racing out the building like that?" She grabbed my arm, and we began down the sidewalk, stepping over dying leaves, and walking against the cool wind. I breathed deeply, letting the sweet smell of my girlfriend fill my nostrils.

"I was just getting some fresh air."

"Well, good news, the Crusaders are actually meeting early today, so we can go shopping afterwards if you want."

"Shopping? For what?"

"Thanksgiving, silly." She laughed as she swatted my arm.

"Well, sure, I'll go."

"Great, then it's a date."

We walked the rest of the way in silence, taking in the scenery around us. Seasons had changed and we hadn't even noticed it. The rest of the world was so consuming that we often missed the beauty in the little things. But when you have everything you've ever wanted, you're no longer consumed. You've got a new journey, to find all the beautiful things in the world and share them with that special person.

I looked down at Carly as she rested her head against my shoulder while we walked to the cafeteria. *She's my special person.*

Inside, the Crusaders were already there. I never checked my email this morning to find out there was a time change, but I was thankful that Carly caught me out there. I took my seat beside her as she led us in a quick prayer and began the meeting. I watched her as she prayed earnestly, spoke gently, and genuinely cared for our group. There was no way Carly wasn't right for me. She was perfect.

"Okay, let's start with old news. An after-action report, if you will," she said as she flipped through her notes.

"The only thing to report is that we got out there at the bowling alley and acted like idiots. No one's going to take us seriously now," Allen said.

"You're acting like you didn't go," Julia commented.

"No, I'm just the only person who's going to say something and own up to my actions."

"What happened?" Phoenix asked. As promised, he returned after Halloween.

"Nothing," Carly said slowly, "we got a little out of hand at the bowling alley."

"Carly invited the gay club," Tabitha said flatly.

"What?" Gertrude sat forward and stared at Carly. It was hard to believe that in the beginning of the semester, Gertrude, Julia, and Carly were side by side at the table recruiting people for this group.

"We needed numbers," Carly said with a hesitant shrug.

"Numbers? And all of you went?" Gertrude looked around.

"Oh please," Sam said, "don't start acting high and mighty."

"I'm not acting high and mighty," Gertrude snapped. "I'm surprised that everyone went despite Love Unlimited being there."

"We couldn't just leave because the LGBTQ club was there," Julia said. "That would've been so rude and smeared our name."

"Well, it would've been better to have the Crusaders' name smeared for the sake of righteousness than to have it smeared in hypocrisy." Phoenix flailed his hands. "You guys literally made a fool out of us. Made us look like we don't believe anything the Bible says."

"No, we didn't." Joe slapped his leg. "We let everyone know we aren't close minded and old-fashioned."

"It's okay to be close minded to the world!" Phoenix yelled.

"Stop shouting," Carly snapped. "I get that you're upset, but it's over now."

"Being disliked because you stood for the Truth is the best thing

158

that could happen to you," Gertrude said firmly.

"Oh please, all that valiant suffering is not as great as it seems," Sam scoffed. "Yeah, we suffer for Christ when we *have* to, not because we decided to be mean and controversial."

"Telling the Truth isn't controversial," Gertrude said. "We've just been told that it is to keep us quiet. We've been told that the Truth of the Word of God, that saying homosexuality is an abomination to God, is mean and hurtful and shouldn't be said." She glanced around at all of us. "We have been labeled and we have *willingly* let those labels silence us because silence is easy. Proving that we're *cool* is fun. We're too afraid to stand for Christ."

With that, Gertrude stood and snatched her things from the chair. Her eyes fell on Carly's. "What happened to you?"

Carly swallowed.

I spoke up for her. "She's fine, Gertrude. Maybe you should just leave."

Gertrude laughed. "You don't have to tell me twice." She started toward the door but stopped. Looking over her shoulder, she eyed Carly. "I thought you were changing."

"I have," Carly answered bravely, "you just refuse to acknowledge it."

"Or maybe she can't see the changes because you're doing stuff like this," Phoenix said as he stood. "I'm quitting too. I just don't want to be associated with a group like this anymore."

"Like what?" Julia asked with wrinkled brows.

Phoenix shook his head. "If you have to ask then you're worse off than your leader." He walked out without saying another word.

Carly's hands were trembling in her lap before she erupted to her feet and grabbed her bag.

"Carly! Wait!" I called.

"Please just leave me alone right now," she said over her shoulder as she rushed out the building.

19

Do the Right Thing

The day before Thanksgiving, I decided to finally call my mother. I hadn't spoken to her in a month or so. She said she wouldn't bug me if I didn't call her, but I think she knew I was avoiding her because she never called or texted. Despite being on a bumpy road with Carly, things were still better in New York than they'd ever been in California. I was having the time of my life, and I didn't want to be bothered with the gloominess of home. Of the case waiting for me when I go back during Christmas break which was only two weeks away now. But I couldn't avoid her and my home life forever.

I sat on the bench outside of the church, the crisp fall air rushing through my jacket. I took a breath and dialed my mother's phone. It rang a few times before her voice came over the speaker.

"Hello? Xavier?"

"Hey, Mom," I murmured.

"Honey!" she exclaimed. "I missed you so much! I'm so sorry I hadn't called. I wanted to, and I felt like a horrible parent for not calling but I knew," she trailed off and the reins of the gloom of home had suddenly reached me, yanking me back to the dark hole I'd been climbing out of this semester.

"It's alright, Mom," I said, filling the silence.

"I'm sorry. Who's the parent here?" She chuckled, but I could hear the guilt and remorse twisting through her words. I really didn't blame her for not calling me. I know she wanted me to have my freedom. She wanted me to feel as far removed from the stress of Matt's case as possible, but it was building a wedge between us.

"I should've called," she finally said.

"Mom, it's no big deal." I tried to sound happy. "Besides, I've been doing really well."

"You have?" She sniffled. "Well, catch me up."

"For starters, I've got a girlfriend."

"What?"

"And before you get upset," I said, waving a hand around that she couldn't see, "she's the leader of the Christian group I'm part of."

"Get out." Mom sounded shocked—a little *too* shocked. "How'd you swing that?"

"Mom," I laughed.

"I'm kidding, X! You're so handsome. I'm happy for you."

"Thanks. I really like her." I paused as I thought about Carly. We'd only texted since the last Crusaders meeting went up in flames, but since we were still on for dinner tomorrow, I figured she just needed some time alone.

"You must actually like this girl." Mom's voice held a twinge of concern. I knew she was thinking of Lia Sunohara and how things turned out with her. Mom never asked me anything about what I had to tell in the interrogation, but I knew she wondered about it.

"I do like her," I admitted. "And she's a Christian."

"Well, just because she's Christian doesn't mean she's the one, Xavier."

"Why would you say that?"

"I just don't want you getting too wrapped up in this girl if she isn't the woman God has chosen for you to be with. Just take things slow."

Even though I knew where her caution was coming from, it still bugged me because it was irritatingly close to the Voice that'd been telling me Carly wasn't the one.

"So," Mom called me back to attention, "what else has been happening?"

I sighed. "I'm attending church now. I'm actually waiting on Bible Study to start."

"Goodness, X, you're really turning around over there, huh?"

A small smile tugged at my lips. "I told you I would."

"And you've kept your word. I'm so proud of you."

"Thanks, Mom."

"Well, I'm going to let you go," she said. "Oh! I forgot to tell you, your brother made the basketball team this year, and he's actually doing really well."

"Really? I thought Jax hated basketball."

"You've really influenced him," she said softly. "The way you stayed strong after everything surrounding the case, and you went to school. I was afraid you wouldn't want to go anymore, but you did and Jax has been really inspired by your strength and courage."

I relaxed against the bench and watched as people strolled by, and the sun kissed the buildings goodnight. "I ... I didn't know I'd influenced him. I thought everyone was secretly angry at me."

"No, honey," Mom insisted. "We love you, Xavier, no matter how many mistakes you make. No matter how costly, we will be with you and love you. That's what families do."

Maybe home isn't so bad, I thought as tears burned my eyes. I thought Detective Vean and Special Agent De Luca were bad omens hovering over the house, and if I called then the bad omens would reach me. But everyone's okay. Everyone's *been* okay, and even though I've got another interrogation coming up, no one's mad at me for it.

I wanted to double over and cry, but I stood from the bench and took a stroll toward the church instead.

"I've gotta go, Mom," I said, trying not to feel emotional. "I love you."

"I love you too, Xavier. We can't wait to see you in two weeks."

"Yeah." I lifted my head with a smile. "I can't wait to see you either."

"Alright, we'll talk soon."

"Bye, Mom."

"Bye, X."

I hung up the phone and took a deep breath. But I didn't get to exhale nice and slow like I wanted because a heavy hand came up behind me and slapped my back.

"Hey," Sky said as he stepped by me and grabbed the door to the church.

"Hey," I said.

"You ready for today?"

"I don't know. Pastor Eli gives me a headache with his teachings sometimes."

Sky laughed and I thought I felt the ground rattling beneath me at his deep voice. "I agree. But, surprisingly, I'm kind of happy with the lessons. I thought I'd resent him for making us learn about being single, but it's actually helped in my life."

"Really?"

He nodded as we made our way to the sanctuary. "I had a girlfriend in September, but after coming here and learning everything, I realized she wasn't 'the one.'" He used big quotations. "I thought she was because she was Christian, but I don't think she is now."

"Why not?"

He shrugged. "I don't have myself together, and I barely knew her.

164

I just thought that since she was Christian, she was alright. But I found out she really wasn't as dedicated to the faith as I am."

I didn't respond. I took my usual seat in the sanctuary, a few chairs down from Julius. Sky, surprisingly, sat beside me today instead of two rows behind me like he usually did. I waved to Julius, and he gave a friendly nod to both Sky and me.

"Hey, what do you think we're doing today?" Daytona bumped Daisy's shoulder.

The cute girl smiled and the whole room lit up. "I'm not sure. Eli's kind of crazy," she whispered.

The two girls laughed, and Eli's voice spilled from behind us, "I heard that, Daisy."

She offered a crooked smile. "Sorry, Pastor Ross."

"It's alright." He smiled as he laid his jacket on his stool at the front. "I know we've been doing some heavy-duty work, so through the rest of the semester, we'll be doing activities and discussing the results."

"Activities?" Marlo repeated.

He nodded. "Yeah. We're only two weeks away from break, so it's easier to finish out the classes with something light. And in January, we'll start back up with the studying."

Kevin groaned and stood. "Do I actually have to stay for this? We're not five, we don't need activities. We need to learn."

"Of course you don't have to stay." Eli nodded. "You are free to go, Kevin."

Kevin glanced around at all of us and rolled his eyes. "Fine, then I'm leaving." He pulled his jacket on and left the sanctuary.

"Now," Eli refocused on us, "we'll be doing two activities today. One is called the Voice of God, and the second is called Your Kind."

"What's the rules?" Daytona asked.

"Simple. We'll start with Voice of God. So, we recently talked about hearing the Voice of God last week and some of you asked how do we hear His Voice, and what does it sound like. Well, we all know part of hearing the Voice of God is recognizing His voice, but also, part of hearing the Voice of God is listening for it *and* paying attention to Him."

"If you're listening for His voice, then aren't you paying attention?"

Eli smiled. "Let's put it to the test. Everyone, spread apart by one seat, and get on your knees like you're going to pray. Listen for your name to be called, and then you can stand."

Sky moved a seat over, and we all moved to our knees. Clasping my hands together, I waited with my eyes closed. I knew that it wouldn't be long before Eli called me since there weren't a lot of us, so I tried to stay focused. But as I sat in silence, I began to wonder about that Voice I'd been hearing. I didn't like what the Voice was saying, and I didn't want to believe it. I'd just told my mother I had a girlfriend, and to lose her so soon would be beyond embarrassing. Sure, our relationship has been rocky, but we're young and still learning,.. that's what I keep telling myself to block out the truth.

I know that Voice is God, but I don't want it to be. I want it to be the doubt in my heart speaking. I want it to be the nervous thoughts just heavy on my mind. How could God say that about Carly? But how could I question God? Why *would* I? He knows best, but I know Carly. I know that's a lame excuse, but I can't think of another reason to keep going with this relationship.

It will bring you turmoil.

Not now, I squeezed my eyes shut tightly, *please, God, not now. Can't you just fix her?*

There is nothing I cannot do.

Then fix her!

I can give her to you, but you will not be happy, and you will no longer know Me.

What? That's impossible! Carly's a Christian, of course I'll always know you.

Because you will love her more than Me. You will forget Me,

and thus no longer know Me.

I sat there, clutching my hands tightly. *God...* I wanted to refute Him, to fight further, but His words were starting to make sense. *I love her more than You right now, don't I?*

Yes.

I'm sorry, God, I took a breath and tried to hold in my tears, *I don't want to lose You, but I don't want to lose her either... What should I do?*

"Xavier."

I raised my head and realized everyone else was standing. Sky was squinting down at me, like he knew something was going on. I stood slowly, nodding at him, and then turning to face Eli.

"You didn't hear me when I called you the first two times?"

"I was... um..."

"It's alright." Eli waved a hand. "That's the point of this exercise. Sometimes we don't hear the Voice of God, even when it's quiet—because we're distracted."

"But I did hear Him," I said firmly.

Eli clasped his hands in his lap, slender fingers interlacing with each other. "See me after class," was all he said to me.

Everyone's eyes were on me now and I dropped my head to look at the floor.

"Hey," Sky whispered. "I know you heard something; you were murmuring the whole time."

"Was I?"

He nodded with big, spooked eyes.

"Alright," Eli clapped, and I sent my attention to his direction. "I want all of you to come up here and pick a word out of a hat. Ladies, pick out the pink hat, gentlemen pick out the blue hat. Without looking up your word, I want you to come up with a meaning just by looking at it, and then find someone who has a word with a similar meaning."

"How will we have a similar meaning if we're making up the

167

meaning?" Marlo Jo called from her seat.

"There is a corresponding word in each hat. So, for example, if I pulled the word *hat* from the blue one, and Marlo Jo pulled the word *cap*, we'd be a match."

"Oh, I see," Emily said, "we're trying to find our match."

"Yes. And I'll take out a pair of words since Kevin left. Since there's only three guys and five girls, Julius and Sky, I want you both to pick two words," he said as he reached into both hats.

"Two," Sky complained as he walked by me.

I walked silently behind him to the front of the sanctuary. Eli gave me his usual unwavering smile as I reached in and pulled out the word, *consubstantial.* I blinked at it, wondering where he even came up with a word like this. It didn't seem hard, but I knew the meaning I came up with—to have a lot of something—was totally wrong.

"Alright, does everyone have a word and their own definition?"

The room nodded together.

"Perfect. Now mingle with each other to try to find who's got your counterpart."

I sighed as I stood and looked around. Daisy and Daytona were crowded around Sky, blinking dreamy eyes at him as he weakly scratched the back of his head.

"Hey," Marlo said as she came over to me, "what's your word?"

"Consubstantial."

"I've got confabulation, but I literally have no clue what that means."

Marlo Jo was pretty up close. She smelled like a girl, spoke like one, and despite her strong physique, her face was quite feminine. She had almond eyes and crisp cheekbones that gave her a womanly appearance, but she was clearly youthful. When she spoke just to me, she wasn't aggressive like she usually sounded, or annoyed like when she spoke with Kevin. She just talked, glancing off so I could see her long lashes, laughing at something I said so her lips curled into a gentle smile. I'm

168

sure she wasn't doing it on purpose, but it felt like she was flirting with me.

I wanted to be liked, to be flirted with. I wanted girls to like me the way they liked Sky. I wasn't ugly, but I wasn't outgoing either. A girl in high school told me that I was the hot guy no one ever spoke to because no one knew what to say to me. But that's because I was always overshadowed by someone else.

Matt was loud and rambunctious, and Sky had two different eye colors and baritone that could cause a minor earthquake, so it was easy to be overlooked when I was around them.

I hated it. But Carly… she looked right at me. And every time she looked at me, I felt something. No one's ever looked at me like that before. It's like she looked at my *soul*, and despite all the bad, she accepted me.

How could I give up someone like that?

"You listening?" Marlo asked.

"Yeah." I nodded, despite how lost in my thoughts I was, I'd heard every word she'd said. "How are we going to figure this out?"

She laughed. "I have no idea. I'm going to mingle a little more." Marlo bumped her shoulder with mine. "You should too, you're pretty funny, but you're so quiet and standoffish."

"You think so?"

She nodded. "We've got to spend the next four years together, we might as well get used to each other." Marlo walked off with a smile and weaved through the seats to Julius.

I took her advice and made my way over to Tracy who looked like she was having a particularly hard time with her word.

"Hey," I said.

"Hey." She looked up at me. "I've got the word genuflection, it sounds like acid reflux to me, or gastritis."

I snorted. "It kind of does. I've got consubstantial."

169

"Is that like, a lot of something?"

"I think." I shrugged.

"Hey." Daytona came up to me with Daisy on her heels. "What's your word?"

"Consubstantial."

"I've got animate, and Daisy's got analogous."

I glanced over at Daisy, her round eyes took me in and then glanced off. Her cheeks were reddening, but I chose to ignore how cute she looked and said, "What about Emily?"

"She's got jovial," Sky said as he came over. "If this wasn't a sanctuary, I'd cheat."

Our group began to laugh together as Eli called, "Alright guys, that's time for today. You have homework from me."

A few groans went up through the crowd, making him laugh. "Just get the definition of your word before class starts next week." Eli smiled at all of us. "Happy Thanksgiving, and stay safe if you're going shopping."

"Thanks, Pastor," we all said as we began to pack up.

I put my things away, but I took my seat in the sanctuary as I waited for Eli. When everyone cleared out, Eli loosened his tie and came to sit beside me. "So, you're coming over tomorrow."

"Yeah." I glanced at him. He was looking straight ahead at the pulpit, where the wooden cross hung, and the glass podium stood.

"And what has God told you about my sister?"

"What?" I adjusted in my seat to move away from him. *How does he know?* I wondered.

"You said you heard from God. I know it was about Carly."

"How do you know that?"

Eli sighed, removing his glasses to rub his tired eyes. He looked worn, like it was hard to always smile, but he chose to anyway because one day, he won't be tired of smiling.

170

"You said something in one of our sessions recently; that you knew you were running into a wall, but you hoped if you ran into it enough times, you'd create a door out of nothing. You'd prove that this was the right way to go, even if it's your own way."

I remembered saying that. It was a few weeks ago, right after bowling, when Carly stopped talking to me. At the time, I didn't want to get over her. I'd been determined to prove to God that everything was fine with her, despite how wrong it felt. And even though I began to get comfortable with the idea of us breaking up, when she came back into my life, I was suddenly uncomfortable without her.

But… I know something's not right with Carly, and I've tried to ignore the feeling. I wanted this to work so badly, I was willing to look the other way. The saddest part was that even though I'm armed with the truth, I *still* want to look the other way.

I swallowed, wiping my hands over my pants to wipe away the sweat. "I remember that."

Eli nodded. "What situation in your life is forcing you to prove yourself?"

"I just want this to work," I said softly. "She's amazing, Eli. The way she can make me feel like time stops around us… How can she not be the one?"

"You think because she's Christian and you're Christian, you two should be together?"

"And because we clicked right away."

"Did you click, or did you like her as soon as you saw her? Because Carly's a nice girl, but she's got her devious side too."

I scoffed. "She's your sister, how could you say that?"

"Because she's my sister I can say that. I know Carly, and I know she's up to something tomorrow. You need to be careful."

"Up to something? Up to what?"

Eli lowered his brows. "What do you know about tomorrow?"

171

"Nothing. I thought it was dinner and shopping."

Eli sat back in his chair and sighed. "I've tried with Carly. I've given it a good effort, but not my best effort. I didn't know how to raise a teenager who was grieving her parents, and still trying to understand herself. All while I was grieving and trying to make things work for myself too. It seems like I've lost her."

For the first time, Eli looked like he didn't have it all together. He wasn't perfect, and even though he strived to be a good brother, Eli was still human, and humans make mistakes.

"Well," I said, trying to find words of comfort, "*I* thought you did a good job with her. I thought you did so well, I was willing to compromise my faith for her."

He snorted and patted my shoulder. "Sometimes we just don't want to be lonely, so we'll do whatever we can to have friends, to have a girlfriend, to have *something*. But that's what singleness is all about. Being alone and realizing you aren't really alone because God is with you. And that will catapult you into a new level in Christ."

"So, you're basically telling me to break up with Carly—your own sister?"

"I'm telling you to ask God one more time about your relationship with her. If His answer is the same, then do what needs to be done."

20

God Has Never Been Wrong

"Happy Thanksgiving, Xavier!" Carly said as she held open the door. The smell of roasted turkey filled my nostrils and raced down to my belly, making it growl loudly.

"Sorry." I chuckled. "I'm a little hungry." I didn't really know if it was hunger or fear churning in my stomach, honestly. I took Elijah's advice, as I usually do, and I asked God about Carly. I asked Him if she was the one for me.

He told me, **No. I fashioned a helper for you, but it is not time for you to receive her yet.**

"When will the time be?" I'd asked.

You have not toiled nor worked. You do not yet know the plans I have for you, Xavier.

"Why won't You just tell me then? I don't want to be alone. I don't want to give up on Carly. Just change her, fix her, do anything, but don't make me break up with her!" Tears were all over the bed as I trembled before Him.

But His voice returned, and a calmness came with it, **I will not** forsake you, Xavier. You are My son, and I have called you out of the darkness. As long as you trust Me, I will protect you.

"But why?" I hiccupped. "Why can't I just have her? Why can't you just take away all the bad that could happen, and replace it with good?"

Every man must choose for himself to serve Me.

"Pharoah didn't! You hardened his heart and created him for that! I heard Pastor Tosh say some plates are fashioned for use and others for breaking. You create people to die!"

Every person serves a purpose on this Earth, yet I am just and fair. I give them the chance to choose Me. I have known every man to walk this Earth before I created it. Therefore, before the heavens and the sky were born, I knew who would choose Me and who wouldn't, yet my Son was sent for everyone.

"So why create them? Why let them come to Earth just to punish them?"

I judge those who reject My Son. Punishment is the judgement. Would it be fair to only create the good and not the bad? Make only the good go through hardships, but the bad would never face anything? There would be no bad and no good had I not created it.

"I just don't understand," I cried. "Why create the bad!?"

Because I am fair and just, and it is fair to give everyone a chance to choose life, regardless of whether they choose it or not.

I laid there in my tears, sniffling and blubbering nothing. I couldn't formulate words, just pain throbbing in my chest. "I don't want to start over," I whispered. "I don't want to be alone again. Can you send someone… anyone?"

Am I not enough?

Silence.

"I didn't mean to insult you, God."

You are very special, Xavier. I do not speak to everyone, but I

174

have chosen you to hear My Voice. Others will learn to look for Me in signs and wonders. Others will hear My whisper. But you, My precious son, will always hear Me clearly.

That was how our conversation went last night. I ended up telling God I'd break up with Carly today at the end of the night. But looking at her cheerful smile, her rosy cheeks, I couldn't understand why she wasn't enough. What was wrong with Carly that I couldn't have her?

She is not your helper.

I stiffened at His voice and Carly frowned, thinking I was upset with her. "Don't tell me you don't like mashed potatoes!"

"No, I do." I waved a hand as I refocused on our conversation. "I just don't always like gravy."

She gasped. "Seriously? Me either! We were basically made for each other, X!" She grabbed my hand and pulled me inside their cozy apartment. It wasn't fancy, since it was just Eli's income supporting them both. But the quaint two-bedroom apartment was filled with a warmth my home had forgotten since Matt's case. The thought made me shiver and I swept the room for something to look at just to take my mind off of things.

A toffee-colored couch and chair sat on a champagne carpet. I walked around the place, looking at pictures of Carly at prom—she went to her junior and senior prom with two different guys—that sat on the television stand.

"Xavier," Eli's voice made me snap around. He was coming from the hallway in his usual sweater and black slacks and tie.

"Happy Thanksgiving," I said, extending a hand to him.

He shook it.

"Same to you. Dinner's almost ready, you can take a seat at the table."

I nodded, following him to the small circular table just beside the kitchen. "Your place is nice," I said as I sat.

175

"It's just slightly better than your dorm," Elijah joked.

"That's true," I laughed.

Carly bounced over to me carrying a tray. Her red hair was pinned back, but her ponytail was full of curls that were bobby-pinned together. I knew we were going out shopping afterward, but I thought she'd dress fancy for dinner. Instead, she was wearing sweatpants and a shirt, a very relaxed look, but her makeup was partially done. Maybe she was just really excited to go shopping, but I wasn't. I was planning to get away from here and tell her the truth of why I came tonight and hoped she would understand.

"I made all the side dishes, but Eli made the turkey and the ham."

"It all looks good," I said, glancing around at the food. My table always looked different at home. Mom was Black and Spanish, and Dad was southern, from Florida. So we had all kinds of food, different types of southern and Spanish foods, and all kinds of stuff my dad hunted. We'd have everything from hush puppies and chitlins, to Spanish rice and pastelitos, all the way to elk gumbo. But the Ross's table looked very different. Peas, spinach casserole, baked turkey instead of fried turkey, and stuffing instead of dressing. There were other dishes I couldn't name but recognized from the time my family visited my father's side of the family for the holiday.

"Let's say grace," Carly said, taking my hand and then her brother's.

We bowed our heads, and I listened as Carly prayed.

"Thank You, God, for bringing us all together. We're so incredibly thankful to have one another for this holiday. Let us enjoy this meal today and share much joy and laughter tonight. In the Name of Jesus, amen."

"Amen," Eli and I said together.

"So, where are you two going tonight?" Eli asked as we passed dishes around.

"We're hoping to get to the mall right after dinner and try to snag some of the best deals."

"Maybe I'll join you." Eli passed me a look.

I chuckled and stuffed a spoonful of peas into my mouth. Eli said Carly was up to something tonight, whatever it was, I was caught in the middle of it. I was hoping he was wrong, but I knew he wasn't because God had already said that Carly was using me. I guess I'm the decoy to make Eli think we're going to do what we say we are. I don't know, and I don't want to know, I just want the night to be over.

"Please," Carly said as she bit her turkey, "you're on dishes duty tonight. You'll have no time."

"I've got all weekend to clean."

"You'd never leave a dish in the sink overnight."

Eli laughed. "Yes, I do like for the place to be clean."

We chatted for a while longer before Carly left to get ready. She dashed out of the room to change while Eli and I set the plates in the sink and began cleaning up.

"Just be careful," Eli said as he opened the dishwasher.

"I will."

"Don't do anything you don't want to do."

"I won't."

Carly rounded the corner in lacey white leggings and a cropped shirt. Her bobby pins were gone, and her hair was loose and curly. She looked sexy … I've never once thought she was sexy before. I always thought she was beautiful, but today, she looked like a totally different woman. I was shocked, but Elijah was even more surprised. His eyes were coming through the frames of his glasses as he stared at his little sister.

"I'm not changing," she said sassily, "so close your mouth, Eli. You ready?" She directed her question to me, and I fumbled to say yes.

"At least wear a coat," Eli finally called from the kitchen.

"Got one," she said as she grabbed a sweat jacket from the coat rack. "I'll be back late."

"Alright." Eli stepped out of the kitchen and came over to the door as Carly left. He shrugged, a bit of shame crossing his face. "I told you I didn't do too well with her," he sighed.

"I'll look after her tonight."

"Thanks." Eli patted my shoulder, and I heard Carly yell, "Come on or we'll miss the next train!"

"Sorry, Eli. Thanks for everything tonight."

"Of course."

I walked out and raced down the hall to the elevators where Carly was waiting. When we stepped inside, the doors closed and for the entire ride down, Carly kissed me. Deep kisses, gasping for air and holding me close. Carly's slender fingers grabbed at my shirt, but I held her hands, trying to gain control of the situation.

When the elevator dinged, she pulled away with a smirk, "We're going to have fun tonight, like real college kids."

I had no words as I let her drag me out the elevator and outside. The cool air whipped by and nearly froze me. Somehow, Carly stood out there in her skimpy clothes and didn't freeze.

"Aren't you cold?" I asked as we made our way to the train station.

"No." She shrugged. "I'm excited for tonight! Let's have lots of fun."

I nodded. "Yeah, okay."

"That was a weak, 'yeah.'"

"Well, it's just, we need to—"

"Madeline! Jocelyn! You guys showed up!" Carly raced over to the girls walking to the entrance to the train station and hugged them both.

I walked up and said, "Hey, I didn't know you guys were coming."

"Of course." Jay smiled. "I wouldn't miss my chance with you for the world."

I gulped and took a step back. I didn't know MJ and Jocelyn would be here tonight, which made breaking up with Carly nearly impossible,

178

and losing my virginity very possible. Jay looked as sexy as she always did. Her hips swayed as she led me onto the train in her miniskirt and jean jacket.

"Carly and I should probably sit together," I said as Jay pulled me all the way to the back of the train. It was mostly empty since stores didn't open until eight today, and the next train would be the busy one. As we made it to the back, an old woman was there with a little girl. The two stared at us as Jay shoved me into the seat and sat on my lap. "Let's finish what we started at the bowling alley."

"I'm glad you're feeling better," I said, eyeing her.

Her mouth twitched into a crooked smile, and she nodded. "Yeah, I was a little sick. Can you tell?" She stood and spun in a little circle. Jay was even thinner than before, but her hips were still round, and her face was still pretty.

"I can tell a little," I said, glancing over at Carly as she boarded the train with MJ. The two of them sat beside us, laughing, and holding hands.

"Now," Jay leaned forward, "let's have fun tonight."

She kissed me and the old woman hissed, "Hey! My granddaughter is right here! Have some respect!"

I tried to apologize, but Jay suddenly pulled away and snapped, "You act like you've never seen a kiss before. Well, get ahold of this."

Jay kissed me forcefully, holding my face in place as she snaked her tongue into my mouth. I gagged and shoved her away harder than I meant to.

"Jay, we can't do this," I said, wiping my mouth. I glanced at my girlfriend, but Jay was still in my lap, cupping my chin so I'd stay focused on her.

"Why can't we do this?" she whispered lustfully. "Carly doesn't care, and I don't care."

"I just can't do this." I moved away from her, pushing her to the empty seat beside me.

Jay rolled her eyes and took her jacket off, revealing a scandalous top that showed everything through the thin material. I gawked at her, but I didn't want to. Jay was hypnotic, the way her body could control my entire mind. She shamelessly crawled into my lap again. I took a big breath as the old lady with her granddaughter nearby gasped and whispered something to the little girl.

"Jay, you have to get off me," I said nervously. The train began to rattle and rock with Jay sitting on my lap, making me dizzy with pleasure. "Please," I whispered breathily. She hooked her arms around my neck, leaning in to lay a trail of kisses down my neck. I was *this* close to doing something I would regret later. I needed to get away from this girl. Right now.

God, I don't want to do this, but it feels so good. Please, help me.

"You were warring within yourself," Eli's words poured into my head, and I realized that this was the scripture I'd lived by. Wanting to do good but doing the evil instead.

A war is not won by complaining, it's won by fighting, I told myself. *I have to want You, God, and I swear I do. So please, give me strength.*

I pulled away from Jay. "We can't do this," I said, pulling her arms from around my neck.

"It seems like you want to do this," she whispered with a smile.

"No, I don't." I pushed her off my lap into the seat beside me. The movement was not as graceful as either of us would have liked. Jay flopped into Carly and MJ who'd been whispering closely to each other.

"What's your problem!?" she snapped, suddenly angry—now that she'd finally gotten it in her head that she wouldn't have her way tonight.

"We can't do this," I told her firmly. "Come on, Carly." I stood and adjusted my clothes.

Yes ... my body had reacted to Jay and her touches and kisses, but I wouldn't let that stop me from doing the right thing. So I ignored the

180

smirk on her face as her eyes flicked over my frame and I gave my attention to my girlfriend again. "Let's go, Carly."

"Xavier, will you just chill out?" Carly snapped.

I stared down at her. "Chill out? I almost had sex on a train right in front of you!" I yelled. "With one of your *friends*!"

I was at my wits' end. I didn't know why Carly was alright with her boyfriend making out with her friend right next to her. I didn't know why she was snapping at me, or why she couldn't be the helper God had picked for me. I didn't know why I went to that stupid party, or why I couldn't stand up to JC or why Lia died, and I lived… but I couldn't take it anymore.

"Just sit down." Carly was frowning like I disgusted her. "You're making a scene."

"And you're not?" I grabbed the silver pole for balance and leaned down, my voice almost a growl. "Let's *go*."

"No." Carly shook her head. "You can go but I'm staying."

"I'm your *boyfriend*! I can't just leave you here!"

"*Boyfriend*," Jay snickered as she leaned forward to laugh into her hand. The train was suddenly quiet, and I could feel everyone's eyes on me, except for Carly's and Madeline's.

"Why is she laughing? Carly, why won't you look at me?"

"Because you're not her boyfriend," Jay said. "Goodness, you're an idiot. It never crossed your mind that these two were actually together and you were just the cover up so Eli wouldn't catch on?"

Mercifully, I didn't fall limp and let go of the pole. I cringed at Jay's words and squeezed the pole instead, helping me stay upright. I didn't want it to be true.

"Carly," I called, "that's not true… is it?"

"Of course, it is," Jay said, but she wasn't laughing anymore, she looked concerned. Her eyes darted to Carly and then back to me. "Oh my gosh, she really never told you the truth?"

All that could be heard was the rattling and humming of the train. Carly had been using me… and God was right. I'd fought against Him for so long for her…

"X, they've been together all semester," Jay said. "I thought you knew. I thought you were okay with helping her keep it a secret from her brother."

"That's enough," Carly said softly, still not looking at me.

"No." Jay shook her head. "Look at him, he deserves to know the truth." Jay looked back at me, her face wrinkled with emotion. She almost looked apologetic.

"Carly's gay, Xavier," she said flatly, nearly shattering me. "Obviously, that's a problem for her *very* Christian brother." Jay sighed. "Madeline and I were together at first, and then MJ and Carly became lab partners. Carly came by the dorm once for some notes, and I was the only one there. While she waited for MJ, I got her to try a blunt, and she got high." She paused and looked down at her feet. "We ended up making out, and when MJ came back, Carly stayed the night with us."

I stiffened as I stood there, clutching the pole so hard my hand was cramping, but I wouldn't let go.

"I honestly thought it was just an accident. Like a one-night stand. Carly seemed really upset about it the next morning because she was still confused about her beliefs, but MJ comforted her." Jay looked at me dead-on, a coldness in her eyes so hostile, I felt a spider walk down my spine. "MJ was there for Carly. She told her it was normal. That there was nothing wrong with the connection they had."

I glared at her, wishing I had the strength to glare at Carly instead. How could she buy any of this? Elijah was her brother. He had helped me so much in my faith and had helped guide me along the path of righteousness—all just from being my counsellor and youth pastor. How much more help could he have offered Carly as his own sister?

I thought of the sad look on his face before I'd left the house. His words rang in my ears. *I tried with Carly.* Sometimes you do try to help someone, but they aren't willing to accept the help.

Jay went on, "Initially, Carly would just come over to get high. She wouldn't do anything if she was sober. She still hadn't fully accepted the fact that she's gay. But then she started getting more comfortable with MJ. That's when she stopped needing the drugs. That's when she started staying the night."

Staying the night...

And here I was, worried about losing my virginity. But Carly had been with two different women already. While we were together.

"All this time," tears swelled in my eyes, "all this time?"

Jay nodded.

"So the time I caught you standing guard... she was...?"

"Yeah, they were together. I was standing guard to make sure no one found out."

"*Carly,*" my voice cracked, but she looked away.

It all made sense now. The way she dressed up for shopping but didn't dress up for dinner. When she invited Love Unlimited to the bowling trip, it was to hang out with her girlfriends in their freaky threesome relationship. The time she kissed me in front of Eli's office, it was just to prove a point—to prove to him that she was straight and Christian. And on the elevator tonight, it was just practice for MJ.

"I'm sorry—" Madeline started, but I snapped, "Don't ever speak to me again."

When the train stopped, I moved as quickly as I could to the doors and stepped off.

For the next week, I skipped the class I had with Madeline and Jay. I just couldn't get myself to go see them. I wrestled all day with wondering what I should tell Eli, or what I shouldn't tell him. I still had a day to figure it out, but in the meantime, I decided to go to the Crusaders meeting to quit the group. I wasn't planning to explain myself. I just wanted to quit and leave Carly with no explanation. However, when I arrived, there was an argument going on… and Eli was present.

I eyed him as he leaned against a table with his arms folded over his chest. He nodded stiffly, before returning his focus to the group.

"Not only did you invite Love Unlimited to our event, but you were seen with two members of that group on Thanksgiving and on Black Friday," Tabitha was saying.

"I can hang out with whoever I want," Carly shrugged.

"But you can't *kiss* whoever you want," Allen said. "I saw you kissing that redheaded girl on the lips and then the other kissed your neck."

Carly pressed her lips together, big pleading eyes shot to mine when she noticed me.

"That's a lie! I was with Xavier on Thanksgiving. Tell them, X."

"I'm not lying!" Allen yelled.

"Let him speak." Eli's eyes lazily lifted to mine, and I knew he expected the truth… He already *knew* the truth.

I looked back at Carly, her eyes begged me to lie, and I wanted to for her. I wanted to protect her, but she wasn't mine to protect. But I didn't want to do this as some kind of payback.

I took a breath and looked around. "Carly and I broke up on Thanksgiving."

Gasps echoed through the room. Carly's jaw was clenched so tightly, she gave me one last pleading look to cover for her.

"We were together initially, but after meeting up with Jocelyn and Madeline, we argued and broke up, and I went home."

Carly's shoulders dropped in defeat.

"So … you really were with them?" Julia asked in a hesitant voice, like maybe she hoped none of this was true.

Gertrude had said it earlier, *silence is easy*. Looking away is easy. But now we couldn't look away anymore. We had to face this problem head-on. A problem I had been warned about and probably could have prevented. But I'd been a coward. I'd done nothing. I let this happen. And now others were hurt because of it.

"No," Carly's voice was hoarse now, "they've got the story wrong. And Xavier is just mad because I dumped him."

"How could you?" I said quietly, but it earned looks from everyone, including Elijah. "I was willing to do whatever it took to make our relationship work. I even fought God over you. He told me that you were using me, but I wouldn't believe Him. I had to find out from the mouth of the same woman you'd been kissing behind my back."

"Stop it!" Carly shouted as she stood. "Just stop it." Tears formed in her eyes. "I have tried to love you, but you were unlovable. I—"

"That's enough, Carly." Elijah stepped forward. "You've sank yourself into enough trouble for today. I'm glad Tabitha called me because I'm putting your leadership to a vote."

"What?" Her tears were suddenly gone, and she was blood red with anger. "I'm the president of this club! You can't do that!"

"Yes, I can." Eli's sternness brought the winter chill inside. I'd never seen him like this before.

"You can't discriminate against me because of who I like!" Carly shouted. "Those girls are the only ones who understand me. The only ones who've ever helped me *grieve*."

That was personal, and spiteful, and her words hurt Eli deeply, despite how hard he tried not to let it show.

"It's not discrimination if you don't follow the code set by the group." Eli stood in front of her.

She backed away, looking crossed and bitter.

He said, "The established rules of this group says that people involved in the Crusaders must abide by the upright living as outlined in the Word of God, and it does *not* include forging my signature to get a school van and steal school funding for events I did not sanction. Nor is it limited to who you are involved with physically. If that person is not a spouse, or is of the same sex as you, that is against the Biblical standards that this group abides by, and this college has passed as acceptable for our religious group."

There was complete silence as Eli looked her over. He looked more like her brother than ever before. He was standing over her, containing his fury as he disciplined his bratty little sister.

"God is merciful," he said. "You may remain a member of the group to receive counseling and healing. But you cannot hold the title of president anymore." His eyes narrowed. "You have not behaved as one."

Carly hiccupped.

"All in favor of Carly being president, raise your hand," Elijah said.

Not a single hand went up.

I almost pitied Carly when her gaze shot to me. Even if I raised my hand, my one vote against the rest of the room wouldn't have helped

"Pack your things," Eli seethed. "You're dismissed."

Without a single tear, and her head held high, Carly grabbed her bag, and walked out of the cafeteria.

21

Work Before Marriage

Elijah cancelled Bible Study the day Carly got removed from office for the Crusaders. Now we don't have a leader, and we're not even sure if we'll keep meeting. We discussed disbanding the group until next year. We felt like we needed a break to reconcile, but we'd still need to figure out who would be president for the following year.

The whole thing was embarrassing, but to make it worse, Junior heard about it and teased me all day about our leader being a fake Christian. My girlfriend was gay and had never liked me. His antics were torture, but I swallowed the annoyance, and let it roll off my shoulders. But the worst part about Carly being removed from office wasn't that Junior had heard, it was that the entire campus had found out.

The Crusaders became the laughingstock of the entire college, and then rumors began about Carly's involvement with some illegal activity. Someone was saying she was meeting people on campus for drugs—buying, selling, using—the rumors were endless. I think they were lying, but there was some truth to at least one of them.

I'd heard that Carly was involved with some unsavory people who'd been around campus before. They apparently asked girls to tutor them, but the sessions were just hookups going on in the dorms. Apparently, the weed made the sex better—which was in endless supply thanks to Jay.

The only thing that made me think that particular rumor might've been true was that Carly wasn't a tutor, and there was no such thing as a sign-up list in the library. But Carly apparently didn't like men, so I wasn't sure how true that rumor was either. Everything was a mess.

I strolled to the church in the brisk cold. California got cold for California, but never *this* cold. It was a new experience that I think I liked. Crushing the leaves as I walked, I noticed a car parked outside the front of the church. A brown-skinned girl with fiery red hair was sitting in the driver's seat looking out the window when we noticed each other. A muscle in my jaw ticked, and I picked up the pace.

"Wait! Xavier!" Madeline called from the window.

I kept walking, ignoring the sound of the car door opening and slamming.

"Please!" MJ was faster than she looked because she grabbed me by the shoulders and turned me around before I could even reach the church doors.

"I told you to *never* speak to me again," I snapped harshly.

"I know," she said. "But I still wanted to apologize. It wasn't meant to be like this. It was an accident, and I…" she held her breath, blinking at me through thick dark lashes. "Well, you're not like who I'd always thought you were. You weren't like him, and I never meant to hurt you."

"Weren't like who?" I stopped reaching for the church doors to stare at her, but MJ never got to answer my question. The next moment, Jay exploded from the parked car, vomiting violently on the ground.

"Jay!" I called as I rushed past MJ. She was on her hands and knees on the sidewalk, her brown skin dewy and pale, her hair sticking to her forehead with sweat. She looked terrible. The worst I'd ever seen her. I

188

couldn't stop myself from caring as I ran to her and said, "Jay, are you alright?" She didn't answer, wiping at her mouth with the back of her hand. "What's wrong with her?" I looked up at MJ for an answer, but Jay grabbed my coat sleeve.

"I'm alright," she said weakly. "I think it's just a bug."

I looked her over, she had somehow thinned even since Thanksgiving last week. Her body looked smaller, and her eyes sagged with exhaustion.

"Jay, something's going on. Something bad." I couldn't stop myself from thinking of the drugs and all the rumors spreading around campus.

"I said I'm fine." She let go of my jacket and wobbled to her feet. "It was nice to see you again, X. I missed your handsome face." She gave me a stiff smile as she climbed back into the car.

"What's wrong with her?" I asked MJ.

"A bug." MJ shrugged and tried to move for the driver's seat.

"Wait a second." I grabbed her arm. "You know something but you're not telling me."

"I know that she's sick, and we've got to hurry up or she'll get worse."

I squinted. "Why are you even here?"

"Carly was grabbing some things she needed. She's moving in with a few friends we met off campus."

"What?" I looked over at the church building, wondering if that was why Eli had canceled earlier this week.

"You should go," MJ said.

I looked down at her, and there was a swirling feeling beneath the anger I'd held onto because of her. Whatever the feeling was, I didn't like it. And when I looked at MJ, I didn't want to admit it even existed. Not now, not ever again.

I sank my hands into my pockets and headed into the church. When I entered the sanctuary, Eli was sitting on his stool, scrolling his phone.

I wondered if he was really okay with Carly moving out. Did he put up a fight? Or did he just let her go? I grabbed my seat beside Sky. He was on his phone looking something up when I remembered the homework Eli had given us. I snatched my bag off and dug through it for my word as Sky asked, "You just remembered the homework?"

"Yeah." I chuckled. "I've had a crazy week, and I'm starting to get nervous about returning home after next week."

"Ah, you're not from here," Sky said.

"Fresno." I pulled the paper out and read over my word, consubstantial. I did a quick dictionary search and found that the word meant *something is similar, or shares similarity.*

"I'm from this city," Sky was talking again. "I want to get out of here sometime soon, but I'm not in a rush."

"You're studying to be a welder, right?"

"Yeah, it's pretty neat work."

"That's a serious career."

"Not any more than becoming a pilot." He shrugged. "I guess I'll be building the planes you fly."

I smiled. "Probably. And when I get my own airport, I'll let you do all the welding."

"Let's do it." He laughed.

"Alright class," Eli said, standing from his stool. He was wearing a grin, one that might've been genuine or genuinely hiding something. I couldn't tell anymore. The last week had taken a toll on both of us, with Carly at the center of it all. Now she gets to run away without a hitch, while Eli and I try our best to keep our heads up. It didn't seem fair or just, but I tried to believe God anyway.

"Did everyone do their homework?"

We nodded.

"Good. So I want you all to partner with who you thought fit your initial definition last week."

190

I never decided on a person, so I sat still, watching the others. But no one moved at all. I looked over at Sky, and he shrugged. When I looked over at Eli, he was beaming.

"No one could find a single person that had a similar definition?"

"I tried," Daisy inserted. "But I didn't understand my word, and I didn't think I could pair off with someone without the right definition."

"That's very good, Daisy," Eli nodded at her. "Anyone else have a reason?"

"Well," Julius said, "I thought I knew what my word meant but no one else knew what their word meant so I didn't pair off."

"Another very good thought. So, Julius, let's start with you. What was your word?"

"I had two, but I'll start with colloquy."

"Alright, was your initial definition, correct?"

Julius chuckled weakly. "No. I was way off."

"So, what does your word mean?"

"Colloquy means conversation or to debate."

"Ooh!" Marlo shot her hand into the air, and Eli waved for her to answer. "I've got confabulation, and it's another word for conversation."

"So, that means Julius and Marlo Jo would be partnered," Eli said. "Alright, so we've got the first pair. What was your second word and its definition?"

"My second word was obeisance which means to bow."

"That's me." Tracy waved a hand. "I've got genuflection, which means to bow."

"Very good," Eli said. "Who wants to go next?"

"I've got animate, which means to bring to life," Daytona said.

Sky raised two fingers. "One of my words was vivify, and it means the same thing."

Eli nodded, and his eyes fell to me. I gulped, raising my word slowly.

191

"I had consubstantial, and it means something is similar."

"I guess we're partners then," Daisy said, raising her hand. She read from a pink notebook, "Analogous; to be parallel, to be similar."

"Which means by default, Emily and Sky would be the last pair. Go ahead, Emily, and tell us your word and definition," Eli said.

"My word is jovial, and it's another word for hearty or cheerful."

"Convivial," Sky added, "and it means to be friendly or lively."

"Good." Eli sat on his stool and opened his arms. "You all have just found someone with similarities. You're all partnered with someone who's like you. Someone who is your kind. But when you had no idea what your word meant, you didn't partner at all. It's the same concept." He bunched his shoulders. "When you don't know who you are in Christ, you don't know your purpose or where you're going. How can you possibly date or marry someone if you don't know who you are?"

"Wow." Daisy ran a hand through her short hair. "So, I was on the right path when I said I couldn't partner because I didn't understand my own word?"

"That's right," Eli encouraged. "Understanding who you are and your purpose in Christ is absolutely necessary before you can marry someone. So being single isn't just about getting married, it's about *you*. And it's about building a relationship with God."

"Well, where in the Bible do we have that example?" Marlo raised a hand.

"Good question, we can take Adam or Jesus or even King David. Each one of these people worked before marriage. They spent time with God before spending time with man, and they all spent time with God *alone*."

"Wait." Marlo shook her head, her bun of dreads swayed with the movement. "Jesus never got married."

"No," Eli nodded, "but He is engaged."

"But I thought we, the church," Sky was circling the room with his

192

hand, "was His bride?"

"We are," Eli agreed. "But it was customary during the Biblical time for the bride and groom to be separated for some time before the marriage ceremony. If you look at Revelation chapter nineteen and verse seven, it says right there that the marriage ceremony will take place. Meaning, once Jesus comes and retrieves His bride, then the church and Christ will be married."

I raised my pencil and glanced around quickly, wondering if everyone else was as confused as I was. "Right now, we're just a bride, but we're not a wife?"

"Exactly. Which is why commitment to God is integral. Our entire life's journey is based on being committed to God no matter what. And that's because we are the bride of Christ. We are preparing for our wedding to the King, and we must be committed during that time because Christ is committed to us. He's dedicated His entire life, death, and resurrection to us, so that when He returns, we can join Him in an eternal unity."

"So, why even get married here if we're going to be married to Jesus?" Daytona asked.

"God allows marriage because marriage is the union between two people that makes them one flesh. So, you and your spouse count as one person, and that one person is married to Christ."

"Oh." Daytona nodded as she flicked her braids over her shoulder. "I see now."

Eli glanced at his watch and nodded in the silence. "Alright, I'll bring this last point home, and then we'll be done for the semester."

"That went by so fast," Emily said.

Elijah laughed. "These four years are going to breeze by, I promise. So, the point I was driving home with this exercise is knowing God before knowing a spouse. And we were touching on Biblical examples of this, like Adam, Jesus, and King David." He smiled at us. "Like I mentioned before, Adam worked the Garden before woman was brought to him. He'd spent time in the Garden with God and spent time in His work which is evident when God puts him in the Garden to tend to it and protect it."

"King David spent time with God alone when he was still young, right? Out in the fields and stuff, fighting the animals," Sky offered beside me.

"Absolutely. King David in his youth had worked and protected, just as Adam did. And it wasn't until after David was anointed as king by Samuel did he find wives."

"And Jesus?" Marlo asked.

"Jesus worked in the Kingdom before receiving a bride as well. He died for her and brought her new life so that she could live eternally with Him. Before we are married to Christ, He has worked on our behalf, and is still working in Heaven for us. He's our intercessor until we reach Heaven."

I slapped my hands over my face as I took in all the things Elijah had told us. We'd spent the entire semester studying singleness, and we weren't even finished. We had four more years of packed study lessons, even the games were loaded.

"Alright," Eli said as I lowered my hands, "Xavier here is exhausted."

Everyone laughed.

"I think all of you are exhausted. You guys did really well and I'm proud of you all for what we accomplished here. When you return, we'll have a review day and pick up where we left off. It'll be the same time, same days of the week."

"Aww," Daisy complained, "I can't believe it's over."

"There's still Sunday service and regular Bible Study, just not group study," Eli offered.

"I know, but I liked our little group." Daisy glanced around the room, her eyes lingering on mine a little longer before turning back to Eli. "I'm going to miss it."

"Well, break is only a few weeks. We'll be back before you know it, and everyone will be complaining again."

The group chuckled and Eli took a deep breath as he glanced at his watch once more. "And that's time, guys. Have a very Merry Christmas and a Happy New Year."

"You too, Pastor Ross," Marlo Jo said as she stood. I nodded at her as she gave me a smile before leaving.

"Hey," Sky patted my shoulder, "you going back to Fresno?"

"Yeah." I sighed.

"Well, safe travels, man. I'll see you next year."

"Yeah, same."

He slung his bag over his shoulder as he eyed Daisy and Daytona who were making their way over to us.

"See you guys later," Daisy said as she glanced over at me. I nodded, and she returned a shy smile before speeding off. Sky nearly drooled on the floor as he watched Daisy leave, and Daytona was only a second behind him in the drooling contest as she ogled Sky.

"Well…" I stood, "I'll see you guys next year, I'm going to say bye to Eli."

"I should go," Daytona announced.

"Me too," Sky said. He waved as he headed for the door, and I waved back before making my way over to Eli.

"Hi, Eli," I said.

He looked up from his phone with a smile. "I didn't expect you to come say bye."

I shrugged. "The semester's been crazy. I thought I should say bye and thanks for everything."

"I'm glad we spent the semester together."

"Me too, actually."

Eli was charmed by that and offered me his hand.

I took it and shook it.

"I'll see you next year," I said.

"Of course." Eli nodded. "I can't wait."

22

I Can't Live with Myself

Everything's been a blur since I came home. Christmas and now New Years, both were blurs that I could barely remember as I sat in an interrogation room staring down at an image of a woman I swear I've seen before.

For four and a half months, I didn't have to think about the accident. Those four months seemed like a lifetime ago, and everything with Carly seemed so minuscule in comparison.

I listened to Detective Vean explain the new evidence they'd uncovered in Matt's case, wondering when it had become me vs. Matt.

Who am I kidding, it's always been this way.

I've always wanted to be better than Matt. I wanted to be cooler than Matt, but I was afraid of the wild parties. Afraid to talk to girls. Hanging with Matt was exhilarating. But it had its downfall. Like the night I covered his most horrible sin.

There was a night Matt committed a crime, one that changed everything about the way I saw him and the way I saw myself. There was a night when Matt's pursuit of girls went too far. When he didn't care that the girl he'd liked had told him no. When he decided he would have what he wanted whether she liked it or not.

I could hear her in her drunken stupor, laughing lightly, though she and Matt had been arguing. She was giggling and telling him *no* in that way that girls do when they don't really mean it. Except … suddenly, she *did* mean it. But Matt didn't care. He kept going.

I heard the shift when it wasn't funny anymore. When it wasn't just Matt being flirty and frisky, or trying to get her to accept his apology. When her voice was pinched with fear, and his voice was full of anger. I heard the shift when she stopped laughing and started crying. Then screaming.

But I just sat there, leaning against the door until he finished.

When it was over, Matt ripped open the door and glanced down at me. He blurred before me as tears filled my eyes. But they weren't for him, they weren't even for her. They were for me. The coward who let a girl get raped.

It didn't matter that Matt and the girl had been sleeping together for the past two months. It didn't matter that she had liked him. Or that she had willingly gone into the room with him. All that mattered was the fact that she'd said no.

She had begged him to stop and wailed loudly as he took what he wanted. And all I'd done was let it happen. Matt was my friend. I couldn't turn on him. We kept each other's secrets, and even though mine weren't as damaging as his, I still couldn't get myself to say a word.

But maybe I should have because neither of us paid for our sins that day. The only person who was truly punished for what'd happened was the victim herself.

A few weeks after that night, the girl took her own life. I remember the day it happened because she did it at school. Went to the boys' locker room and tied a rope around her neck. Someone found her body swaying limply in the showers. She was naked and written in permanent

198

marker on her legs and stomach was the message: **He did this, and I can't live with it anymore.**

I always wondered why she never said who. Maybe because even in her death, she knew no one would believe her since they hadn't bought her story in life. Rumors had gone around that she'd been raped, but no one took it seriously.

She's a loose cannon.

She's got a reputation.

She probably asked for it.

I remember the things people said in response to the accusation. No one had believed her.

But I knew the truth, and I've lived with the fact that my best friend is a monster, and I let a girl die because of that.

Her name, I thought as I stared at the picture, *I can't remember her name or her face anymore.* The girl who'd been assaulted by Matt. I swore I'd always remember it, but I couldn't anymore. The accident took parts of my memory away but left other parts I wish it'd taken. But as I stared at this picture, this girl somehow looked eerily familiar. Like I'd seen her before, or maybe this was the face of the girl Matt had forced himself on.

I didn't know because I felt numb the moment Detective Vean said that Matt's DNA was found in a semen sample they took from the victim. And they were looking into the possibility of Matt being the assailant of the other victim at the party.

"Were you with him the entire time?" Special Agent De Luca's fiery eyes were burning as I stared blankly at her.

"I … I … don't know. I can't think right now."

"You have to think," she said. "A girl's life depends on this."

"Special Agent," Detective Vean snapped, "that's enough."

She sighed and nodded at me. "Can you think of any time you weren't with Matt at the party?"

I lifted a shoulder slowly as I tried to recall as much of the party as possible. The accident had managed to knock out parts of that night too, but I could remember Matt leaving me when we'd first arrived.

"When we got to the house," I said quietly, "Matt went to get us drinks, but he didn't come back for a long time, so I mingled with the crowd until he found me."

"And then what happened?"

"He told me to go after Lia, and I don't know what happened after that."

"But you went into the bedroom with Lia, and didn't see Matt again until he picked you up when the cops came?"

I nodded.

Her soft eyes found mine and the detective sighed as she took a seat across from me. "You seem distant today, like you're thinking a lot. You want to talk about what's on your mind?"

"He's finally been caught," I whispered as I stared at the picture.

"I'm sorry?" the detective said.

"Matt's finally been caught."

"*Finally* caught? Isn't this his first offense?"

My hands became slick with sweat, and I was beginning to feel dizzy.

"Xavier, we need the truth," the detective urged. "I know it's scary, but I promise, it's better to tell the truth than it is to lie right now."

God? Will telling the truth make up for everything I've done? Everything I've hidden?

I have already forgiven you.

Why? I let someone die! Tears pricked my eyes, and I began to sniffle.

Because with sincerity, you asked Me to forgive you, and I have. Your sins are far from you, and I do not recall them.

He remembered that I asked Him to forgive me the night that girl was assaulted by my best friend. But He won't remember that I let it all happen. *Why? Why be nice to me? Why forgive me?*

200

"Xavier?" I looked over at the special agent. She was extending a tissue to me. "What happened? Let's talk about it."

I took the tissue and wiped my nose. "There was a girl. It was supposed to be a double date, but my date didn't show. So, we went to his girlfriend's house and…"

"Do you remember the name of Matt's girlfriend at the time?"

"I can't … I can't remember her name, but I think she looks like this girl right here." Shakily, I placed a hand on the picture and stared into the eyes of the smiling girl. Dimpled cheeks and a little overweight, but she was adorable. Her smile was to kill for.

"You think she looked like this girl?" Detective Vean tapped the picture.

"Yes."

"What happened that night?"

"They had sex."

"Was it consensual?"

I paused. "No." The word melted out as a whisper, and I heard the special agent exhale.

"Are you sure you don't know the name of the girl in that picture?"

"Yes," I said as I stared at it.

"This girl is Adeline Jones. There's a chance that she is the other assault victim from the party. She had an identical twin, Madeline Jones. Both attended your high school. Unfortunately, Madeline took her own life a few weeks after she was assaulted. Her sister and her family were never the same."

"Wait a second…" I froze. Lifting the picture.

"What is it?" Detective Vean asked.

"This girl in the photo… who is she?"

"She's Madeline's identical twin, Adeline."

I squinted until it hit me, and I dropped the picture. "No," I whispered. "Madeline's alive. I … I had a class with her."

The detective and the special agent passed each other a look before looking back at me.

"Madeline died, Xavier. Her sister, *Adeline* Jones, is alive. Her father isn't cooperating with us, so if you know anything—"

"I know Madeline!" I shouted. "Madeline Jones, *MJ*, she has bright red hair and loves Mary Jane Watson from Spiderman! She has that sticker..." I trailed off as I struggled to remember the difference between Madeline and Adeline.

"Alright," Detective Vean said, fanning a hand at me, "calm down. Tell me what you know about the girl at school."

"Her name is Madeline Jones and she loves Spiderman, that's all I know."

"Ok, can you get in contact with her for us?"

"No." I shook my head. "I'm not bringing these problems across the country with me. It's enough that I'm even here!" I shot to my feet, but Special Agent De Luca shot to hers too.

"We had a deal," she snarled.

"I don't care!" I shouted.

"Enough!" Detective Vean snapped. "I know you're stressed, Xavier, and this is a lot to take in. But I want you to do me a favor, okay? If you happen to see Madeline Jones, ask her where she's from. We know where she's from, and if what she tells you matches what we have on record then it's a match."

"You'll bring her in for questioning if it's a match?"

"We have to, she's a victim."

"Sometimes victims just want to disappear," I said tiredly.

"I know, but if she ever wants justice to be served, then we have to ask her some questions."

"Justice." I almost laughed at the word. "You don't know Matt; he does what he wants. There's no order or way to do things. He just does them," I said as I finally lifted my eyes to see them both.

"He's not a first-time offender," the special agent said. "And he does have a pattern." She leaned over Detective Vean and opened the folder in front of her. Tossing a picture down on the table, she pointed. "Brown skin, curvy, pretty smile, brown hair. She looks similar to the twins, doesn't she?"

I shrugged.

"She's the victim who provided his semen sample. Her name is Naomi Brown."

I grabbed the chair to steady myself. I was dizzy suddenly as I stared at the victim because memories flooded back of a conversation I'd had with Matt once.

"His type," I whispered.

"What do you mean?"

"One time, Matt said he had a type of woman he truly wanted, and a type of woman his parents wanted for him." I sighed. "He really liked women of color."

The detectives exchanged a look. Vean finally said, "But his parents didn't approve. Did they?"

I shook my head.

"So, were his parents racist? Have they ever made any comments or done anything?" There was a pause. "You're half Black, right? Did they say anything to you?"

"Honestly? I've never had a problem with his parents. Then again, Matt and I didn't hang around them very much."

There was a stern silence in the room before the detective cleared her throat and stood. She extended a hand to me. "I think that's enough for today."

I looked at her hand and then back at her face. Without a word, I pushed from the table and left.

— ❦ —

I went home and packed my things. I couldn't stay any longer. MJ not being MJ. Matt being a rapist. Me confronting my past. Yet, God had forgiven me. It was too much chaos all at once and I felt like I'd drown if I tried to stay any longer.

Dad didn't put up a fight when I told him and Mom I was leaving after the interrogation. Unfortunately, Jax was out with his friends at the arcade, so he didn't know I was heading out early. To my shock, my parents agreed with the idea of me going back to college early. Mom took me to a bus station to catch the last one back to New York City. It would be an almost three-day ride, but I didn't care. I just wanted to get away, I wanted to breathe and, thankfully, Mom understood that.

"You're not coming home again, are you?" she asked as we stood in the station.

"I don't ever want to come back here again," I told her. "But I can't leave you."

She smiled and took my hand. "Xavier, I've done what I could as a parent. I tried to raise you right, tried to hold tightly to you. But this case, it's taken everything out of me, and out of you too, and I just don't know what else to do."

"Mom, you did fine," I said earnestly. "I'm not so bad off."

She laughed. "No, but a good parent would be able to stop you and give you direction. I'm just lost right now." She reached up and touched my cheek. Mom and I looked alike, and Jax looked like a cross between Mom and Dad. I was always grateful that I'd gotten Mom's good genes but now, as I looked down at her, I knew that every day I looked in the mirror, I'd remember this day.

"I am not letting you go," she said sternly, "but I am letting you walk away. I think the distance helps you, and I want you to be okay more than anything. You still have to contact me, and at least visit for the holidays."

"I'm not dying, Mom, I just need to be away from here," I said as I leaned down and hugged her.

"I failed you," she whispered. "I'm so sorry, X."

"Mom, you didn't—"

"Your bus is pulling up. You'd better go get a good seat." She pulled away, and I studied her a little longer before I leaned down and kissed her cheek.

"I'll be back before you know it, Mom."

"I know, and we'll be laughing about the day I cried when I took you to the station."

I chuckled as I reached out and wiped one of her tears away. "We'll be laughing because we'll be happy again. I'll call you more, and I'll keep in contact with you, I promise."

"I love you so much, Xavier."

"Momma," I smiled, "I love you too."

23

Something Permanent

He placed a hand on the tall door. It was made of white gems with a beautiful glow that reflected around his hand. Benny had never been here before, had only heard of it. It wasn't the Throne Room, where Jehovah sat and watched the Earth's activity. The children of the Light weren't allowed in that room because of the adversary. He often came before the King, making a plea to test one of His children. Jehovah was a confident God, One who sometimes allowed His children to be tested because as they had faith in Him, He poured His own strength into them.

This door led to the Testament Room, where angelic beings were given assignments and the children preparing for Earth were instructed to go if they had any questions. It was Wisdom's home.

From the stories of the Realm, Wisdom was a beautiful woman, more beautiful than *any* woman, and she was very kind. Benedict had never seen her before. She was one of the spirits chosen by God to roam the Earth. Whenever someone prayed for wisdom, she was notified and went to pour her kindness into those who sought her Master. Now,

Wisdom's home was Gabriel's workplace until she returned. He was a messenger angel and was assigned by the Great God Jehovah to take over tasks in Wisdom's stead.

"Wait," Adar said as she grabbed Benny's shirt.

"What is it?" He turned to her, vaguely aware of the dark emotion surrounding them. It was an emotion he could feel but didn't know how to name. He'd heard it called 'nervousness' during his Earth training, and as he looked upon Adar, he recognized it in her expression.

"Are you sure about this?" she asked.

He took her small hand in his own. "It won't hurt to ask."

Adar nodded, and Benny led her by the hand into the big room. The warmth in the room buzzed as flowers of all sorts sat around the room. There were no books, like Benedict thought there'd be. On Earth, he learned that people became smart because they read many books. But as he stood in Wisdom's home, he remembered that wisdom and comprehension were different.

They took slow steps, wandering through the twists and turns of Wisdom's home. The joyous wind brought a greeting to them and guided the young children of God to where Gabriel sat. He was a tall being, with curly blonde hair and a handsome face, the total opposite of Michael—as he was only a messenger and not a warrior.

"Adar, Benedict, how can I help you both?" Gabriel asked kindly.

"I have a request," Benedict said as he stepped forward.

The kind angel only nodded in response and Benedict said, "Please don't send Adar to Earth. It's too scary, and too hard. She can't go."

Gabriel watched with eyes as blue as the ocean below. He could feel the joy of his Master tickling all over as he understood more of the plans of God for His children. "You are a precious child of Jehovah," Gabriel said, "and because of your concern for Adar, my Master will certainly reward you. You feel the way God feels, and I am unable to feel that. I do not understand what it is to love someone. I know what it is to feel joy when my Master's plans succeed because my only desire is for His success."

"Why are you telling me this?" Benny asked.

"Because I cannot show you compassion for your suffering. I don't quite understand why one would question or fight against the plans of Elohim. He is the One who knows all and knows best. Who are we to question His desires?"

"I … I don't mean any disrespect," Benedict began to explain. "I just… I want to protect Adar, that's all."

"Adar must learn that the Master is a protector and guardian of all. But He has given me knowledge of your placement in the Earthly realm." The winged creature stood and looked at the children of God. "You two were one spirit God made into two. Your spirits will reunite on Earth, as Adar is a part of you, Benedict."

"So that means, we'll find each other?"

He nodded. "And you will reunite into one flesh, so that the Master can welcome you back as one spirit when the time comes."

Benedict looked back at Adar who was smiling. It was bright and wide, and her perfect teeth were beautiful. On Earth there was a saying Benny had heard in his training. When something was great or deeply loved, whatever it may be, it is considered worth giving up the fleeting life the Earthen vessels have. *Her smile,* Benny thought, *it is to die for…*

I sat up and took a deep breath. Being in the dorm room alone was creeping me out and making those dreams come back. I hadn't had one in a while, but it didn't matter. I always forgot them all. *Except the time Madeline…*

A sigh escaped me as her name left my mouth in a whisper.

Everything I'd learned about the accident was disturbing. The man who'd lost his life because of our reckless driving, Lia who'd lost her life because of our reckless driving. My lost memories. Plus, there were two girls who'd been sexually assaulted and an injured person at the party.

How could Matt be at the center of everything that'd unfolded that night?

Crushing my palms into my eyes, I rubbed away the sleep before throwing the blankets back so I could go freshen up. It was two in the morning, but I couldn't stay here any longer. I'd returned to campus two days ago, but I'd only sat in my room, begging God to help me feel better, to forget it all, but He's been silent.

Shoving clothes and shoes into a duffle bag, I slung it over my shoulder and headed out. It was cold in New York City. The freezing winter air, and the mounds of snow. I'd never seen snow before I came here for school, but it wasn't until the Christmas décor came out that I fell in love with the wintery weather here.

NYC looked like a Christmas town during the season. It felt like it too. The way people huddled together and stayed close to keep warm. The smiles on everyone's face, the kindness and joy. I admired the beauty of what was left of the décor in the New Year as I walked the sleeping streets of the city.

With a hesitant hand, I knocked on the door... twice. I was ready to knock a third time when a voice called out, "Just a second."

Clutching my bag, I braced myself as the door opened and Elijah emerged. He wasn't wearing his glasses, but he was wearing a confused face and a white t shirt with pajama pants.

"Xavier? It's almost three in the morning. What's going on?"

"I don't know." I shrugged. "I don't know what's wrong with me or why God's not talking to me."

"Come in." He waved me inside. The apartment was cool, but I took my jacket off anyway as I walked in. He lit the small fireplace and disappeared down the hall. A few moments later, he returned with his glasses before heading into the kitchen to bring me a bottle of water. He sat on the couch beside me as I glugged the water before he said, "Start from the beginning."

"Everything was going fine at home until I had to go to another interrogation."

He bobbed his head.

I took a breath. "During my sophomore year of high school, my best friend Matt … he—he raped this girl. They'd been seeing each other on and off, and I was there when it happened. But I didn't stop it, I just sat there outside the door until he finished." I felt a familiar lump in my throat as I stared at the dancing flames of the fireplace. I'd cried or fought tears so much this year, I didn't want to cry anymore. Thankfully, the tears were all shed in private, so no one really knew that I wasn't keeping it together—besides God and Eli.

"That girl killed herself, Eli… *I* killed her."

"No, you didn't."

"Yes, I did! Because I let my friend hurt her."

My breaths were short and stiff, and I fought tears that tried to fall, but it wasn't fair to cry now, not after sitting on this secret, convincing myself that I deserved happiness. How could I?

"What you did was wrong, Xavier, but I don't have to tell you that. You just want someone to say it so you'll feel like you've paid for what you've done."

"It's the only retribution."

"Okay, so now you've paid it. What else is the problem?"

"Wait … that can't be it." I sniffled. "You have to yell at me!"

"Xavier, you've yelled at yourself and beat yourself up about this for the last two or three years. You have to stop *wanting* to be punished. It doesn't make you admirable."

"I don't want to be admirable!"

"Then what do you want?"

"To stop him!" I snapped. "I want to stop him… I want to go back and help her. But I wanted to have a friend so badly, I let someone die. How do I move on from this?"

Eli took a deep breath, adjusting against the couch. "God's love will be your comfort as Jesus' blood will be your stain remover. But you have to allow Him to love you past your wrong doings, X. If you hold on to this guilt, you'll never forgive yourself. And if you're not forgiving yourself, God can't forgive you."

"But… I can't forgive myself. That's not fair."

"Do you know why God's love is the only cure for guilt?"

I shook my head.

"Because when we are loved by God, we stop judging ourselves, and picking ourselves apart. We leave the conviction to the Holy Spirit, so that He can show us our errors and how to correct them. So that He can remind us that we are loved. Loved so much that we don't have to sin."

"But why? Why can God forgive me like that?"

"His love is unconditional. Which means there's nothing that can disqualify you from His love or qualify you for His love. He loves because God *is* love. And there's nothing we can do to stop His heart from beating for us."

Wringing my hands, I took a breath to try to calm down. There was a feeling of peace knocking on my heart, but I was afraid to let it in. I was afraid that if I was at peace then I didn't care and wouldn't feel sorry. Yet, I knew that wasn't true.

The sleepless nights, hoping that I'd done the right thing were proof of my remorse. The years I've spent tied to this guilt was even more evidence of it. I just wished I could tell her; I wished I could tell…

"Madeline…" I paused and looked at Eli. "Madeline was the name of the girl who committed suicide. They weren't lying."

"Who wasn't lying?"

"The interrogators. They said Madeline Jones was the girl from high school who killed herself. I remember her name now. I couldn't remember anything about her at first, but it's coming back to me now. Like her red hair. And her backpack with a Mary Jane sticker on it from Spiderman."

I trailed off as I moved to the edge of the couch. Madeline Jones had been the girl who sat in front of me during global history, and AP English. But she had a sister, I just never had classes with her. Everyone always called Madeline *Maddy* because she was wild, like a madwoman, or MJ because that's what she wanted to be called. She'd dyed her hair red one summer and came back as Mary Jane Watson. But not much was ever said about her identical twin. The only way the two of them could be told apart was because of MJ's red hair.

"There was a sticker on Madeline's notebook," I began to explain to Eli, "and it said, *face it Tiger, you just hit the jackpot.*"

Eli frowned. "X, you know you're describing Madeline Jones who attends classes here, right?"

"That's the thing," I said, "the detective told me that the girl who committed suicide had an identical twin sister. The sister's name was Adeline, and the twin who passed away was Madeline."

Eli stirred for a moment, his brows tensing as he glanced off.

"What is it?" I asked.

"I can't share confidential information."

"Eli, please," I begged. "I think the girl who goes to school here was raped."

He sucked in a breath and tried to maintain his calm demeanor.

"I think she was assaulted back in my hometown and she somehow came here and changed her identity. Pretended to be her dead twin sister." I took a breath. "I know you can't tell me things, but this information is for the police, not just for my own good. Madeline's case is still open. The man who hurt her could get away with all of his crimes

212

if Madeline doesn't come forward and help the police."

Elijah bristled and then his shoulders sagged like he'd just given up. He looked at me with a glum expression. "Madeline's name on my student roster is *Adeline* Jones, but she told me that they missed the 'M.'"

I blinked at him, my heart breaking, my gut curdling. "So, Adeline is Madeline's twin?"

"If what those investigators say is true, then yes."

"But why does she pretend to be her sister?"

"If she was truly assaulted, she might be trying to gain distance from everything—even from herself. Becoming her role model, or the person she loved the most may help her cope."

"So you're saying that Adeline pretends to be her sister as a coping mechanism?"

He shrugged. "It's the only explanation for her behavior."

"What do we do?"

"We have to wait until classes resume."

"And then what?"

"I don't know. There's nothing I can do until the police come knocking." He yawned and stared off as we both soaked in the mystery in the air. If everything was true, that MJ from college was Adeline Jones, that meant she was a potential victim if investigators could confirm her story with the other bystanders' stories. Special Agent De Luca said they'd spoken with a few more students from the party who ultimately pointed them to Adeline.

"Just get some sleep for now," Elijah said into my thoughts.

I looked up at him as he stood from the couch, and I asked meekly, "How's Carly?"

"I haven't heard from her."

"Before our last Bible Study, I saw Madeline... or Adeline?"

"Just call her Madeline for now," he said as he made his way into the kitchen.

I moved from the couch to follow him. Resting against the doorframe, I continued, "Well, MJ said that Carly was going to stay with some friends of hers." That reminded me of seeing Jay that day too. She'd exploded from the car, vomiting violently, and she'd looked even frailer than I'd ever seen her.

Something was wrong with Jocelyn, but MJ was keeping everything a secret. I needed to see her if not for Carly's sake, or even Matt's sake, but for Jay's sake. I was worried about her, to say the least. I found myself mildly attracted to Jay beyond our normal sexual tension, after all, she was the only one who told me the truth on the train, which was pushing me to be more worried about her. I'd been ignoring that attraction since I was in no place mentally to have feelings for anyone, plus the fact that she wasn't straight.

Elijah's sigh rang out and called my attention back to him. He turned on the stove with a skillet on it. Smearing butter over a bagel, he tossed it into the pan, and it began to sizzle. "Carly's run away before. She'll be back."

"She has?"

"Unfortunately, yes. She ran away a little while back. I had to go looking for her. Now, things are different. She's eighteen, and if she left with friends and the police knows this when I ask them to investigate, they'll tell me she's an adult and doesn't have to tell me where she's at."

"I see the problem."

He flipped the bagel and there was a nice brown hue across the front that made my mouth water.

"Tell me about your vacation besides the case, how'd everything else go?"

"Oh," I said, "well, it was fine. Christmas was good and New Year's was great until I had to be interrogated."

"Sounds like a typical break."

"It was." I laughed.

He slapped both sides of the fried bagel with jelly and passed me the plate. "You looked hungry," he said as he walked out the kitchen.

I smiled down at the food before rushing to his couch. "Carly said you don't like dirty dishes."

"I don't, but I'm too tired to take care of them right now."

My shoulders lowered, and I could feel the weight I'd placed on Eli's shoulders smothering my own.

"No," Elijah waved a hand, and there was a tired smile on his face, "I'm actually tired. Not mentally or physically, just tired from being abruptly awakened."

"Oh," I blew a sigh of relief, "I thought I was becoming a burden."

"You're fine. Blankets are behind the couch." He pointed. "Just leave your plate on the table."

"Elijah," I called before he hit the hall.

He stepped back with a raised brow.

"Can I... Can I..." I struggled to ask him what I wanted. I didn't want to go back to the dorms, but I also didn't want to barge in on him.

"You can stay." He nodded.

"Really? We're not breaking any rules?"

"I'll contact your mother and she'll have to let the school know you're staying with me. But, if a counsellor feels their student is in serious need of mental help, and their home is the safest place, they can, with your permission, bring you to their residence."

"Really?"

"It's frowned upon because of all the sexual misconduct that's happened between counselors and students in the past, but it is something that's reasonable."

"Well, what if I just stopped seeing you as a counsellor?"

"It's a week or so," he shrugged, "you don't have to stop seeing me."

My gaze avoided his and I heard him whisper, "Oh," as he understood that I was thinking of something more permanent.

"You're not going home for summer break, are you?"

"I just want to be away from there."

"We'll talk in the morning, your bagel's getting cold."

24

BFFs?

"Do you always clean your entire apartment before the semester starts?"

Elijah chuckled and wrung out his rag. "Of course. Usually Carly helps, but since you're here squatting, I'm putting you to work."

"I've been thinking about that," I said as I started scrubbing the wall again. "I'm going to start applying for jobs."

"Really? Thinking of moving out already?"

"No." I waved my rag and suds flew everywhere. Eli's laser vision spotted each one, marking where I'd need to clean up. He was a stickler about having a clean place and eating dinner together. Other than that, Eli didn't impose many rules. He had a lot of expectations, though. Like when my first Sunday here rolled around, he didn't even wake me for church. He came out, made coffee, and went back to his room. Thankfully, I was awake and slipped into the shower before he did, but we never even talked about it. I was just ready when he was, and we left for service.

"I just don't want to be a burden. And it's not fair to move in and expect all my expenses to be taken care of."

Eli stopped cleaning and leaned against the counter. "You know you're not a problem for me, Xavier. There's no need to rush into anything you're not ready for."

I wondered briefly if he was this nonchalant with Carly. "I appreciate that," I said as I stood, "but you've already put a roof over my head, I can't ask for anything else."

He smiled and patted my shoulder. "You're doing very well. I'll be sure to let your mother know."

"Thanks," I said.

Break ended and I returned to the dorms. My mother ended up cancelling the rest of my sessions with Eli since I'd be living with him during the summer and could go see him on my own. It was bittersweet when we finally talked about it. But she said she trusted Pastor Ross— which I thought it was funny that Elijah introduced himself as Pastor Ross, and then as my counsellor. I think he knew my mother was worried about me spiritually and mentally, and seeing that he covered both areas, she certainly felt more secure about my living arrangements—and she said she was learning to trust me in the hands of God again. She had held on to me so hard, she believed she'd squeezed every ounce of life out of me, so she let me go, but ended up pulling her hands too far away in our separation.

I sighed as I pushed open the dorm. I wanted to stop by Jay's room just to check on her, but I didn't want to see Carly at all even though I needed to see MJ. My head was spinning. I didn't know if I'd be able to make it through the semester. So much had transpired last semester, I planned to keep my head low and just make it to the summer.

But that was easier said than done.

"Well, well," Glenn said as I walked inside.

"Hey, Glenn." I tried to ignore the scowl on his face.

"I covered for you and JC found out and exploded on me."

"I—"

"I told you to tell him!"

"Glenn, I'm sorry." I set my bags down and kicked the door closed behind me. "I just missed the chance, a lot happened at the end of the semester."

"Yeah, well now everyone hates me because JC keeps telling everyone that I'm a liar and he's started some rumor about me wanting to be a Crusader and that's why I covered for you."

"I'm sorry. I'll go talk to him right now."

"The damage is done." He shrugged. "Just don't ask for any more favors. You stay on your half of the dorm; I'll stay on mine."

"Glenn, come on, I'm sorry."

"I don't care." He shook his head. "You can be friendless, but I don't want to be. I had the hardest time making friends here, and now they're gone because of you. Just don't involve me in your business." He brushed by me and headed out the door before I could say anything else.

I squeezed my eyes shut and took a breath before leaving the dorm.

Glenn was my friend and I'd screwed him over. I really meant to tell JC, but I never got the chance, and it just didn't come up. I was dealing with a lot, but I know I avoided the topic when I did see JC. Granted, he started blowing me off for his other friends, so we weren't seeing each other much outside of classes. Occasionally, he'd swing by the dorm, but he and Glenn were getting closer as he and I became distant.

I stopped at his door and pounded on it.

"JC, come on, open up."

I pounded again.

"Junior! Come on!"

The door was snatched open, and JC was standing there glaring at me before I even spoke.

"I know you're mad at me, but what you're doing to Glenn is—"

He slammed the door shut.

"Junior!" I hollered, but he didn't respond. "You're just being childish! All this over friends! What are we, five!?" I yelled at the door. A few guys passed by before I grunted and left JC's door.

I took the shortcut through the girls' dorm and decided to stop by Jay's dorm anyway to see her and MJ. When I got to the door, it was slightly ajar. I knocked twice, but when no one answered, I pushed the door open and stepped inside.

The room was clean. No clothes, no shoes, not even the girly scent that usually filled the small area. The blinds were closed and the beds bare. Classes started tomorrow, I had hoped they'd be here, or at least one of them would be here.

Elijah was contacted to retrieve some things from the dorm the officials thought were Carly's the last week of break. She had officially unenrolled, and her things had to be removed from the premises. The only reason they knew Carly had been on campus was because it had been reported that she'd been staying in Jay and MJ's dorm before everyone completely disappeared and illegal activity started going on.

Since no one had heard from Jay or MJ, their parents were contacted. Some kind of way, Elijah got saddled with retrieving MJ's things as well since no one could catch up with any of the numbers listed as emergency contacts except Elijah's.

"Here I was, thinking you were actually remorseful."

I whirled around and Junior was standing in the doorway.

"It's not what you think, JC. There's something wrong with Jay," I said as I rushed out the room to him.

With his face pinched, he snarled, "Yeah, I'm sure you know all about what happened to her. Even though I don't know how she told you anything with her mouth always glued to yours."

His words made me flinch and left me speechless.

He crossed his arms. "You've got nothing to say, *best friend*? I thought you liked Carly?"

"I did like Carly. But things happened and—"

"And so, you marched into another man's turf. You're garbage, you know that?"

"Junior, it wasn't even like that with her."

"Don't lie. I'm not an idiot. I heard about her grinding on you in the back of the train! You guys were basically having sex in public! And you think I didn't hear about the way you threw yourself at her at the bowling alley?"

"Hold on," I waved a hand, "the train thing was … I don't know. She caught me off guard, just like the bowling alley. She came up to me and well…"

"Well, what? I wasn't there to remind you that I called dibs?"

"Would you stop acting like we're twelve and are talking about toys!" I snapped. "Jocelyn is a *woman*! Not your turf or your toy to lay claim to."

He dropped his arms, eyes shooting over me quickly before he yelled, "Of course you say that! I'm sure you know how much of a slut she really is now, don't you?"

Something in me ticked.

I lunged at JC and shoved him into the wall. He hollered and there were squeals in the hall of passing girls.

"Stop it!" I heard someone yell.

I punched Junior so hard my own hand hurt, but I couldn't focus on the pain. We tussled until we fell to the floor, punching each other and rolling around in the hall.

"Someone, get help!" a voice called out.

I couldn't afford any trouble, so I shoved Junior away. He rolled over, panting as he stared up at the ceiling. Slowly getting to my feet, I wiped the blood from my mouth and pulled him up by his shirt.

"Stop spreading lies about Glenn." I dropped him and turned to leave.

"Some kind of best friend you were!" he called behind me. "You took my girl and you're going to pay for that!"

I turned and looked down at him as he struggled to get to his feet. "She was never your girl, Junior. She never even liked you."

He couldn't speak.

I turned and made my way out of the girl's dorm and headed back to my own.

25

Review: Being Single

"Welcome back, everyone," Eli said as he stood at the front of the church.

Everyone had returned for the new semester, even Kevin came back—despite him missing the last few Bible Study sessions.

"Daisy," Eli called.

The small woman perked at her name and focused on him as he spoke.

"How was your break?"

"It was fun when I wasn't working. We're understaffed right now, so every time I was at work, it was a horrible, time."

"But outside of work you had fun, right?"

"Yes." She nodded with a smile.

"Very good," Eli said. "Kevin, welcome back. How was your break?"

He grunted. "Fine."

"Good. Anyone want to share anything exciting before we dive into our review?"

"What did you do?" Marlo asked.

Eli hesitated. He looked thrown by the question but regained his thoughts quickly without even making a sideways glance in my direction.

"I spent Christmas and New Year's alone this year." He shrugged.

"I didn't know you ever spent it with anyone," Marlo said.

He chuckled, slipping his hands into his pockets. "Well, it's usually just my sister and I, but she wanted to spend the holidays with friends."

"Oh, well, I was alone too. We could've spent the holidays together," Marlo teased. It made Elijah flush red and let out a weak chuckle as the rest of the room laughed lightly.

"Marlo Jo," he said quickly. The young woman was sitting with her legs crossed and her arms folded over her flat chest. She raised her chin with a smirk as Eli continued, "Name one thing we talked about before break."

"Being lonely," she said.

"And what about being lonely?"

"That we're never alone. God's always with us. And you said that being alone is good for nurturing our spirit."

"Very good." Eli pulled out a red ball from his pocket and held it up. We all knew we'd have a turn, but no one really wanted one. He tossed the ball to Kevin first. He caught it and sighed.

"We learned about spiritual warfare."

"What is it?"

"It's when we have inner turmoil. Like when the Spirit wants to lead but so does the flesh, so it's a fight to do the righteous thing."

"Very well said," Eli complimented.

Daytona caught the ball next. "Hearing the Voice of God?"

"Is that your answer or are you asking me?"

"My answer."

"Correct. We did learn about listening for God's voice. Name one more thing."

She thought for a second. "We went over how it's okay to never get married. Some people have assignments that require them to work alone and not with a spouse."

"And how do we accept that?" Eli pressed.

"We start by accepting the call to singlehood. It's a gift, not a punishment; since in our singleness, with no other distractions, we can get very close to God."

Eli nodded proudly. Daytona glanced around until she spotted Sky sitting beside me. With a gentle toss, the ball sprang from her hand to his. He nodded and stood.

"We talked about the place of men and women in a marriage and how knowing our roles helps us prepare for that during our singleness."

"Excellent. Can you tell me something specific about the roles?"

"Well, I remember you saying women are like helpers, and men are protectors."

Eli bobbed his head and Sky threw the ball to Daisy. She caught it clumsily, and her big, embarrassed eyes looked right up at me. I sucked in a breath. Daisy was cute and short. Dainty hands and slender fingers tossed the ball back and forth as she looked away from me to Eli.

"Knowing ourselves before knowing someone else."

"That was a fun activity, wasn't it?" Eli asked.

"It was." Daisy nodded playfully, then she turned from Eli and locked eyes with me. I wanted to tell her no, but she weakly tossed the ball before I could say anything. It didn't make it to me. Emily caught it by accident since it was so low and slow. Daisy blushed and sat in her seat. Nothing got past Elijah, though. He glanced at her, but not at me, before giving Emily his attention.

"You taught us that women were the rib, and our work is internally within a marriage."

"And why is that important?"

"Because women are natural intercessors, so it is vital in our singleness to spend a lot of time in prayer."

"What about the husband?"

"He has to spend time in prayer too, but that's because he's going to lead, and he can't lead without the Spirit of God."

"Well said."

"We discussed women are equal to men under grace," Julius said as he caught the ball.

"Nice one, Julius."

He passed the ball to Tracy, and she held it for a second. Unfortunately, that meant I had to go last. Everything I remembered had been discussed already. I scratched my head nervously as I watched Tracy stand and struggle to remember something. At least I wasn't the only one.

"I'm pretty sure we talked about appreciating walking with God on our own."

"We did," Eli nodded, and Tracy sighed a breath of relief. "Can you elaborate?"

"Well, our singleness is to bring us into a deeper relationship with God, which benefits us. So, walking with Him gives us the chance to be refined and purified with no distractions."

"Good, I like how you explained that."

"Thanks." She smiled and turned to me to toss the ball.

"Xavier," Elijah said as he looked at me. "You're up."

I cleared my throat nervously. "We talked about our calling before being married."

"What about your calling?"

"That we need to walk in it, knowing what God wants us to do in our life."

"What example did I use?"

I paused and glanced around. *That's too specific,* I thought.

"I think you used the scripture where God takes Adam to the

226

Garden and places Him in it. And He gives the command, but that command relates to both Adam and Eve because she came out of his side."

Eli was glowing now. "Very *very* good, Xavier. You remembered well—*all* of you did." He turned to face the entire group. "I think we only missed the part about wives being gifts. But that was more of a tangent than an actual lesson. That's definitely something we can dive deeper into as we move forward. But I really want to stress for the rest of this semester, enjoying our time with God as single people."

"It's hard," Daytona said. "I want a boyfriend. I want friends in general. I don't want to just hear my own thoughts all the time. I know I'm supposed to be alright with it, but I'm not."

"And that's alright," Eli said as he crossed the room to her. "We are, by nature, beings that long for interaction. God said it right before he made Adam a helper that it's not good for man to be alone. However, there are seasons in our lives where being alone is the only way to produce and cultivate the Fruit of the Spirit."

"But I hate it," Daytona was frowning now. "But I also hate that I hate being alone. Why can't I just be comfortable with who I am?"

"Because you're rushing," Eli said gently.

Daytona lowered her head, and I saw Daisy's small hand reach out and grip hers.

"We become unsettled when we try to race time. It's something we can't beat because we operate in the function of time. It is a universal measurement of the human race. However, God's time is not our own, so when we try to force something to happen, we become unsettled."

"Question," Sky raised his pencil, and Eli nodded. "What if you just don't like being alone? Like, I just don't like pineapples." A few students chuckled. "There's nothing wrong with pineapples, but I don't like them, and I never will. What happens then?"

"Then you have yet to understand that you are not alone." Eli smiled. "In other words, you've only tried pineapples from a can. You haven't had them fresh and ripe and in season."

Sky chuckled. "Maybe so."

Eli nodded, addressing the rest of the group. "We seem to forget that because God doesn't answer us right away, that means we're totally alone. But, the Creator of the universe, the One who knows all things, walks with us, dwells with us, watches over us and protects us. What more can we ask for?"

I stirred within as I jotted down notes. When he put it that way, it seemed like the world was inappreciative of God. Walking with Him alone was something most people didn't want to do. Because we know that in being alone, you make tons of sacrifices for God. You give up hanging out, being popular, even having money sometimes.

Sometimes walking with God drains you before it gets better, but it *always* gets better with God. And during our singleness that is what we learn. That through the ups and downs, God is there, even if it feels like He isn't. We learn patience and we learn trust, although those are attributes that continuously improve in our walk, the basis of our belief stems from our trust in God and the patience, the endurance, to wait on Him.

"You can't know who you are if you don't know who God is. And that's because every part of life is supposed to come from God," Eli was explaining. "Our desires, our thoughts, our jobs, everything part of us is a part in the bigger plan of God."

"It's just hard," Julius spoke up, "being around all my family and their girlfriends and wives and husbands, even kids now. And then there's just me. But it's not so bad. I mean, I'm really the only one in my family who's saved. So, I know I've got to just stick it out."

"That's very good, Julius," Eli comforted. "But I hope you see that if you hadn't been walking with God, you'd have no idea how to be still and abide despite the situation you were in. Knowing that we're part of something bigger should always be our motivation. We're part of the plans of God, don't ever forget that."

26

Accidents Happen

This second semester has been harder than the last one. Not because of the drama, it's quite the contrary, honestly. This semester has been hard because there's been no drama. There's been schoolwork and there's been Bible Study, occasional phone calls with Mom, and visits with Eli.

I've got no friends, no one to hang out with. Sky's cool, but he works a lot, so we haven't been able to hang out. Kevin isn't friendly, and Julius is alright, but he's just *alright*. We've barely spoken, so I can't say much about Julius. The only person I've talked to recently was Daisy to help me get a job at her café. I'm supposed to have a second interview soon which is great, but I … feel so alone.

I know I'm not supposed to. I've been beaten over the head plenty of times with the fact that I'm supposed to enjoy being alone and walking with God. But I don't always enjoy it. It's not always fun. It certainly hasn't been fun lately. It's easy and fun in Bible Study and at church. But when I'm here at my dorm, alone, like I am now, it isn't fun.

Glenn barely stays here anymore now. He and JC are miraculously on good terms again, and he stays at JC's dorm since Junior's roommate is never there. I'm left here, alone.

"God," I whispered, "will things ever change for me?"

Have I ever left you?

"Why do you sound so close today?"

Because I am here with you.

I looked up from my hands, glancing around the room, until my eyes landed on a man with glowing skin and flowing robes standing beside me. My heart began to pound, and I felt like I'd pass out, but He reached out and touched my head and suddenly, I was calm.

"I have come to comfort you," Jesus said.

"Why? Why now?"

"Your desperation called to my Father, and He sent Me."

I continued to stare at Jesus as He walked around my room, exploring the details of the tight space. If I would've known He was coming, I would've cleaned up a little more…

"There is a journey ahead of you, Xavier, one that requires you to be in this season a little longer than others."

"Why me? I'm always by myself." I sniffled.

He smiled and reached out to touch my tears. "Moses, a servant of My Kingdom, spent forty years alone with my Father. Samuel spent time alone as a child before he was raised to be the prophet my Father called him to be. The impact of your life determines the length of your journey alone."

"The impact of my life?"

He nodded. "Moses's years alone were in preparation to lead a nation. King David spent his childhood and early years alone, even after he was anointed to be king. But he needed that time to walk in the anointing My Father placed on him." He knelt before me, placing a hand on my head, He pulled me close to Him. When my head met His, there was a numbing feeling all over.

"Benedict, you will finish the race. Do not lean unto your own understanding, but trust that My Father's Spirit is guiding you."

I heaved a deep breath and sat up. I'd fallen asleep on the floor of my dorm. But how? I glanced around, and I almost remembered something when a pounding sounded at the door.

"Glenn?" I called as I got my feet under myself.

"Please!" the voice was desperate, spearing me in place.

I couldn't move for a moment. What was going on? I woke up on the floor and now someone was banging on my door?

The pounding erupted again with a screeching cry for help, and I jolted to the door. Ripping it open, Madeline was standing there. Scraped and scratched. Covered in blood and dirt. She was holding her arm as it bled onto the floor in front of my dorm.

"Madeline?"

"Please! It's Carly! I tried to get Eli, but I can't find him! She's hurt!"

I was moving before I realized it. Rushing around the room, stuffing things into a bag, I snatched a jacket and raced out the room, grabbing MJ's hand on the way out the door. We left school, greeted by the thin air outside. It froze me to my core, but I ran across the slippery ice anyway. Crunching freshly fallen snow beneath my boots and fighting against the wind as I rushed to find Carly.

MJ led me to a place not too far from campus where a car was flipped upside down off the road. There was a car nearby with their blinkers on and the doors open. A man and woman were at the car, trying to get the door open.

"There's someone inside!" the man called to me as I ran over and slid to my knees.

"I've notified the police," the woman was saying over my shoulder.

232

Shakily, I grabbed my phone from my bag and hit the flashlight button. My heart nearly stopped as realization set in.

"Carly," I whispered.

She was in the vehicle, her head leaning back with blood leaking from it. It looked like she was pinned between the steering wheel and the seat.

Not again.

I stared at Carly as the world around me fell silent. In my peripheral, the man was screaming at me, and I knew the woman and MJ were behind me shouting too. But I couldn't move. I was paralyzed. I never had a single memory of the accident I was in, but seeing Carly took me back to the hospital bed, where I found out I'd been part of a murder, part of a car accident.

Was this what it looked like? Was I pinned in the backseat? Was no one able to help Lia? Was it all my fault, again?

God... please not again.

Suddenly, there was a warmth surrounding me. A barrier blocking out the cold and closing in the heat. The world was quiet, and I was transferred to a place I'd only dreamed about. A place I could never remember, but I was suddenly there now.

The car was gone, and it was replaced with a field of poppies. The sun was shining and there was no snow or wind. I was kneeling with my hands over my face, feeling a whirlwind of emotions I'd never felt before. It was too much, I thought it would crush me, but her arms wrapped around me. She pulled me into her embrace, and in my ear, she whispered, "Benedict, come back to me."

I inhaled and the sound clicked on. The poppies disappeared and the car came back into view.

"Xavier! Please!" Madeline was holding on to me, her arms gripped around my waist, holding me as she wept into my back. "Please snap out of it!"

I shook my head, trying to regain myself. *God, please, help me.*
Remove the belt.

"MJ," I whispered suddenly, "I've got to unbuckle the belt."

"What?"

I turned to the man beside me. "We've got to unbuckle the belt!"

"We tried, but we can't get it loose."

The wind had picked up and the snow was getting thicker, falling faster. The ambulance probably had another five to ten minutes before arriving, and I didn't know if Carly had that long.

"We've got to cut her loose then."

"Baby!" he yelled to the woman. "Get my tool bag out the back!"

"Already got it," the woman said as she knelt beside the man. I watched as she dug through the bag for him. He was shining a flashlight in the bag for her to see, and I caught a twinkle of the diamond on her ring.

They're married… She's his helper.

The woman had known what to do before her husband had even asked. She had known what he'd want. She had known what he would do next before he'd even done it. When the man had called out to her, he'd known he could trust her to bring exactly what he was asking for.

This is marriage. This is why it's a gift.

"Young man!" the man's voice snapped me out of my trance, and he was waving a knife at me.

"Thank you," I said as I grabbed it and crawled into the car.

"Light!" I called. "I need—"

MJ shoved herself through the car window with me to shine the light for me. I blinked at her as blood trailed down her panicked face. Her features were morphed into a ball of anguish, and she was fighting the tears begging to fall.

"Thanks," I muttered as I began cutting away at Carly's seat belt. It took a minute to cut through, but when I cut the final piece, she fell into the dashboard and heaved for air.

"She's breathing!" MJ shouted.

Carly began to cough as blood came from her mouth.

"We've got to get her out!" I yelled as sirens cried over us.

MJ backed out of the window, staring down the street. "They're here!"

I crawled out behind her, just in time to see the medics rush onto the scene.

The man and woman from the scene drove me to the hospital where I thanked them tremendously for their help. The old man let me keep his hunting knife, and he told me that it was a memento for being a hero.

I didn't think I was a hero. I didn't think anything as I stared at the bloody knife in my hand. My clothes were soaked, and I was shivering like crazy beneath the blanket the medics had given me as I waited in a private room. The images of Carly lying in the car wouldn't get out of my head.

"Why did this have to happen? Is this some kind of punishment for her?"

Silence.

"God! Please, say something."

This was not punishment.

The door opened and Elijah stepped inside.

"Eli!" I shot to my feet and hugged him tightly. He was calm, just as he always was, just as I needed him to be right now.

"You saved my sister's life," Eli said as I pulled away.

I could see the puffiness of his eyes, the red hue from tears previously shed. I looked away from his sullen eyes as he said, "The doctors said if you hadn't cut that belt, she would've suffocated."

"It wasn't me…" I paused. "It was God. He told me to remove the seatbelt. But I don't understand why He saved her. Why let her go through all of this just to save her in the end?"

Eli sat in a chair and took a breath. "Carly needed a reawakening. This will be it."

"So, God caused this accident?"

"No, but He did protect her to bring her to repentance. He could have stopped it, but He allowed it to happen."

"I don't understand, why would He do that?"

Eli patted the chair beside him, and I sat. "God told me last night that trouble had come for Carly, but there was no prayer that could stop it." He scratched the light stubble on his chin as he went on. "Do you remember in the story of Job, how Satan had to come ask God for permission to mess with him?"

"Yeah."

"God allowed Satan to cause sickness to be on Job because Job was strong enough to handle it. God allowed this accident, but not because Carly was strong, it was to rope her back into His arms."

"So, He let her almost die just to get her to come back to Him?"

"He let Job almost die just to prove a point," Eli said sternly. When he saw the look on my face, he added, "Some people are slow learners, Xavier. Some people can only learn through tragedy. There's always a kid who sticks his hand into the flames, even when you warn him not to. It's like he won't understand until he's burned."

"And that's okay with you?" I asked sharply, but Elijah didn't move. He pushed blond strands of hair from his face and looked plainly at me.

"I don't like what happened, if that's what you're asking."

"Then why aren't you mad at God!? You never cared about Carly! Did you?"

"I love her."

"Then why!?"

"Because God saved her!" he nearly yelled. The sound of his voice silenced me immediately. I'd never seen Eli this emotional before.

His hands balled into fists as he went on. "This was part of the plan for Carly's life before she was even born. Satan was allowed to take everything from Job, just so God could prove that Job wouldn't curse Him. Is this situation any different? You think I don't *want* to be angry? But I know better." Eli sank against his seat.

My hands fell from their tightened fists as I understood Elijah. He was angry, he was hurting, but he was right. His position was no different from Job's, except, Eli wasn't the one being tormented. He had to sit by and watch his family fall apart and keep his head elevated. But I heard him say once that our crosses are only as heavy as we are strong.

Some people can handle more pain than others, while some people can take more mental anguish than others. Eli was clearly strong enough to handle this, but he was also weak. A heavy cross also meant that your endurance was high, high enough to carry it through life's journey. But that only came from spending time with God, and letting His strength hold you in your weakness.

"I'm sorry, Eli," I said slowly. "I don't know what I was saying or thinking."

He didn't speak for a while. He exhaled sharply and looked up at me. "It's alright, X. I know it seems like I don't care. I just have a hard time showing my emotions."

"Really?" I asked as I sat beside him. He passed me the blanket back and I wrapped it around my shoulders.

"Yeah. Carly used to tell me all the time that she couldn't grieve around me after our parents died because I never cried. I guess for her it seemed weird to be the only one crying over the loss."

"I think that's a little different."

Eli snorted. "I know it's weird."

"Sorry."

He waved a hand with a sigh. "I'm just glad I didn't lose Carly too."

"Yeah." I agreed. "I'm glad she's going to be okay."

PART II

Two years later
(Senior Year)

27

Who Is Your Helper?

Xavier

"X! Can you cover for me?" Daisy asked as I leaned against the wall, picking dough and other sticky things off my smock.

"Right now? We're in the middle of a shift."

"I know," she pleaded, "but I've got to get this now or I'll never get the preorder deal!"

"Fine." I rolled my eyes as I pushed off the wall. "But you owe me."

"Yes! Of course!" She skirted off to the back and hunkered down with her phone. Daisy was an avid gamer. Today was the preorder date of some new game she'd been telling all of the café about since the game released its first trailer. The game seemed interesting, but I didn't care that much, not as much as Daisy.

We'd gotten close since I started working here two years ago. I got the job after God blessed me to save Carly from that accident. Eli was so thankful, he was willing to let me stay with him forever—for free. Unfortunately, Carly wasn't as thankful. When she was released from

240

the hospital, she left without contacting anyone. She was eighteen and an orphan, she didn't have to tell anyone when she'd gotten out. So she didn't. And she also didn't return home.

Eli gave me her room, I guess as a thank-you. But I wouldn't let him take care of me for free. Daisy helped me get hired at the café. It's good pay, even for parttime, but the catch is that we're worked like dogs. I've always got overtime which gives me up to twenty more hours added to my normal schedule, so I'm really working a full-time job during the summer.

Daisy was the best waitress at the café. Her girly looks and perkiness always charmed even the angriest of guests. She's a manager now but she works even harder than the rest of us. I like working here with Daisy. We started scheduling all our shifts together once she became a manager last year, and lately we've been spending time together outside of work and Bible Study.

She's a sweet girl who aspires for much more, and even though she doesn't want to get married, I'm hoping I can change her mind.

Work ended and Daisy and I walked home together. The sun was winding down, but it was summer, so it didn't fully set until after eight. We had plenty of daylight as we walked our normal route home. We never talked about much, but it was nice to be around her. I liked Daisy. I always thought she was cute, but now things have changed between us, and I think I want something more with her.

She's perfect, I thought as I watched her laugh until she turned bright pink at my joke. She threw a small hand over her mouth; pink glossed lips were smiling widely as she tried to regain her composure.

Maybe… I paused as I looked at her. I hadn't thought about anyone really in the past two years. I'd been trying to walk the straight and narrow. But maybe the season had come for me to finally fall in love. *Maybe this time—*

Daisy is not your helpmate.

I stopped walking abruptly, earning a raised brow in confusion from Daisy.

"X? You alright?"

"Yeah." I shrugged. "I was lost in thought."

"So, you weren't listening?"

"I was."

"Was not," she corrected. Her frown flipped quickly into her dainty smile, and she giggled as she grabbed my arm. "Come on, you should get home before the heat gets to you."

— 🌿 —

"Marriage can't be the goal," Eli said with his Bible open. This semester, he's been teaching us about dating and about not giving in to the pressures of society. "Many people think you've got sin in your life if you're still single by a certain age. They think marriage is a prize for the pure of heart and only those on a wayward path are still alone. But that's absolutely not true. Jesus tells us that some are called to being single." He shrugged. "Not everyone is called into singlehood, but some are."

"How will I know if I'm called to be single?" Marlo asked. Her dreads were pinned into a twist, where each dread looped over the other to make a pretty impressive bun.

"Matthew chapter nineteen and verse twelve tells us that some men had been eunuchs from birth, others were ordained eunuchs, and then some made themselves eunuchs for the purpose of the Kingdom." Eli crossed the room to give Marlo his full attention. "Being single is a calling that everyone has to answer because it is a time of growth. However, after that growth period is over, and you move on to the next stage, you have a choice. You can move on with a spouse, or without one."

"Then how can we be so sure that there's someone for us if some people *choose* to be single forever?"

"Ms. Joanna, you mentioned during our first Bible study together that you wanted to be married," Eli reminded her with a smile that made her blush.

"You remember that?" she asked softly.

Elijah looked stunned for a moment, as if to say, *'of course,'* but he only nodded. Our group had gotten close, but no one knew Eli like I did. How he was very close to God, and he kind of knew *everything* with the help of the Holy Spirit. I had never understood what it meant to be gifted with the wisdom of God until I met him.

"I feel like I might be special," Marlo joked, but Eli's sudden red cheeks and embarrassed grin made it seem like there was some truth to Marlo's words. But I knew there wasn't. Elijah was passionate about his work, which made Marlo's jokes embarrassing for him. The good thing was that she was the only one who ever joked that way. For whatever reason, Eli never told her to stop. But he also never encouraged her.

"You are *all* very special to me," Eli said as he turned to the group. "Which will help you understand just how much more you mean to God. I remember that Marlo wants to get married, and I also know that Daisy doesn't want to get married, and even though Tracy and Julius are no longer with us, I remember their stances on marriage and some things they felt passionate about during our class time." He crossed the room again to stand by his stool as he flipped through his Bible.

I remembered when Tracy left. She'd gotten a job opportunity which would begin during our last year of college, so she moved out to the area to spend senior year at a college funded by the company she'd be working for. Julius left our junior year. There an accelerated program for his masters, so he switched schools and went across the country to southern Texas.

"Your Father in heaven takes care of the birds and the flowers." Eli looked around at all of us. "How much more will he do for you? God knows our hearts. He knows who's going to want to be single, and who's going to want marriage. He knows what's best for us and how to take care of us. He already planned everything out. So we don't have to worry if we think we want to be married today, but in the next three years we realize we want to be eunuchs."

We all laughed together with Elijah as he closed his Bible. "Like I said before, marriage cannot be your end goal. If, right now, you're thinking that marriage is the final step, that marriage is what'll bring you the happiness you don't have right now, then you're not ready for marriage."

"Isn't marriage a gift, though? It's supposed to make us happy," Kevin asked.

I was seriously surprised he'd stayed in the group, considering how much he'd always challenged Eli. But Pastor Ross always took his questions and comments in stride, and never let Kevin ruffle him.

"It is a gift, and it can bring happiness," Eli replied. "Marriage is a gift for your work. But your work doesn't stop because you get married. Your work continues and even *deepens*. Being married means double the laborers in the field, which indicates an expansion in your work."

Daytona raised a hand. "Is that why men used to work or trade for the woman they wanted to marry?"

"Yes." Eli nodded. "A woman's job was to bear children and raise those kids to take over the estate or the farm. So, men paid for a woman with cattle and jewels because they were taking a laborer from that family's field and adding her to their own fields. Some women even came with land, so the man who was asking for her hand in marriage would pay a hefty price for her."

"God paid for us too, didn't He?" Sky asked beside me. He seemed a little teary eyed by that, but I was in no position to point that out. My life had been full of tears, an emotional rollercoaster for all of college. Learning to trust God, walking away from things, losing friends and people, it was all so overwhelming. But I learned that every burden was carried by Christ, and my tears eventually turned into tears of gladness, not just pain.

"He paid the ultimate price for us," Eli said.

I sat on my bed, staring at the wall. I thought about what Eli said about marriage not being the end goal. Maybe that was why I wasn't with anyone yet. Maybe I'd been seeing marriage through a tunnel and not as a picture.

Marriage was an enlargement; it was an expansion for the Kingdom of God. Which meant that you had to have something to enlarge, which is why we have to know our calling before we find that special person. And why you must have your own source of joy, your own source of love to share. Everything in a marriage is shared, even emotions, but if yours are broken, then there's no way to share a thing. If your source isn't Christ, then there's also no way to share anything.

Rubbing my hands over my face, I exhaled heavily. All the thoughts of sharing, expansion, and marriage were making my head hurt. I just wanted a wife. I wanted someone to share my life with. So far though, Carly was a no, and now it's a no to Daisy.

Carly had her own problems, but Daisy was literally perfect. I didn't want to understand, but everything Eli had taught us was filling my head and I couldn't ignore it, not like how I had with Carly and nearly died of a broken heart.

As scary and as lonely as that time was, getting over Carly, I still wanted Daisy, despite the no. God always had a good reason for His answer, even the answers we didn't want to accept. But we had to.

Elijah taught us that what really prepares us for marriage is accepting God's will, and the only way to do that was to fully submit to Him. I was having a hard time submitting. It was way easier said than done when I was basically dating Daisy already.

What was wrong with putting a title on it?

You'll become too attached.

I jumped at His voice, standing abruptly to my feet. God didn't always answer, and sometimes I didn't know for certain if what I'd heard was Him, but when it came to dating, God had been clear.

I stood there a moment, trying to ignore the fact that dating Daisy wouldn't be innocent for me. I would become attached and be just as brokenhearted when God's Voice never changed and His answer was still no to Daisy being my wife. Sighing, struggling to formulate my own response, the phone rang and caught my attention.

"Hey, Mom," I said as I answered.

"Well, if you're glum now you'll definitely hate what I have to say."

"Sorry, I'm just…" I ran a hand over my hair before flopping onto the bed, "I don't know why God keeps rejecting every girl I like."

"Maybe you just keep liking the wrong girls."

"I don't know how. They're girly, and polite. They've been Christian. I don't get it."

"I've told you before that just because someone's Christian doesn't mean they're *the one*. You've got to let God do His work."

"Of course, you can say that." I laid back and sighed. "It's easy for you, Mom. You're married already. You've got everything."

She cleared her throat. "Do you know what your name means?"

"What?"

"Your name, do you know what it means?"

"What does this have to do with—"

"In Arabic, it means 'new house.'"

246

"Okay?"

"Names mean something, Xavier. They're part of us in some way. I knew that, and I had a name for you, but I let your father choose your name when you were born. We weren't really Christian, so he picked a name he liked."

"Why does this matter?"

"Because the name I had for you was from God. He showed me in a dream; I was holding a baby boy and a name was whispered to me. But I ignored the dream so that your father could be happy." I could hear her adjusting the phone on her shoulder like she always did when she was talking and working. "I valued your father over God, though, in my defense, I still didn't know Him very well. Not well enough to be as certain as I am now that that was His Voice in my dream. But I didn't even consider asking about that dream. We'd been going to church here and there, but no real commitment." She sighed.

I scratched my head, still trying to figure out where exactly she was going with this when she said, "Your wife will need to be strong enough to choose God over you. She'll have to trust God in order to trust her husband. These young women you've been interested in may not be strong enough to do that in the long run. And just because they're girly doesn't mean anything, X. That's a preference."

I was sitting up now, clutching the phone against my ear. "Oh," I managed.

Mom chuckled on the other end. "That's just a little piece of information to keep in the back of your head."

"I will," I said.

"Well, I have to go, Xavier, but I needed to tell you something."

"What is it?"

"Special Agent De Luca called, there's been a trial date set."

I slowly closed my eyes. "When is it?"

"April."

247

"I'm going to have to testify, aren't I?"

"That's what she said. But you knew that when they brought you in last month and you had to meet with the prosecutors. They told you there was a possibility you'd have to testify if they couldn't catch up with that Adeline girl."

"MJ," I whispered. I hadn't seen her since the accident our freshmen year. She disappeared from the hospital and even Carly said she didn't know where MJ had gone before she too disappeared. Neither of them ever told the story of what'd happened the day of the accident. When everything was over, Carly left without a word. She contacted Eli weeks later and told him she was in Springfield and had joined a Christian retreat group for those wanting to reconnect with God away from the rest of the world. No one's heard from her or MJ since.

I hoped they were safe. I'd even prayed for Jocelyn, hoping that one day I'd see her again. I hadn't heard from her since that time she'd vomited out in front of the church.

"X? You still there?"

"Yeah," I said as my drowning thoughts dispersed.

"I know it's hard, Xavier, but once this is over, you'll be done for good."

"Yeah," I repeated.

"I'm sorry, honey," she said.

"Yeah… me too."

— ❧ —

Two weeks later, I had another one of those dreams and woke up screaming for Adar again. Before I could even register what'd been said, Elijah burst into my room and flicked on the lights. There was a panicked expression on his face as he stared at me. We sat in this awkward moment for longer than I would've liked. Finally, though, Eli broke the silence and asked, "Who's Adar? This is the fourth night in a row, the second *week* in a row that you've woken up like this. What is going on?"

Eli told me each dream was the same every time. I scream for Adar and then I can't remember anything. I told him I'm not sure where it's coming from, but I've been lying. I just haven't wanted to talk about it. I don't want to talk about anything. Ever since Mom told me a trial date had been set, I'd been avoiding talking to everyone. At Bible Study, at work, even once classes started, I didn't participate in the icebreakers. I gave my name and told my professor I had a very private life. It was enough for her to back off, but the way her brow ticked up in disbelief was noted.

"I … I've been having these dreams."

"No kidding," Eli said as he sat down at the desk. His glasses were gone, and his handsome features weren't hidden behind his sloppy blond bangs as he watched me attentively. Elijah had become more of a brother to me while we still somehow maintained that counsellor and patient relationship. It was odd but it worked for us.

"It's like I'm dreaming about something and when I first wake up, I can almost remember things, but when I realize I'm awake it's like I can't remember anything anymore."

"Well, clearly you're dreaming about Adar," Eli said with folded arms.

"I know. MJ told me once that I called her Adar when I woke up."

He raised a brow and I waved frantically. I didn't realize how that little detail would sound until I said it aloud.

"No, not like that. I fell asleep outside your office once, and when MJ woke me up, I called her Adar."

"Right," he said flatly.

"I'm serious, she's… you know," I shrugged.

"Gay?"

"Yeah." I glanced away.

He sighed. "I know."

"Oh." I folded my hands in my lap and waited for him to speak again.

"I can't tell you what she and I have discussed in our time together, so how about you tell me a little more about the dreams you can't remember."

"Well, Adar's the only name I can remember, and for whatever reason, I'm certain it's a name, not a *thing*, not a *place*. Adar's a..." I paused, trying to search my thoughts, "she's a woman. I'm sure of it."

"Alright. Adar's a woman. Anything else?"

I shifted uncomfortably. "I've never really talked about it, so I don't know."

"Maybe talking about these dreams will help you figure things out."

"How, when I can't even remember them?"

"You just remembered Adar was a woman. Try thinking of something else."

I sat forward, resting my elbows on my knees, I closed my eyes to think. Images were resurfacing in my mind. "A woman, and she's standing in some kind of fire field, or flower field, but it's all red. But I feel like..." I opened my eyes, "I feel like I love her."

"Or *will* love her."

I raised a brow, and he casually lifted a shoulder in response. "Our lives are predestined. God determined long ago that there would be an Xavier Miles today, waking up from these dreams."

"I don't believe that." I folded my arms. "There's no way God would predestine bad things to happen."

"He predestined for Jesus to be brutally beaten, stripped of all His clothes, and die a criminal's death, though He was innocent." Eli shrugged nonchalantly. "And to make it a little sweeter, He let Jesus have

250

a good life. Make friends. Enjoy His work so much that He didn't want to leave. And then Jesus had to die, had to give up those friends. So, give me a better reason why you don't believe in predestination."

I gulped. "Well, God gave us free will, so there's no way we can make choices if it's already planned out."

"We are allowed to make choices, but God already knows the choices we're going to make."

"So why does He let us make these choices then?"

"Because He wants every opportunity to prove to us that He's God and we're not. So every time something bad happens, God can get the glory for rescuing you. And every time something good happens, He can get the glory for blessing you."

"All He wants is praise, isn't that a little…"

"You want to say selfish, but you can't when He gave up Jesus, knowing you'd sit here on this day, thinking God was selfish."

"I'm sorry." I hung my head. "I'm just apprehensive about predestination. That means there's nothing I can do to change myself, doesn't it?"

"Though it has been planned for some dishes to be tossed away and others to be preserved, every dish is made to serve. Which means every dish has a chance to be used. God gives everyone a chance, even though He knows some of us won't take it."

"So why create us then? Why allow us to come to Earth just to be sent to Hell?"

"Because He's fair and just."

"How?" I wanted to scream, but my voice came out weak and soft. "How can that be fair? If He's all knowing, shouldn't He just keep us from coming to Earth?"

"God *is* all knowing," Eli corrected sternly, and I looked away from his piercing gaze. "And in His wisdom and knowledge, God being all knowing allows those of us who will turn from Him to come to Earth."

251

"But my question is, why?"

"Is it fair to only let the ones who won't give up on God be tempted and tried? That's not fair to make them go through that but no one else. The point of free will is the basis of God's justice. You may be a sinner, but God will always give you the chance to be saved."

"So, you're saying that by sending us to Earth, God is abiding by His own rules of justice? Earth is God's way of being fair." I stopped to think it over, but I found myself mumbling aloud anyway. "We're sent here, though we may not make it back, because God is bound by His Word. He's bound by His laws of justice, so giving everyone a fair chance at life is actually justice and free will."

Eli leaned forward and patted my knee. "There you go."

I sighed. "So, predestination *is* real."

"In every aspect, even in who we'll marry. Maybe this Adar girl is your wife."

"No way." I shrugged, but for some reason, I wanted to agree with Eli. "Well ... Maybe she is…"

28

A Death in the Family

Madeline

I told him my parents were dead because they are. To me. When my sister passed away, I was blamed by my own parents. And when my grandmother asked me why I ran away, I was blamed then too. It was an endless cycle I never thought I'd get out of. So I disappeared. I was too much of a coward to die, but too lonely to live, so I became someone else. I became the only other person I could be, my identical twin sister.

Madeline Jones, my sister, my very best friend, committed suicide when we were in high school. She loved Mary-Jane Watson from Spiderman. She claimed that one day she would find her own Peter Parker in high school, and went full blown crazy, dyeing her hair fire engine red, and flirting with all the nerds in school. Of course, she was beautiful, and nerds weren't the only ones giving her attention.

Everyone loved MJ. They adored her. She was friendly, outgoing, and apparently, she was good in bed. I was quite the opposite, though. Brown hair, an introvert, heavyset, a virgin. We were twins, but there was always an ugly twin, or a fat twin. I wasn't ugly, but I was definitely bigger than my sister.

Eventually though, things mellowed out and I began to lose weight. But that didn't matter. I wasn't flaunting fire engine red hair and sleeping with the football team … or basketball team … or the baseball team. So no one cared.

It seemed like my sister and I were worlds apart. We were truly night and day. Naturally, I was night, the quietness surrounding the world as darkness hung over. But Madeline, she was absolutely the day. Burning so brightly like the sun, she could cause a heat wave, and everyone would still rush to be washed in her rays. But when you stand in the sun for too long, you get heat exhaustion. People get frustrated when they're overheated. Arguments break out, and before you know it, everyone's wishing the sun and its sweltering heat would go away.

That's exactly what happened to Madeline.

There was never a time I doubted my sister when she came to me crying that she'd been raped. They say that twins are connected, and we sometimes feel things the other feels, and I believe that. The night my sister was assaulted, I was at a friend's house. But out of nowhere, it felt like someone had touched me. It left the hairs on the back of my neck standing on end, and I was filled with horrible discomfort all night.

I couldn't sleep at all. I sat in one spot, gripping a pillow, crying, and wishing for someone to save me. It was the oddest thing, but when I left my friend's house later that night—after I couldn't take the overwhelming fear—I realized my sister and I were closer than I thought.

Our parents were out of town for the weekend, so I went to the station with MJ. She gave a statement to the police and an investigation was supposed to be launched, but it got twisted into something else—into that heat exhaustion I mentioned earlier.

MJ was the sun, sizzling the entire Earth, but when you're always so bright, people get jealous. They become exhausted, and the first opportunity for a cloud to block out the sun, they welcome it. The girls at our school were vicious with rumors. Suddenly my sister wasn't the joy of the school, she was the slut of it. A reputation she didn't earn alone. But no one ever called out the boys who helped give her that name. Then again, they never do.

The boys were protected. They were basketball players and football players and baseball players. The stars of the school. While they shined, the rest of us stood back and watched my sister's light wink out like a dying star.

Home life had already been miserable for my sister, which was why she wanted attention. Our parents did everything they could to show me that I was as beautiful as she was. They would buy me things and not her, take me places when Madeline was busy. They doted on me.

Their attention was only meant to be an innocent confidence boost, but it quickly turned into a dark pit of neglect for Madeline. Despite that, we grew close because of it. She tried not to let it bother her, but I saw the way she beamed when our parents paid attention to her. I saw the way she hugged our mother, as if each hug was the last hug. It was sad to watch, and it became unbearable when she began to wither like a rose. But like I said, twins share things, and when Madeline had faded away completely, I began to as well.

Adeline Jones was a withered rose. My thorns had been clipped by our parents, and I had no way to defend myself against the predators of life. Roses blossom and are picked because of their beauty, and I was no different. I blossomed and was picked, but there was nothing left to start the life of the next rose in my absence.

I began hating myself, and I wanted to be done with the world. But I was just as weak as Madeline. She wasn't strong enough to stand against the turmoil and the rumors, so she committed suicide.

I was afraid to die, I was too weak to rid the world of myself, but that wasn't necessarily a *weakness*, I guess. I don't praise my sister for what she did, I believe there's always another way to overcome your troubles. I just haven't found it yet.

Starting over, that's what I named my freshmen year of college. I wanted to give Madeline another chance because Adeline had run out of life. When my sister died, the love my parents had for me ceased. My father began drinking because the case had ruined his career. His daughter was a lying, suicidal maniac. His daughter was the loose girl of the school. None of that looked good for the dean of a prestigious college. He stepped down and picked up a bottle. The alcohol made him abusive in more ways than just physical.

I should've been by my sister's side—that's what my parents told me. They were projecting their own feelings onto me because I was there and that's what made things so hard for me. I was with Madeline every day, and I even though she was getting a little stronger. Her suicide was just as surprising for me as it was for my parents. But they didn't care enough to ask me how I felt. I was somehow their punching bag, whether physically, or emotionally, and I was losing my mind.

The last night I spent at my parents' house, my father came onto me. He wasn't in a drunken stupor; he didn't reek of alcohol like usual. He came into my bedroom and told me what he wanted. When I refused, he tried to take it, but I got away.

My grandmother was good to me until I finally told her why I ran away. How dare I accuse my father, her *son*, of doing something so outrageous. That was her complaint. But since my parents wouldn't take me back, I spent the last two years of high school in a shell looking for happiness. I tried to get out of that shell, to shed the old skin. I even applied to college and got accepted. I went out, trying to force high school into my past, but history repeats itself, and the past is only ever a second away.

The night I went out with my friends, I was assaulted. Just like my sister had been. And I wasn't strong enough to fight back, like my sister.

My attacker was stronger than me. And he enjoyed using his strength to overpower me. I didn't think it would ever end. I fought for as long as I could, but eventually I went numb. I lay there, letting the last part of me drift away. I wanted to hold on to the bit of Adeline Jones I had left, but she was taken from me, by the same man who'd taken Madeline.

When he finished, he lay beside me and told me about how much I reminded him of Madeline. He told me he'd loved her more than anything, and he missed her. He was hoping I could replace her, but no one compared to my sister, not even her identical twin.

Suddenly, it was clear to me that I wasn't even good enough to my own rapist. My sister was the twin everyone wanted. They got shortchanged with me.

When I went home that night, I packed my bags and headed for New York. I forgot my locks of brown, purchased a fire engine red wig, and disappeared.

Adeline Jones had officially died.

29

My Attempt

Madeline

I raced through the night, carrying Jay who was thin as a rail now. Her bony arms, her ribcage showing, Jay had wilted just like my sister, just like Carly, just like me. I couldn't save anyone, but Jay had been too good for me to not be successful this time. I loved her, but not in the way everyone thought I did. I loved Jay because she knew the truth.

"Madeline, right?"

I nodded.

"Jocelyn," she extended a honey-toned hand, "but you can just call me Jay."

"Nice to meet you," I said as I shook her hand.

"So, we're roommates which means we're best friends now."

I blinked. "Okay."

"You know anyone here?"

"No, I just got here." I tried to sound nonchalant so she wouldn't ask about my past. I hadn't thought much about how to explain who I was. I convinced the administration office that I preferred to be called Madeline. It was easy to do since they had a *don't ask, don't tell* policy. That meant my real identity was washed and I would be Madeline Jones, a registered student.

Everything went smoother than I had expected. Convincing the school, and even the bankers in New York was easy. Their offices had to be professional; they couldn't question why I preferred a different name. For all they knew, I was a confused girl transitioning into whoever I believed I was meant to be. Thanks to that, the offices took my name, Adeline Jones, on paper but my account name was under Madeline Jones. I could be whoever I wanted to be if I was transitioning. Of course, I wasn't, but they didn't need to know that. But I digress. Convincing someone who didn't have to be professional or risk losing their job, their income, their status, was totally different.

"Must be so nice," Jay almost whined. "I've been in the Big Apple all my life, but at least this school is new for me. I felt like I was being squeezed, stuck here in a bustling city. It'd be nice to actually have an identity, I just feel like I don't exist sometimes."

"Yeah," I said as I unpacked one of my notebooks. "I know what you mean."

Jay appeared beside me and looked over my notebook before she asked, "Who's Adeline?"

I clutched the notebook to my chest and backed away.

"Calm down," she waved. "I don't care if you're Adeline Jones or Madeline Jones." She shrugged. "You've gotta do what you need to do to be happy, and I'm not getting in the way of that."

That was the first time anyone had been concerned for my own happiness in two and a half long years and that changed me.

They call us queer because we're weird for being unhappy. So unhappy that we want to be someone else. But we call ourselves gay because we don't want anyone to know that we're so miserable.

Being gay is supposed to make you happy. You go around being the total opposite to the natural way of society, and it honestly makes you kind of feel good about yourself. You're finally standing up for yourself. You're different and, for once, it's okay to be weird or queer.

Being queer becomes good because you're not like everyone else. You're not stuck in a gender, or the frame of what society tells you is okay. For once, you're telling society what to do. You're telling all the world to accept you, and if they don't, they're penalized. Now, every single time someone doesn't like you, hurt you, or makes you cry, they are repaid by the cruel world. They are the ones at the sharp end of the stick now, getting stabbed by the ever-changing views of our world.

Being a homosexual meant I got to sit on the world and dictate to it what was an offense and what wasn't, because I was the only one who understood myself. Even in the gay community, we tell each other that we understand each other, we accept each other, because we've been so hurt. But we only understand the pain that brought us all here, not anything more.

We get that something pushed us over the edge, and as we dangled by a thread, all we really wanted was happiness. But, if Madeline was the light in the day, that meant I was the darkness in the night, and everyone like me was too.

Feeling in the dark, you can't see anything. You're so afraid for the light to come on that even though it's pitch black, you still close your eyes in case there's a spark somewhere in the distance.

I'll tell you a secret though. We're always searching for the light, we just hate to be burned. Stepping into the light for the first time always burns. We don't want that because that's why we're here. We've been hurt so badly before; the consuming darkness of this predatory world was easier to slip into because no one can see anything or feel anything.

They can't see that we're unhappy, they can't see that we're losing our minds, they can't see that we're worse off here than where we were before. No one can see the other person scrambling for the light. But we can hear it when the match is struck, when the flint and steel are sparked, and we can hear it when we begin to run for the light... So we don't. Our pride gets in the way, and we stay in that darkness, letting the moments of happiness that spring up every now and then, strap us in and keep us there.

We feel nothing but regret and anger. We miss the way things used to be, but we don't want to be ostracized from the only people who've ever accepted us. And for some, they came to this realm seeking something, but they just don't know what. They weren't bullied, or mistreated, they came over because they were told they should. They were told there was something to gain, but no one ever tells the truth. Not in this world.

We lie because we're still looking to hurt those who've hurt us. We lie because we're empty, and we hope you are too. We tell everyone we're happy, hoping that it'll affect the ones who pushed us here. But it never does, and we can't get over ourselves. We can't forgive those from the past, or bear to face the present or the future. So, we hide behind being different, forcing our acceptance onto others because, for once, it feels like everything is alright.

Jay and I had become lovers by accident. She didn't care that I didn't even know who I was. She loved me because I needed her, and she just wanted to be needed, to be cared about. And every night we slept

261

together, I never once thought of the man who'd taken Adeline from me. I didn't feel his hands on me, I didn't feel his weight crushing me. Jay was gentle with me, caressing me, telling me how much she loved me.

How could I give that up? Was it wrong to be in love with Jay because I was a woman, and she was too? But I already knew the answer. It was wrong because of the natural order of things, or so someone had told me when I asked them why I felt conflicted about being with Jay.

Eli Ross, my counsellor, explained that whoever told me my conviction came from the natural order of things was only *partially* right. He told me that the only reason why natural order was convicting me was because God created it. He decided what would be 'natural' and then wrote it on the tablets of our hearts.

He gave us insight before we were even coherent on what was wrong and what was right, and every time we kicked against that, the carvings in those tablets were etched a little deeper.

That was the first time I was exposed to God. When I asked Eli why he risked his job and told me about Him, he smiled. It was so radiant that I broke into tears. He told me that there was something stirring in me, and if I let God in, He would change things for me.

I wasn't going to until his little sister entered the picture.

Carly Ross was like Matthew Leslie. What she wanted; she took. She wanted me, and she took me. Initially, I was fond of her as a friend. I even pitied her when she told Jay and me about her parents, and about her brother. Mr. Ross had been nothing but kind to me, and I had a hard time believing her allegations of cruelty about him, but I said nothing. I listened, and when she finished, Jay comforted her. But she wasn't there for Jay, she was there for me. A girl who didn't weigh more than me had felt just as heavy, if not heavier than Matt. But I didn't know what to do besides give in. If I resisted, she'd be able to tell, and I didn't know how she would react.

And then there was Jay, who wasn't really in love with me like I thought, but I wasn't offended. I was tired of kissing her, sleeping with her. I'd truly begun to see her as a sister, and it just so happened that a crush knocked her right off her queer feet.

He was handsome. Broad shoulders, tanned skin, hazel eyes, and dark curls that faded into a sexy haircut. Xavier Miles… he was Matt's best friend, and when he first reentered my life, I was afraid of him. On my way out of Cali, I'd heard on the news that he and Matt had been in a terrible accident.

At the time, I didn't really care, had even thought they deserved it. Right up until he appeared at school. Like a gentle breeze on a summer night, the past had returned. But this time, the past returned like most of history—without a memory. History only retells what the world needs us to know, not all of it, and certainly not the truth of it. It seemed like the same had happened to Xavier; he had only been left with need-to-know information.

"Where are we going?" Jay whispered as I set her down to rest. The sound of her voice snapped me from my thoughts and memories. We'd been running blindly through the night, something we'd been doing more and more often these days. We had no home, we had no friends, we had nothing but each other. That was about to change too.

Jay was sick. She's been sick for the last two years—back when we were still in college. But I can't take it anymore, she can't take it anymore. The drugs, the alcohol, the hard life we lived. Jay needed help but wouldn't take it, so I was improvising. Getting her the help she needed the only way I knew how.

"I'm getting you help," I told her.

She blinked at me weakly. "What about you?"

"I'll be alright."

She reached up and gently caressed my cheek. "No one has ever loved me the way you have, Adeline."

263

I fought tears as I watched her hand retract to her side. She wasn't dying, but this was certainly goodbye for us. We'd been through so much from Carly, to dropping out of school, to now. We were only in this mess because of Carly.

Jay and I visited a gay club not far from campus quite often, some of the people we knew would come by the campus to hang with other members of the club and to hang out with Carly. She'd known a few of them from the previous year; they always claimed to be students needing tutoring which was the cover for them to get on campus. A guy named Kasey had been selling weed to our campus and would let his guys have fun with the students. Carly had too much fun and that became our downfall. Our reason for running through the night looking for help.

Jay and I had always stayed away from the heavy drugs until Carly got involved. The year before, she'd only gotten a taste of what pills could make you feel, and she had committed that to memory. When these guys came back around, she wanted to do everything, and she wouldn't do it alone.

Jay had always been outgoing and was a daredevil, so she followed Carly's lead—because whatever Carly wanted, she got it, or she took it.

Carly didn't get addicted to the drugs, Jay did though, and there wasn't anything I could do for her. The withdrawals were too hard to watch, and I caved every time she asked me to get her a fix. Eventually, when Carly left and I made it home from that wretched car accident, Jocelyn got mixed up with some dealers, and we ended up spending the next two years paying off debts the only way we knew how.

We had no money to offer. No drugs to trade. So we gave them ourselves. The nights were no longer full of parties and fun. They were full of pain and misery. Jay was hardly recognizable. I was hardly recognizable. That's when I began to pray. I will never forget the night I whispered a prayer to God, just to rescue Jay... and He answered. The following day, I caught a glimpse of a familiar boy, the one Jay was in

264

love with, Xavier Miles. It was late, and he was walking home, wearing a uniform from that diner up the street.

I hadn't seen Xavier in two years, since the day he saved Carly's life by cutting her loose from the car she'd crashed. The accident had been my fault, but Xavier didn't know that. He didn't know anything—nothing about the drugs or the alcohol or us selling our own bodies. But I doubted that would make a difference. Xavier was a good man. He would have helped Jay no matter what.

That's why I started planning right away. Finding a way to get him to help me save Jocelyn, the last withered rose.

30

Taking Out the Trash

Xavier

Daisy went home before me today, like she always did on Friday nights. I worked until nine and helped out a little with closing. The diner didn't actually close—it was open 24/7—but things slowed down a lot after ten. I usually wiped down the counters and bagged up all the trash for the day and dropped it at the dumpster on my way out.

Tonight was no different. I cleaned down the counters, bagged up the trash and wished everyone a goodnight as I left work. The bags were heavier today, but the weekends were always our busiest days, so I wasn't surprised.

Rounding the corner to the dumpster, I set the bags down to get the top open on the can, that's when I noticed a foot poking out from behind the garbage dump. I didn't see anyone as I glanced around. Shakily, I grabbed my phone from my pocket, and fumbled with it for the light as I got closer to the body.

I flashed it on, and nearly shrieked as I stepped back. The foot was

266

attached to a leg which was attached to a woman. She had sunken cheekbones and a frail body. She looked like she would stop breathing any second.

"Oh my goodness," I whispered as I leaned closer. The light shined right on her, and she sniffled, raising her head slowly to see me.

"Jay?" I didn't even know if I'd said her name aloud. But it didn't matter. Jocelyn was sitting there, frail and bruised, barely coherent. She was in the trash, like someone had thrown her out.

"Help!" I shouted as I shoved my phone back into my pocket to pick her up. "Help! Somebody, help me!" I was screaming it now as I raced back around the corner to the diner.

I burst inside, carrying Jay's mostly limp body. Her head hung over my arms, she looked deranged and sickly. Leathery skin, and a bony frame, just looking at her brought tears to my eyes.

"Help me!" I croaked, sucking in a sob that was trying to escape.

The entire diner erupted into chaos. Someone was shouting directions, another person was calling the police, and then there was someone else just screaming in the background.

"Okay," Jason, the night shift manager said, "I need you to put her on the table, okay? Where was she?"

"In the trash," I said as I laid her on a table. "She was just lying there, dying." My breaths were short, my words staccato.

"Do you know her?"

I nodded. "She went to my college. She stopped showing up one day, and I haven't seen her since then."

"Jason, we called the police," another coworker said.

He nodded. "Put everyone out. We'll reopen at midnight."

The coworker obliged but not before gawking at Jay, which made me snap, "What are you staring at!? She's a human being!"

"Xavier, calm down," Jason said.

"No! I just found my friend in the trash! Don't tell me to calm down!"

"I understand the weight of the situation, but I'm going to—"

"No, you *don't* understand! You have no idea what I'm going through!"

Jason held his hands up defensively, nodding as he took a step back. He was whispering something, but I didn't hear it, and I didn't try to. I burst into the sob I was holding in, gripping Jay's hand as I dropped to my knees beside the table.

"God, please do something. Save her, please!"

"X?"

My head snapped up, and I could see Jocelyn trying to open her eyes.

"Jocelyn!" I nearly screamed as I got to my feet again.

Slowly, she took a breath, parting her chapped lips to speak again. "Where am I?"

"At my job. Jay, you're going to be alright."

She grunted, a jagged smile etching onto her brittle skin. "She told me the same thing. I guess this was her plan."

"Whose plan?"

Her breathing became labored. I was shaking, and when she began to fade from consciousness again, I turned to the crowd of onlookers and yelled, "Where's the ambulance!?"

"They're almost here," Jason said. "Two minutes maybe."

"She can't wait." I grabbed Jay off the table and moved for the door.

"Where are you going!?" Jason shouted behind me.

"To meet the ambulance!"

"Xavier, listen to me. Even if you rush out there, you're still going to take two minutes to find the ambulance. It's better to just let her rest, too much movement might make her injuries worse."

I stared at Jay in my arms. She was nearly lifeless. I could still remember the bowling alley night … Thanksgiving. The way she'd teased me and drove me wild. The way she'd almost seduced me. She wasn't frail, she wasn't small. She had curves and slender legs. I was addicted to her body, the way it was so commanding. I was intrigued by her confidence, the way she knew I was hers. I was enamored with her beauty, the way her smile melted me. I never wanted to admit to it, but one wrong night, a time when I was sad, or unhappy, and I would've given myself to Jay.

She was hypnotic, but that's what I liked about her. I'd never encountered someone like her, and I haven't since then. But looking at her now, at her frail body, at her sunken cheeks. She wasn't even a shell of the woman I once knew.

"Just leave her on the table."

I came back to reality, nodding but never looking away from Jay. I carefully placed her back on the table as the police and the ambulance's wailing filled the room. They rushed in, pushing me back as I held her hand. I watched it slip from my own as she lay there breathing slowly. I pleaded with God in my heart for her to make it. I begged Him to give her a chance to make things right with Him. Jocelyn still had a place in my heart. She was everything I thought Lia Sunohara would be. She was like a sponge, soaking up all my anxiety about girls and trading it for comfort and confidence.

"Xavier!" Jason's voice got my attention.

The paramedics were hunched over the table, placing a breathing mask on Jay as another paramedic wheeled in a cart.

"X, the officer needs to speak with you," Jason said.

I looked over at the lady officer, feeling distraught.

"Just going to ask you a few questions about the girl—"

"Jocelyn," I corrected, "she's not just a girl."

"Of course. Can I have your name?"

"Xavier Miles."

"Alright, Xavier Miles, about what time did you find Jocelyn?"

"It was almost ten. I think."

She nodded as she wrote. "And where was she?"

"In … In the trash."

Her hand froze, but the next second, she nodded and kept writing. "And what happened after you found her?"

"I brought her into the diner."

"Did you see anyone? Or anything out of the norm?"

"No," I shook my head, "but Jocelyn woke up and said this was part of someone's plan."

"Did she say who?"

"No, she passed out again."

"Anything else you can remember?"

I shook my head as I watched them wheel her by. "Is she going to be okay?"

"They'll do their best."

31

The Unnatural

Madeline

I found my way back to the apartment complex before anyone woke up. This place had been our prison for two years. When Jocelyn got mixed up with the dealers, she developed a full-blown addiction. She only got 'mixed up' with these guys because she was trying to steal some products and had gotten caught. With no money, no skill, no nothing, my lover was suddenly their trick, and began to fall apart, just like my sister Madeline had.

I couldn't watch Jay wither away the way Madeline did. I couldn't let this world blot out the sun again. So, I asked for work. Of course, Jocelyn's much prettier than I am, so my work was different from hers. She slept around to help the guys make deals in exchange for a fix. She was so far gone, it didn't matter who she slept with—men or women. But I was only asked to count money for the most part, make sure they weren't duped. If they ever were, it would've been my skin. I didn't care what I had to do, but I kept a close eye on Jay until I finally mustered up the courage to get her out of there.

Coming back alone was the only relief I had. I knew that when they discovered Jay was missing, they'd go looking for her, but at least for now, no one knew where she was, and probably wouldn't know if Jay was smart and kept her head down. I was worried, but I watched her from across the way get carted onto an ambulance, so at the very least, she's getting the medical attention she needs. And finally, she'll be off the drugs.

I lay in bed, staring at the wall beside me. Jay and I stopped sharing a bed a while ago, I don't even remember the last time I really held Jay before last night. We were no longer lovers, but she truly became my sister, my lost sister.

We'd been separated most days. Sometimes I didn't see her for weeks at a time. She always returned more strung out than she'd left, but I was thankful she returned at all.

I sighed, pressing a hand to the wall. It was cool against my warm palm. I wondered if I would ever get away, if this was it for me. Maybe I deserved this for letting my sister get washed down the drain, getting Carly into an accident, and letting Jay slip into an addiction. Who knows.

"Aye!" Dagon, one of the guys who worked closest with Jay, called outside my door, "Wake up! That little slut is missing!"

I flinched at the word, *slut*. I remembered when my sister and I returned to school after the accusations were released that Matt Leslie had raped her. He came right up to us as we entered the building and shouted at Madeline. He called her all kinds of curse words, but I'll never forget the way he seethed *that* word between his teeth.

It was like fog rolling over a river, like if he opened his mouth fire would come out. I didn't understand how he could be so angry at the truth, but it didn't matter. That morning was always memorable, but not just because of Matt's outburst on Madeline, it was that he came alone to address her. It wasn't until later that day, when I saw Matt again, that

Xavier was with him. I always wondered why he chose not to be by Matt's side that morning.

Tossing the covers back, I hopped out of bed and rushed into the bathroom to clean up. It was dinky and small, but there was running water, and the toilet flushed, so I couldn't complain. As I made my way into the living room of the small apartment, I realized it was quiet all except for one voice.

The living room was filled with people, Dagon and his escort crew. Jorge and some other useless guys, and of course, Kasey, the leader of this little group. He was a tall lanky man, with no backbone. He was always worried sick about his money which made him aggressive and dangerous. If he didn't have the money to give to the main boss— someone I've never met before—he'd be killed and our whole operation would be over.

He was the same guy who sold drugs to college kids, but never really showed up to do the dirty work himself. Just sent word for his guys to sell to us, sleep with us, have parties to get us to buy more. As long as the money was rolling in, Kasey didn't care who he sold to.

You can't make people feel bad for selling drugs to others, because everyone who bought from Kasey or used his products were consenting adults. I wouldn't have even cared if Jocelyn hadn't been involved, if she hadn't gotten strung out. It's sad, things never really matter until they affect you. That is what's wrong with the world, we simply don't care.

Kasey was hammering the remote, turning up the volume on the television as everyone watched in silence. A few women dressed in ripped dresses, and fishnets were watching with hopeful eyes, while everyone else looked angry. Finally, turning my attention from the crowd to the television, I nearly fainted. A picture of Xavier was right next to Jay's. They were calling him a hero for saving this missing and sick girl.

I could've died. Kasey finding out who 'saved' Jay was the last thing I expected to happen. I didn't think that far, I didn't plan that far ahead.

I just wanted to get Jay to safety, but now I've realized I just put X's life in danger.

Xavier Miles had been good to everyone in my life. It was obvious he liked Jay, but even when he didn't know it, he was kind to her and loved Carly. He was kind to me, but most of all, X was kind to my sister. She mentioned him a few times whenever she'd spend the night at Matt's house. She and X loved Spiderman. He was the only person in class who knew exactly where the MJ quote on that sticker from her notebook was from. And even now, he still remembers that quote with a smile.

I wondered if Xavier ever remembered my sister, who would he remember her as? He was kind, and handsome. The only reason Madeline didn't claim him as her Peter Parker was because she was too busy with Goblin Junior, or rather, Matt Leslie.

Kasey swore loudly, pulling me from my thoughts. I could feel my eyes peeling back in surprise as he shot to his feet. I tried to remain calm as Kasey paced the floor.

He stopped abruptly, swiping thick red hair from his face as he shouted, "I'm going to kill him for taking our best girl!"

"Yeah!" the men shouted back.

"He thinks he can take from me and be a hero?"

"Yeah!"

"He can't!"

I was fading from the loud conversation, trying to think of something to say, something to do, when I was literally snatched back to reality.

"Hey!" Kasey was shouting at me as he shook my shoulders.

"Y-Yes?" I muttered. Sweat rolled down his head, he was always sweating from nerves.

"You're going to help me, aren't you, sweetie?" He raised his hand to my jaw, caressing my face like I was his. Jay had the attention of every other man except for Kasey. For some reason, Kasey was obsessed with me. I'd spent more nights with him than I care to share, though some nights he made me share them with another woman for his own pleasure. I did what he said without question or argument, and I think that's why he liked me. But I didn't obey because I enjoyed it. I obeyed because I was afraid for my life.

No part of me enjoyed this world I lived in. I wasn't actually compliant. I knew that being Kasey's girl meant I'd be safe, and that gave me the security I needed to figure out how to get Jay out of there.

"Help you do what?" I finally responded.

"Help me catch this little kid who thinks he can steal from me. You know how much money just went down the drain? I've gotta make that back."

I swallowed. "Do you really think beating him will make you money?"

He glanced up at the ceiling before dropping his cold eyes back to me with a smile. "I never even thought to rough him up. I was just going to capture him, bring him in and put him to work. But I think I'll give him a lesson first."

I didn't even get to react. He pressed his lips over mine sloppily, kissing me until he groaned, shoving me into the wall. "Do you see why I love you?" He pulled away, panting.

I looked away.

"Come on, sweetheart, I promise tonight I'll make it up to you. I know you hate the violence, but I can't let someone stomp on my turf. What will the guys think?" He turned my face to see him. A soft smile was there, but his eyes were greedy.

I nodded without a word, and his smile turned wicked.

"Good girl. Now I want you in my room all day, getting ready for me." He leaned closer. "I want you all night."

I raised my chin and took a breath as he leaned down and kissed my neck. The wetness of his kisses made me feel like a dog's chew toy, not someone's lover.

He pushed me against the wall a little harder. "I wanna take you right now."

"Please," I whispered as I looked at the men behind him, "not right here."

He grunted, pulling back. "Fine. Privacy. Don't worry about working today, alright? I just want you relaxing all day. Eat whatever you want, do whatever you want, I'll be back by six."

I almost jolted in surprise. "You're going to take him during the day?"

He shrugged. "I gotta send a message."

I tried not to panic as I took another shaky breath. His eyes narrowed on me, but I chewed my lip, like I was really trying to think of a way to help. Nervously, I asked, "How will you even find him? And it's dangerous during the day—"

He slapped a hand over my mouth, shoving my head into the wall. A pain swelled in the back of my head as he whispered, "You seem worried. You know this kid or something?"

I shook my head. Feeling the panic I'd been fighting clutching my chest.

"You'd better not," he warned. "I'll kill you if you're lying, and I don't want to do that." He moved his large hand to cover my nose and mouth. His eyes grew dark as he said, "Do you see how easy it would be to kill you?"

My nails dug into the wall behind me as he pressed harder against my face until I couldn't take it. I grabbed Kasey's arm, pleading with my eyes for air, as my chest tightened, and I began to tremble. He watched my eyes the entire time as I suffocated beneath his hand. I tried to fight, but I was feeling lightheaded, and I thought I'd pass out when he let me go. I fell to the floor, and I heaved deeply.

"Next time, I'll kill you," Kasey said as he stepped over me. The rest of his men followed behind him and I stayed there coughing and crying until I was all alone.

Even when I was alone, I couldn't stop crying. I didn't know if I was relieved to be alive, or angry I hadn't died. It didn't matter. Xavier's life was on the line now, and I had no time to think of my own.

Pulling myself together, I made my way to Kasey's bedroom. The only way I could save Xavier was by putting my own life on the line. All I needed to do was make one phone call to the police. Ask them to watch for an attack on Xavier's house, or the diner, but that meant giving up who I was. They'd want to know how I knew the plans of a gang affiliated group, and even if they gave me immunity for my information, the streets never would.

When I stepped inside the room, the bed rocked and the blankets shifted. "Kasey?" a woman with wild hair and bronze skin was lying in his bed, naked.

"Sorry," I said, closing the door behind myself, "it's just me."

"Madeline? Did he send you in here to entertain me?"

"No." I glanced around the room. Dominique was in love with Kasey, but Kasey didn't love her. He used her when he was angry with me, or too busy for me. Dominique served no purpose here except to please him. I'd never met someone who was so proud of that.

"Then why are you in here?" she asked.

"Because…" I paused as an idea came to me. Maybe I could make it out of this alive, maybe the blame didn't have to rest on me anymore. I moved to his dresser and ripped open the drawers.

"What are you doing?" Dominique snapped. "You're not supposed to go in there!"

All the phones we used were tapped so we couldn't call the police. But, if I could force Dominique to make the call, then I could possibly get away. I just needed something to blackmail her with… and I'd just found it.

In the top drawer under Kasey's clothes, hidden in the bottom hatch of the drawer was a safe. I took a breath as I reached inside. There was money in a plastic bag, but the coolness of an automatic made my fingers twitch.

"I'm going to get Kasey if you don't get out of there!" Dominique shouted at me.

I ignored her. Slipping my hand from the drawer, I rushed back to the door to listen. When I didn't hear anything, I moved to the bedroom window. Below, I could see Kasey and some guys laughing as they climbed into a truck. And when they pulled off, I sprang into action.

"I'm going to call Kasey," Dominique murmured as she scooted from the bed. She would've been faster if she wasn't naked and holding blankets to her chest, but it all worked in my favor.

"Don't move." I extended the gun from his drawer at her, and she stopped.

"What are you doing?" Her face strained and tears were ready on command.

"I want you to call the police. Right now."

"What?"

"Pick up the phone and call the police."

She glanced over at the cellphone on the bedside table. "You know I can't do that."

"You have to." My voice was trembling now.

"I can't—"

"Call the police!" I screamed.

"Okay! Okay! Please don't shoot me." She was crying now, and I felt my stomach turning flips. Even if I didn't get caught, Dominique would, and as I watched her trembling hands grab the phone, I stopped her. "Hold on," I said, "get dressed. Put some clothes on, we're getting out of here."

"What?"

"Do what I say or you're going to die!"

She nodded, moving from the bed to grab her clothes. Kasey had fits like this often, sending Dominique and I, or whatever other woman he was with, scrambling from his fury. I hated doing this to her because it'd been done to us for too long. Being on the opposite end of the barrel was supposed to feel good. But all I felt was guilt and pity for Dominique.

If I let Dominique take the fall, I'd be swallowed whole by the guilt, but Kasey would still come for me. He'd know I put her up to it when he returned and she was here, but I wasn't. I could make it look like a crime, make it look like a hostage situation, but I couldn't do that to Dominique. No one actually walks into this life willingly. Even if Dominique loved Kasey, she didn't belong here, nobody did.

I watched her slender legs step into her skirt. I was supposed to be focused when aiming a weapon. It wasn't really the time to be gawking at her physique, but I guess that's the only thing that was the same between Kasey and me when you're behind the gun; you can't help but notice the woman in front of you.

Trembling and scared, she looked so helpless, like she needed me… needed someone to comfort her. I wanted to lower the gun, to tell her that everything would be alright, and let her cave into me, but inside of my heart, it all felt wrong.

I'd gotten used to looking at women, being attracted to them. Watching Dominique dress herself was making my heart pump like crazy, and I knew I was a monster just like Kasey. You make someone feel small, less than you, and then you salivate for them because they're inferior to you. I wish I didn't feel like this. I didn't want to be like this anymore. I was getting out of control, heck, I'd *been* out of control.

I'd been in Dominique's position yet, I couldn't stop watching her dress herself. I couldn't stop myself from being the kind of person I've lived my life running from. The kind of person who took advantage of

279

the weak, preyed on the broken and insecure. Right now, I was no different from Kasey... and no different from Matt.

Taking a breath, I looked down at my feet. I didn't want to admit how out of control I'd gotten with my attraction and desire for women. When Jay started becoming more like a sister, and I stopped being forced into a relationship with Carly, I'd gotten lonely again. But there was woman after woman who was just as lonely as I was, and we made things work. Even Dominique. She loved Kasey, and Kasey liked me, but when the two weren't getting along, I was suddenly both their love interest.

I didn't like Kasey so much, but Dominique was different. She had round hips, full breasts, and could be really nice. I secretly began to like her company, and standing here now, I wanted to keep looking at her as thoughts of her raced through my mind. But that force of nature, or *God*, was knocking on my heart, and telling me everything inside of me was wrong. Looking at her like that was wrong. I needed help.

When she finally pulled a shirt over her bare breasts, I looked up at her face. She cowered as I clutched the gun.

"Find a bag or something and dump all the money from the drawer in it, and then call the police."

"Why? Why are you doing this?" she asked.

"Because I have to save someone else."

"What about Kasey?"

"I don't have time for Kasey!" I shoved the gun at her, and she screamed, dropping to the floor with her hands raised.

"Get the bag!" I shouted.

She moved, racing to the closet, and digging through it. She emerged with a bag and dug through the drawer until she felt the money. When she filled it, she went back to the bed and grabbed the phone.

"What do I say?"

"Tell them that Xavier Miles is in trouble. Either on a college campus, at his home, or at his work. I don't know which one they'll hit but…"

No, I thought, *they're going to the diner. College is closed and campus police would stop them. The news didn't release his home address, the only place they can go is the diner.*

"No," I started again, "tell them that they're going to the diner to hurt Xavier. And when they ask how you know, tell them you've been kept hostage here. You and one other girl."

I have to get to the diner…

"No." She shook her head. "Kasey will kill me."

"That's why you're going to take this bag of money and get away from the city. Go as far as you can, and never come back. Change your name, cut your hair, do whatever—"

"I love him," she whispered. "I love him so much."

"Dominique…" I sighed, feeling impatient but also heartbroken for her. "Kasey doesn't love anyone but himself."

"He loves you. He always has." Her eyes flicked over me, a very cold look growing in them. "But I don't know why."

"It doesn't matter why." I grew cold too, pointing the gun at her again. "Call the police."

"Why? I'm dead either way."

"You have a chance," I tried to sound convincing, "you can fall in love again. You don't have to suffer for love."

"But I'm not suffering now."

"Yes, you are. Every time he sleeps with someone else, you suffer. Every time he's with another woman and he neglects you, you suffer." I lowered the gun. "All the times we've been together, the tears you've shed over him." I shook my head, feeling indignant now. "He has never deserved your tears, Dominique. He's never loved you. What happens between you two is not love."

"What is it, then? Because it feels like love."

281

"It's not love, its domination! It's control! It's forced! There is no love in that!" I paused and almost chuckled. Who was I to speak on love? The very next thing I said was the gauntlet of my confusion. "It's not natural."

She was blinking at me, tears rolling down her cheeks.

"I got into something because I wanted to be loved, I wanted to feel happy, and I thought I was until I realized I wasn't. I'd just been using the few good moments to put bandages over all the bad ones," I said as I finally looked up at her. "But I haven't actually been happy in a very long time. The confusion I feel every time I look at a woman, and then at a man, the way my heart flutters when a girl looks beautiful, but my heart does nothing when I'm kissed by a man. It's wrong, and it's confusing."

"Why is it wrong? You can't help it." She shook her head. "You can't help who you fall for."

"Yes," I nodded, "you can. Because what you feel now, and what I felt then has been driven by something I've never addressed. A lack of attention. I just wanted someone to see me and not my sister for once, and the first person who did was a girl." Tears were rolling down my own cheeks. I wiped at them and raised my gun again. Unfortunately, I didn't have any more time to spare. I'd messed up, and X's life was on the line, I had to at least try to save him.

"Call the police right now. Or I'm going to call them and pretend to be you."

She raised the phone, a blank stare on her face. I think in that moment, she realized that there was a chance she didn't love Kasey.

32

Fair

Xavier

"Adar," Benedict whispered. She was standing at the edge of a cliff; the water below was so crisp and clear it made the precious stones trapped beneath the currents shimmer like diamonds. She stared at the world beyond the cliff, a chasm that separated them from those who had already conquered Earth.

"Michael told me that our Father does not send us without preparing us. All of the training we've gone through was for this moment."

"They've called you," his words were barely on his lips when Adar turned, the grass parted for her sudden movement.

"The space between our realm and theirs," she pointed toward the heavens, "is where we prove that God is real, and He is faithful."

"No." Benedict stepped forward. Adar had summoned him to the place where the rivers ran into space, and the realms stepped apart. This cliff was a rock, carved by angels as a last reminder of the solid foundation upon which the earthlings and all the world stands on. Only those ready for departure could come here, along with the ones summoned to make pleas to meet again.

"I'll find you." She laid a hand over the place where a heart would be knit for her. "I'll find you again, and when I do, we'll remember together."

"Wait!" Benedict began to panic, becoming more human by the second. His fears were setting in, becoming real. Anxiety had reached him. The matters of the Earth had touched him deeply, and though he had not been called yet, his human demeanor was an indication of how much time he had left.

"Let me go to Him who knows all," he pleaded. "Maybe He'll let me go too!"

"Everything has a time, and a place. Mine is now, and yours will be later." Adar took one step back, bringing her closer to the edge. In a moment, she would fall freely, letting the Realm transition her spirit into the earthen realm. When the transition was complete, she would be born into the world below.

"Please!" Benedict tried to move, but the vines beneath his feet were holding him in place. The Master had whispered to the vines long ago, setting them charge over the ones whose human emotions were strong. "I'm begging you, please don't go." He dropped to his knees, wishing he could dig his fingers into the dirt, wishing he could stop what was unfolding. But the plans of God were unstoppable.

Tears were swelling in Adar's eyes as she took one more breath of the realm around them. This was the last time she would be here, unless summoned by King David for the final battle. She had received her assignment, had seen the path her life would take, and had prepared herself to find Benny again. The only plea in her heart was that she would not face this world alone until she found Benny.

Groveling, Benny reached a hand forward, wishing to touch her just once more. She stared at his open hand, his trembling figure, and she reached forward and touched him. Their hands knit together, uniting them permanently as one spirit, one soul, and soon, one body.

"We will meet again," she whispered.

"Don't forget me," he hiccupped as the two embraced.

Pulling away, Adar got to her feet. "Look for me, Benny, and find me!" She turned quickly, the flowers turning away, the grass moving aside as she raced for the edge of the cliff. Reaching the tip, she whirled around, flailing her arms open and holding her breath, Adar tipped over into the abyss.

"Adar!"

— 🌿 —

I heaved, jerking out of my sleep. The white room became clear, and a beeping noise chimed around me.

"Where... am I?"

"X?"

I moved slowly, blinking at the blurry figure. She was leaning over me now, brown skin, dimpled cheeks. She looked familiar as her worried eyes watched me.

"Adar," I whispered. "I found you."

"Xavier," her hand was around mine now, "do you know where you are?"

The voice sounded familiar, the face looked familiar, but as her red hair fell loose from her ponytail, I realized I wasn't dreaming anymore.

"MJ?"

"Yes," she whispered in relief. "It's me, MJ."

"No." I shook my head as the blurriness cleared, and the grogginess faded. "You're Adeline."

She took a step back, her eyes wide with fear. The warmth of her hand had gone.

"Adeline." I tried to sit up, but my entire body ached; I felt like I'd been run over by a truck… twice. "No… Not Adeline. Who's Adeline?" I groaned in confusion.

She glanced around before grabbing something from the empty chair and moving for the door.

"Wait! Please! Don't go," I called, extending a hand across the bed.

She stood there a moment, clutching the door handle. As I stared at her, more of today's events surfaced in my head; the name Adeline was disappearing into my subconscious, and I could remember more clearly that the girl in front of me was Madeline. The past seemed so foggy; it didn't help that I'd already lost part of my memory from the accident.

"Please, I promise, I just want to ask something."

"What?" she said over her shoulder.

"What happened to me? Why am I in the hospital?"

Her hand loosened until it dropped to her side. Slowly, she turned and returned to the bed. Taking my hand that was still extended, she sighed. "Do you remember saving Jocelyn?"

I nodded—her name summoned a memory of the frail girl sitting in the garbage, and more memories returned as MJ continued.

"She was mixed up with some people, and they came after you."

I swallowed. "How'd you know? How'd you get here?"

She shrugged. "The news. But I got here as soon as I could."

I shook my head. "No—how did you know about Jocelyn, and who she's mixed up with? How do you know anything? What is going on?"

"Calm down," she said.

"No! Where have you been? Why did you disappear? Why…" my breath hitched, and a lump formed in my throat. My words became quieter as I said, "Why now?"

She pulled her hand from mine and backed toward the door. "I had to find you, I had to save you." Without another word, she opened the door and left.

My mind was clear again. I'd been jumped. I was on my way to work, though Jason had asked me not to come in. I couldn't sit around, I needed to do something other than worry about Jay. A car pulled up on the sidewalk, but I kept walking, little did I know … They were there for me.

It wasn't until they got out the car, and another pulled up with more men getting out that I realized something was wrong. Before I knew it, I was getting pummeled, but the faint cries of sirens in the background gave me hope. It seemed like hours before they scattered, trying to avoid the police. That's when everything began to fade.

I sighed at the memories. None of them told me why I'd called MJ Adeline besides the conversation with the detectives from Matt's case. Eli had told me that her paperwork said Adeline, but it felt strange, like I just couldn't believe it or didn't want to. However, that wasn't my real problem. After two years of not seeing MJ or Jocelyn, I saw them both in a matter of twenty-four hours, ended up in the hospital, and I called Madeline Adeline. If it wasn't for the soreness, I would've freaked out completely at the coincidence, but I settled for a deep groan as I tried to turn over.

A few hours later, Eli showed up with a change of clothes and food. "Hey," he said as he set the food on the little table beside me. "How are you feeling?"

"Sore." I tried to shrug.

"You look pretty bad," he said as he pulled a chair over. "A black eye, a couple of bruises on the face. They're only keeping you another day because you had a concussion and a bruised rib."

"Yeah, they told me after…" I paused.

"After what?"

"MJ was here," I said slowly. "She was here when I woke up, but I called her Adeline, and it made her leave. But she knew things about what'd happened to Jocelyn and who hurt me."

"Why would you call her Adeline?"

I groaned, turning away from him. "It doesn't matter." Really, what I meant was 'I don't know.' I said it without even thinking, had even thrown *myself* off. I vaguely remembered the name from the case, but the association was foggy when I tried to remember it past that.

"It does matter." Eli's voice was hot with annoyance. "It matters because your mother called me two weeks ago to thank me for helping you with the case. She said you'd been confiding in me." He crossed his arms. "You haven't said a thing. Now you're wrapped up in a gang retaliation, you're calling Madeline by another name, and you nearly called God selfish. Not to mention the dreams and how much talking you *haven't* been doing."

I looked over at him and he was scowling. He didn't do that often, but when he did, it was terrifying.

His normally calm face was twisted into an anger that made me feel incredibly guilty. "So, tell me what's wrong, or I'm going to call your mother and tell her that you're lying in a hospital bed," Eli threatened.

"Please," I sat up without thinking and fell back against the pillows in pain. If my mother found out I was in the hospital, she'd make me come home and I didn't want that. "It's just… the trial. They set a date, and I'll have to testify. I'll have to confess in front of the whole court to messages, evidence, all kinds of things. I don't know if I can do it right in front of him."

He sat back, his scowl disappearing. "Is it the messages and the evidence that bothers you, or is it seeing Matt?"

"I think it's both."

"Why both?"

"Because the evidence they have on him, some of it was from my own phone."

"But that's not really the root of the problem here."

I nodded. "It's evidence, Eli, that means he did it."

"Are you shocked, or did you think it would never catch up with him?"

"Matt always got what he wanted. I just feel like it's all my fault that he's in so much trouble. He's going to get a long sentence. Vehicular manslaughter ... sexual assault." I shrugged. "Driving under the influence. He's got a stack of things against him."

"Is God not just?"

"Is God not fair?" I snapped back.

"Are you saying that because you think it's unfair for Matt to be charged for the things he did?"

I gripped the blankets. "I don't know."

"You do. You'd charge another man, want him to go to prison, serve time for taking lives, and things that women can never get back. It just feels horrible because he's your friend."

"Yeah," I said.

Elijah sighed, rubbing a hand over his neck. "You remember the story of the golden calf?"

I thought for a moment. "Yeah, the one when they made a calf while Moses was on the mountain?"

"Yes."

"Why?"

"Do you remember what Joshua said when Moses was coming down the mountain?"

I shrugged. I honestly didn't even remember Joshua was in that story.

"Joshua said there was a sound of war in the camp. But Moses corrected him, advising that it wasn't a loss, or a win, it was singing."

"Ok, why is that important?"

"Because people sing when they're happy. They dance, they do as they please. But when Moses came down the mountain, he broke the tablets, burned the calf, and forced the Israelites to drink the water where the calf's ashes had been thrown into."

"So, they were punished?"

"Not right away, actually. Drinking the water with calf ashes was actually foretelling of another scripture. Numbers chapter five, and verse twenty-four."

It always amazed me how many verses Eli knew, especially ones that seemed like they were part of a story, not a commandment, or an encouragement.

He continued, "That verse outlines what happens to a woman who cheats on her husband. She drinks a curse for her sin. It's dubbed the *adultery test*."

"She had to drink cursed water?"

"Essentially, yes. And it was bitter, and made her stomach upset. But do you know why the Israelites had to drink the water with the ashes in it?"

I shook my head.

"Because they were adulterers. They'd worshiped something that wasn't God, they cheated on Him, so they had to drink cursed water."

"But I thought they died?"

He nodded. "Some did. Others were swallowed up by a plague."

"So, why did He punish them twice?"

"God didn't punish them twice. He sentenced them once and they received their judgement through the plague."

"But they drank the bitter water."

"That was their sentencing. That was God's way of marking the Israelites as adulterers. The judgement He brought down on them was a plague."

I chewed my lip, trying to recall the story. "But didn't we say that some of them died? So that's two punishments, right?"

He smirked, and I knew all the other information was just Elijah explaining things, but what he was about to tell me was something to help me.

"Those who died were killed by their own family members. The Levites." He nodded. "They were instructed to kill their own kin, neighbors, and friends."

"But why?"

"Because nothing is supposed to come between you and God. If your right arm offends you, cut it off. What that means is, anything that'll pull you from God must be severed and cut away. Not family, not loved ones, not a job," he paused, "not even a friend."

My eyes drifted from his to stare at the wall ahead of me as his voice came again, "Who is on the Lord's side? Come to me. Those were Moses's words in the camp that day. Those who came, the Levites, they had to grab their sword and kill from one end of the camp to the other, family, neighbors, and companions."

"So, you're telling me this because I have to let Matt go?"

He nodded. "And I'm telling you this because God is fair and just, and He will repay evil. If the Israelites weren't excluded, then neither is Matt, no matter how heavy the sentence."

I clutched my sheets, trying to make the frustration go away. I knew he was right; I knew Matt was guilty, but it hurt. I was hurting, I didn't want this for him. But what could I do?

Even in that story, Moses had pleaded with God to turn from His anger, and even though He didn't reign down the terror He initially proposed, the sin of the Israelites could not be overlooked. Forgiven, but still punishable. Just like today. Jesus's mercy is ever enduring, but judgement is still due, justice must still be served. The mercy of Christ will always be extended to Matt, he'll always have the chance to be saved. However, until one repents and turns from evil, the door of wickedness is left open, and punishment is swift to pass through.

"So, let me ask you something, in modern terms," Elijah tossed his hands behind his head and asked, "Who's on the Lord's side? Will you stand with me for justice to be served?"

33

It's a Door, *Not* a Jar

Xavier

"X?"

"In here," I called from my bedroom. After being released from the hospital last week, Eli wouldn't let me go to work for a full week. Jason understood why and still paid me for that week, and he's not going to count it against my vacation time. The only places I was allowed to go were to classes and church.

"Hey," Eli pushed open my door and leaned in.

"What's up?"

"Carly just called." He looked as uncomfortable as I felt. "She needs a place to stay for a few days, just two or three. She's passing through to catch an international flight."

"Oh." I nodded. "Does she need her room back?"

"No." He waved. "She'll probably crash on the sofa. But I am going to pick her up now from the train station. It was kind of last minute."

"Oh."

"Are you going to be alright? I can put her in a hotel."

"No." I shrugged. "I'm fine."

He sighed, and it was the first time I'd ever seen Eli look so relieved. "Thanks, X, I'll make it up to you."

"It's fine." I waved. "You didn't call my mom until I was released from the hospital, so it's all good."

He chuckled, a faint red glow on his cheeks now. He nodded before stepping out and pulling the door shut.

I flopped onto the bed with a loud sigh. I hadn't seen Carly in so long—not since the accident two years ago. She left the hospital, gathered some things, and skipped town. I wondered what she looked like now, what she acted like. Had she changed? This was frustrating, but at least my eye had gotten a lot better since being jumped last week and I looked somewhat presentable now.

A knock sounded outside my bedroom door about two hours later. I clutched my pencil for a second before I answered, "Yeah?"

"It's me."

Every hair on my body stood up.

"It's Carly."

Swallowing, I laid my pencil down and moved for the door. I stared at the handle, wondering what opening this door meant.

Pulling it open, Carly was there, like she'd never left. Her hair was the same strawberry red, her button nose, and girly smile. It was like I'd opened a door to get a good peek at my past before letting it all go.

"Hi." I cleared my throat.

"Hi." Big eyes were blinking up at me, her innocence had never left, it was just tainted. "Can I come in?"

"Sure." I backed up and she stepped inside. "Where's Eli?" I asked as I closed the door.

"He's grabbing dinner. I think pizza."

"Nice."

She clasped her hands and walked around the bedroom. I forgot it was hers, but now the room looked like it had never been an odd shade of pink or smelled like flowers.

"You really made this place look like you, X."

"Really?"

She smiled, casting her vision to me for a nod. "You've always been this way. Eggshell white, grey desks, and nude colors."

"I've been boring?"

She laughed. "Not at all. You've been fascinatingly you." Her voice had a softness to it I didn't remember. The former leader of the Crusaders always had an edge to her innocence. But now, she was as gentle as she always wanted people to believe she was.

"Carly, why'd you come back?"

"I have a flight to catch—"

"No." I shook my head and stepped closer to her. "Why did you come back?"

Her mouth opened the slightest bit before she snapped it closed.

"I wanted to see you one more time." She reached up and touched my cheek. "I wanted to see my rescuer who I never properly thanked, and I wanted to tell you goodbye for good. I need to close this chapter of my life, but I didn't think I could unless I saw you."

I clutched her hand against my cheek, but I couldn't speak. I just watched her as she fought the tears swelling in her eyes.

"For the last two years, I've cleaned up my life. I spent every day proving to myself that God is real, and I'm a product of His saving grace. But I also spent every day trying to prove to myself that I didn't have feelings for you." Her lip was caught between her teeth when she paused. In a whisper, she pleaded, "Tell me I'm wrong and I'll stay. Tell me I'm wrong, and I'll stay right here with you."

My shoulders dropped. This was the woman I thought I was dating two years ago. This was who I wanted right now, but I knew I couldn't have her. If she wasn't for me before, then I knew she still wasn't now. But my heart was begging me to ignore what I knew. It was threatening to stop beating if I let her go. But today, it would have to make good on its threats.

"Carly," I whispered, "I needed you so badly. I would've done anything to have you. But now—"

"Don't say it, please don't say it."

I took another step, closing the gap between us. "I love you so much," I whispered as I leaned down to press my forehead against hers, "but I cannot reopen that door. I love you because you were a teacher to me. But you've only got one shot at a test. If you fail it, you'll be stuck repeating. I don't want to repeat again."

She was shaking, sniffling, crying. I pulled her into my chest, letting her cry loudly against me. It was tearing me apart to listen to her sobs, but I knew I was doing the right thing.

Before, I was angry at Carly, but along the way, I learned to forgive her and move on. Now, she was here, just when I felt more solid, she reappeared. But scars don't reopen unless you cut them again. I couldn't do it. Not to God, and not to myself.

"I wanted you to need me," she was whispering, "I wanted you again."

Taking a step back, I leaned down to look at my crying ex-girlfriend, and for the first time, I kissed her because I truly loved her. Before now, I kissed her because I thought she was pretty, I thought we were supposed to express physical affection. But kissing her now was different. There was depth to it now, meaning behind the way she clung to me, the way I held her close. It was a goodbye, a permanent one. But there was a promise somewhere in there to never forget each other.

The door to the apartment opened, and I could hear Eli coming inside.

"Guys?"

I pulled away and lifted Carly's chin. Her pink lips were puffy, which made her pouting even harder to resist. "One day, you won't look for me. A lock of dark hair, someone my height, or hazel eyes, they won't bring back memories. One day, you'll try to remember why you loved me so much, until you can't remember who I was to you. Promise me that day will come."

She nodded. "I promise."

"Guys? I got pizza," Eli called again.

"Coming!" I called back.

Carly grabbed my hand and kissed it. "One day I'll forget; that's my promise. But for now, I want to keep remembering."

"Okay." I was in the middle of kissing her forehead when the door to my bedroom opened.

"Hey, X—oh! I'm sorry!" Eli slammed the door shut and Carly and I exchanged a chuckle.

"Goodbye, Xavier," she said.

"You're not staying?"

She shook her head. "There's a hotel up the street with some vacant rooms. I planned just in case."

"So, this is it?"

"Yes. This is it."

I took a deep breath, slipping my hands into my pockets as she moved for the door.

"By the way, try not to be a hero anymore," she said.

I laughed. "Roger that."

She opened the door and stood there a moment, taking one final look around the room before her eyes fell back on me. "Goodbye, Xavier Miles."

"Goodbye, Carly Ross."

All that time, the door had been ajar for Carly to come back into my life. But finally, that door closed.

34

What Do You Live For?

Xavier

I stepped out of class, moving through the crowd to head to the library when I heard someone calling my name. I scanned the crowd of students until I found Glenn waving from across the hall.

"Hey, Glenn," I called as I jogged over to him.

"What's up, Mr. Superhero?"

I snorted. "Shut up."

"It was all good until you got your butt handed to you."

I shoved him playfully. "All I did was find her." I shook my head, trying not to let the thoughts of that fight swarm me.

Glenn rolled his eyes as we started down the stairs. "I've got some news for you."

"What is it?"

"Junior joined the frat here on campus."

I stopped on the stairs, earning some grunts. "Seriously?"

"Yep."

Glenn and I had made up our sophomore year. We had a class together each semester, and we were chem partners in lab. It was really awkward at first, but eventually things worked themselves out and Glenn and I were cool again. I never did make up with Junior. I tried twice, but he refused to see me. I stopped caring though and moved on. Every now and then Glenn gives me updates on JC. He'd been doing well, I guess. Passing classes, joining the basketball team, going on exactly one date. Things were looking up for JC, which was nice for him.

"When's the initiation?"

"Not sure, I think after New Year's."

"Isn't it kind of late for him to be joining a frat? It's our senior year."

"Yeah, I said the same thing." He shrugged. "I think he's only able to join because someone higher up quit or swapped colleges so there's an upperclassmen spot."

"Well, I'm glad for him."

"Me too. All he's ever wanted was to belong to something, I think. And a frat's the best thing for him."

"You sound like a proud father."

He cackled. "Do I?"

"Yeah."

"Well, I'd rather be a father than a superhero."

I laughed as we stepped onto the lawn, nodding goodbye before Glenn headed to another class. I trotted across the lawn to our library. It was a large building with big glass windows that allowed you to see our studious student body hard at work... that's what the pamphlets always said at least.

There were some students who actually studied in the library, way in the back where, incidentally, there were no large windows. The front of the library was the choice spot for the frat boys to hang out. Loud idiots who weren't even that smart, but somehow made it into the fraternity that required a 3.5 GPA to get in, and a 3.6 to stay in. I guess next

300

semester JC would be hanging out there too.

It was quiet in the back of the library. Our librarian never really made the frat boys leave because they were the pride of the school. I didn't care, honestly, I just stayed out of the way.

I tossed my backpack onto an empty table and grabbed a chair. I wanted to think about the previous night, seeing Carly again. My hand subconsciously went to my lips, I'd kissed her. It was like they remembered before my brain did. Carly was still beautiful, she was still girly, she was still innocent. Rather … she was *actually* innocent now. And it wasn't that I was looking for her innocence, but I was attracted to it. She was kind, and she seemed naïve, like the whole world was laughing at her because she still wore pink skirts, and fuzzy sweaters. She was a girly girl, and that was new to me. Lia Sunohara was such a tomboy, but I loved seeing how strong she was on the volleyball team. Carly's girliness rivaled Lia's tomboy style. Both were wonderful, but both of them were doors I had to close. Lia's by force, Carly's by choice.

Freewill, it made an appearance last night. I had three options; ask Carly to stay, ask Carly to leave, have sex with Carly and then decide after that. That last one was throbbing in the back of my head the entire time she was there, but I ignored it. I knew I couldn't ask her to stay, but I had the chance to, the freedom to. But would it have been worth it?

Sometimes we make the wrong decision, and the only penalty is guilt. I truly believed that staying with Carly as she is now, would've been different from our freshmen year. I believed that I could've married her and had a happy life, but that wasn't the will of God. And I would've lived a life of disobedience.

Dropping my head to the table, I sighed. It was hard, doing the right thing, but in the end, I know it'll be worth it. When is the end? When will I stop waiting? When will I be rewarded for the righteous things I've done? Everyone always tells you to just hold on, to just see it through,

301

but I have, for almost four years now. I've waited, I've endured, I've prayed, I've fasted. I've done everything I'm supposed to do, so why haven't I been blessed? Why does it feel like I've been ignored by God? These were questions I was always asking, always searching for an answer to, but only because I didn't like the actual answer; to just wait.

Habakkuk the second chapter, and the second verse, Eli had explained that those were instructions from God to Habakkuk. *Write the vision*, is what God instructed first. Each one of us must write down our vision. We need to see our own vision and believe it.

Writing the vision down is an act of faith. We believe that what we've written has come from God, and this vision of God will be fulfilled. The next part of that verse tells Habakkuk to make it plain on the tablets. Write it plainly but engrave it into the tablets on our hearts so it'll never be forgotten. And the final part of that verse, God tells His prophet that these instructions must be followed because someone will come later and will believe what is written and run from their sin.

Our visions are not our own because they come from God. Every righteous desire within us has come from God. But these visions are not just for us, they're for the people around us. Believers will always be looked at, observed in the spotlight, because we are the light. So our visions from God must be plain, they must glorify Him, and allow our faith to prove that God is real, God is unchanging, God is loving. So, I wondered more, what the dreams and visions of Adar meant. Why was she important? If I was supposed to fall in love with this girl from my dreams and visions, how could that help others?

One thing I knew was that Elijah has always had an answer for everything.

"Spouses do a few things for us." Eli held up three fingers as he walked around the front of the sanctuary. "The first thing, for men, your wife protects you spiritually. Your prayers will be hindered if you don't treat her right. But, as your spiritual protector, God does give her the chance to cool His anger on your behalf. Remember Abigail? She went to David on Nabal's behalf."

"He still died though, didn't he?" Kevin challenged, but that night Eli was on a roll.

"Yes, he still died. But he didn't die by David's hand, who Abigail pleaded with."

"But it doesn't matter if he still died."

"That's where you're wrong. It matters because Abigail made atonement with *David*, not with God, for her husband. Nabal had offended a man of God, and it wasn't going to be overlooked. Abigail asked David to overlook her husband's offenses. But no one ever asked *God* to."

Kevin was silent now, and Pastor Ross smiled.

"I guess you understand now, Kevin? That your wife doesn't just go to David, she goes to the source, the One who will make the final judgment."

Kevin had only nodded, and Eli went on. "Now, women, you are protected by your husband's name. That's why you take his name, join his tribe, become part of his clan. Your husband is supposed to be in right standing with God, just as King David was when Nabal offended him. Now, I told you there were a few things spouses do, and this is the third one." He paused and held up three fingers again. "A Bible believing marriage, centered on Christ, is an example of God's relationship with Christ and the Church."

"His relationship with Christ?" Marlo Jo raised a pencil, and Eli nodded.

"Jesus is our mediator. He goes to God on our behalf the way a wife goes to God on her husband's behalf. God also loves Jesus, and anything asked through His name is given to us. Which represents a husband's hard work, his reputation built off his name giving his wife and their family a chance at a better life."

"So, it's kind of like the same thing with the church, right?" Daytona asked. "The church prays on behalf of the world, going to God for justice and for mercy. And the name of Jesus is our power. Anytime we're in trouble or need something, all we have to do is call on Jesus."

"You are exactly right, Daytona." Eli walked over and bumped fists with her. "As your fellow student has explained, calling on the name of Jesus, and going to God on behalf of others, that is the depiction a marriage brings to onlookers. If your marriage is not a replica of the peace between God and man, the love between God and man, and the praying power given to man from God, then your marriage is a false doctrine to the Kingdom."

So that was it. Marriage is representation of God's own relationships, and if our marriage is bad, it makes Him out to be a liar, to be no good, and He is incapable of lying and being no good.

So… we wait.

We wait because there's a grooming process. We wait because there's a cleansing process. We just wait.

But I hate it, and it's hard, and I don't want to wait anymore. I don't want to be encouraged; I want to be *blessed*. However, my mother always told me that we are trees planted by the river Jordan. Trees don't grow overnight, or even in a year, they take years of growth and maturity. And then one day, they begin to produce fruit or flowers, and that's what we have to look forward to.

No matter how hard it is to believe, if you write your vision on the table of your heart, those who read your story one day will believe. They'll see that you never gave up, that you never stopped believing, and one day they'll believe too.

For me, the day someone believes because of my vision, I think that's the day I'll live for.

35

I Want to Feel Something

Madeline

The holidays had passed, and the darkness of winter was beginning to yield to the light. I spent the winter in and out of shelters, keeping my head down. Kasey and a few of his gang members were arrested on Christmas. It was a relief, but I still didn't feel safe since the gang would undoubtedly search for whoever turned in their operation. However, with the cops investigating, I knew they would lay low for a while. Either way, Dominique's voice was the one on the phone recordings from their tapped phones, not mine, so I'm sure they figured I ran away with her. And with no way of finding us, they would eventually stop looking.

I gave all the money to Dominique, and she bought a one-way ticket to Australia. She said she wanted to see all the wildlife there, and she wanted to be alone. I understood better than anyone. I hadn't always wanted to be alone until I realized I was the one who made things bad for everyone else. The night I spent in the hospital watching over X after he got jumped—because of me—I vowed in my heart to be alone. But the truth is that I wanted to be loved, no matter what I vowed.

I was accepted into a women's shelter for the abused. I was protected and I wasn't asked many questions. But I couldn't stay there, even though I wanted to. Women were kind, and gentle. Always hugging you and talking sweetly to you. Those bits of affection weren't meant to make me feel the things I did.

A touch, a hug, someone holding my hands, telling me it would be alright, it all made the confusion within feel silly. It felt like I wasn't confused at all, it felt like it was alright to feel these things. But I knew it wasn't. I knew it was wrong, not only because of God, but because everyone here was just as broken as I was. How could I take the last bit of kindness they could summon after being shattered, and use it for my own passion? I was selfish.

What I told Dominique was the truth. I was hurting, and the first person to ever care was Jocelyn. And because of my need for attention, my craving for happiness, I fell in love with her. And then out of love with her, and into love with every other woman until I realized I was searching for that feeling.

Whatever glint of affection Jay had given me, gave me a high I couldn't find anywhere else. I tried, but there wasn't anyone like her, though some days Dominique had come close. Maybe it was because she meant it when she said she didn't care. And maybe that's what I was searching for. I was searching for someone who didn't care about my past, who could look past who I was, choose me over the fragment of my sister I'd become. I wanted someone to revive Adeline, to rescue her. Jay came so close, and I craved that.

But I wasn't sure.

When Xavier called me Adeline in the hospital, I didn't know how to react. It scared me. It didn't feel the same way that I thought it would. Being recognized didn't make me happy, or maybe it was just that being recognized by a man was different than being recognized by a woman.

Women saw me, they understood me. Men just looked at me and wanted me to forget my problems and cater to theirs. Maybe I was judging every man but at this point, I wasn't really sure of anything anymore.

"Maddy, wake up, they're doing an inspection today because of the new girl."

I sighed as I rolled over to see my roommate Kimberly. She and I had shared my bed a few times since I'd been here. She was nice. But we'd been notified that we were getting another roommate, so we'd been trying to keep our distance.

She tossed freshly washed blonde hair over her shoulder as she made her bed. I watched her small hands tucking the skirt of the blanket into hiding. She was slender, but she was pretty. Her green eyes were so mystifying, but I enjoyed looking into them. I enjoyed Kim, but that was it. I didn't care for our conversations, I didn't care for anything serious with her, except at night when she would climb into bed with me after lights-out.

"Kim," I called as she fluffed her pillows.

"What?"

"Do you love me?"

She stopped fluffing and looked at me for a moment. Her raised brows lowered in concern, and she tossed the pillow onto her bed. I made room for her to sit on the bed with me, but instead, she laid down.

"Of course, I love you, Maddy. Where's this coming from?"

"Well, I'm supposed to meet with the counsellor today about finding a good place for me to move in and get a job. I'll tell him I need a space for two if you want to stay with me."

"Yes!" she squealed. "I want to stay with you, Maddy! We've been through a lot alone, we should stay together."

I could only produce a half smile as she snuggled closer to me. I'd been through a lot, but Kim just couldn't keep a job. She confessed to

308

hating to work, and would sometimes quit because it was too hard, but being here had changed her—at least that was what she'd told me. I don't know, and I'll never know, because I didn't mean anything I'd told her.

I wasn't actually meeting a counsellor from the shelter; I was meeting Elijah today. I called him yesterday from one of the phones downstairs and asked him to meet me today. I was tired of the knot in my stomach. The confusion. It was draining me, and I wanted help. I *needed* it.

The hours ticked by slowly until, finally, three o'clock rolled around, and I was sitting in a café in the heart of Queens, waiting on Eli. I didn't want to meet in Brooklyn where I was staying or Manhattan where I presumed Eli stayed since that's where the college is.

I absently tapped my mug of hot chocolate, trying to keep myself from getting nervous. It's been a while, years actually, since I've seen Elijah. He was good to me, and the only person I felt like I could still count on.

When the bell jingled, I knew it was him.

"Good afternoon, sir, table for one?"

"No, I'm looking for—"

"Hi…" I'd tossed a few dollars on the table and made a beeline for Elijah. He looked well, not a hair out of place.

"Hi." He smiled at me.

"Can we walk?" I asked.

"Of course." He opened the door for me, and we stepped out into the streets of Queens.

We didn't speak much while we walked, I didn't know what to say, or what he would think of me. But Eli wasn't judgmental, he always waited for me to open up.

As the slush sloshed around our feet, we walked beside each other until we reached an alleyway. I grabbed his hand and rounded the corner. Then I shoved him into the wall and forced my lips over his.

Elijah was the only man in my entire life who made me feel things the way a woman could. I was so tired of being confused, so tired of fighting against God, that I didn't know how to stop the feelings women gave me, the feelings that were absent when men touched me or approached me. My heart didn't race, my palms didn't sweat. But, whenever I saw Elijah, they did.

Even today in the café, the moment the bell rang, my heart skipped a beat. I wanted to see him. I couldn't wait to see him. He could make me feel things... He made me feel loved.

I was sure Elijah loved me, so that meant he'd want me. He'd want sex from me, and maybe sex from a man I loved would make my feelings for women disappear. Maybe if we did this, we'd love each other without anything holding us back. We could set our passions free, and hopefully that would change me. Maybe that would satisfy God, and He'd cut me some slack.

I pulled at Eli's clothes, forcing his arms around me, not breaking for air. But I could tell he was only going through the motion. He just stood there as I forced myself onto him. He wasn't holding me, he wasn't caressing me. He didn't groan, he didn't gasp in pleasure, he didn't even kiss me back.

I moved to his neck, kissing the tender skin there, trying to get a response, trying to make him react, but he didn't. He stood there, and I felt exposed before him. Like, somehow, this was his fault.

He should've reacted. I don't know why I thought he would. No one has ever reacted to me; they only ever reacted to my sister. So why would I think Eli would react? Why would he touch me and try to make himself feel good?

"Am I doing something wrong?" I muttered against his neck. "I can do something different."

310

"Adeline."

My name.

I stepped back. He looked embarrassed, but there was also a twisted look of pity on his face.

"How do you know my name?"

"I've known who you were since the first day we met."

"How!?" I shouted. "You've known it was me and you still…"

"And I've still cared." He stepped forward but I backed away.

"Don't touch me."

"Adeline, please—"

"I said, don't touch me!" I shoved him back, but I didn't run. I was tired of running. Dropping to my knees, I sobbed. But I should've felt relieved, someone knew who I was all along, and they still cared.

"So why?" I blubbered. "Why does it still hurt?"

"Because you won't forgive yourself. You won't love yourself. You want to be punished, so you do your best to pity yourself."

"That's not true!" I snapped my vision up to him and he knelt in front of me. "Just go away." I scooted against the wall, the wet ground soaking through my ragged pants.

"I won't leave until you can stand on your own."

"I have legs," I murmured. "I can stand."

"Then get up."

"No."

"Come on, Adeline, get up."

"No! Just leave me alone!"

"Alright." He moved to sit beside me against the wall. "Then I guess we'll be here a while."

We sat for what seemed like hours on the slushy ground. Thankfully, though, spring was close, so it wasn't freezing. It took me a while to calm down, to convince myself that I could trust Elijah. He'd come all this way to help, and all I'd done was suck his face and cry.

One big sniffle, and then a sigh. I tried to steady myself to talk finally.

"Eli?"

"Hmm?"

"I like girls."

"You've told me before."

"And I want to fall in love."

"You've told me that too."

"But I've never told you why I became my sister, so how did you know who I was?"

He shrugged beside me, keeping his gaze fixed on his boots. "I got your file. Yours said Adeline 'Madeline' Jones. I had instructions to call you Madeline, and that your real name was not to be used for any reason."

"So, you didn't know that Madeline was my sister?"

"I guessed it after our conversations, and the times you mentioned her, you were always particular about not saying her name."

"Was it that obvious?"

He chuckled. "Yes, but that wasn't the point of our talks. You needed an outlet, and I was happy to be that for you."

"Can I ask you something?"

"Go ahead."

I clasped my hands together nervously. "Do you ever get lonely?"

"Not really, especially since X lives with me now. I find his company quite fulfilling."

"Fulfilling." I nodded. "Is that what I've been looking for? Fulfillment?"

"Could be, if you've been feeling lonely."

"I've been wanting someone to love me, that's all I want, but no one loves me. Everyone loved my sister, not me."

"Is that why you became her? So that someone would love you?"

"I think so. I lost myself. Well, really, I felt like my life had been

312

taken from me."

"Go on."

I leaned back against the wall, the coolness of the bricks reaching through my sweatshirt. "I was raped a few years back, by the same man who raped my sister."

Eli was silent.

"Before that, I'd had a rough time with my parents, but I've already told you all that."

"It's alright," he shrugged, "tell me again anyway."

"Well, I thought my parents loved me until my sister died. Then they hated me, and I ended up with my grandmother who hated me too. But I tried to stay optimistic, and I went to this stupid party…" I trailed off, trying not to remember Matt's weight on me again.

"I think part of you shut down," Eli said as the dark memories threatened to consume me. "What happened that day was unbearable, and to preserve yourself, you shut down and became someone else. Someone who people liked and wouldn't take advantage of. Someone the complete opposite of who you truly were."

I sniffled and nodded. "Yeah, I think so."

"But the part of you that was closed off reopened when you fell in love with Jocelyn, right?"

"Yeah."

"She gave you attention, and it felt like love. But, really, you fell in love with the attention she gave you."

"I don't know." I scratched my head. "I loved the way I felt when I was with her, whether in bed or out of it. And then things changed, Carly came along, and Jay became like a sister to me."

"And at that point, Adeline had returned, and Jocelyn filled in for Madeline."

I looked down at my bracelet, the cloud-shaped charm dangling against my wrist, and for a second, I wondered if Adeline had ever really left. This bracelet was the only thing tethered to who I really was, and for some reason, I'd clung to that through this small piece of jewelry.

When Eli noticed my silence, he looked over at me and grabbed my hand. "Carly didn't make you feel the way Jocelyn did, did she?"

I shook my head, embarrassed to talk about his sister. "No, she was nice, but she didn't…"

"Carly didn't care enough, she wasn't focused on you the way Jocelyn had been, so you chased that feeling. But where did this feeling, this attention seeking feeling, come from?"

"I was hoping you would tell me."

He laughed. "I will. It stemmed from your parents. They had loved you for so long. Remember how they favored you over your sister?"

I only nodded.

"You told me once that your parents always tried to make you feel good about yourself, so when they stopped, you stopped too. You stopped feeling good about yourself. You stopped being happy. You stopped feeling anything and searched for something that would replicate the love and joy of your parents. And Jocelyn just happened to do that for you."

I clenched my jaw. I knew he was right; I'd known all along I was searching for something, I just didn't know it had to do with my parents.

Tightening my grip on his hand, I said, "What do I do, Eli? How do I keep going?"

"You really want to know?"

I looked over at him, and he was smirking. He only smirked like that for one reason, or rather, one person.

"You're going to say *God*, aren't you?"

He nodded happily. "I am. God is truly the only one who can make you feel better, Adeline. He's the only one who can help you stop blaming yourself for Madeline's death and stop dwelling on your parents. He's the only one who can help you forgive your rapist and

314

move forward. And He's the only one who can change your desires."

"You mean, He's the only way I won't want women and attention?"

"I do. Because He'll give you a love stronger than your parents. Attention more focused than Jay's, and He'll never leave you, nor forsake you."

"But how? Everyone needs God. How can He just focus on me?"

"Because you mean that much to Him. And because all of our lives are intertwined. There's a reason Jesus called us sisters and brothers and not friends and companions."

"Jesus," I felt every hair on my body raise, "I've got goosebumps," I said as I dropped his hand to pull up my sleeves.

"His name is powerful enough to break every chain, if you believe."

"But it's so simple. Won't I still have these feelings?"

"God can take away your pain instantly, and He can draw it out like the dross of silver that takes time. It depends on your level of faith."

"I don't have any, so I'll never be better!"

He was laughing now, cheeks turning pink and bunching. "Faith only needs to be a mustard seed to move a mountain. How much less do you need to believe that God can change who you're attracted to?"

"Oh, I didn't know that."

"Healing can take time, it really all depends on you. And even if you start small today, with just accepting Jesus as your Savior, things will begin to change for you."

"But I'll still be a lesbian, I'll still like women."

"Accepting Christ changes you, Adeline. God will send His Holy Spirit to fight that desire, to beat it down like dust until it flies away like chaff in the wind. Until your faith and trust in God outweighs your worldly desires."

I touched my heart; I could feel it beating faster. Did I really want God's help? Could I finally stop running from Him? Would He truly love me?

"I have one question."

"Alright."

"Why do I love you, Eli?"

"Oh, that's easy." He smiled brightly, almost like he was flattered. "Because we have a relationship. We are connected to each other through interdependence. You rely on me for help. I rely on God to help you and I rely on you to trust me. Remember when I said everyone in the entire Body of Christ are brothers and sisters?"

I nodded.

"That's because families help each other. They depend on each other to operate in a familial unit. The Body of Christ is interdependent on each other and on God."

"So, if I join, people will depend on me, won't they?"

"You'll be needed, and you'll be loved, but not just by us—you'll be needed and loved by God."

I shook my head. "God doesn't need me."

"But He wants to use you, if you let Him."

"I'm scared," I whispered.

"Only because freedom is beckoning for you. For years, you've depended on the bad, and your own pity to keep you going. But now, you'll have to give that up to allow God to take care of you. You think you're ready for that? Are you ready to depend on God?"

I took a deep breath. "I … I think I'm ready."

36

All the Pieces Are Coming Together

Xavier

Someone knocked at my door.

"Yes?"

"Hey," Eli said as he stepped inside. He was holding a bag in one hand, and his glasses in the other. It took me a moment to register he didn't have them on, then I realized his eyes were more noticeable. Sheepishly pushing blond hair from his face, he said, "I was supposed to make a run into Queens, but I think I'd better go to the optician, so I can have my normal glasses back sooner than later."

I sighed as I set my pencil down. "You want me to run the errand?"

"If you don't mind." He extended the bag to me.

"What are you even doing in Queens?"

He laughed, waving me off. "Just make sure everything gets to the address I wrote on a sticky note inside the bag."

"Do I just walk up and hand over the bag?"

"Yeah," he said slowly.

My brow arched before I squinted. "What's going on, Eli?"

"I've gotta run, so get that done, ASAP."

"Eli…"

He waved and left the room. He never left like this, and when he was all mysterious, he was always up to something. Last time he acted this way was my first birthday I celebrated here. He'd planned a surprise party with the church and had me running around the city until I reached the party. It was fun, but my birthday wasn't anytime soon, so I had no idea what to expect now.

Opening the bag, I peeked inside. There was a box and a yellow sticky note that gave an address and read; **Adeline Jones**.

"Adeline Jones… Adeline Jones!" I was shouting now as I pulled the box out of the bag. I remembered Elijah was tasked with collecting some of Adeline's—at the time *Madeline*'s—things from the dorm during our freshmen year when she disappeared.

I snatched the top off the box to find some jewelry in a pouch, a folded shirt, perfume, and some notebooks. I pulled out the notebooks, flipping through each one until I stopped. There was a blue composition notebook with bubbly handwriting and a white sticker.

"Face it, Tiger," I read the sticker aloud, "you just hit the jackpot."

That was Mary-Jane's first line to Peter Parker in the comics.

I chuckled. "Madeline swore she'd be—" Slapping a hand over my mouth, it felt like I'd been hit by a racehorse or something incredibly powerful.

"Madeline … she's not the same person."

I grabbed one of the other notebooks. It was a regular black and white notebook, fine print, different from the bubbly print that said Madeline Jones on the blue one. *This* one said Adeline Jones. I flipped through them both, searching for any correlation to the twins mentioned by the detectives. They told me to look for an address, but I found something better. On one of the pages of the notebook that had

318

Adeline's name on it, there was a note.

Missed you in class, mostly because I had to take double notes for me and you. It was lonely today without you, but Xavier had a vintage Spidey comic he's letting me borrow so that was cool. I don't know why I'm writing this, it's not like I won't see you when I get home. Whatever, I love you, and I miss you.

"I remember that," I whispered as I read over the note again. "I remember that vintage comic, it was a special addition sale Jax had convinced Mom to get for me. I let Madeline borrow it because I felt guilty about Matt."

It was true then, that the Madeline Jones I met here on campus was actually a twin sister named Adeline. The real MJ had died, and the reason that girl in the picture that the detectives showed me looked so familiar, was because that was Adeline.

She didn't have red hair, she had curly brown hair, and it was the only way we could tell the twins apart once we got into our sophomore year. Adeline was heavier than Madeline at first, but when they returned, one had lost weight and the other had red hair and was seen hanging with the football team. Adeline faded to the background as her sister took the lead, and that's why I'd forgotten her.

I was panting as the memories came back. Bits and pieces of things I'd remembered before suddenly made sense now. It was like I was slowly knitting together my broken memory.

I needed to see Adeline, to tell her I remembered. I was thankful for Eli now, thankful that his glasses were broken.

Jolting to my feet, I tossed the jewelry and the perfume back into the box. As I piled the notebooks in, I dropped one. It hit the floor with a splat, pages folded and sprawled. Snatching it up quickly, something flew out of it. A picture. It was a polaroid on the floor of my bedroom, the dark side facing up. When I turned it over, I felt winter's ice pouring into my room, freezing me to the floor.

In the center was Matt and Madeline. His arm was draped over her,

319

she was hugging him and kissing his cheek, a red mane flowing behind her. I was standing on the other side of Matt, making the best smolder I could, but there was someone else in the picture. Another girl. She was identical to Madeline, like a photocopy had been made, except she'd matured a little differently, possibly because she'd been heavier before.

Round hips, a little belly, big breasts for a high schooler, dimpled cheeks—two, not one like Madeline—chocolate brown skin, and thick curls that hung over her shoulders. Her eyes were so pretty they seemed to shine, but it was the glimmer of her bracelet that caught my attention. A cloud-shaped pendant that hung from her wrist, the exact same shape as the birthmark on my own wrist.

Everything became clear. Adeline was the same girl from the picture the detectives had shown me, and the same girl I saw that day at the graduation party.

I had stepped out after Matt told me there were plenty of girls wanting to lose their virginity at that graduation party and bumped into a girl. It was such a casual interaction, I never once thought more of it until now. Now, it means something. Now, I know that girl was Adeline, she was at the party. And I can't forget the way Matt eyed her as she made her way through the crowd after I bumped into her. Just like I'd bumped into her on my first day on campus.

"No," I whispered. "*No.*" I choked on the second 'no' because it was undoubtedly true. Matt loved Madeline, and he'd always said he wanted to try Adeline, and he would if Madeline stopped loving him. My best friend had assaulted a set of twins, one had killed herself because of it. The other had tried to become someone else because of it...because of *him*. I couldn't defend him anymore. I couldn't ignore what was staring back at me.

Slipping the photo back into the notebook, I placed them inside the box, and headed out to Queens.

The entire way from Manhattan to Queens, I prayed. I asked for

God's help, for His guidance, for His favor. I was about to confess to Adeline that she wasn't to blame for what'd happened to her sister. *I was to blame.*

In my heart, I wanted to be strong, and I didn't want to ask for forgiveness, but I knew I would. I would do anything to make things right, even in the smallest sense. I had to repay Adeline, help her make up for the lost time, and do something to make up for all the pain I know I caused her and her family.

God? I pleaded within. *Help me make this right. Please allow her to forgive me.*

A vision rolled out before me in my mind. I could see her, Adar—no—*Adeline* was standing in a field of red poppies. She leaned down and picked one, lifting it to her nose to smell it. When the vision faded, my memory did too, and I was still on the bus, heading to Queens.

37

Roses, Poppies, and the Lily of the Valley

Adeline

Roses ... They were my favorite until Madeline died. For the longest, I hated flowers until I read an article one day about the poppy flower. Red poppies have been associated with death since ancient Rome and Greece. These cultures used the poppies to represent a loved one had passed on to eternal sleep. But by the time the legend of the poppies reached the US, their legend had been altered and they became symbolic of hope for peace, for better times, and for remembrance of fallen soldiers.

Madeline Jones was no hero, but she was worth remembering. So, I began planting poppies around the house, growing them under lamps so they'd blossom around her birthday and around the anniversary of her passing. It had been my tradition until I moved to New York. I never stopped loving poppies because I knew deep within that Madeline was gone, and my charm bracelet reminded me that I was still alive no matter how long I pretended to be her.

For the last month or so, I've been seeing Eli consistently. He's been teaching me things about the Bible, teaching me ways to cope. I'd never faced reality, but I already knew that. Most of us in the gay community won't face our fears. We won't address the root of the problems, just the surface because it was too embarrassing to dig any deeper.

Well, I guess it's not 'we' anymore.

Elijah told me to stop thinking of myself as a member of that community; I had to believe and know that I was adopted into the family of God. And that meant forgetting the things in the past. Forget who I used to be, forget the things I used to want, and ask God every day to fill me with His desires for good. It had been challenging, but since I moved out of that group home and into a different shelter—a Bible based shelter recommended by Eli—I've had an easier time accepting my salvation.

I checked my watch. Eli was late. That wasn't like him. I leaned against the building, waiting for him. He told me last night on the phone not to leave until he got there, he promised he would show. Which I guess I should've taken as he'll be late, but it was going on twenty minutes, and I'd only have about two hours before I needed to be back in the shelter. I tried not to worry as I clutched the strap on my bag.

After another fifteen minutes had passed, a bus pulled up in front of me and people filed off. I was thinking this was it and, technically speaking, I was right. My gaze met Xavier's as he stepped off the bus. He was holding a bag in one hand and a sticky note in the other. If I hadn't made undeniable eye contact, I would've just gone home. But, putting it all together, Eli probably set this up, and there was a reason X was here and not him.

"MJ," he said as he came over.

I'd stopped going by Madeline, though I hadn't let the red hair go yet. It was a process, and I wasn't in a rush.

"Hi, X." I hadn't seen him since the hospital, and now he was here, looking stressed and exhausted.

"We need to talk."

"Do you want to go inside?" I looked back at the café, but when I caught his pinched expression, I knew something was going on. "Come on."

I took him to the alleyway where Eli and I talked the first time we met a month or so back. It was dry now, and the sun was shining more than before, so I was fine with talking there today. I was just a little worried about what Xavier would need to talk about in private with me.

"I know you're not Madeline Jones." He dug through his bag and pulled out a box. I was wondering how he'd found out, hoping Eli hadn't broken the last bit of trust I had.

"I have to tell you how I know you're not her."

"What are you talking about?"

"I ... I'm the reason your sister was raped."

I stepped back. "X, I think—"

"No," he was breathing hard, "I just need to say this." He waved his honey-toned hand around, cutting me off. I gulped as his hazel eyes lifted from the ground to meet mine. "I was there when it happened."

A numbing pain gripped me, and he looked away.

"I didn't stop it. I didn't stop Matt. I should've stopped him, but I didn't. I don't know why, but..." His eyes flicked back to mine. "I'm so sorry, Adeline."

"You let my sister get raped." It wasn't a question, more like a statement, one I couldn't believe. I fell into the wall, my legs failing me, the world closing in on me. How could this be? The one person I risked everything for, the one person I began to trust and believe that he was nothing like his best friend... but I was so wrong. He was identical to him. Just as closely patterned after him as I was with Madeline.

"Adeline! Adeline!" Xavier was calling for me, but I couldn't respond. I'd just begun to heal, and now this... *What do I do? What is even happening?*

The world began to fade, and the last thing I saw was Xavier leaning over me, tears falling from his eyes to my face as he yelled for me to stay with him.

— ❦ —

Slowly, I opened my eyes, but there was nothing to see. It was cold, the bed, the blanket, the room, wherever I was.

Where am I?

Adeline.

That Voice… Whose is it?

Come.

Where?

To Me.

To You? Who are You?

I make burdens light, and darkness flee. I make the mountains bow down in worship, and the captive free. I heal the sick, and the blind to see. I am the forgiver of sins, and the One who made all things to be.

Jesus… why can't I see You? Why are all these bad things happening to me?

My child, I have lifted your burdens, and made all the darkness in your heart disappear. I have made the mountains bow to Me, so that you may cross smoothly onto the path of righteousness. Your chains have been broken, and you are no longer a hostage to sin. The confusion within has been healed, and your eyes have been opened. I forgave your sins, died for your freedom, and made all things possible for you.

You've never been there for me!

I have always been right beside you, Adeline, though you

would not seek Me.

Why!? Why didn't You save my sister?

Madeline did not want to be saved.

It's not fair! How can I go on!?

I am the door; you must go through Me.

I can't take the riddles! Tell me what I am supposed to do!

There was silence now. No voices, no response. The silence was deafening. I could feel myself writhing in place, my mouth stretching as far as I could open it to scream, my hands balled into shaking fists, but there was no sound. No one could hear me, no one could see me. I was alone, I was in pain, it was the way I'd always been.

The next moment, light burst through the emptiness. A warmth washed over me, and the sound of birds singing, bugs chirping, and the world awakening filled my ears. Slowly, I sat up. The world I was in was not the same one I'd left. There was a sky a color I couldn't describe, and a green so pure, it looked greener than the chlorophyll beneath a microscope. And the wind, it was neither a breeze nor a howling tug. It felt like arms wrapping around me as it danced along. The flowers popped their heads up, one red poppy at a time. They looked like they were greeting me, the way they waved in the wind.

"Do you remember this place?"

I turned suddenly, looking for the Voice.

"It's You," I whispered.

"I am." He nodded as He walked through the grass. The blades stood taller, and every flower tried to expand her petals, rolling her leaves out a little wider to present herself to the Maker.

She wanted to be noticed, and the kind and gentle One acknowledged the flowers and the grass. He stopped short of me and leaned down, waving a milky hand through them all, and they seemed to bloom a little bigger at His touch. Weaving between his fingers, and winding up His arm, the flowers rushed to greet Him, as the grass

326

swarmed around His feet.

"My preciousness, I adore you."

It seemed like this entire place was coming alive as He stood in the field. The wind danced a little more, rippling through His clothes and playing in His dark locks. The rest of the field for miles stretched and bent to reach Him. Even the bugs moved through the dirt, carrying leaves, and other findings to present to Him.

"What is this place?" I asked finally.

"You don't remember? You and Benedict grew up here."

"How could I have grown up anywhere but Earth?"

He chuckled as He straightened. The grass and flowers returned to the ground, and the bugs made way for Jesus to move. He placed a hand on my shoulder, I thought I'd melt from His touch, as He sat beside me in the grass.

"This is the realm in which spirits live before they are sent to Earth."

"Before they're sent to the Earth?"

He nodded. "My Father won't send you without first preparing you, and the canal which brings you to Earth is your final preparation."

"You mean the birth canal?"

His cheeks stretched into a smile. "That's the earthly realm. The canal you follow from here humanizes your spirit. You're given skin, and a form, a shade from Our Father, and your tablets are written."

"My tablets?" I wanted to frown, but I couldn't, not sitting beside Jesus. He was calm and friendly, I really wanted to hug Him, to touch Him, but at the same time, I wanted to fall flat before Him. There was a raw power, and a strong anointing rolling off Him as He sat beside me.

I thought I'd faint.

"Yes…" He looked out at the fields before us. "Your heart is a tablet, written with our Father's guidance on it. He takes His time, writing the things He wants you to know, the things you'll need in order to choose life and not death."

"I don't understand any of this and it's not fair. Nothing in my life has been fair."

"My sweet Adeline." He took my hand, and my heart went with it. "You want to believe, but you're still angry, and you're still hurt. You think I've wronged you, and that I took Madeline from you."

"Why?" I took a breath. "Why didn't You save her? Why did You let all these bad things happen to me? How can I trust You now if You weren't there before?"

"I have always been with you. You did not recognize Me, and so you had forsaken Me."

"How is that fair? I didn't even know You were there!" My voice cracked, anger bubbling in my chest. His grip on my hand was now a little firmer, and I couldn't help but glance down at our hands.

"There's a hole." I raised our hands closer, staring at the hole in His hand. "You have a hole in your hand!"

When I looked up at Him, Jesus was wearing a smile. He didn't look glum, His face didn't portray pity. He was beaming and I didn't understand why.

"My servant Elijah, he's taught you about Me, hasn't he?"

"Elijah... like Eli Ross, my psychologist?"

"Yes."

"Well, yeah. He told me that You were nailed..." my words grew quiet as I looked back at His hand. The wound still looked fresh, like the nailing happened only moments ago.

"My scars are a reminder that God is faithful," He began. "Before the cross, I was betrayed, ridiculed, beaten. Then I was made to carry my own cross, and before I was nailed to it, I was stripped of my clothing, and humiliated."

I could feel my breath getting caught in my throat. My hand trembled as He held it.

"Couldn't You have saved Yourself?"

328

"I could've, but then I couldn't save you, and you mean more to Me than life itself."

Shaking my head, I was now clasping His hand a little tighter. "You did this all for me?"

"Every nail, every lash, the crown, it was all for you, Adeline."

"Why didn't God help You? Why didn't He stop the people from beating You?"

"Because it was all part of Our rescue mission. Your life is valuable to the Father, and there is a plan for your life. For the heartache and every struggle, there's a plan. God could've intervened at any moment, but My pain was so that you wouldn't have any."

I shook my head. "But I've had so much pain. I've been so hurt, and now…" I tossed my free hand up. "Now Xavier is telling me he didn't save my sister."

"You must forgive him as I have."

"But you're Jesus, You can forgive so easily."

He chuckled and it was such a sweet sound, it reminded me of a song. "You can forgive too, Adeline. Forgiveness is a choice. God chose before the foundations of the world to forgive you for your sins, so He sent Me to qualify you for forgiveness."

"But you're Jesus. He's God! You can forgive!"

"When I went to the cross, I died for everyone to have a chance at eternal life, and I knew that not everyone would take it." This was the first time I saw His expression change. A grim look crossed His face as He looked around the field. "I gave up my life so that all could be forgiven, all could receive salvation. Yet, many have rejected Me, and a day will come when I'll have to reject them for eternity."

I swallowed as I watched Him. His words were painful. He didn't like rejecting anyone, but He'd done all He could… literally. Jesus had died for the world, prepared us for the world, gave us instructions, and sent the Holy Spirit (per Elijah's teachings), to be here with us, and we still reject Him. And what's worse? Punishment doesn't always follow sin.

Some of us live happy lives, feeling like we've got the world spinning on our own axis as we live in sin. And every breath we take is another chance to get things right, but we don't… I didn't or hadn't.

"What do I do? How do I forgive Xavier?" I asked earnestly.

His smile slowly returned as He faced me again. Glowing eyes, and radiant skin. There was no way to describe the King, other than beautiful.

"Confess to the pain his actions caused you, confess to being unforgiving, and then choose to forgive him. He wants your forgiveness, Adeline. It may not seem like it, but Xavier suffered for a very long time after your sister passed. And even now, he's still suffering, struggling to forgive himself and accept that I've forgiven him. But your kindness to him will help him."

"I … I didn't know he's been suffering."

"Many suffer in silence."

Looking around at the poppies, each one still in full bloom before the Maker. I took a deep breath, inhaling their scent on the wings of the wind. "This smell, it's familiar."

"You grew up here, and you've always loved poppies."

"Have I?"

He grinned. "You have."

"Jesus, when I wake up, and I've forgiven Xavier, what happens next? Do I just keep living?"

He nodded. "You must. There's still much work for you to do in my Father's Kingdom on Earth. You will be an example to many that there's hope in the darkness."

"Eli told me I'd have to die to myself, but I don't know how."

"You already have. You're not who you used to be, you gave that up, and now you are My child."

330

"Is that why You had to die, to get new life?"

He lifted my hand to His lips and kissed it. "Yes, that's right."

38

When Things Began to Change

Xavier

I called Eli when Adeline passed out in the alleyway. I couldn't afford to be caught with another woman in a shady situation. I barely got away with not being a suspect in Jay's attempted murder case. Thankfully, the diner's cameras caught everything, and I was ruled out as a suspect, but they never made out the figure who carried her over to the garbage and disappeared.

With my head on my desk, I waited for Adeline to wake up. I wasn't sure how she would feel, or if she would even want to talk to me, but I had to tell her the truth. And with the case coming up, I had to make a decision; convince her to testify in my place or follow the plan and take the stand myself. The only problem is that if I don't tell the detectives that I found her, I could be charged with something along the lines of withholding information. A groan escaped me as I raked my hand through my hair.

"What am I supposed to do, God?"

He didn't respond, and I knew from His silence what I needed to do. This was my chance to finally make things right with Adeline, to make some kind of peace offering for what I've done. Living and knowing that someone else wasn't because of my cowardness almost made me an even bigger coward.

"But God has forgiven me," I whispered. "I'm forgiven." Though it didn't feel like it, I had to believe it.

The rustling of my blankets caught my attention. I glanced over at the bed to find Adeline sitting up, holding her head.

"Where am I?"

"Adeline," I came to the edge of the bed and knelt beside it, "you passed out and I brought you back to my place."

She wouldn't look at me. Her hair fell forward, forming a red curtain dividing us and hiding her from me. I should've been the one hiding.

"Do you know what it's like to be alone?"

"I don't know how to answer that," I said.

She grunted softly, a single bounce of her shoulders. "Then you've never truly been alone. I have. I've been in a space where nothing exists, screaming for someone to hear me. But no one did. Losing my sister took nearly everything from me, but the last part of myself I'd been clinging to was taken by Matthew Leslie."

I flinched at his name.

"And then, his best friend came stumbling back into my life when I thought I'd gotten away from all of Fresno. I was afraid at first, but you were nothing like him. I realized it on my own, but the person who vouched for you was my sister."

Lowering my head to the blankets, I listened to her. I couldn't face her when she was advocating for me because of her sister.

"I had this memory of her, gleaming, because you were the only person in the entire school who knew that line by MJ. She danced all around the house, proclaiming that you were likely Spiderman in plain sight, or just Peter Parker." She chuckled, and it was a broken one, filled with too many emotions. Happiness, nostalgia, bitterness, they were all swirling in her voice now.

"Madeline lost her footing, fell for a guy who was no good for her. But you were still the same good guy you'd always been, even after Matt was accused. I used to think you were so nice to my sister because you were different from Matt, but now I know you were just as guilty as he was." She stopped, and I was doing everything I could not to break down right in front of her when I felt her hand on my head. "But I remember my sister smiling from ear to ear the night before she took her life. She told me that you were the only guy in the world who deserved love, and she hoped that one day you'd have that."

She was crying as her hand ruffled my hair. I didn't move or raise my head, I just let her tears drench me.

"I didn't know Madeline knew you were there that night, even so, she wouldn't have wanted you to intervene and see her in that situation. She wouldn't have asked you to pick between her and your best friend, and she'd forgiven you." Her trembling voice was weak now as she whispered, "Because of Jesus, I have to forgive you. But because of Madeline, I *want* to forgive you, and I do. I forgive you, Xavier."

Raising my head, I had my own set of tears, but she was covered in them. Pulling her close, I held her, whispering gratitude and apologies, muttering anything I could formulate to show my thankfulness.

I've been forgiven, I thought. *Adeline has forgiven me. I can let it go now... I don't have to hold on to this pain anymore, right?*

I have already forgiven you, My son.

Sobbing. That's what filled my bedroom for at least an hour. I wouldn't let her go, and she couldn't let me go because I was holding her close. When we finally pulled apart, she made room for me on the bed, and I sat beside her. There was nothing to be said right away. It was a liberating moment, yet a sorrowful one as I could almost put high school behind me.

"Adeline," I said softly.

"Yes?"

"I have something else to tell you now."

She nodded, and I reached for her hand. She let me take it, my fingers sliding between hers. Her fingers fit perfectly between mine, like my hand had been fashioned for hers, and hers for mine.

"I want you to know first, that you don't have to be alone anymore. I know you've only just forgiven me, but being alone is hard, and I want you to call me if you ever need anything."

A small smile dimpled one of her cheeks as she nodded.

I exhaled. "Secondly, Matt Leslie is on trial for vehicular manslaughter … and sexual assault."

She looked at me, almond eyes filled with shock.

"He's on trial for the rape of Naomi Brown and," I paused, almost afraid to say her name, "Adeline Jones."

"*Me* … How did they know?"

"They pulled people from the party and asked us to identify anyone they saw at the party. The prosecutors told me that three different people pointed you out. Two remembered seeing Matt leaving a room, and some time after that, you left the same room in a rush."

She placed a hand over her mouth but didn't let my hand go. She sat there, staring ahead at my mostly empty room. I couldn't tell if she was relieved or afraid.

"They want me to testify against Matt."

"What?" She looked devastated, like testifying wasn't an option.

"I have to, because if I don't, they'll drag you back to California and make you stand trial."

"I'll do it." She pulled on my hand, leaning away on the bed to see me fully. "I'll go back there and tell them that he took everything from me."

"You can't because I'm going."

"No—"

"I have to do this for Madeline!" The entire room was still for a heartbeat. "I have to tell her story because I was there and no one else can tell it but us. It's not about me anymore, Adeline, it's about the truth."

Slowly, Adeline shifted beside me again. Within the blankets, she felt for my hand as she said, "Thank you."

"What?"

"Thank you for telling her story. I think she'd like that you were the one who told it. She'd really think you were Spiderman, swinging in to save her."

Leaning her head on my shoulder, we stayed that way in silence, undoubtedly both of us thinking about Madeline.

The trial was only a few days away now, and Adeline had been staying with Eli and me for a week. I'm used to being here with her and Elijah, we were like a family. Returning home to my real family was going to be overwhelming because I knew when I left them this time, I never had to go back again. Matt's trial would be the only thing I had to do in California. I'd be liberated from my past once I left the stand, and I planned to run to the doors of freedom.

I had to make it through the trial first though, and every day it got closer, I felt more anxious about it. Eli had been making me and Adeline share our feelings about the case every day this week like we were in group therapy. To be honest, it helped. My anxiety had been through the roof, but Elijah gave me scriptures to pray, and breathing exercises, and I was admittedly feeling a lot better.

Coming down the hall, I could hear AJ and Elijah chatting in my bedroom. AJ had been staying in my room while I slept on the couch. I didn't mind, but Eli said we'd need to start looking for a new place to stay with AJ joining us.

"And you see yourself in a field of red flowers, waiting on a boy?"

"I've never seen his face but I'm always calling him Benedict in my head."

A field of red flowers?

Instinctively, I crept closer to the door to listen, but the floor beneath me creaked—for the first time ever—and both of them stopped talking. Awkwardly, I pushed open the door, trying to play it off like I hadn't been eavesdropping.

"Were you—"

"I'm heading out," I cut AJ off. She was sitting on the bed, legs folded, wearing my oversized hoodie. I'd given it to her last week when I thought she was returning to her own place. But she ended up staying and I never asked for it back.

"Adeline, why don't you go with Xavier? I think he could use the company right now," Eli suggested out of nowhere.

"Oh … Uh …" AJ glanced back and forth from Eli to me, wearing the same surprised expression I had on. Though she'd been staying here, we didn't do *that* much together. AJ and I had mostly been like two passing ships in the night. It felt like family because Jax and I were the same. My little brother played sports and I hung out with Matt, but at the end of the day, we sat down as a family with our parents for dinner—most days. Here had been no different. Adeline did whatever while Elijah and I went to work and classes. When we all came home, we had dinner together if I didn't have a late shift, or we'd just do a little counselling.

"It's alright if you don't want to go." I waved. "I'm just going to pick up my check from work. They're having a system update, so there's no direct deposits right now."

"You should go," Eli encouraged. "It'll be good to get you out of this place. You haven't left since last week."

Adeline told me she didn't want to leave the apartment because nowhere else had ever made her feel quite as comfortable as Eli's place. I couldn't blame her; I'd felt the same way when I decided to stay here. She promised to leave soon, she just needed time to get her head together. Eli didn't mind, and neither did I. He'd told her that if she stayed any longer than a week, she'd have to start going to Sunday service. He was more lenient on her about that since he didn't want to force her into church. Surprisingly, Adeline had agreed to his terms without a fuss.

She'd told us both about her experience when she passed out. How she saw Jesus and spoke to Him. Without full details, she told us they'd had a conversation about her sister and forgiveness. It was shocking to me, since I thought she wasn't straight. But Eli clarified later that a month or so ago, Adeline had let her former lifestyle go and accepted Christ.

It wasn't an easy or fun transition—abandoning her attraction to women and living the life of a straight Christian. Her thoughts and mental capacity were in need of serious reframing. Seeing the Bible as truth, and not just a book of stories took someone like Eli to make things plain and clear for her, but she seemed to be adjusting well. It was obvious this was something she wanted, not a phase or an interest. Adeline truly understood that her life as a lesbian had been wrong and was over, but it was only over because she had trusted in Jesus to set her free from the spirit of homosexuality and all the bondage that came with it.

Eli had explained the Bible to me in a way I would never forget. He'd said that Abraham believed God, and that was it. Moses thought his faith was remarkable and under the influence of the Holy Spirit,

338

wrote down Abraham's story. People in the Biblical era were no different from us. Writing things down so they wouldn't forget them, retelling a story to encourage someone else. People were inspired by Abraham's faith, moved by King David's passion, impressed with King Solomon's wisdom, and baffled by Job's endurance and patience. These were stories worth remembering, lives worth memorializing.

None of the people in the time that these events occurred knew that God was going to single their lives out and place it in a Book for us to read later. God could've taken any person's story, and added even more stories to the Bible, but He was specific in His choosing. Intricately telling the story of Jesus from beginning to end, Old Testament to the New Testament. Who could doubt the Bible when you know that it's the truth? No one doubts a biography, so why is it that we doubt Jesus's?

Regular people inspiring other people, impacting those around them, so much that someone thinks to write it down, award them, document their deeds. Eli said the Bible had been no different on a basic level. Of course, it's holy and divine, equipping us with the tools we'd need forever, however, if one can marvel at the wisdom of some poet, or the accomplishments of a military war hero then, surely, belief in the Word of God was no different.

39

Making Things Right

Xavier

Adeline didn't go with me to pick up my check. Instead, the day before I left for Matt's trial, she asked if we could hang out. I had nothing better to do, instead of biting my nails and trying to ignore the anxiety drilling deeper into my gut with every inhale. Taking my mind off facing Matt and standing up for the righteous thing was certainly welcomed.

"It's windy today," I said as AJ and I walked through Manhattan. She was wearing my hoodie again, paired with some sweats and sneakers. Her iconic red hair was pulled into a bun, leaving nothing but her dimpled cheeks and piercings for me to see clearly. Adeline had always been pretty to me, even when she wasn't straight. And she always had this aura about her, like something was always drawing me to her. Whenever I looked at her, it felt like I'd seen her before, or maybe I'd just found something I've been missing.

If I'm honest with myself, AJ was prettier than Carly and Jay, but I never paid her much mind since boys weren't her thing, and Carly had commanded every iota of my attention. I couldn't stop myself from glancing at the cloud pendant on her bracelet as she brushed a strand of hair from her face. I felt my pulse quicken, blood pumping through the thick vein of my wrist, right against my cloud-shaped birthmark.

It doesn't mean anything, I reminded myself, though I couldn't stop my mind from summoning an image of a field of red poppies all of a sudden. I almost stopped right there on the pavement if it weren't for AJ touching my shoulder.

"You good?" she asked.

I nodded dumbly. "The wind."

"Almost blew you over." She laughed.

I laughed too, though nothing was funny. "It's always a little windy during the spring and the fall."

"I guess so."

"Where are we going?"

"Just walking," she said. "I used to walk all of Brooklyn when I was living in that group home. I needed something to do."

Nodding, I glanced down at her as she looked ahead. "So, can I ask you something then?"

She shrugged.

"How did you end up in a group home?"

"The same way Jay ended up in the trash."

I stopped walking. "What?"

Shoving her small hands into the pocket of her hoodie, she turned to me. Adeline looked thinner now. Like the stress of everything had taken her appetite and her strength. So much had changed in four years for me, I couldn't imagine what four years had done to her.

"What do you know about Jay?" I asked.

"I was the one who left her there for you to find. She wasn't doing good, so I got her out of there and got myself into a home."

"I don't understand."

"Of course, you don't." She turned and continued walking and I jogged to catch up.

"Wait, AJ, I don't want to fight about this. I just want to know what happened to Jay."

The corner of her mouth flinched before her brown eyes reached up to mine. "It never fails that whoever I talk to is always concerned with the wellbeing of someone else. Why even bother talking to me?" She shoved past me, but I grabbed her arm at the last second. A brutal look of frustration and resentment washed over her as she glared at me. The rest of the crowd passing by watched us too.

I let her go. "Can we just talk about this?"

"No."

"*You* brought her up." I ran a hand through my hair. "So don't play victim like this. I just want to know what happened to her."

AJ took a step back, looking me up and down before she chuckled, "You still don't get it." She turned away, stepping forward to blend into the crowd to be forgotten, but I wouldn't let that happen again. I knew how she felt, like she'd been overlooked. I'd felt like I'd been overlooked by every girl I ever wanted to date. Lia never paid me any attention until she thought I wanted to have sex with her. Carly was using me, and I didn't mean anything to her until it was too late. Jay liked me, but Jay liked *everyone*, I don't think I was special.

I even considered Daisy, but after she and Sky cozied up together at Bible study during the hot chocolate party Eli threw for us this past Christmas, I've been avoiding her. And what's worse, none of these women were God-approved. He'd told me no to Carly. I never thought to ask about Lia, nor did I care enough at the time. I figured Jay wasn't right because she wasn't straight, and God was very clear about Daisy too. But it all still hurt, it all felt like I was no one but a passerby, like the concern was always elsewhere and never on me.

"Adeline," I grabbed her wrist, "I see you, and I hear you, and I'm listening. You're not just a face in the crowd to me. You're not your sister's replacement. You're no one but you."

Her wrist was trembling in my grasp. Her chocolate cheeks were drizzled with strawberry syrup as they reddened. Tears began to swell, and I pulled her into my chest. Small hands with chipped nail polish gripped my jacket as she cried. Hearing her cry was easier than seeing her cry. She always looked so broken and devastated, though her hiccupping now rivaled her expression. Pain had been twisted in her belly for longer than I could ever know and seeing her take her life back every day after wanting to lose herself seemed wonderful to me. But for Adeline, it was probably the most challenging thing she'd ever done.

"I'm sorry," she whispered. "I'm sorry for getting angry at you. I just… I still feel like everyone's looking at me but not seeing me."

"I know how you feel." She stepped from my embrace, drying her tears on her sleeve. "I'm sorry that I was only concerned with Jocelyn."

She shook her head. "Don't be sorry. You were right, I brought her up. It was stupid of me to get all emotional about it."

"Nah, Eli said you're still healing, so I should take everything slow with you."

Her sadness was murky now as she squinted. It took me a second to realize what I'd said before I tried to explain. "I didn't mean sex!"

A woman walked by, eyeing me, and a couple passed by on the other side laughing to each other as they both looked us over.

I sighed. "I didn't mean take it slow *that* way."

AJ laughed. "Come on, let's grab dinner and go home."

When we returned home, Adeline and I spent our Friday night without Elijah. He wouldn't be home until the morning since he was participating in the church's shut-in. The only reason Adeline and I didn't have to go was because this was for the pastors only, to build up their faith and strengthen their prayer lives.

Adeline and I actually had a lot of fun, laughing and talking about high school. We even talked about our professor from the class we had together our freshmen year. Adeline was hilarious and super goofy, which was the total opposite of her twin sister, Madeline. From what I could remember about Madeline, she was loud and in your face, but you knew it was only a façade. She never actually enjoyed anything, but it always looked like it.

When I think about it, I think I know Adeline better now than I knew Madeline while she was alive. I'm sure, though, if someone knew her best, it was probably Matt.

"So," AJ said as she flopped onto the couch beside me, "how long will you be gone?"

"The trial is three days in the middle of next week, so I'll be back home by Sunday. I think my mom wants me to stay an extra day with her."

She scooted closer to me before she leaned over to rest her head on my shoulder. I wanted to hyper-ventilate and set off proximity alarms to scare her away, but I swallowed thickly and sat stiffly beside her. This wasn't the first time Adeline and I shared a moment like this. The first time we were caught up in tears and apologies, but now, we were just talking, and she was sitting beside me, leaning her head on my shoulder.

It was surprising, considering how closed off Adeline was, but it was also not surprising, since I knew she was just trying to comfort me. Her warmth beside me soothed the nerves rattling within my gut. The ones she stirred from sitting so close, and the ones that'd been growing every day the trial grew nearer.

"You don't have to do this," her voice was small in the stillness of the apartment. "She's already gone, nothing can bring her back."

"I know." I shied away from her now, moving further to the arm of the couch. "But I owe her, and every other girl who's been wronged by Matt. I've protected him for too long, now's my chance to set things right. And I … I owe you too."

I could feel her eyes roving over me. It wasn't a burning glare, or an icy look, the heat of her gaze was filled with pity and sorrow, but I wouldn't look at her. I couldn't. I was afraid I'd see Madeline and be lost for words.

"X," she said, "thank you."

My eyes flitted to hers without my consent. The dim lights of the apartment let the sun trace her stunning figure. Her skin was radiating, like glitter had been poured all over her, and I couldn't look away. She moved on her own, closer to me until she was right beside me, taking my hand in hers.

"I thought she would disappear and be forgotten. Then I lost myself and tried to make myself be forgotten. But somehow you noticed us both." She squeezed my hand, a small smile tugging at her puffy lips. "You remembered my sister when we met in my dorm, and you saw that notebook. And then you noticed me, the *real* me, in the hospital room, and when you met me from the bus last week. You remembered me, remembered that I wasn't a copy of my twin sister, that I was a real person with my own thoughts and feelings. That means more to me than any case, or trial."

Without a word, I adjusted on the couch, and let her in. Fitting perfectly beneath my arm, Adeline rested against me, keeping her fingers interlocked with mine.

"Xavier, it's time to wake up."

I snorted, inhaling the smell of breakfast in the apartment. Eli stood over me, and I realized I was asleep on the couch with AJ. She was still curled beneath my arm, slumbering away quietly.

"What time is it?" I asked.

"Almost ten. Your train leaves at noon, doesn't it?"

"Yeah." I nodded and glanced back down at Adeline. I didn't want to move. Last night had been one of the best nights in my entire life, and it was spent mostly in silence until we fell asleep. Though we didn't speak, a new bond had formed between us. Adeline's fingers laced with mine, our breathing steadying to make pace with each other's, it felt like the entire world was finally right.

But now, I sat awake with the weight of reality pressing on my shoulders. I'd be traveling the whole weekend for Matt's trial. I'd miss the first day to rest once I arrived back home, but I didn't need to be there until the second day to hear the testimonies per the prosecution's request. However, I didn't testify until the last day of the trial.

"You should get ready soon," Elijah said as he moved for the kitchen.

I wondered if he was mad that he caught us like this. Technically, we hadn't done anything, but it was probably something Elijah wouldn't want us doing again.

Carefully, I moved from the couch, lying Adeline down as I stood. She adjusted a little, and I pulled a blanket over her. Before leaving to get ready, I leaned down and brushed Adeline's hair from her face. A few red strands had sprung free from her bun, and as my hand swept them away, her eyes sleepily opened for a second. My heart stopped when I thought I woke her, but she only adjusted again and went back to sleeping.

My bags were already packed, I just needed to shower and grab everything I needed for the trip. It only took forty-five minutes to get ready, and Eli had finished breakfast. A whole table full of food;

pancakes, sausage and bacon, eggs, cream of wheat, and toast. There was also a bowl of fruit in the center of the table.

"What's all this for?" I asked as I set my bags down.

"It's breakfast." Eli shrugged as he took a seat.

Adeline rounded the corner, stopping short to glance me over and then Eli. The room was suddenly awkward, and I couldn't avoid the pressure any longer. Adeline had run my nerves up the wall while simultaneously gathering them to calm them. But I could deal with something normal like pretty girls giving boys anxiety. But, this case, it was breaking me.

Gripping the top of the chair, I stared down at the empty plate in front of my spot. "I'm scared." The words echoed through my head as I spoke again, "I'm scared that he'll get sentenced, and I'm scared that he won't."

"You don't have to want anything bad to happen to him to do the right thing, X."

I looked up to find Adeline. Right across from me, she looked shy like she always did, but her words had an air of confidence surrounding them.

Eli scooped eggs onto his own plate, and then looked up at me. "Who's on the Lord's side?" It wasn't really a question, more of a way to snap me back to attention. "You don't have to be afraid that he'll be angry with you, Xavier. Doing the righteous thing is all you can do. Don't give up this opportunity to do the right thing, to stand for something."

"It's easier said than done," Adeline added, "but I promise, it'll be worth it in the end. It was hard to choose to think on Godly things, and not think the way I used to," she said softly. "But when I finally surrendered to God, He helped me feel better about the change. He can do the same for you, X." She reached for my hand, and I stared at hers.

I wanted to snap and tell her that deciding something like this was harder than not being gay. But Adeline had made decision after decision, choosing to do the righteous thing even when she didn't want to—even when it felt totally opposite of what she had been told was natural and normal.

I couldn't yell at her because she had faced the monster already. She knew how hard it was to defeat the villain within, the pangs of guilt that burst in your chest when you thought of the effects of your decision. However, if I wanted to win the civil war on the inside, I had to put down my own weapons, and cling to the Word of God, allowing Him to win this battle.

Slowly, I reached for Adeline's hand and held it. With her touch, the world seemed right, and I felt a little stronger. Like the small delicate hands in my own needed me to protect them. And I would. I wasn't only going to do the righteous thing, but I was going to make things right for Adeline and her sister.

Everything's going to be alright.

40

Fam(ily)

Adeline

"Are you worried about him?" Eli asked from the dining room.

I slid a plate into the dishwasher and slapped a hand to my hip. "I just want him to do the right thing, but not because of me."

"You two seem to have gotten a little closer," Eli's voice reached me before he entered the kitchen holding a skillet with chicken and gravy leftovers we'd have for dinner tomorrow.

"I don't know what you're talking about." Grabbing another dish, I placed it into the washer. He chuckled as he pulled containers from the cabinets only he and Xavier could reach, they were both so tall.

"It's not a big deal if you guys like each other." Eli smiled. "I would prefer you guys didn't sleep together while I'm *gone*." His emphasis on 'gone' was a dagger to the heart. "But everyone's clothes were still on, so I wasn't *too* upset."

"I don't…" I struggled to get the words out. Words that I'd been avoiding since Eli let me stay here. A topic I'd been dodging because I didn't want to confront it. "I don't like Xavier like that," I grinded out.

"Alright." Eli lifted the pan to pour the gravy into a separate container from the chicken. "You don't like him like that, but you do like him."

"*You* like him, Eli."

"I'm very fond of Xavier."

I rolled my eyes and got the last few dishes and silverware into the dishwasher before rinsing my hands and leaving the kitchen. I had choices, I could either flop on the couch where Xavier and I had fallen asleep together, or I could go to Xavier's bedroom where all his belongings were... I only went to his room because I'd been sleeping in there, and I was avoiding Elijah.

Sitting on the bed, I looked around the room. Xavier was such a plain guy, nothing special about him except his looks. He was attractive. Square jaw, lovely hair, honey crisp skin with hazel eyes that held all his emotions. He didn't have a lot of facial hair, just a slight dusting of stubble that appeared whenever he was too lazy to shave it.

Xavier was the furthest thing from an eye sore, but he never called attention to himself. You just happened to look up one day and catch his eye from across the room. Then you suddenly realized he was handsome.

I lay back and I heard a crinkling noise. I'd heard it all last night when I slept in X's bed. I was trying to avoid snooping, but I couldn't help it now. Lifting the mattress, there was a folded piece of paper under it. Reluctantly, I reached for it and opened it.

I love you.

My breath hitched for a second when I thought X had left the note for me. But that wasn't it at all. I recognized the handwriting, it was Carly's. She'd written this note to me and asked one of the nurses to give it to me when we were in the hospital.

Before I knew it, I was out the door and in the kitchen where Eli was wiping down counters in his casual jeans and button-down.

"Eli, what's this?"

He looked up, adjusting his glasses to see. The moment of recognition was easy to see on his face. The way his brows flattened, and his eyes sank away. "He told me before I left for the shut-in that he was going to leave that note for you when he went back to California."

"How did he get it?"

"From the hospital. We went in to check on you and you were gone. The only thing left was that note. He always had plans to return it to you, but considering what'd happened, that seemed nearly impossible."

"Okay, but I've been here a week, why didn't he give it to me?"

"Did you read the letter?" Eli pushed blond bangs aside and removed his glasses.

"Yes, it's a note from Carly, telling me she loved me."

"Do you really think you needed something like that right now?"

I stepped back. "How dare you assume I'm that weak? How dare you assume I'd go running back to Carly or women at all!"

"Calm down, Adeline. I know you're stronger, but *Xavier* doesn't." He shook his head. "He was so confused over whether or not to give it to you. He didn't want to push you back into something you've been fighting to get out of. X was just looking out for you."

Looking down at the note in my hand, I felt dumb, but only because X was right, and Eli was wrong. I had gotten stronger, but I don't know if I could've seen this note a week ago, when I'd learned the truth about my sister, and not crumble back into that dark pit.

People relapse because that's the only way they know how to cope. Without God, it's impossible to truly be set free from the dark feelings and the tormenting mindset I had.

"I'm sorry." I sighed. "I'm not angry at you or Xavier, I'm angry at myself. Embarrassed that this is who I used to be, and embarrassed that X was right to keep this from me."

"Why do you say that?"

"Because I think I would've tried to find Carly."

"You would've been unsuccessful," he said as he grabbed his rag from the counter to start wiping again. "Carly moved out of the country. She took an international flight a while back to somewhere—I don't even know where. She called me once from a private number just to tell me she had landed and moved into a nice place. She gave me no scenery, no hints, nothing. Just let me know that she was alright."

"Really?" I stepped into the kitchen and leaned against the wall.

"Yeah. She's trying to start over, wants to be better, so she left."

I smiled as I looked down at the note. "Carly always wanted better. That's how we got into that accident."

He stopped wiping and looked over at me. I'm sure no one had ever told Eli the truth about how that accident happened. Carly left a bogus statement that she was sick and veered off the road. I wrote down that I couldn't remember anything about the accident and left the hospital through the night. I was more concerned for Jay, though the concern increased after Carly sent me this note.

"We'd gotten in bad with some people. Jay got addicted to drugs. Carly had tried them enough to like them, but she didn't get addicted for some reason. Jocelyn's addiction was out of control, and we were low on money."

"What happened?"

I took a deep breath; this was the first time I had told the truth of what'd happened in that accident. "Carly and I were working little gigs here and there, and we were going to try and get some work from some people we'd met." I spared him the details and gave him the cleanest version of the story I could give. "But that was a lie. Carly got into the driver's seat and headed onto the freeway in the opposite direction of our friend's house." I glanced down at the note and opened it. "She wanted to run away with me. Leave Jay behind because she was too much of a problem. But I couldn't leave Jocelyn—"

"Because that's who you really loved," Eli interjected.

"Yes, she was."

"You guys fought?"

"I grabbed the steering wheel, and it sent us spiraling." The lump in my throat felt like a rock as I swallowed. "I was so desperate to see Jocelyn, so angry that Carly would try to take me away from the only person who'd ever loved me without realizing that Carly had loved me too. But when I did realize that she loved me, I ran. I had to get away because I didn't want to hurt her by staying. By giving her any idea that I loved her back."

"So you left when she sent you that note."

"Mmhmm." I folded the note and finally raised my head. Eli wasn't looking at me. He was leaning against the counter, arms folded, looking at the pictures on the fridge. I stepped closer, seeing Carly in almost every single picture except three. One was of Xavier at his desk, laughing with his head back. He was smiling so hard; it was a beautiful picture. But the last two froze me in place.

Shakily, I reached out and touched a picture of myself. I was sitting on the couch, daydreaming as I looked out the window. I was there, part of the family. The other pictures were of Carly and people I assumed were Eli and Carly's parents since the two siblings were younger as they posed in the picture with the two adults. In the center of all the pictures was the word, *family*, and I was part of it.

Tears began to blur the final picture; it was clearly his latest addition to the fridge—which I had never noticed until now. We were asleep, X and I. On the couch, our hands were knitted together as X's arm was wrapped around me. I didn't know what we looked more like, siblings or lovers.

That's a lie. I knew what we looked like, but I wanted us to look like siblings because it was safer that way. What I felt right now was just jitters from being here, nothing more.

"I'm sorry," I said as tears rolled down my cheeks.

"There's nothing to apologize for, Adeline. Carly's fine, you're fine, even Jay's fine—she took six months of rehab and is starting her life over now. What's there to be sorry for?"

"I almost ruined everything."

"But you didn't, and now I've got a family again."

41

Make an Effort

Xavier

Returning home was draining. From the long train ride to the beady eyes of my family, and the pity they all had on me. I appreciated their gentleness and concern, but it was also frustrating. I wanted my family to act like nothing major was happening, and though they tried, they couldn't help themselves and showed me pity not support.

How could I blame them? My family knew I loved Matt like a brother, and standing against him would change that forever. But I had lov*ed* Matt… I didn't still love him.

It was on the train ride when I prayed for God's support, His strength, that I actually felt soothed. I'd taken Adeline's advice and submitted to God and paired it with everything Eli had told me about not letting anything get between God and me. He'd been there for me, guided me, and helped me. I had to do this for Him, I wanted to do this for Him. Not to prove to myself that I was actually a Believer or to anyone else. I wanted to do this for God, to stand up for Him.

355

Many times, I've read articles about celebrities, or stars who said they believed in Jesus. And when the opportunity was presented to them to take a stand for righteousness, they never did. They dodged questions and gave lukewarm answers in interviews and hoped that God would understand.

But He doesn't, and He never will because for eternity God has stood for us. Protected us, fought against the enemy, sent His Son for us. Jesus defeated death, hell, and the grave for us. All just to sit on the stand and tell the truth. I was going to do it... I had to do it.

I also wanted to do it for Adeline and Madeline. Madeline had died because she was broken beyond repair. She didn't know that Jesus could've fixed her, so when I go to the stand tomorrow, I will make it clear that Madeline saw no way out. And I won't let Adeline be forgotten.

The prosecutor told me that they really want to hammer at Madeline's suicide, but I can't let Adeline be overshadowed again. She'd spent her whole life in her sister's shadows, had even taken on her sister's persona and completely let go of her own. Adeline will not be another name on a legal document. She won't be plastered on a poster or become a hashtag. She won't be attached to a list of names where people beg others not to forget them. Adeline's story will be told, and she will be recognized as a human being who's been violated just as darkly as her sister had been. The difference between the two, Adeline found the still small Voice in the storm, and answered Him.

In the courtroom the next day, my leg bounced beside me as we waited for the guards to bring Matt inside. I sat on the prosecution's side, that meant when Matt came in, he'd know I wasn't there to support him. He would be shocked, just as shocked as he probably was yesterday when I wasn't there for opening day. Matt had always assumed I'd be right behind him, patting him on the back and supporting all his endeavors. But when I encountered God, I changed.

"X…" My mother placed a hand on my knee, and I looked at her. She gave me a tight smile. "It's going to be alright."

I nodded and took a deep breath. Jax and Dad couldn't be here today. Jax had school, of course, and Dad had work. But the two of them and Mom would be there tomorrow to hear me testify. I wasn't surprised when I didn't see Matt's parents. They were either confident he was going to get off with a warning, or too embarrassed to show their faces. Either one had to do with their pride but, like I said, that didn't surprise me.

The back doors opened, and I looked back quickly. It was Special Agent De Luca and Detective Clora Vean. The two ladies walked in, nodding at me as they took their seats behind me. Suddenly, my nostrils were overloaded with the most girly fragrances I've ever smelled. The two agents looked tough, both brandishing badges and guns, but they smelled heavenly.

"Hey, kid." De Luca patted my shoulder. "We came to make sure you were here."

"No, we didn't." Detective Vean rolled her eyes. "We came to see the case. Watch everything roll out."

I nodded, and turned around, though I only believed Special Agent De Luca. The two of them really had no reason to be here. They weren't testifying until tomorrow, so I knew the special agent was telling the truth when she said they were there to make sure I was too.

The creak of the back door made me stiffen. I knew this was it. There were heavy footsteps that undoubtedly belonged to a guard. The officer stepped forward, holding open the small door, when Matthew Leslie appeared. Blonde hair perfectly swooped back, a fitted suit, grey

357

with a light blue button-down—no tie, and his cocky demeanor ever present. He limped a little as he walked out, and I remembered one of the detectives told me that he'd broken his legs in the accident. Matt didn't see me as he walked by, replacing my perfume-stained nostrils with his expensive cologne.

Matt took a seat at the table where an older man with grey hair was setting down binders. He leaned over, whispering something to the old man with a slight smile on his face, when he noticed me. It was like he didn't know if he was imagining things or not when he stopped speaking immediately. His smile disappeared, and his mouth fell open.

Yes, Matt… I'm here.

And he knew if I had anything to do with the case, there was a possibility that secrets had been told, confidential information between us had been bribed out of me. The wave of lies he'd rode in on had just pulled away from the shore back into the darkest and deepest part of the ocean.

Matt stared so long that his attorney grabbed his shoulder, and I felt Mom grabbing my hand, and one of the detectives behind me gripping my shoulder. He moved, jerked forward, before rising slowly to his feet. His attorney jumped to his own, mumbling something to him, and I heard the Special Agent whispering behind me, "Don't let him startle you. If you get thrown out, the prosecution may not be able to call you to the stand tomorrow."

"Baby," my mother's voice got my attention. I didn't even know I'd been panting. Matt and I had entered some private arena momentarily, like two dogs barking through a fence at each other in the open, but to the dogs, the only focus they had was on each other.

"Greater is He that is in you, than he that is in the world. Say it with me," my mother whispered.

"Greater is He that is in me," I paused to take a breath, "than he that is in the world." I felt a spiral of emotions. I was heartbroken and angry because Matt had gotten us into this mess. If he hadn't done these things and put me in this predicament, I wouldn't be here right now. Or maybe I would, I'd just be sitting on the opposite side. But I wasn't. We were best friends turned enemies in a matter of days. The moment I woke up out of that hospital bed and spoke to the detectives, Matt and I were no longer friends. And after four long years of his parents tying things up in legal battles, we were total enemies.

Mom squeezed my hand and then exhaled slowly. I looked down at our hands intertwined, at the matching birthmark we shared. I felt glad she was here with me instead of my father or Jax. No one else would've known what to say just then, no one else would've told me to quote a scripture to calm down.

I squeezed her hand back.

"All rise," the bailiff's voice boomed into the room, snatching Matt's eyes from mine. "The honorable Judge Sidwai is now presiding."

A short woman, dark skin with flowing hair, stepped inside the courtroom and up to her bench. Setting files down and placing glasses onto her nose, she said, "You may be seated."

As we sat, I caught Matt staring at me again, but I looked away. The judge looked over the rim of her glasses at Matt as she said, "Excuse me, Mr. Leslie, your case is up here. Please face forward."

Matt grunted and turned away.

"Now," the judge began, "we will continue where we left off yesterday. We went over the evidence pertaining to the vehicular manslaughter charge and the drinking under the influence charges. Now, we will be moving forward with the charges of sexual assault. Rodrick, you may begin with your opening statement."

Mom had been keeping up with the case and she told me that the vehicular manslaughter account was solid, but they were considering dropping the DUI counts because he was 'still young.' The defense had built their whole case on Matt's youthfulness and making mistakes, as well as trying to find a reasonable mental issue from his past to make up for his shortcomings. It seemed like it was working so far since Matt came in with a smile on his face before he saw me.

Rodrick, Matt's attorney, stood to his feet and buttoned his expensive black suit jacket. He stepped around the table, reading his notes for a second longer before looking up at the judge and nodding. "Yesterday, you heard how the defendant was in a car accident resulting in the lives of others being taken. The prosecution will have you believe that the young man has been riding a white horse his whole life with a silver spoon in his mouth, so he thinks he shouldn't be punished." He raised a hand. "The truth is quite the opposite."

Rodrick gestured to Matt. "Matthew Leslie is a young man with a bright future. His family has been well-off, but doesn't that also mean Matt hasn't been exposed to much? He's a sheltered kid, who made one mistake, one night, trying to have the time of his life with his best friend. An accident is an accident, no matter how you paint it." Rodrick nodded firmly once more at the judge and took his seat.

"Alright, Belle you may make your opening statements."

A woman leaned over and touched the arm of her counterpart before standing. "As you all have heard, Matthew Leslie is a kid with a future. However, a man's future was taken from him. A young girl's future was snatched away before it ever really began. Is it fair that when you paint the picture of an accident, you only paint the victims lying in their own blood, but not in the blood of the one responsible?" She shook her head, and looked over at Matt. "This young man may have gotten into an accident because, by law, accidents presumably happen without intent to harm someone. However, when you get behind a three-ton vehicle, with alcohol coursing through your system, and the cops are hot on your tail, a girl kissing your face off while you drive; yeah, it's an *accident*." She crossed the room to Matt and stood right in front of his table, staring him down as he glared back.

"But Matthew Leslie was sober enough to realize the cops were raiding the house and fled. So maybe he had no intention of crashing, but he had every intent to drive under the influence and make out with a girl with no regard to anyone else on the road." Belle turned back to the jury with her hands raised. "When you listen today, I ask that you look at the picture being painted and decide what's missing. Decide what doesn't fit in this painting. Take into consideration the deliberate actions of the defendant and the victims he left behind. Thank you."

I was sweating after that. The prosecution was strong, using the defense's own argument to crush them. I kind of felt relieved, like maybe my testimony wasn't going to be that important, like they could do this without me.

Gripping my pants, I took a breath. *No. I have to do this, I can't back down now.*

"Today we will be opening the case for Naomi Brown and Adeline Jones."

I flinched, looking up at the judge. She was still reading off her paper, explaining the court's agenda today, but Adeline's name was all I could focus on. I didn't know they went forward with pursuing Matt for her assault. They told me they were going to use Madeline's case to support Naomi, and if they could add Adeline, they would. No one told me they had done that, though.

Belle stepped forward again. "I'd like to call Naomi Brown to the stand."

Naomi stepped out of the pew in front of us. She wore a flowery dress, and her hands were clasped as she walked to the stand. I thought she would faint before she got there with how nervous she looked. Large eyes avoided Matt's as she stared only at Belle.

"State your name please," Belle said.

"Naomi Brown."

"Thank you. Now, Naomi, can you recall what happened the night

361

of your assault?"

She shifted. "I was dancing with my friends, and he came over—"

"Who is *he*?"

She hesitated. "Matt."

"Is he in this room?"

She nodded.

"Can you point him out to me?"

With a trembling hand, Naomi could barely raise her eyes to see Matt. She pointed to him sitting across the courtroom, and he dropped his head. But I knew that move. Matt always did that when he felt like he'd been wronged. He wasn't sorry or pitiful, he was angry and annoyed.

"Very good. Go on."

"He came up to my friends, and he told us he was looking for the bathroom. Abigail told him it was down the hall."

"Abigail, she was one of your friends?"

"Yes."

"And what was Matt's response?"

"He said, 'Abbey, why don't you walk me there?'"

Belle nodded. "And what did Abigail say?"

"She said, 'No, we're going to play beer pong, but join us when you're done.'"

"And then what happened?"

Naomi paused, her eyes flicking to her hands in her lap.

"It's alright, Naomi, we need the truth, okay?" Belle's voice was gentle as she tried to convince Naomi to speak.

The small girl took a breath and nodded. "He turned to me and said, 'Why don't you walk me?' And I said, 'Okay.'"

"What happened once you got down the hall?"

"Matt and I stopped at the bathroom, and he put his hand on the wall beside me and stroked my chin. He told me not to leave him, so I waited there for him. When he came out the bathroom, he was smiling."

"And then what happened?" The quietness of Belle's voice told me that it was coming. Matt's brutality was here, knocking at the door and all I could imagine was Madeline the night of her assault. The way he pushed her against the door, kissing her until she couldn't breathe, telling her how much he missed her and needed this from her. She'd only struggled a little then, but that didn't matter as he pushed open the door and shoved her inside.

"Matt told me I was beautiful and that he'd always had a thing for me, I was just too quiet. I told him I didn't know he liked me, and he said that he always had. Then he… he stepped forward and kissed me. He kissed me and told me that he *needed* this more than he wanted this."

"What was the 'this'?"

Naomi's eyes were leaking tears. "Sex," she whispered.

"Go on," Belle said.

I was trembling, I could barely listen. All I could see and hear was Madeline's agitated sighs, her whining for him to stop. It was replaying so loud in my head; I hunched over and covered my ears in the courtroom. I was falling apart right there. My mother's hand was on my back, rubbing small circles beside me.

Breathe.

You are with me, aren't You?

I am.

Following His instructions, I took a breath to slow my panting. His words had soothed me, anchored me, and I raised my head again.

"He opened the door behind me and pushed me inside," Naomi said. "I told him no. I fought and scratched at him, but he told me to be quiet. He put his hand over my mouth when he shoved me onto the bed."

"And then what happened?"

"He lifted my dress … and he … unzipped his pants." She

363

hiccupped. "And then he…" She couldn't say it, but she knew she had to. "He raped me."

Complete silence fell over the room as Naomi curled over at the stand and wept loudly. It had been years, but the pain of it all was still present like the party had happened last weekend.

"Naomi, I know this is hard," Belle said as she came to the stand, "but I want you to tell the jury what happened when he finished."

It took her a moment to compose herself, but when Naomi raised her head, her words weren't sorrowful or painful, they were angry, they were words I'd heard Matt say all the time.

"He said, 'you were such a good screw.'"

A few jurors wiped their eyes as a few others covered their mouths.

"I'd like to present evidence to the court, Your Honor."

"Proceed."

Belle came forward with a plastic bag containing a tube, and some other things inside. Opening the bag, she took out the contents and set them before the judge.

"That's Naomi's rape kit. The semen sample taken from her the day of the party matches Matt's DNA perfectly."

Judge Sidwai read over the paperwork and nodded.

"No further questions, Your Honor."

Judge Sidwai turned to Rodrick who stood immediately. Making his way over to Naomi, he took a second to look her over. "Ms. Brown, is it true you were drinking that evening?"

"Yes."

"And is it true that you and Matt kissed?"

"Y-Yes."

"Very good. So, Matt came out the bathroom, complimented you and the two of you started kissing. Then he moves you to the bedroom, where he gets a little rougher than you'd like, but you didn't mention screaming for help. You said you scratched him, but everyone knows

364

scratches during sex means you're doing something right." He turned to the jurors with a smug look on his face, but it was the jurors' reaction that made my stomach knot.

Some of them laughed... right in Naomi's face. They laughed. Their giddiness sounded like the squealing of thirsting pigs. They were disgusting.

"How dare you?" Naomi's words were vicious. "How dare you mock me? I was raped!"

"Settle down." Judge Sidwai banged her gavel and turned her attention to Rodrick. "Not in my courtroom. We don't make jokes about serious situations."

"My apologies, Your Honor," Rodrick said unsympathetically. "However, Ms. Brown, it's true that you didn't scream for help, isn't it?"

"I couldn't, he was covering my mouth."

"And you didn't bite him, or anything else?"

"Objection, Your Honor." Belle raised her hand.

"Overruled," Judge Sidwai said. "Continue, Rodrick."

"Thank you, Your Honor. I was asking Ms. Brown if she took any action to remove Matt's hand from her mouth."

"No." Naomi looked away.

"Right, so you were drunk, you kissed Matt, he took you in the room and when the act of sex began, you scratched him, but didn't make an effort to remove his hand or scream for help."

"I couldn't, I was hurting. Everything hurt... I was a virgin."

"Wow, virgin sex at a house party, sounds like a typical high school party."

"I was *raped*," Naomi said coldly, "it wasn't just sex. I have a rape kit."

"I'm not denying that Matt's DNA is in the kit. I'm not denying that you and Matt had sex. I'm just simply stating that rape is a little farfetched when there was intent for sex from the beginning."

365

"Objection, Your Honor, please. He can't tell my witness what her intentions were."

"Sustained." Judge Sidwai nodded.

Rodrick threw his hands up defensively. "I'm saying there was a lack of effort made on Ms. Brown's part to remove herself from the scene that would make it seem more plausible as rape, and not just sex she regretted later. The police weren't even called that day for her, which further points to my defendant being a victim of false allegations." Rodrick slipped his hand into his pocket, giving Belle a cheeky smile before looking back up at the judge. "No further questions, Your Honor."

42

How to Stand Without a Crutch

Xavier

Day two ended with more witnesses coming to the stands. Abigail showed up, she testified to Naomi going off with Matt and never seeing her again until two weeks later. Naomi came to her house and admitted to her that she'd been assaulted but was afraid to press charges because of what'd happened in high school. No one asked about what'd happened in high school, but they didn't have to because, today, everyone would know.

A few more witnesses were called, one for the defense who was a girl that claimed she and Matt spent most of the party together. She had a perfect outline of their day; the only problem was that I was excluded from her outline. There was never any mention of Matt and me hanging out, except that she said there were times she lost track of him in the crowd, which I supposed was meant to be filled in by his time with Naomi. It didn't matter because today I'd finally take the stand, and today I'd finally be free.

"If you all would turn your attention to the screen, I'd like you to read along as I play the 9-1-1 call placed the day of the party," Belle said as she clicked the button on the remote.

White noise buzzed. Then words appeared.

Operator: 9-1-1, what's your emergency?

Female voice: My name's Macy, and I think my friend Addy is being raped.

Operator: Alright, Macy, can you tell me what's going on? Where are you?

The sound of a door opening, music booming.

Macy: I'm leaving the bathroom now, but I saw Adeline go into a room and Matt followed her inside.

Operator: Who is Matt? Did she know he was following her?

Macy: I think so. But a few minutes later I heard her scream 'no.'

Operator: Okay, and where are you right now?

Macy: I'm at a friend's house, I can't think of the address. *(Macy began to sound frantic as she tried to think, heavy breathing for a moment)* I'm trying to remember but I'm drawing a blank and Adeline's in trouble!

Operator: Calm down, Macy, I need you to take a breath, everything's going to be alright. I can see your location on my map from your cellphone ping. Are you at *** *(the address has been blurred from the video and the audio silenced).*

Macy: Yes! Yes!

Operator: Alright, Macy, can you describe your friend to me so I can tell the cops who to look for when they arrive?

Macy: She's short, she's pretty, she has brown skin, brown hair, um…

Operator: You're doing great. What is she wearing? Can you—

Screeching. Screaming.

Female voice (presumed to be Adeline's): Stop it! Help me! No!

Male voice (presumed to be Matt's): Come here!

Macy: Adeline?

Operator: Macy, I need you to stay where you are. The cops are on their way.

Macy: Adeline!? Adeline!

Thumping and rattling noises, presumed dropping of the phone.

Operator: Macy? I need you to stay where you are.

There was white noise, and music thumping in the background. But through the chaos, you could hear the thrashing in the background and then a voice.

Male voice: Get out! You're such an annoying little—— *(the language has been blurred).*

Macy: Adeline!

Female voice (presumed to be Adeline's): Macy, just go!

Male voice (presumed to be Matt's): Where are you going!?

Operator: Macy? Are you still with me?

Shrieks of madness went on, a crashing noise, and then more shrieking and screaming with music and laughter in the background until the operator finally ended the call.

The courtroom was stiff. It seemed like all the life within the jurors had gone as we listened to the chaotic phone call. Adeline had never gone into detail of that day. All I knew was that she'd been raped by Matt, how it'd happened had never been told, and now I understood why.

"Ladies and gentlemen what you just heard was the 9-1-1 call placed the day of the party, at the time of Adeline Jones' assault," Belle said. "Macy, a brave young woman, and Adeline's dear friend, tried to rescue Adeline from Matt. Macy clearly stated that Matt followed Adeline inside the room. We aren't sure whether she knew he followed her inside, but it's very clear that she no longer wanted him there."

It was Rodrick's turn now as he came to the jurors.

"What you heard was a chaotic call that the prosecution wants you to believe happened because the defendant was assaulting the woman in subject, Adeline Jones. If you look around, you'll notice that Adeline Jones is not here to testify and has never given a statement. All they have is a phone call." He shrugged, suit bunching quickly around his shoulders and then every wrinkle smoothed out as his shoulders fell. "For all we know, Macy could've had something against Matt and made this call. And the fighting you heard in the background could've been between Adeline and Macy. There's no real proof that Macy was fighting with Matt. He could've been yelling at her because she attacked Adeline."

He stopped and glanced around the jury for a moment. "I just want you all to remember this was a house party, which means other people were around, they would've heard the chaos and the screaming."

With that, Rodrick found his seat beside Matt who couldn't keep his eyes off me again today.

"Belle, do you have any more evidence for the court?" the judge asked.

"Not at this moment."

"Rodrick, do you have any more evidence for the court?" the judge asked.

"No, Your Honor, not at this moment."

"Alright then, Belle you may proceed with your next witness."

Belle nodded and my heart sank. My mother was sitting on my right, and my father was sitting on my left, both holding my hands. I was so nervous, I was the last witness to be called today after Detective Vean and Special Agent De Luca were called, and I'd be cross-examined by the defense right after giving my turn of events to the court with Belle's questions and coaching.

"I'm so scared." I squeezed Mom's hand, and she leaned over and kissed my cheek.

"Don't be afraid, baby. God is more than the whole world against

370

you," she whispered, "And Matt is not the whole world."

Facing Matt was one thing, telling my story was another, telling the twins' stories was completely different, being questioned by Matt's attorney was totally another thing. Yet, none of it meant more to me than the results that would be reached today.

If Matt wasn't found guilty of the rape of Naomi Brown and Adeline Jones, then, did that mean I somehow made a mistake? Did I forget to say something? Was everything I went through for nothing? But then, if he got convicted, how would that make me feel? Is it okay to be happy when he was supposed to be my best friend? Will I even feel happy?

"I would like to call Xavier Miles to the stand." My name rang like a train's horn through the room, and when I looked up, I felt like I was standing in a boxing ring. Facing off with myself to do the right thing, and with Matt to do what was wrong.

Slowly, I stood. My dad patted my shoulder. A look of concern washed over him, and that almost made me feel confident and happy that he was showing some emotion for once. This case had definitely changed my father, made him more approachable and likeable. He was still a little cold, but he wasn't like ice anymore. A small smile traced his thins lips and his normally milky skin reddened now with nerves.

"You look good."

"Thanks, Dad." I nodded as I stepped past my mom who tried to hold my hand forever. As I passed Jax and stepped into the aisle, he nodded at me and so did the detectives behind us. They each gave me a reassurance that I needed as I turned and stepped into the court.

Methodically, I walked, taking a breath with each step. I was stopped by the bailiff, sworn in and seated at the stand. The entire room looked different from this angle, even my parents looked like faces in the crowd, not family. There was no one I could look out at and know that everything was going to be okay. It was just me... or so I thought.

As I scanned the crowd while Belle got her papers in order, I spotted a man, blonde hair, black-rimmed glasses, in a starched suit. He was handsome, and he looked as calm as the ocean.

Elijah.

He nodded, and I felt my heart settling, the racketing it was causing began to still, and internally, I thanked God for blessing Eli to be here. His words rang through me as I looked over at Matt for the first time since I took the stand.

Who is on the Lord's side?

I am. I'm on Your side, God. I will do the righteous thing today. I will tell the truth.

Elijah told me that everyone had a purpose in life. Abraham's was to have faith, Moses' was to lead a nation, Isaiah's was to prophecy, Paul's was to teach, and Jesus' purpose was to save. We all have an assignment, and I felt like mine all along had been to sit in court today and do the righteous thing. To stand, and to let justice roll on like a river.

"State your name for the record," Belle began.

I took a breath, looking away from the storm in Matt's eyes. He was brewing darkly, and his smothering gaze was nearly killing me.

"Xavier Miles," I said shakily.

"You nervous, Xavier?"

"A little."

"As long as you tell the whole truth, you've got nothing to worry about."

"Yes, ma'am."

"Good."

Yesterday evening, Belle, Special Agent De Luca, and Detective Vean came by my house after the second day of the trial. I decided to tell them that I'd spoken to Adeline and could give them more information about her. Of course, they jumped at the chance, but they wouldn't let me tell them what I knew. I was told that they wanted the information to be presented as new and fresh information. And since

Adeline wasn't there, more than likely Judge Sidwai would allow me to give my complete testimony so that both the prosecution and defense could hear the information for the first time together.

It was risky, but since they'd granted me immunity for withholding information about Adeline, and Madeline, I was willing to take the risk. I knew that my testimony would be critical today, and Belle had told me yesterday evening to just tell the truth.

"Now," Belle started again, "let's start with the basics. How do you know Matt?"

"We grew up together. Played on the same little league soccer team and then we started going to school together."

"And have you ever noticed anything peculiar about Matt?"

"No." I glanced over at him, but the anger shrouding his face almost made me jump in fear. He looked like an angry bulldog with how pinched his face was. Every wrinkle possible to mankind had made grooves into his face, even in places I didn't know a wrinkle could be.

"Mmm." Belle nodded. "This case is about Adeline Jones." She clicked a slide and a picture of Adeline appeared. She was smiling, big curly hair, brown eyes that were glowing. I guess I couldn't recognize the Adeline I knew today because she no longer looked like that. Not because she had red hair, but because her eyes didn't glow, and her smile had faded long ago.

"She was the twin sister to Madeline Jones." The next slide was a picture of both girls. "But I can't tell you about Adeline without telling you about her identical twin sister, Madeline. They say twins share a lot of things, but I bet you'd never guess they shared the same rapist."

"Objection, Your Honor, my client has not been proven a rapist."

"Can I rephrase that then, Your Honor?" Belle asked.

Judge Sidwai nodded. "Objection sustained, you may rephrase your last sentence, however, jurors, you are not to use the previous sentence Belle said in your deliberations."

373

"Twins share many things, but I bet you'd never guess they shared the same experience, being raped by someone they knew."

"Objection!" Rodrick was standing now, pointing at Belle. "She's insinuating that my client was the rapist."

"Your Honor, that's why we're in court. The prosecution believes Matt was Adeline's rapist, and it's my job to prove that beyond a reasonable doubt."

Belle was good, she was really good.

"Objection overruled."

Belled exhaled. "Thank you, Your Honor. Now..." she turned to the jury, "you are about to see disturbing photos released to us by the Fresno County Police Station. These photos were not used in the first case against Matthew Leslie because they were ruled unnecessary. However," she looked at me, "they are very necessary for where we're going today. Your Honor, the pictures were submitted to the courts two months back and were approved for use today."

Judge Sidwai nodded, and Belle clicked the button.

There was an audible gasp. I didn't look because I already knew what was up there. I focused on Matt's reaction. His eyes were wide, just as big as the first time we saw MJ's body hanging in the boys' bathroom.

"He did this to me, and I can't live with it. Those are the words written in black marker on Madeline's naked body. She was ashamed of what'd happened, and she couldn't live with the embarrassment. This was Madeline's last photo taken. Ever."

The room was quiet. I couldn't look at the screen, but I could see my mother crumbling as she fell into my father, and Elijah only looked away.

"Xavier, do you know why Madeline was so ashamed of herself?"

"Yes."

"Can you tell the court why?"

I stared down at my hands as I tried to catch my breath. When I

374

raised my head, I forced myself to look Matt in the eye. But he wasn't angry... he was pleading with me. A strained look of desperation. I closed my eyes and prayed.

God, please, help me.

I am with you, My son.

"Matthew Leslie raped Madeline Jones."

"Let that sink in," Belle said. "Matthew Leslie raped Madeline Jones six years ago." She clicked to the next picture, and there was a picture of Madeline beside a picture of Naomi. "They look similar right? Like sisters, or cousins. Matt has a type. If you look here..." she clicked and now Madeline, Naomi, and Adeline's pictures were on the screen together, "we've got identical twins and another brown-skinned woman who looks just like them. Doesn't that seem like he was looking for someone?"

"Objection," Rodrick raised a hand, "she's telling the jury the intentions of my client."

"Sustained."

Belle nodded. "Matt had a type a girl, didn't he, Xavier?"

"Yes."

"And what did you admit to the detectives about Matt's type?"

"That he wanted to date Black women, but his parents didn't approve of his tastes."

"Hmm..." Belle looked down at her paperwork before her head popped up to look at me. The longer I was on that stand, the harder the questions got. "So, Xavier, I want you to tell me what you witnessed the night Madeline Jones was assaulted."

"Well, I didn't see it happen, but I saw everything up to them going inside, and I heard everything from outside the door." I stopped and hung my head. "I was a coward that night... but I guess I had always been, I just didn't know it."

"But today makes up for that night," Belle said.

375

"Nothing will make up for the loss of Madeline's life, but I don't want her to just be a victim in a case. The night Madeline was raped, Matt and I were supposed to be going on a double date. Matt's date was Madeline, my date was another girl, but she ditched me at the last second, so we just went to Madeline's house."

"Was that something you two did a lot? Hang out at Madeline's place?"

"Yes. Adeline had her own friends, so she was never around. That particular night, it was just Madeline home alone. No parents, no sister, just us and Madeline."

"And what happened?"

"We arrived at her house around eight, and she let us inside. We hung out, drank a few beers, and then Matt started touching her, and she didn't like it."

"Did she storm off?"

"Yes, and he followed her up the stairs. They actually kind of argued."

"What do you mean?"

I shifted as I recalled that night. "Madeline was telling him that he never cares about anything else. Just beer and sex. And he was telling her that she meant more to him than just sex."

"So, they were arguing about sex? Did this happen a lot?"

"Yes."

"Go on."

"He ran upstairs behind her, and I followed them, trying to mediate between them. When I reached the top of the stairs, Matt had Madeline against the wall, telling her how much he loved her, and how much he needed... this."

"And is that the same *this* he told Naomi he needed?"

"Yes."

"What is it?"

376

"Sex."

"Continue."

"She was telling him no, but he kissed her anyway. The two would get rough, but this time Madeline didn't look like she liked it. She tried to pull away, but he shoved himself against her a little harder, and told her he wasn't leaving without having her."

"Then what happened?"

I took a breath and glanced out at Elijah. He was nodding, and I said, "He pushed open her bedroom door, and took her inside."

"Did you try to stop him?"

"Only once."

"How'd that go?"

"I told him that maybe he'd had too much to drink, and maybe tonight we should just joyride, but he shoved me away and told me not to interrupt him ever again." My eyes slid to Matt, and he looked dead. He'd paled and was sitting stiffly.

"You sat outside the door, or did you go back downstairs?"

"I sat outside the door."

"What did you hear?"

"Matt was enjoying it, but Madeline wasn't. I remember her crying, begging him to stop. She had even said that she couldn't breathe once. But Matt wouldn't stop. He never stopped. He always took what he wanted."

"And after the sex ended, what happened?"

"He came out like nothing had happened. Told me to go downstairs and get the car. And we spent the rest of the night joyriding."

"Did he ever say anything? Or did you ever say anything?"

"No." I shook my head. "I was a coward."

Belle tapped her pencil on the desk and turned to the jurors. "Madeline Jones was raped, and when she went to the police, things fell apart, and just weeks later, after constant bullying, Madeline Jones tied a rope around her neck and hung herself."

"Your Honor—" Rodrick began, but Belle's counterpart came through the door rushing with papers and a flash drive in his hand. He waved Belle over, whispering to her and the entire court fell silent as they watched the interaction.

"Your Honor," Belle said, "we've just received new evidence. Can I submit it to the court?"

"You may approach the bench."

Belle passed me a look that tightened the feeling in my chest. I was beginning to feel accomplished after finally telling the truth about Madeline. My family had never heard that story, and each one of them did their best not to pass me a judgmental look. Thankfully, the initial surprise of it all pushed the judgement away from them. However, Belle's look, the new evidence randomly submitted while I was on the stand, made me sweat bullets.

"Rodrick, approach the bench please."

I glanced over at Matt. He was in a state of shock. Possibly because he never thought I'd tell that story, or maybe it was because he'd been trying to forget Madeline. Matthew had been through a lot in the past four years, I'm sure. And I'm also sure that with rape surrounding his name—again—he remembered Madeline. He thought he wouldn't ever remember her, but now they were showing pictures to a courtroom full of people who weren't bias schoolkids and easy to push over jocks. We were all adults in this room, with no one to sway us left or right. How would Matthew stand when he didn't have the world as his crutch?

Belle and Rodrick moved back to their respective places behind their tables as Judge Sidwai began, "New evidence has been submitted to the court that I am allowing. I have discussed with the defense and prosecution, and both have declined breaking for time to evaluate the new evidence. The prosecution will continue, and then the defense will speak." She shuffled her papers. "The defense also brought an objection to my attention that there was a concern of relevance pertaining to Madeline Jones' case. However, the prosecution has convinced me that Madeline's death, and the reason for her death plays a role in Adeline Jones' case. And since Adeline Jones is not here to speak for herself, I am allowing the material presented to be used in this court. Therefore, the objection is overruled."

"Thank you, Your Honor." Belle stood in front of me. "Before I display some new photos we received from an anonymous source, I will address the use of Madeline's case for her sister's case. Madeline and Adeline were very close siblings, and as you heard earlier from various witnesses, Adeline changed after her sister passed. One witness even mentioned Adeline had shut down. But high school had ended, and she wanted to come out of that shell, so she went to a house party expecting to leave it renewed, not ashamed."

She clicked to the next slide; it was a picture of Adeline with brown hair. "The last time anyone saw her, Adeline had left the party in a rush. No one has seen or heard from her since then." She paused to look over at me. "Except for you, Xavier Miles."

"Yes," I admitted. "I've seen and spoken to Adeline."

"Can you explain that to the courts, as this is new information for us, Your Honor."

Judge Sidwai raised a brow which made my palms sweat so much they were glued to my pants. "Go ahead, I want to hear this."

"Objection!"

"Overruled," she growled darkly.

"Xavier, you told the detectives that you hadn't seen or heard from Adeline, is that true?" Belle asked.

"Yes."

"Was that a lie?"

"Yes—well, not intentionally."

"Explain that."

"Adeline doesn't look like that anymore, so I didn't know it was her. And she doesn't go by Adeline either."

Bell squinted, and I could tell she was genuinely thinking about that. "When you say she doesn't look like this picture, what do you mean?"

"Madeline had red hair. She dyed it over the summer between our freshmen and sophomore year of high school. She made everyone call her MJ, like Mary Jane from Spiderman."

Belle nodded.

"When the detectives asked me if I'd seen Adeline, I'd told them no, because I'd met Madeline Jones at my college. We had a class together and I'd visited her dorm from time to time."

"You met Madeline Jones? But that's impossible."

"I know." I exhaled slowly, looking up at Eli. He smiled, and I began again. "But the accident had caused my memory to become a little foggy, and I didn't remember Adeline until the detectives told me that Madeline Jones had passed away, leaving a twin behind named Adeline. I thought that was impossible, even after seeing pictures. But when I got back home, I realized that the girl I'd met was Adeline, pretending to be her sister Madeline."

Belle didn't respond for a moment as the jury shifted uncomfortably. My story seemed outlandish, but I promised God and Belle I'd tell the truth, and so I did.

"How did you discover that the Madeline Jones you met on campus was actually Adeline Jones?"

"She disappeared in the middle of freshmen year, and when her dorm was cleaned out, the school asked if anyone had known her well enough to know where she'd gone. An investigation was launched, but with no leads and no interest, it died. My guardian was listed as an emergency contact for Adeline, and he was asked to pick up some things from the dorm. He took a few items, notebooks, jewelry, papers." I shrugged. "And inside one of the notebooks, I found a picture of

Madeline and Adeline."

Belle clicked to the next slide. It was that picture. Madeline with her fiery red hair standing beside Matt, with me on one side and Adeline on the other side of the couple.

"Do you recognize this photo?"

"Yes."

"Can you tell me when this was taken?"

"About two weeks before Madeline was assaulted."

"Correct me if I'm wrong, pictured here with red hair in the middle with Matt is Madeline, and Adeline is beside her? And you're beside Matt, right?"

"Yes, that's right."

"So, when you saw Adeline with red hair, you thought you'd met *Madeline* Jones?"

"I did. But, honestly, I didn't even remember the case from high school until the detectives triggered the memory."

"Oh!" Belle exclaimed. "So seeing Madeline Jones in a picture or hearing about the case reminded you of the real Madeline Jones and her sister? You thought you were just meeting a *new* woman named Madeline."

"That's correct."

"Hmph. Is this what Adeline looks like now?"

The slide clicked, and there she was. Adeline Jones was sitting on the couch in Eli's apartment looking out the window.

Eli... I thought. *He submitted these photos.*

"Yes, that's her."

"Where is she?"

"She's in my apartment. My guardian and I had given her a place to stay for the last week or so."

"So, Adeline went missing off campus, and then just last week you ran into her?"

381

"I did. Well, she called my guardian from a phone in a shelter and was asking him for help. And he sent me to meet up with her, and we let her stay with us."

"And that's when she told you the truth about impersonating her sister?"

"Yes."

"Why was she doing it?"

I swallowed. "She said Matt had taken every part of Adeline Jones, and she just wanted to disappear." I glanced off, remembering a few of our counselling sessions with Eli, where Adeline shared a little about her past and the night of her assault. "She said that even her own rapist wanted her sister, and since the world loved her so much, she became her."

"Wow." Belle placed a hand over her heart. "She wanted to disappear. And when you say her rapist didn't want her, what does that mean?"

"Adeline said after Matt had assaulted her, he didn't leave right away. He told her that he missed Madeline and hoped she would replace her, but she didn't."

"Adeline couldn't replace Madeline?"

"No," I said.

"Cold words." Belle shook her head. "Well, I've just got one more question for you, Xavier. Why did Adeline confide in you?"

I paused...

"Because I confessed that I was there when her sister was raped."

"She then became honest and vulnerable with you, despite knowing that you were there during a crucial time in her sister's life?"

"Yes."

Belle nodded. "She forgave you, didn't she?"

"Yes," I nearly croaked.

"I believe it."

382

Two pictures appeared on the screen side by side. The first was of Adeline and I asleep on the couch the night before when Eli was at the shut-in. I didn't know he'd taken this picture of us. And the picture beside it was another photo of me and Adeline. We were at the train station before I left.

We'd shared a teary goodbye, and in this picture, her hand was on my wrist as I was clutching her face with one of my hands. I was promising her that I'd tell her story, and that I wouldn't forget about her. But the picture seemed so much more intimate. The way we were gazing at each other, with our free hands clasped together. We looked like... we were in love.

43

I Am Broken, a Withered Rose, and a Fractured Diamond

Xavier

Rodrick read from a yellow notepad before he nodded to himself and walked across the room to me. "Mr. Xavier Miles, how are you today?"

"I'm well."

"Very good. How were you feeling the day of that party?"

I rubbed my hands together. "A little anxious. A little excited."

"Why?"

I palmed the back of my neck, trying to avoid remembering Lia Sunohara. "Because I was going to talk to this girl I really liked."

"Lia Sunohara, correct?"

"Yes."

The corners of his mouth dropped for a second with an approving nod before Rodrick went on. "And, Matt, what was he like?"

"Well, we were both excited, I guess."

"You guess?"

"Yes. We were both excited."

"And do you mind if I read some text messages submitted to the court?"

"No," I responded.

Clicking through the slides, he stopped at a screen with messages between Matt and me.

Rodrick read them aloud. "Matt said, 'Hey man, I'll be there in 10 minutes.' Xavier replies with two celebration emoji hands. Matt texts again and he says, 'How many times do you think I can get laid at one party?' Xavier replies with a laughing emoji and says, 'I don't know. I think all the girls will probably be willing since they all think they won't see you again, laugh out loud.' Matt's final response, 'I know, right? They'll melt for me, just like chocolate always does when it gets hot.' And Xavier replied with two face-palm emojis and says, 'Man, the chocolate references really make me hate you, haha, just kidding.'"

He turned to the jury and shrugged. "Matt wanted to get laid, is that a crime? No. Most teenage boys do. And Xavier backed him up right here." He picked up a laser and circled my response. "He told him the girls would be willing. So, it begs the question, how willing were Adeline and Naomi? We can't write off that the two girls were probably willing to sleep with Matt, they just didn't like how aggressive he got, and called it rape. Is that fair?" He looked at me. "Is it fair, Xavier?"

"No, but—"

"Exactly. Now, I'm having a hard time getting an understanding of Madeline's character. The prosecution told us her story, but there's no way to connect to a story if we don't have any characterization, right? The only characterizing they were doing was demonizing Matthew."

"Objection!" Belle yelled.

"Sustained. Jurors, please dismiss that last sentence."

Rodrick rolled his eyes and pointed to a picture of Madeline on the screen. "This is Madeline with the football team." He clicked. "This is her with the basketball team. I spoke with a few members of each team, and they each gave a statement to the court about her character, and they stated how many times they'd slept with her. Each one of them."

A few gasps sounded through the court, but I took a stilling breath to keep myself from flying off. He was trying to cut Madeline down, call her loose and say that it was all in her head just like everyone had in high school.

"The prosecution used Madeline's case to try to show how much her death affected Adeline." He wrung his wrist. "Madeline's passing made her shut down, and then she tried to come back to life, but then my client, according to the prosecution, took that from her. But, if we're going to look at Madeline to support her twin sister, let's look at her completely."

Rodrick clicked the slide, there was a picture of Madeline on the screen now. She held a drink in one hand, sandwiched between two guys at a Halloween party. Everyone was dressed in costumes. Hers was a sexy version of Mary Jane Watson from some special edition Spiderman comic. Everyone loved her outfit that night, even I hadn't been able to stop staring.

"Here she is, having a good time." Rodrick clicked again. "Here she is dancing with three other guys, and here," he clicked again, "she's kissing someone, and you'll see in the next slide," he clicked once more, "Madeline's finally with Matthew, kissing him. So, Xavier, you want to tell me a little about Madeline?"

"Objection." Belle stood. "Madeline's not on trial, knowing her character has nothing to do with how it affected her sister."

"Oh, but it does, Your Honor." Rodrick clicked through the slides quickly. "There's Adeline right there, holding hands with Matt. There was obviously some sister rivalry or jealousy."

"Your Honor—"

"That's not Adeline."

I could feel everyone's eyes on me as I looked at the picture. "That's not her. That's Madeline."

Rodrick squinted. "No." He looked back at Matt, his eyes were filled with worry—he must've lied and told Rodrick that the girl in the picture was Adeline. "That's Adeline."

I shook my head. "Adeline has dimples in both her cheeks, Madeline only has one dimple. And…" I pressed my thumb into the inside of my wrist. "Adeline always wears a bracelet with a cloud-shaped pendant on it."

Rodrick's head whipped back toward the screen to stare at the picture. Sure enough, the hand clutching Matt's *didn't* have a bracelet on it at all.

Collectively, the courtroom shifted in discomfort.

"Well," Rodrick's swallow was audible.

"The objection from Belle is sustained," the judge said. "The case is for Adeline and not Madeline. Use of Madeline's situation surrounding her must support your defense. Since your evidence is not clear, it must be rejected from the courts." Judge Sidwai leaned forward, tenting her slender brown fingers, hunching her small shoulders, letting a scowl stretch across her pretty face. "And may I remind you, Rodrick, we do not tear down potential victims in this courtroom. The insinuation that follows a story like the one you prepared for the court about Madeline is not allowed here where I preside." She took a moment to let that sink in, and Rodrick tried to keep a smug look, but Sidwai's raised brow was chipping away at him.

"I remember this case very well. It was horrifying," Judge Sidwai recalled. "But the case was not closed, the charges were dropped, meaning a verdict was never reached. And that means there is a chance that Madeline was telling the *truth*. However, we don't know for certain. But we do know that this young girl took her life, and I will not allow you to shame her, is that understood, Rodrick?" She glanced over at Belle. "Belle?"

"Yes," they answered together.

"Good, now you may continue, Rodrick."

"Your Honor," he said, "may I present this argument in a different direction?"

"If you know how to be decent about it," Judge Sidwai responded.

"I do, Your Honor."

"Very well, you may proceed."

He nodded. "Xavier, you mentioned that you didn't see Matt assault Madeline, you just heard it, correct?"

"Yes." I nodded.

"And they were arguing before that?"

"Yes."

"Then, couldn't it have been that the two of them were possibly fighting?"

"No." I shook my head. "What I heard was not fighting."

"Can you prove that it wasn't?"

"Can you?" I snapped back.

"Hey," the judge said to me, "take it easy."

I took a deep breath and nodded.

"I'm just asking because the 9-1-1 phone call sounded like a fight. Naomi's story sounded like a fight. Why couldn't Madeline's have been a fight?"

"Because it wasn't."

"We can't be sure. Loud noises, grunts, and things like that sounds like fighting to me."

"I am sure," I seethed.

"Then why now? Why decide to tell the truth now when your best friend's life is on the line? Why turn on him? Seems like there's been some secret jealousy going on."

"What?" I was so baffled I almost fell out my chair. "I'm not and have never been jealous of Matt. Intimidated," I shrugged sheepishly,

388

"yeah, I can admit that. But jealous? Never."

"Then why turn on him now?"

"Because I couldn't take it!" I snapped. Closing my eyes, I whispered, "I couldn't take it. I didn't even know I'd forgotten about Madeline until I saw her picture. And then I felt so bad, like I had betrayed her. I promised to never forget her, but the accident and school and just life happened, and I forgot…" I wiped at my tears.

"So, you're telling me that out of the goodness of your heart, you'd turn in your best friend? I want you to look at Matt and tell me how lying to a court full of people is doing any good."

"I'm not lying!" My voice was raised and tears were gushing when I looked over at Rodrick. He wore an arrogant expression, raising a shoulder like all this was child's play.

"The detectives and the prosecution didn't bribe information out of you to make Matt look worse?"

"Objection, Your Honor!" Belle stood but Judge Sidwai waved a hand immediately.

"Overruled."

Rodrick raised a brow as he waited for my response.

"No one bribed me for anything."

"Not even with a deal? Tell us this and we'll keep your college record clean?"

"I don't have a record," I answered quickly.

"You could've, though. Who is to say *you* didn't rape Madeline and are putting it on Matt now?"

"That's ridiculous! There was a case against him. Madeline pressed charges!"

"They were dropped after she passed. The family didn't wish to pursue him any longer, or maybe they found out you were the real culprit and decided to just let Madeline rest in peace. You were the only one there, the only person to tell what'd happened. Isn't that suspicious that

389

you were involved in both assumed assault cases of twins?"

I shook my head as I looked over at Matt. He was grimacing, but I no longer cared, because I remembered this was bigger than he and I.

"Do you know how they fix a fractured diamond?"

"I'm sorry? Are you asking *me* a question?" Rodrick sounded indignant, but I never lifted my eyes to see him.

"They use a glass-like resin to slip into the cracks of the diamond that makes the fractures nearly invisible to the naked eye. It's almost like magic for a diamond."

"Objection, Your Honor, I don't know what this has to do with my question." Rodrick nearly laughed, but Sidwai's lack of joy in her voice silenced him.

"Overruled. Go on, young man, I want to hear where you're taking this."

I looked up at the judge and she gave me a warm smile. "Your Honor, a rose and a diamond are totally different. Roses wither, but diamonds can only be broken under immense pressure. A rose is a lot weaker than a diamond, and that's the difference between Madeline and Adeline." I looked up and found my mother in the crowd nodding along as I spoke. "Madeline is a withered rose. She was plucked because of her beauty and died because she was so beautiful. But Adeline ... she is a fractured diamond. Stronger than her sister, strong enough to keep going despite her circumstances. But every time she was hurt or broken; every single time someone wouldn't believe that she had been raped, her diamond was fractured. But unlike Madeline, Adeline kept going." I sniffled as I looked over at the pictures of Adeline and me.

"Madeline withered away, and everyone saw it. But Adeline hid her scars so that no one could see them unless they looked closely. The glass resin filling the cracks of the fractured diamond made Adeline's brokenness seem like it didn't exist. But that was only until you looked beneath a microscope and found that the woman before you was not a reincarnation of Madeline Jones, it was a shattered woman who hid her identity because of all the pain."

Forcing my attention to Rodrick, I raised my head a little higher. "I was a coward the first time, but the second time, I swore things would be different. In that picture," I pointed to the screen, "I promised Adeline that I wouldn't let her story go untold or be swept away under the rugs of shame to be overlooked. I will honor that promise."

"You already have." Judge Sidwai nodded, her chair rocking with her. She turned back to Rodrick whose mouth was clenched shut. "Anything further?"

His eyes lingered on mine a little longer. "No further questions, Your Honor."

The deliberation took two full days, and since the courts were closed over the weekend, we didn't get back into the courtroom until Tuesday. Eli wasn't present, and I didn't get to see him when the trial ended for the day on Friday. It was alright though, because I couldn't have asked for any more support than what he'd given me. Submitting those pictures to the courts last minute, being there to hear my testimony, it was overwhelming, and I couldn't wait to return to New York to thank him.

I stood in court between my mother and father, with Jax on my mother's other side. I didn't know what to expect, but I knew justice would be served.

The jury filed in and took their seats as Judge Sidwai returned to the bench.

"Has the jury reached a verdict?"

"We have, Your Honor," one of the jurors said as he passed a slip of paper to the bailiff. He took it to the judge, and she read it over quickly before passing it to the speaker for the jury.

A man in a too tight suit unfolded the paper and read aloud, "We the jury, find the defendant, Matthew Leslie, guilty of vehicular manslaughter on two counts." He turned the pages, and I saw Matt gripping the table, realizing that his life was over, and the only person here to witness it was me, and a bunch of people he didn't know. His parents had never stepped foot into the courtroom. Matthew was all alone.

"We the jury," the juror began again, "find the defendant, Matthew Leslie, guilty of the sexual assault of Naomi Brown and the sexual assault of Adeline Jones."

The room was spinning now, and I could hardly breathe. It was over... The case was over. The trial was over. I never had to see the prosecution or the detectives again... It was all over.

I looked over at Matt to find that he was looking at me.

"You did this," he snapped. His voice was like lightning whipping through the room to shock me. "You did this! You ruined me! I'll kill you!" He jumped over the little door and raced at me, but the bailiff was on him before he reached my seat.

"Get out of here!" my dad shouted at me.

My mom nodded and kissed my cheek. I took their advice and patted Jax's shoulder as I squeezed by and raced for the doors.

"You took everything from me!" Matt shouted behind me. "You took her from me! She fell in love with you, and you never even knew it because you were such an idiot! Madeline wasn't enough, so you took Adeline too!"

At the door, I looked back at the guards wrestling him down to the floor, fighting and tearing at him to stop. Then, I stepped forward and left.

On the train ride back to New York, I realized Matt was just being Matt. Angry that he lost, so he blamed everyone but himself. He'd always been that way. When he was guilty, he would wiggle his way out of trouble with his parents' money, or his good looks. I won't bash him now that the truth is out there. Matt had been my friend, my *best* friend. There was some good in him; unfortunately, the bad outweighed the good.

When I stepped off the train, Elijah was there. Standing against his car, dark aviators replaced his frames as he waved me over. I thought I'd squeeze the life out of him when we embraced.

"Thank you." I was so close to tears now. Four years ago, I walked into Eli's office because I was forced to by my parents. I never thought I'd depend on him so much, that he'd become family to me.

"Thank God not me. It was your mother who called at the last minute."

"What?" I backed away, wiping tears and sniffling.

"She called and said you needed me. She was afraid the case wouldn't be strong enough with the way the defense was retaliating in there, and she said she didn't know how strong you'd be on the stand. I caught the next flight I could."

"So, it *was* you who submitted those pictures." I made a mental note to remember to send Mom a thank-you text for reaching out to Eli.

He shrugged. "I was just thankful God blessed me to take the photos in the first place. I never thought they'd be used in the court of law."

"Me either." I chuckled. "I don't even know when you take pictures." I grabbed the door and slung my bag in the back before hopping into the front.

"I have my ways." Eli laughed as he came around the car and got inside. "Alright, what was the verdict?"

"He was found guilty," I said as I watched the buildings pass by.

"You texted and said you were going to be home a little early. Did something happen after the verdict?"

"He had an outburst."

"At you?"

I grinded my teeth. "Yeah."

"How did it make you feel?"

"It shocked me at first. And then it kind of scared me. I couldn't believe that he blamed me for the verdict."

"Why did it scare you?"

I looked over at Eli's side profile. "At the time, I was doing everything I could not to blame myself, and to feel proud. Hearing him say that just made reality weigh on me. I realized how devastating my testimony was."

"Well, don't let yourself be conflicted. You know you did the right thing. God's proud of you for standing. I'm proud of you too."

"Thanks a lot, Eli."

He smiled as we turned onto our street. "You know, Adeline's been worried about you."

"Has she?"

Eli's brow raised at my quick reaction. "Does that mean something to you?"

I swallowed… did it?

"No," I said slowly.

"Are you sure?"

"Why?"

"I'm just wondering. Those pictures presented in court made it look like you two had gotten pretty comfortable with each other."

"Why did you pick those pictures?"

Turning into the parking lot, his wolfish grin began to make me nervous. Eli was always brewing with his own plan that somehow worked in perfect alignment with God's.

"Because I wanted the court to believe that Adeline might've actually told you the truth about herself the last week she'd been with us. They needed to see how close you two had really become, and so did you."

I didn't speak as we exited the car. Why would I need to know how close Adeline and I had gotten? We *weren't* close, we had just bonded over the case. It was a stressful experience for both of us. We needed each other, and so we depended on each other. There was nothing more to it. But was that the truth?

Now that I stood on the elevator rising to our floor, I wondered why I was suddenly feeling nervous to see Adeline. My heart was pounding in my chest and in my head, but not just with nerves, it was also in excitement. I *wanted* to see Adeline…

When the doors opened, I tried not to sprint through them or down the hall for that matter. I walked slowly behind Eli, listening to him whistle as we made it to the door. The pounding steps vibrating through the hall, jingling of the keys, the twisting doorknob.

"Adeline? We're back." Eli stepped inside, and I could hear Adeline moving around in my bedroom before the door creaked open. A patch of light was splayed on the hall's floor before her shadow appeared. She stepped out, and I dropped my bag at the door.

"X?" she whispered.

My feet were moving, but my eyes didn't stop focusing on Adeline. She was standing in the hall in an oversized sweater and a long skirt. Red locks were flowing like rolling lava over her shoulders as I came to her. She stood there, waiting for me.

"Adeline," I pulled her into my chest in an instant. My heart stopped rattling; the nerves soothed. I was cleaving to her like she was a buoy on the lake, and I was threatened with losing my life if I didn't hold on.

"He was found guilty."

"You did it," she whispered.

I shook my head, and she stepped back. "God did it. We did it together. God, me, you, and Eli, we did it, Adeline. And now it's over."

Tears were misting her brown orbs as she searched me for a response. She was happy, smiling almost like she was in that old picture. But I think the smile she had today was even better than the old one. It came with relief and maturity, pain and growth.

"It's over now." She pressed her forehead against mine. "You never have to go back."

"I don't ever have to leave." I swallowed. "Adeline, I don't ever have to leave you again."

Her nose brushed mine and then our lips brushed. Mine against hers. I was hesitant to kiss her, but I wanted to. My hands were holding her by the small of her back, gripping her and pulling her against me. I didn't want to lose her ever again. I didn't want us to be apart again.

I would protect her from the world. She was a fractured diamond, but she was worth more to me than anything in the universe.

"Adeline," I whispered against her lips, "I'm home."

"Welcome home, Xavier."

44

My Acceptance

Adeline

I ended up leaving X's and Eli's apartment two weeks after the case ended and Xavier returned home. I promised him I'd come back, I just needed to clear my head completely. I wanted to make sure that what I felt for X wasn't desperation or just loneliness. I wanted to get out on my own and tie up any loose ends in my own life before I could be part of his. He told me he'd wait for me, and I told him I'd return. I wasn't going to disappear this time... I really didn't want to.

Missing X's graduation was going to be hard on him, but I knew he would forgive me. That was my only regret for leaving. But I didn't let that slow me down. I spent the next month and a half working on myself and growing in my relationship with God. I went back to the shelter and started working with the counsellors to get a job and find my own place.

Kim had left, and I was given a room to myself. I stayed long enough to get a job and save up enough money to get my own place and buy a train ticket to California and one back to New York. There were things

I needed to do in California in order to move forward with my life here in New York with Xavier and with Elijah.

Stepping off the train with nothing but a backpack and a couple hundred dollars and a ticket to return home, I glanced around at the place I used to live. Fresno. Everyone says you come to California to make it big, but they don't know that the heat of the California sun is nothing compared to the raging of those who live beneath it.

Everyone's trying to make it, *everyone's* hungry to become something, except who we're supposed to be in Christ. I learned that since I stopped pretending to be Madeline and stopped living a life where I never faced my own problems.

Homosexuality, it's a gaping hole of destruction. Reeling you into a darkness that makes you crazy and starved for anything. But I think the worst part about that lifestyle is that no matter what anyone says, we all know it's wrong. Maybe we didn't initially, but the deeper we get into darkness, the harder we look for a way out.

God is always the way out, and He has always been the way out. So what stops us from taking His hand? The same thing that got Satan kicked from Heaven… Pride.

Pride is at the root of our sexual sin. The ungodly acts that are shameful and disgraceful, the behavior that is Biblically explained in Acts chapter one as a crime against our own bodies. And that's so heavy because our bodies are temples to house the Holy Spirit. How can we house Him if we are unclean and disgraceful?

Our pride keeps us there in the dark, and our ungodly desires pervert our temples. We're selfish, we want what we want, and we become prideful about it. But there's something even deeper than the pride… Fear.

We're afraid we'll never be loved, afraid we'll never fit in. So, we give in to darkness and hope that the cold clutches will satisfy us in some way. However, it never does, and that's why we search the darkness for something that'll fulfill us.

I learned that Christ is the ultimate fulfillment. Having a purpose and a destiny in Christ is beautiful, because it's never as simple as being a chef. Or being a mechanic. Our purpose is intertwined with the Kingdom's purpose, to further the spread of the Gospel. We have to reach every lost soul, and the best way to do that is to be a light that draws them.

A dim light or a flickering light cannot draw anyone. But the light of Christ can. And at the basis of Christ's redemption plan, is what's even deeper than the pride and the fear, it's forgiveness. God's forgiveness draws us to Him, and forgiveness opens the door for life to begin.

Most people are like me, stumbling into homosexuality because of a past pain, or dumb decision we've made. And we remain unforgiving of our mistakes or of those who hurt us. But today, I was going to make things right and be completely set free.

Xavier was just the beginning, I thought as I waited for a bus to zip by. *But now, I can finish this journey.*

I jogged across the street. I had two more blocks before I reached my old house. The place I grew up with Madeline, with our parents. Our household had always been complicated, but losing Madeline made matters worse. I tried not to think about that as I climbed the steps of the house. The porch had a big crack in it, and there were old chairs sitting out. Torn seats of the chairs, and ripped siding on the house, it looked like the house had been through more than I had in the past six years.

On the chipped white door, I raised a fist and knocked.

"Who is it?" My father snapped almost immediately. I didn't know what to say. I'd planned it all out in my head, but standing there now, maybe I wasn't as ready as I thought I was.

Just as I turned away, the door was snatched open and my father hissed behind me, "What do you want?"

I turned back and the smell of alcohol made the nostalgia in my stomach churn at the sight of my father. He'd aged more than six years, more than ten if you asked me. Deep grooves created a map of wrinkles that even the greatest of scholars would have trouble following. His brows lowered and his eyes widened as he stared at me.

"Who… who are you?"

"It's me, Dad. It's Adeline."

"Adeline? But you look just like—"

"I know."

There was a long silence, and then he stepped back and said, "Do you want to come in?"

"Sure."

Up the stairs, I went inside and found the house didn't look much different. There were more empty beer cans, and a layer of filth everywhere now. But I said nothing as I sat on our old red couch.

"Don't mind the cans," my father said as he shoved them aside. "I just hadn't had the chance to clean up."

I nodded, glancing around. "Where's Mom?"

He stopped mid-motion, holding a can in his hand and a few others in his other arm. "Your mother left me two years ago. And I haven't heard from her since."

"I'm sorry."

He stood up straight. "No, it was my own fault." The words were weighed with guilt and sadness as he went back to picking up some of the cans. "How have you been?" he asked after a moment of silence.

"I've been alright." I glanced at the television; the news was on. My dad always watched the news, no matter what. I wondered if the trial had aired, but I doubted it. Xavier told me it was private, and cameras weren't allowed inside per the Leslies request—only journalists from esteemed papers. It worked out for X, though; it kept things from traveling to his school.

"That's good."

"How's Grandma?"

"She died a few months after you left," Dad said as he poured the cans from his arms into a big garbage bag. "Buried her in the same cemetery as your sister."

"I see."

He stood, a grim look on his face as he stared blankly at the creaky wooden floor. "I know I never—"

"Matthew Leslie was found guilty for the rape of Naomi Brown." I paused as I cut him off. "And Adeline Jones."

His eyes were wide, white holes against his dark skin. "You... You were..."

"That's why I left. But Madeline's case is being reopened as well, and he's looking at facing another two years if the prosecution can prove Madeline committed suicide because of the assault."

My father slouched onto the counter, crying into his palm like a child. "I'm so sorry! I'm so sorry!"

I watched him crumble and moved from the couch to stand beside him. It'd been six years since my father had touched me. I didn't know if I was ready for him to touch me again, but I was ready to forgive him.

"Dad," I said quietly over his tears. "I forgive you. And I forgive Mom and Grandma, too. You guys didn't believe that Madeline had been raped, and I knew you'd never believe me. It hurt to run away, but I needed the space." I wiped at my nose, trying to hold in my tears. "And I forgive you for what you did to me." I paused as he stiffened beside me. "I couldn't bring myself to face you, and I never thought I'd come back. But I didn't get stronger on my own and returned. I got stronger because in my darkest time, I met Jesus." Twisting my backpack over myself, I unzipped it and pulled out a Bible. "I brought you something. Keep it and use it, Dad. And if you ever need anything, I left my number on the sheet of paper with some scriptures I outlined for you." Placing the Bible on the counter beside him, I slung my pack over my shoulder and headed for the door.

"That's all you came back for?"

I opened the door, making it more than clear to myself that I couldn't stay. I hadn't returned to be his daughter, that would come later. I returned to open the door that I'd closed and to invite him into my life again. I never planned for that to happen overnight. I was still healing, and I still needed some space to grow to trust my father again. For now, this was the best I could offer him.

"Not all I came back for, but you were my priority."

Stepping out of the house, I closed the door behind myself, and headed down the sidewalk to a motel. I picked the first one I saw since I was only staying overnight. Tomorrow evening would be another two-day journey back to New York City. I wasn't sure if I'd go see Xavier or maybe take a few more weeks to myself but I wouldn't know until I returned.

In my motel room, I stood in front of a mirror and took a deep breath. For years, I've worn a red wig. Changing it out regularly to keep the image of Madeline alive. It was an adjustment at first. I initially just wore a red wig, no lace. But the hair got matted so easily, I invested in a good one that lasted me a little more than six months. And then I continued to buy them, keeping myself in my sister's shoes. However, it was time to change that.

I began rubbing a solvent along the edge of the lace. Tomorrow, I'd wear it once more, but I didn't need it laid down. I'll wear it glue-less so that I can remove it quickly. The adjustable band in the back of the wig was fraying on the edges anyway. This wig's life was nearly over, which meant, so was mine as Madeline Jones.

Taking hair scissors and other supplies I brought with me, I began cutting my real hair. I needed a change, a breath of fresh air, and as I watched the brown curls fall to the floor, I felt relieved.

The following morning, I packed up and left the motel, returning the key to the front desk. I walked a few miles before I hopped on the bus and rode out to Fresno's penitentiary. I'd called ahead and set up an appointment to see Matthew a week after his sentencing. He got almost fifteen years in prison for the assault and vehicular manslaughter charges.

His previous four years on house arrest (which was swung by his parents' money) were counted towards his time and took him down to eleven years. The judge said it was mandatory that he finished six years in prison, and if his behavior was good, he'd get out early and spend one year on house arrest. But, if things worked out in Madeline's case, Matt was looking at possibly another mandatory two years, and he'd spend a total of eight years in prison.

Eight years is a long time, I thought as I waited at a round table for him. I asked for my identity to remain anonymous so he wouldn't reject my request to see him. And thankfully, it worked. Matt came out in an orange jumpsuit and cuffs. His hair had grown in pretty good, and he looked tired, though his exhaustion probably came from the beatings he'd been taking.

His eye was swollen, lip busted, and purple and green blotches decorated his face. I'd always heard adjusting to life in prison was hard.

Matt glanced around as the guards uncuffed him, trying to figure out who'd want to see him. But today the room was full, people were sitting everywhere talking with inmates, so Matt didn't see me.

"This way," the big burly guard said. Matt followed him until they reached my table where he stood stiff as a dead man.

"Sit," the guard commanded, and like a man who feared for his life, Matt sat quickly across from me. "No touching, no yelling, no fighting. If any of these occur, you will be removed from the facility, and he will be taken back to his cell."

I nodded up at the guard. "Understood."

"You have one hour."

"Thank you."

As the guard walked to the wall, I realized this was the first time Matt and I saw each other since the party… since he raped me. Four long years later, we were sitting across from each other, speechless.

"I didn't need an hour," I said.

"Why are you here?" His words were agitated, but I ignored his aggression.

"I never thought that I could face you."

"Well, now you have." He went to stand, but my words captured his feet, sealing him to the floor.

"I'm here because I want to move on."

He stared at me, almost amazed, but he was too angry to feel anything else.

"You're just like her. Dramatic, and an idiot."

My eyes traced the welt beneath his eye as he adjusted in his seat. It was red and bloody, like they tried to clean him up to come out here. But the big welt was sitting on a swollen knot on his face, making it so noticeable I couldn't stop looking at it.

"Does that hurt?"

"Do you suddenly care how I feel?"

"Have you ever cared about how anyone has felt? Me? Madeline? Naomi? You just take what you want and expect everyone to be okay with it."

"I didn't take anything from anyone."

404

"Look at me!" I snapped. "I tried to become someone else because of you. Because I couldn't stand what'd happened and I just wanted to stop feeling used. So, I became the only person I knew the world loved… the only person *you* ever loved."

"Stop it." He looked away. "Don't do that."

"Don't tell you that you loved her? That no one ever replaced her, the same thing you told me that night."

"I said, *stop* it!"

"Hey," the guard stepped forward, eyeing Matt, "watch your tone."

"Yes, sir." Matt's eyes dropped to the table, and I actually felt bad for him… He'd been through so much just after a few weeks in prison. It was probably equivalent to everything I'd been through the past six years. However, I wasn't here to compete with him to have a more troubled life, I was here because I needed to be.

But it was just like extending the gun to Dominique. When you're on the opposite end, you're supposed to feel everything your torturer felt, the goodness he felt. But all I felt was sadness…

Maybe I've been wrong. Maybe Matt and even Kasey had never enjoyed their own brutality. Looking at Matt now, I had no idea what to feel besides miserable.

"I think I understand you," I said after looking him over. He stared at his pale hands folded on the table but didn't respond. "You can't accept it. You don't want to accept what you've done. You can't forgive yourself."

"You don't know what you're talking about." He gritted his teeth. "There's nothing to forgive because I didn't do anything." His words were like claws on a board, piercing me deeply as I watched him push away all the responsibility.

"Guilt will make an hour seem like a day but lying can make a moment last for eternity."

He frowned, but I cut off his snarl.

"The longer you pretend to be innocent, the longer this jail time will be."

"Who do you think you are?"

"I was hoping you'd ask that." I reached up and pulled my wig off and laid it on the table. "For years, I tried to be Madeline. I tried to kill the girl inside. But she was much stronger, and she was loved. Because of that love, she was able to forgive herself and be the person she was meant to be."

"I don't care," he said as he looked away.

"You can't even look at me."

"I don't want to look at you."

"Why not?"

"Because I don't."

Grabbing my bag, I pulled out a plastic bag and a Bible. "I brought these for you."

He still wouldn't look.

"If you won't look, then I'll just tell you what they are," I said as I picked up the first item. "It's a withered rose. I let it dry out myself." I twirled the dead flower in my hand. "This represents what you did to Madeline." I picked up the next flower. "This is a red poppy, used for remembrance. This one is so that you'll never forget us, the victims of your own hand." I pushed the dried flowers forward and grabbed the Bible. "This is special." My hand ran over the golden letters printed on the front. "Because this is what saved me. The love found here will save you too. And it's why I'm here today."

Finally, his blue eyes reached mine.

"I came here to tell you that I forgive you, Matthew, for everything. For raping me, for forcing me into a dark corner, for never admitting what you did to me and my sister and Naomi. And I also forgive you for hurting my sister so badly that she took her own life." I glanced down at the Bible and patted it. "God's love is so liberating. I found it easier

406

to let go of the old." I paused, trying to fight the burning tears. "Recently, I found out that Xavier was there when my sister was raped, and he did nothing. I forgave him for it, but I still needed to forgive you too. Not just for hurting my sister, but for forcing Xavier into an impossible situation. Because of you, he took the stand and pulled the rug from beneath your feet."

He didn't speak, his eyes just stayed fixated on the Bible in front of him.

"My forgiveness is nothing compared to the forgiveness of God. If you'll allow Him in." I tapped the Bible. "Then you'll make it through the next six years."

Matt's lips were sealed shut, never muttering another word as I prepared to leave.

"One more thing, Matt; I know you think it was easy for him. You think he turned on you, but that was the hardest decision X ever made. To him, it was a matter of life and death, choosing the life of Christ, or the death of your friendship. Obviously, you know which one he chose."

Pulling my backpack on, I grabbed the red wig from the table. "Matt," I whispered, "you can forgive yourself because you didn't destroy Adeline Jones."

I looked at the guard and nodded as I turned to leave.

"Wait," Matt called.

I didn't look back, I stood still, looking through the exit gates.

"Will I ever see you again?"

"I'm not disappearing like I did before." I glanced back. "I'll come back, and next time, I'll bring him with me."

Without waiting for a response, I headed for the exit, tossing the red wig into the garbage on my out.

Adeline Jones had officially returned.

45

See You Soon

Xavier

I stared at Junior Calliway's picture. I told Eli and my parents that I'd meet them at a restaurant a little later. It gave them all enough time to catch up and finally meet. My parents had no idea that Eli had even shown up at the trial since they'd never seen him before. It was funny, watching Elijah and my parents interact.

"JC," I said aloud in the empty auditorium, "we never got to make up."

I could still remember when I saw Glenn after the trial was over and I returned to school. He'd been out for a month, and I took some time off when I first got back after the trial just to recuperate. Thankfully, I had good enough grades to get me through missing those classes at the end of the semester, and my scores were high on finals, bumping me up from Magna, to Suma Cum Laude.

Glenn had been out with the flu and when we finally met up again, he told me that JC had died. He passed away in the frat's hazing event...

he was drowned. Junior died and there was no vigil on campus.

I knew all this because today was the three-month anniversary of Junior's death in March. The trial had been in April. I was still going to classes regularly up until I left to testify. I wouldn't have missed something like that. I know I didn't.

Our college swept it under the rug because our fraternity was its moneymaker. This picture of him and a moment of silence during the graduation ceremony was all that our school held for him.

I was angry and I was hurt. We never patched things up, we didn't get to at least end things the way we started. We were supposed to be best friends, doing everything together in college. But things went awry, and now it's all over. College, the trial, everything has ended and moved on. Junior will never know how much I wanted to fix things between us. He'll never know the real secret my parents and I were whispering about my first day on campus.

After leaving the auditorium, I headed out back into the parking lot where Glenn had arranged a memorial service for Junior. The auditorium was kind enough to let him do it, and I was grateful to at least have a moment to say goodbye.

Holding my cap under my arm, I stood closer to the back, and watched Glenn speak through a blowhorn about how much he loved JC. People were crying on our graduation day. It's supposed to be one of the happiest moments in our life, but doing this day without JC, without making things right, was eating me alive.

The only good that came from graduation was not just graduating—duh—but also Glenn told me that he's planning to get his masters and he asked about the Bible study I always had him covering for. He said realizing that Junior was gone made him think about the afterlife, which spooked him a little. And since his gods had never answered when he'd prayed, and he'd caught me plenty of times praying and talking openly to God Almighty, he invited himself to church this coming Sunday.

I didn't oppose. I was excited. I felt kind of like an idiot for never picking up on Glenn wanting to convert all this time.

Looking ahead at the wreaths of flowers twisting to spell JC, I whispered, "I'm sorry, Junior." Though, I knew he'd never know.

My high school graduation had ended with a party that resulted in the death of two people, critical injuries, and the assault of two women that haunted me for my entire four years of college. But college wasn't any better because graduation ended with a vigil.

When will it get easier for me?

"Hey, stranger."

I recognized the voice immediately and whirled around.

"Jocelyn?"

She smiled. I hadn't seen her since she was admitted to the hospital back in September. She was a rail, barely clinging to life. The drugs had left her in a really poor condition and her family had asked for privacy. So, after September, I wasn't allowed to see her anymore. Then more drama broke out and I never had a chance to check in on her again. But seeing her now, she almost resembled the old Jay. She was healthy again, not completely, but definitely getting there.

"Don't just stare." She giggled. "Give me a hug or say something."

I snorted as I leaned down to hug her tightly. "I can't believe you're here."

"I can't believe I'm here either. I knew you'd be here, so I came to say thank you for saving me."

I pulled away. "Well, I'd say you're welcome, but I wasn't the one—"

"I know." She looked out at the crowd, the warm breeze rustling through her golden curls. "She saved me, and I'm really thankful."

Jay smiled, hiding the brokenness she was feeling inside. Knowing

410

someone risked their life for yours was hard enough to swallow. But never knowing if they made it all this time was probably the hardest thing for Jocelyn.

"You know, she's doing good." I paused. "Adeline—I mean—*MJ*, is doing good."

She crossed her arms, her leather jacket creasing with the movement. "I always knew there was something about her that was different from everyone. I just didn't care that she didn't know she was different."

"I think she really admired that, and because of you, she tried to love herself in the confusion."

"And I squandered that."

"Jay—"

"Will you tell her for me?" Her lips pressed into a thin line and her eyes glistened with tears. "Tell her that I'm figuring it all out because she gave me the chance to."

I nodded sympathetically. "I'll tell her, Jocelyn."

She reached up and patted my cheek. "You've always been such a good guy, haven't you, X?"

"Well, not exactly."

As our eyes locked, a melancholy wave of nostalgia brushed over me on the hem of the breeze. At one point, I thought I would never find someone like Jocelyn, though I knew I could never truly have her. I thought that when she got better, and we saw each other again, maybe things would work out. But seeing her now, I knew goodbye was better than 'see you later' for us. Jocelyn needed to figure herself out, and only she would know when she had accomplished that.

"I love you so much," she whispered as she caressed my cheek, "more than I can even understand."

"Jay," I started, but her hand fell from my face to her side.

"I know. Someone else has your heart. I just wish it could've been me."

I squinted. "No, I'm not in love." The thought had definitely tugged on my mind, but I ignored it. I sighed. "I'm sorry."

"Please," Jay waved a hand, "be happy for yourself for once. Okay?"

A small laugh escaped me. "Okay."

"I'd better go. But I wanted to pay my respects to Junior."

"He'd be so happy to know you came all the way back to see him."

That made her smile reappear. "He was a pretty good kid, wasn't he?"

"Yeah, he was."

She stared an extra moment at his picture. "Well, X, I don't know when I'll see you again, but hopefully next time it won't be for something so sad."

I nodded as I felt a rush of sadness washing in. I'd said goodbye one too many times this year, and it hadn't gotten any easier.

"Come on." Jay lightly punched my arm. "You're making this harder on me."

I shook my head. "Sorry."

"Just one more time, let me see you genuinely happy."

Sniffling, I nodded. Then I took a deep breath, and produced the best smile I could for her, and she smiled back in approval.

"There he is. That's the guy that stole my heart. I guess that's why thieving is wrong. It leaves the other person empty with nothing to replace what's been taken."

No words could form as my smile began to fade.

"See you never, X," said as she turned on her heels and walked through the grass to disappear into the crowded parking lot.

"See you never," I replied.

"Alright," Elijah said as he sat on his stool in the front of the sanctuary. "We've made it through four years of Bible study together. Can you all believe it?"

"NO!" Marlo Jo exclaimed with a hearty laugh. The rest of us laughed along with her and Eli chuckled too.

"We lost Tracy and Julius along the way when Tracy moved for work, and Julius for school. But they both check in from time to time and they're both in very good churches."

We clapped for a moment at the announcement.

"So, what did we cover?"

"Singleness," Sky said as he elbowed me. I laughed now, but a few months back it would've taken everything in me not to roll my eyes. He and Daisy were still going strong.

"Excellent," Eli nodded.

"We talked about finding our purpose in God as single Believers," Daisy waved her pencil, sitting on the opposite side of Sky. It took effort not to take thing personally when I found out she and Sky were getting serious after Christmas. Now, it was like we never liked each other, and our past had been forgotten.

"Very good."

"Dating," Kevin said next.

"What about it?" Eli challenged him, for once.

"How to pick a partner by not picking a partner. Letting God bring us to who He's created for us and then going from there."

"Good, good. And how do we go from there? Anyone?"

Daytona raised her hand and Eli acknowledged her. "It's different for men and women. Men have to prove that they can provide for the woman they want to marry, and women have to prove their value spiritually."

"Excellent. Marlo, want to elaborate?"

"Yeah." She nodded. "It was like the way Jacob worked for Leah and Rachel. They both were valued at seven years, though, technically, he did all that for Rachel, so she was valued at fourteen years."

Eli nodded for her to keep going.

Brushing a brown dreadlock over her shoulder, she went on. "And you also used the church as an example. How we are so valuable to God that He gave Heaven's best and His only Son for us to be able to live with Him eternally. You also mentioned how smart Abigail was. We discussed how a woman's value was based on her spiritual covering and how well she decorated her husband," Marlo said as she flipped another page in her notebook.

"Good. But let me reiterate that women are not just brooches men wear on our suits. They are our *most prized possessions*, and that's why we, as men, have to make sure that once we invest our entire life to protecting and providing for our wives, we know that she's the one from God. And what did I say about men knowing?"

"That because of Adam's recognition of Eve, we can recognize our ribcage, or the part of a man that's missing."

"Good, Emily, though I was expecting one of the gentlemen to answer."

We all laughed.

"Alright, X, that leaves you. Tell me something we learned about marriage."

"We learned that we each have roles, and it's not to lock us in a box, but to set guidelines to a Biblical and successful marriage. Men honor their wives by protecting them and serving them, taking care of them. Women honor their husbands through submitting to their protection, and constantly praying for them."

"I love the way you put that." Eli smiled from ear to ear. "Go on a little more into that."

I wanted to sigh but I nodded. "Women protect their husbands spiritually, so they're always praying and petitioning God on their

414

husband's behalf. For strength, for courage, a better job, spiritual needs." I shrugged. "That's what wives do. And they also allow their husbands to be the one whose name they wear. His name is the protection and the provision for them, so that if something goes wrong, they always have someone to fall back on."

"Very well said," Eli agreed. "Now, tell me about the husband's role."

"He's supposed to have a good and honorable name so that his wife and children will have a good name to fall under. And we're supposed to honor our wives by serving them and supporting them the way Christ does. We kind of make our life revolve around our wives because she's our reason for everything."

"Aww," Marlo teased from across the room.

Eli laughed. "Very very good." He took a deep breath and gave us a nod of approval. "Alright guys, well, we sure did cover a lot. And I hope you guys took good notes so that when that special someone comes along and you're not sure about something, you can refer back to the notes you took."

"So, is this it?" Emily said as she set her notebook beside her.

"This is it. If you guys decide to join the other Bible study I teach for young adults from twenty-two to twenty-five, you will be welcomed."

"Man," Sky said, "I feel sad, even though I'll just see you all on Sunday."

"I know!" Daytona agreed with a laugh. I wondered how hard it was for her to accept Daisy and Sky together. She never seemed to let it show if she was bothered.

"Alright guys," Elijah glanced down at his watch and for the last time, he said, "God bless each of you, and that's it for today."

46

A Blessed and Noble Child of God

Xavier

"Adar," Benedict whispered as he stood at the edge of the cliff, ready to fall over. His time had finally come, his name had finally been called. He had been selected to begin his earthen journey back to heaven. "I'll find you, I promise," he breathed as he tipped over the edge, leaving the Realm behind to enter the world.

— ❦ —

"Adar." I sat up out of bed and immediately grabbed my head. "Adar," I whispered. A sigh escaped me as I stared at the blank wall ahead of me. It'd been nearly two months since I last saw Adeline, and I was beginning to think she wouldn't return. *Maybe the stress of wondering about her triggered those dreams,* I thought as I climbed out of bed.

Before I reached the door, a field of red poppies filled my head, and

I could see Adar clearly, standing there like she was waiting for someone.

Benedict…

"Hold on…" I stepped back from the door. "How'd I know that? Who's Benedict?"

Benedict.

I snatched my phone up and sent Mom a text message.

Me: Mom, weird (and random) question, have you mentioned someone named Benedict lately?

Mom: No? Why?

Me: I don't know, I just remembered the name randomly.

Mom: Call me.

Mom always preferred calling. I sighed and gave her a ring, she answered on the first one.

"Hello?"

"Hey, Mom."

"Hey, X, how's it going?"

"Pretty good. Sorry for the random text about that name, I just felt like I'd heard it before, recently, I think. But I don't know from who or where."

She was silent for a moment.

"Mom? You still there?"

"Did I ever tell you what I planned to name you? Or the name God gave me for you."

"You told me you let Dad name me Xavier. But you never mentioned the name you and God originally had for me," I said as I sat on the bed.

"It was Benedict."

Silence.

"What?" I blinked.

"I was going to name you Benedict."

"Wait a second…" I stood up. "You were going to name me

Benedict?"

"Yes."

I raked a hand over my head. "But why do I feel like that still doesn't answer my question and I feel like I knew that was my name already."

"Have you spoken to Elijah?"

"No, he's out right now."

"Well, when he gets back in, ask him where you're getting this from."

"Alright, Mom, I'll call you when I have an answer."

"Love you," she said.

"I love you too."

Hanging up the phone, I sat on the edge of my bed. My head was hung, and my hands were covering my ears as I tried to focus.

"Holy Spirit," I whispered, "bring back to me where I heard that name from."

Sitting still had always been a challenge for me, but through more prayer, I found that God often speaks when you're still. So, I sat there on the edge of my bed, trying not to think about anything, but Adeline kept popping into my head.

Adeline… her name was just a thought at first, and then it was a reality. *Adeline!*

I snapped my head up. The week of Matt's trial, she and Eli were in my room discussing a dream she had, where she was standing in a field of red flowers waiting on someone named Benedict. I've been dreaming about a woman named Adar standing in a field of red poppies.

"No way." I shook my head. "Nope. She can't be Adar and I can't be Benedict." I laughed. "That would make… perfect sense and it shouldn't."

We learned that God brings us to our spouses, He has someone designed perfectly for us. Could it be that Adeline had been Adar, and I had been Benedict and from the beginning, we've been a match for each other?

418

God… You've never said a thing about Adeline.

He didn't answer.

I snatched my phone from the bed and did a quick search of the name *Adeline*. In Hebrew, the name meant *noble or someone with nobility*. Cross checking the name Adar… in Hebrew, that name shared the same meaning as Adeline… noble.

But Benedict didn't match Xavier, so this couldn't be right… unless my name was different because I wasn't named correctly. Had I been named Benedict, or something similar, Adar and Benedict would've been able to find each other.

I slapped a hand to my face. "There's no way this is real." But deep down, I knew it was. Even when I dated Carly, I felt attracted to Adeline—MJ at the time. I always thought she was so pretty. I wasn't sure of my feelings because she didn't swing the way I did, and Jocelyn was also a distraction.

Carly and Jocelyn were just so much louder than Adeline that I never paid my feelings for her any attention. I let them fade to the back of my head. Just like everyone had always let Adeline fade to the back for the sake of Madeline. But now, my feelings were banging at the door, trying to get me to let them inside.

This can't be real, I thought.

Why do you doubt?

God? I can't believe this! How can I?

Because you are not honest with yourself, you cannot accept *My* will for your life.

Honest with myself… I took a breath; I'd been dodging my feelings for Adeline. I knew I liked her, but I was so afraid that God would tell me *no* eventually that I'd been pushing away everything I felt for her. I wouldn't acknowledge it, hoping that maybe she wouldn't return, even though I wanted her to. Even though I missed her and talked about her all the time with Elijah. We reminisced about our time with Adeline, both concerned about what condition she would return in.

I needed to be honest with myself. The way it feels like I can't breathe when Adeline's around but, somehow, it gives me an ecstasy I never want to stop. And when she's gone, it feels like I'd suffocate without her, as if I'm drowning because she's no longer the buoy I'm clinging to. She makes me feel like the world spins because if it slowed or stopped, it wouldn't matter that gravity fluctuated, or that chaos ensued. All that would matter is our lives ending and I'd never get to see her smile again, and I can't live with that.

All while she'd been gone, I've tried to better myself, so she'd have no reason not to accept me. And the only reason I hadn't brought her up to God was because she was special to me. I put myself on the line in Matt's case for God, and for Adeline. I wanted to protect her the best way I could in that courtroom. I didn't want her to be demeaned or for the case to be washed away like Madeline's was.

So… is it true, God? Do I really like her?

No. You love her.

The doorbell rang out through the entire apartment, and I flinched so hard, my shoulders began to ache.

"Eli must've forgotten his key. This is the second time this week," I grumbled as I stepped out the room. "One second," I called, walking down the hall.

I pulled open the door to find a woman standing there. She was wearing my red hoodie, smiling up at me with dimpled cheeks and almond-shaped eyes. She was the most beautiful woman I'd ever seen. Her short pixie cut made her dimpled cheeks look sassy and not innocent like they had before. When she lifted her hand to wave at me, the cloud-shaped pendant on her bracelet winked in the sunlight.

My breath caught in my throat. We'd been connected from the very beginning. My love for her knit into the very fabric of my being, brandished on my own skin. I had always been hers and she had always

420

been mine. So close, yet so far away.

Until now.

"Adeline?" I whispered.

She stepped forward. "It's me, Xavier... I'm back."

"No..." My voice was soft as I grabbed her hands and kissed them. "You're home."

The End

Thank you for reading this novel!

More books by A. Bean & TRC Publishing!

Christian Fantasy

The End of the World series

The Scribe

Cross Academy series

Christian Science Fiction

I AM MAN series

Christian Romance

The Living Water

Withered Rose Trilogy

Fractured Diamond

The Woof Pack Trilogy

Christian Children's Fiction

Too Young

ACKNOWLEDGEMENTS

Jesus is the Christ, Son of the Living God. He is the One who gave me the idea and enabled me to write this story, thank you.

I want to recognize my pastor (and mom), Pastor Cyndi, for being there for me spiritually and emotionally as I wrote this book. I hope I make you proud with this one!

Follow me on Amazon to get updates on new releases, pre-orders, reduced prices on my books.

The Rebel Christian Publishing

We are an independent Christian publishing company focused on fantasy, science fiction, and romantic reads. Visit therebelchristian.com to check out our books or click the titles below!

Made in the USA
Monee, IL
20 February 2024

53850028R10243